D1036790

THE LIGHTKEEPERS

TRIPLE SIX : THE LIGHKEEPERS, BOOK 2

Published by 

Front cover design by Hoffman/Miller Advertising
Printed in the USA.

Back Cover and Interior Format

ERICA SPINDLER

TRIPLE SIX

The Lightkeepers #2

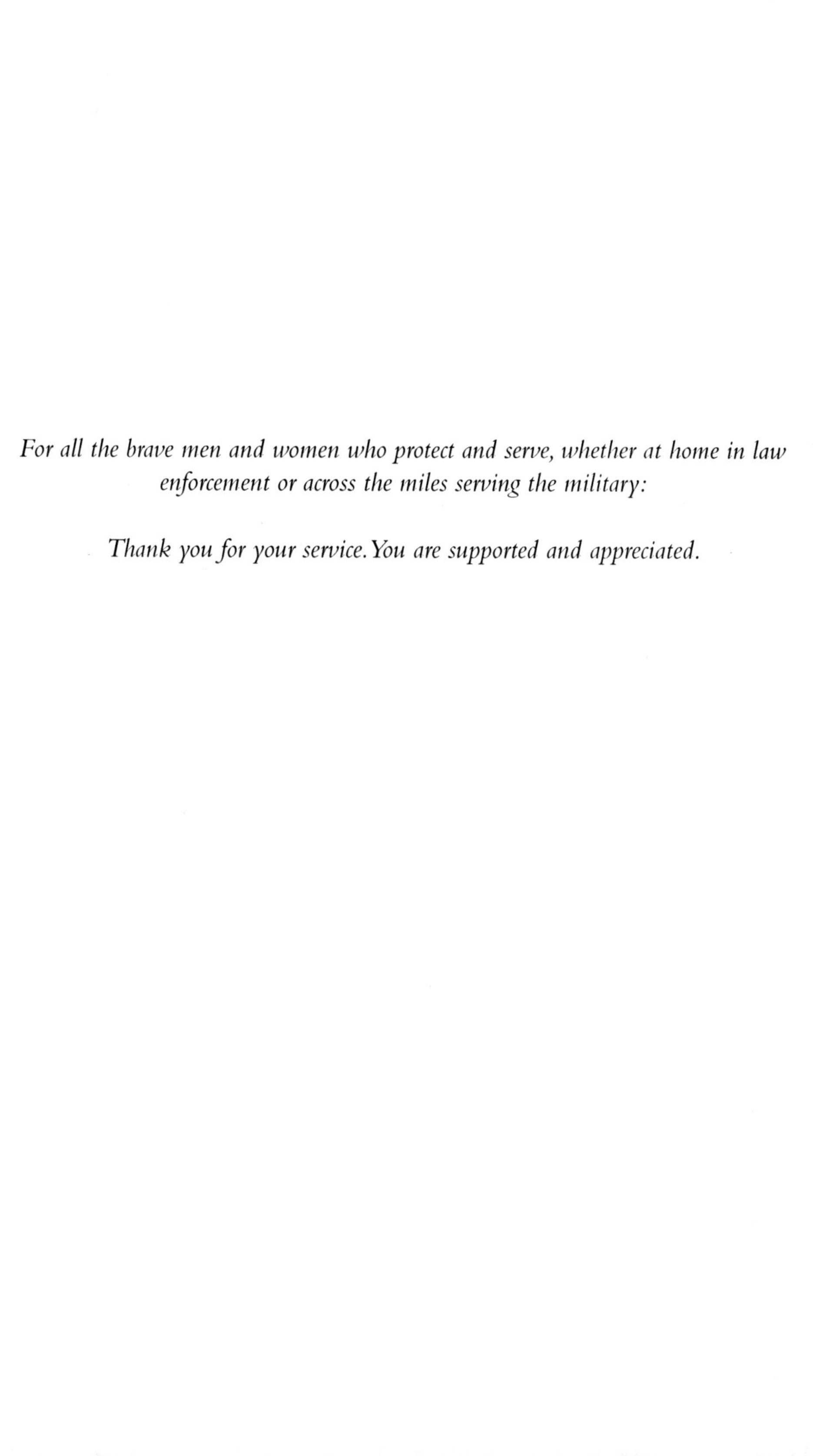

For all the brave men and women who protect and serve, whether at home in law enforcement or across the miles serving the military:

Thank you for your service. You are supported and appreciated.

PROLOGUE

New Orleans, Louisiana
Monday, July 22
3:00 P.M.

LOST ANGEL MINISTRIES. ZACH HARRIS stood at the wrought iron gate, gazing at the sign as it swayed in the breeze. The iron fence circled the property, a Victorian home from days gone by, repurposed into a center that helped lost and disenfranchised youth. Youth who were . . . unique.

The front door opened and a teenager darted out, calling 'Bye' over her shoulder. She was small with a spiky, pixie haircut, the spikes dyed Irish green. She met his eyes as she reached the gate. Beautiful eyes. A brilliant green that matched her hair.

Like him, was she a Half Light? A product of the co-mingling of the human and Lightkeeper races? Or could she be Full Light, one of the rapidly dwindling number that remained?

"Hey," she said, slipping past him.

"Hey," he responded back, and headed through the gate and up the walk. It felt weird, thinking of himself as not completely human. Part light, enrobed in human flesh, sent to guide the human race? Part mortal angel, locked in a life-or-death battle with an ancient evil?

It felt like total bullshit. It pissed him off. He might not want to buy in, but at this point, he didn't have a choice. Like it or not, his eyes had been opened.

From the neutral ground behind him came the rumble of the streetcar. He glanced over his shoulder at it, bright, shiny red, windows shut tight to keep the heat out. He reached the door, looked directly at the security camera and was buzzed in.

Eli met him in the foyer. He looked totally unfazed, as if saving lives and battling the forces of darkness had the rejuvenating properties of a spa day.

"Zach, buddy—" he clapped him on the back, "—great to see you. Come, they're in the conference room."

They started in that direction. Eli turned his extraordinary gaze on him. "You've been to the hospital and seen Michaela?"

"Left just a little bit ago."

"How is she?"

"Healing quickly. Very."

"I do good work."

The cockiness annoyed the crap out of him. "She says she remembers being surrounded by a beautiful, healing light. Like being wrapped in an angel's wings."

Eli stopped and cocked his head. "Did she? That's curious. And what did you tell her?"

"That she had lost a lot of blood, was in shock or hallucinating."

"Good. Here we are."

"Wait." Zach laid a hand on his arm, stopping him. "I thought you said she wouldn't remember anything."

"That's why it's curious." He smiled. "I don't think it's anything you need to worry about."

Famous last words, Zach thought as he stepped into the conference room. Only two at the table: His Sixer point man, Parker, and Professor Lester Truebell.

"Zachary." Truebell stood and held out his hand, smiling.

Zach took it. "Professor."

"No worse for wear, I see."

"Tell that to every muscle, joint and bone in my body." He indicated the four of them. "We're it?"

"For today, yes."

"No Angel?"

"She's not ready."

The comment rankled. More secrets. More need-to-know bullshit. "I see nothing's changed since the last time I sat across this table from you."

The elfin Truebell shook his head. "Everything's changed, Zachary. Sit. Please."

He did. Parker spoke up. "No hello for me, Zach?"

Zach looked at him, not masking his anger. "I may have to work with you, Special Agent Parker, but I don't have to like you. And I sure as hell don't have to respect you."

Parker leaned back in his chair and folded his arms across his chest. "You don't think that's a little harsh? And formal, considering we're family?"

"From our first meeting, everything out of your mouth has been either a lie or a manipulation. Or both." He arched his eyebrows. "So, no. Not too harsh."

"Sixers wasn't a lie. There was just more to the story."

"There always is, and that's the problem." He shifted his attention back to Truebell. "Why am I here today?"

"You know why."

"Do I?"

"Are you in," Truebell asked, "or out?"

Zach wished he could say he was out, shake this whole experience off, and go back to the life he had known before. But that life was gone forever. "Saturday made a believer out of me."

Truebell nodded. "You know it's destructive power now. You understand our urgency."

Zach's head filled with the memory of the power turned on him, his helplessness against it. "Yes."

"And now you know our power as well."

The joining of the Lightkeepers. The explosion of light. The howl of rage as the Dark Bearer had been forced out.

Darkness cannot exist in the light, Zach.

But it could put up a hell of a fight.

"How many of us were there that night?" Zach asked. "A dozen?"

"More. Fourteen."

"Fourteen to overcome one? I suppose you've noticed those odds suck for us."

"They do, indeed. So, Zachary, now that you're a believer and you know the odds, are you with us?"

He held the professor's gaze. "I'm in. For now."

Professor Truebell smiled slightly. "Not quite the gung-ho response I'd hoped for, but it'll do. One last thing—" he folded his hands on the table and leaned toward Zach "—I have to have your word. You'll do what you need to do, concerning Michaela?"

He hated this. She was his partner. Secrets put her in harm's way.

No, Zach. They make her safer.

He looked at Eli. *Get out of my head.*

You have to trust us.

I trust her.

"Zachary? Your answer."

"Yes. I'll tell her nothing of the Lightkeepers and nothing of the true nature of the events of that night."

"You won't regret it."

He regretted it already. "What's next?"

"We wait."

"For what?"

"A Dark Bearer to strike."

CHAPTER ONE

New Orleans, Louisiana
Friday, October 16
11:25 P.M.

"YOU'RE SURE IT'S COOL IF I go?"

Angel Gomez smiled at her fellow barista and waved her toward the door. "Girl, go. Have fun."

Ginger hesitated. "Micki'll tear me apart if she finds out I left without you."

"I won't tell her, so she'll never know. And you've got to admit, Micki's a little over the top when it comes to her rules. It's kinda stupid, considering that before moving in with her, I'd been living on my own for years."

"Still—" Ginger glanced at the clock, "—it's only a half hour—"

"And only five blocks home for me. I've got my phone, my mace and a set of loud-ass lungs. Go. And tell Bryan I said to be good."

Ginger laughed and snatched up her backpack. "He always is."

"*That's* not the kind of good I'm talking about."

A moment later, Ginger was gone. And Angel was alone. She made herself busy completing the last of the day's clean-up and the next day's set-up. Ironically, Friday night was the quietest night of the week at Sacred Grounds. During the week, nestled within biking distances of both Tulane and Loyola Universities, they were non-stop with students either caffeinating to cram for tests or caffeinating to not crash after cramming for them. Friday, by this time, everyone was decompressing. Parties, dates, movies, gaming. Study hall was over. Let the good times roll.

Angel smiled to herself. So much had changed since that terrible night three months ago. So much that was good. She was happy in a way she'd never been before.

She could almost forget what it had been like to have that Dark Bearer in her head, to be at his mercy.

No, she thought. The nightmare was over. Eli, the professor and the other Lightkeepers had sent it packing.

Angel hadn't told anyone about him being in her head, not Micki, or Zach or even Eli. She didn't want them to know. She was afraid they'd look at her differently, like she wasn't *really* one of them. Like they couldn't trust her. But she'd promised herself she would, if he ever came back.

"You still open?"

She looked over her shoulder. She hadn't heard the door open, hadn't heard the chime that announced the arrival of a customer.

Gorgeous. The guy in the doorway was simply gorgeous. Dark, wavy hair. Bright white smile. Beautiful hazel eyes she could see from across the cafe. He took her breath away.

"I surprised you," he said, "Sorry about that."

"No, I—" She cleared her throat. "I was just closing up. What can I get you?"

Was that hopefulness in her voice? Geez, she was pathetic.

"Whatever's easy."

"I could do a pour over if you want hot? I've already emptied and cleaned the machines—"

"How about cold?"

"Iced tea? Iced coffee? A bottle of water or juice?"

"A bottle of water's fine."

She retrieved it from the cooler behind her. "I haven't seen you in here before."

"It's my first time."

She handed him the bottle. "You a student?"

He shook his head and took a long swallow of the water. Angel found herself staring at his neck, the way the tendons stretched with the movement.

"Finished with all that," he said. "Out in the working world."

"What do you do?"

"I'm in sales."

"What do you sell?"

He laughed. "You're a very curious girl, aren't you?"

She flushed. "Sorry. I guess I'm being rude."

"How old are you?" he asked.

At the question, her heart skipped a beat. She wanted to say "old enough" but that would have been *really* rude. "Almost nineteen."

"I'm twenty-two." He reached for his wallet. "What do I owe you?"

"It's on me."

"You already closed out your register, didn't you?"

"I did, but that's my bad. Don't worry about it."

He took a five-dollar bill from his wallet and stuck it in the tip jar. "I've got to go. Thanks— what's your name?"

"Angel."

"Angel," he said. "I'm Seth."

That smile again. For a split second she couldn't breathe. When the second passed, she returned the smile. "Hi, Seth."

"See you around, Angel."

She watched him leave the coffeehouse, a strange sense of loss rolling over her, and bringing with it the urge to run after him, ask him out.

She got her cell phone and texted Ginger.

u missed the cutest guy ever. he just left.

u get his #

got his name. Seth.

u should have asked him to party

Angel tried to picture that and laughed. Right. That wasn't happening. Ever.

gonna finish closing talk 2 u tomorrow

She pocketed her phone and quickly finished doing just that. Five minutes later, she flipped off the neon *Open* sign and locked up.

The cool, damp night settled around her like a cloud. She shivered and started home, thoughts turning to Seth. Ask him to party? Ask him for his number? Odd, unwanted Angel Gomez with a guy like him? Never gonna happen.

What was it about him, she wondered? She'd never been super-interested in guys, not that she was gay or anything, but she'd been able to take them or leave them. Until him. Tonight. His smile. Something about his eyes. Looking into them, she'd felt like the two of them were . . . connected somehow.

She suddenly became aware of another person coming up behind her. She glanced back. A kid in a hoodie, head down, hands in the jacket's pockets. She stepped to the right so he could pass her.

But instead of breezing by, he slowed down, fell into step with her. "You want to party?"

A kid. Maybe sixteen. She thought of what Ginger had texted and almost laughed. This kid clearly had no trouble doing what her friend suggested. "With you?"

"Why not?"

"You're too young, kid."

"How about some weed?"

"Not interested. Get lost."

He followed her. "Pharmies? A little crank or coke?"

She stopped and turned toward him. "I don't do drugs and I don't like people who push them. Take a—"

In that instant, he grabbed her purse and yanked hard. The strap snapped; he turned and ran.

"No!" she cried and took off after him. Her phone was in there. Her ID. Today's tips.

The mace.

She never saw the other kid. He leapt out from behind a pick-up truck and knocked her sideways, into the bushes. Angel went down, her head snapping back, hitting the ground with a thud.

Seeing stars didn't stop her from fighting him. She kicked and clawed. "Get off me, creep!"

The first kid had doubled back. Her purse landed on the ground near her head.

"Gimme a hand," the guy holding her said.

"What's the problem? You can't handle a *girl*?"

"She's stronger than she looks, okay? Lemme have your jacket."

"What for—"

"I'm gonna shut her up!"

In the next instant, the sweatshirt was pressed over her face. Angel fought. Squirming. Kicking out. When the jacket slipped, the guys came into focus. Both so young. Why were they doing this to her?

She sucked in a lungful of air and screamed. Once, then again.

"Shit!" The one on top of her howled. "Shut her up!"

"Dammit Pong, how am I—"

"Idiot, hold the jacket over her head!"

The first one smashed the hoodie over her face again, this time so tightly she couldn't breathe. The smell of sweat, stale tobacco, and something cloyingly sweet filled her head. She thought she heard her name being called. *Eli? She answered. Is that you? I need you!*

"Get the fuck off her!"

In the next instant, the kid was dragged aside. She heard the sound of a blow, then a grunt of pain and footfalls on pavement.

"That's right, you'd better run!"

She clawed free of the hoodie, gasping for breath. Seth, she realized. It had been his voice she'd heard.

He knelt beside her. "Are you okay?"

Angel blinked. "Your nose is bleeding."

He laughed softly. "And yours is running."

She wiped it with the back of her hand. It was a mess. "I guess it is," she said and burst into tears.

He gathered her against his chest and just held her, letting her cry. Every once in a while he awkwardly patted her back.

After a minute, she pulled herself together and wiped her tears with the heels of her hands. "Sorry for being such a cry-baby."

"Are you serious? Those creeps attacked you. If you didn't cry, I'd be a little freaked out."

She tried to laugh but it came out as cross between a whimper and a hiccup. "What're you doing here?"

"I heard you scream."

"But how, where—"

"I'd gone back to Sacred Grounds, hoping you were still there. To get your number."

"You did?"

He laughed. "Why do you sound so surprised?"

"Are you serious?"

He looked confused by the question. "Think you can stand?"

She nodded and he helped her to her feet.

"We better call the cops."

"No." She shook her head. "No cops."

"Those guys—"

"My roommate's a cop. I'll tell her." He didn't look convinced. "Please. I just want to go home."

"Where do you live?"

"A few blocks up. On Dante."

"You think you can walk it?"

She nodded, though her legs felt rubbery. "I'm fine. Thanks for your help."

His eyebrows shot up. "You don't seriously think I'm just going to leave you to walk home alone?" He must have read her expression, because he frowned. "No, Angel, I'm not."

He put an arm around her. "Let's take it slow to start."

She nodded. They went a few steps before she remembered and suddenly stopped. "Wait, my purse! The first guy snatched it—"

"And you ran after him."

"Yes."

"And the other guy was waiting and jumped you. Classic move."

It was. And pretty stupid of her, falling for it. She was smarter than that.

"There it is," he said, pointing toward a cluster of azalea bushes. "I'll get it."

When he handed it to her, she looked quickly through and let out a sigh of relief. "They didn't take anything."

"They must not have had time." He put his arm around her again. "Come on, let me get you home."

CHAPTER TWO

Saturday, October 17
1:16 P.M.

BEFORE HER LAY A TOPPLED angel. Split in two, but wings intact. Micki stared at the angelic victim, then shifted her gaze to the apocalyptic landscape. Desolate and ruined. A place where all good had called adieu, leaving behind nothing but the moldering scent of death and decay.

Her death. Her eventual decay.

She was going to die tonight.

Before the panic of that took hold, the shot rang out. A bullet entered her chest, exploding magnificently and reverberating clear to her marrow. She teetered on the edge of a cliff, so high she could see nothing but dark below.

A second explosion sounded. It blew her wide open, shattered her into a million sparkling pieces. Over the edge she went, plummeting into the abyss. Blood, she realized. Her blood. Gushing. Gurgling noisily out. It quieted as her pumping heart slowed.

Still she fell, barreling toward the darkness below.

Cold. She was so cold.

Suddenly, brilliant light broke through, spilling over her, drawing her into its warm cradle. Someone with her . . . She strained to make out the face. A beautiful face, she knew without seeing. Because of the voice, as rhythmic as the ocean waves, as soothing.

"Not yet, Michaela," the one with her whispered. *"Not yet . . ."*

With a gasp, Detective Micki Dare opened her eyes. She went for her gun, tucked under the edge of the mattress. Her fingers curved around the grip; her gaze flew to the bedside clock.

1:16 a.m.

She shifted her attention, taking in the details. Moonlight filtering in around the edges of the blinds. Absolute quiet. The still of deep night.

She brought a shaking hand to her chest. No gaping wound or blood gushing out. No pain or stench of decay.

No brilliant light. No angelic voice calling to her.

Micki's grip on the weapon eased, but she didn't release it—she couldn't, not just yet.

She sat up, laid the gun on her lap and dropped her head into her hands. Breathe, she told herself. In through the nose, out through the mouth. Slowly, deeply. She followed her own instructions until her trembling ceased and her heartbeat slowed.

You're in control, Micki. You've got this.

She straightened, snapped on the bedside lamp. Light enveloped her, reaching into every dark corner and cranny. She'd awakened from the same nightmare a couple nights ago.

She drew her eyebrows together in thought. She got it. The night she'd been shot had been the most frightening of her life. She'd almost died. What she'd seen and heard had shredded her beliefs about good and evil, about truth and fiction.

Evil existed. Not just through the acts of men, but as entities on their own. They had a name.

Dark Bearers.

This one had known her. Her history. Who she loved and who had hurt her.

Pull it together, Micki. Think this through. A bout of PTSD shouldn't be a surprise. Hell, yeah, she should have expected it, all of it. The nightmares and self-doubt, the heightened sense of the beauty and fragility of life.

What she didn't get was, why now? It'd been three months. Life was good. Her body had healed. Her partnership with Zach had fallen into an easy camaraderie. Their cases had been straightforward; she hadn't landed on YouTube, or been shot again, and the Nova was still in one piece. There'd been no sign of a Dark Bearer.

Micki reached for the elastic band she kept on her bed stand and gathered her shoulder length, dishwater blond hair into a messy ponytail. She was a fighter. She fought as hard and as smart as she could. If that wasn't good enough, it wasn't—she'd go down without regrets.

But what was this? Not regret. Not fear or hesitation. A feeling of unfinished business, of waiting for the other shoe to drop.

Of something more.

A missing piece of the puzzle.

She shook the thought off, turning her attention to Zach, their partnership, the Sixers program. Hard to believe it'd only been this past July that Chief Williams had informed her she'd been selected to be a part of a new FBI initiative to curb street crime using agents with psychic abilities. After they'd convinced her it wasn't a gag, they delivered a second bombshell: she'd been chosen to partner with one of the recruits.

Since her return from medical leave, they'd had amazing success. Robberies closed in hours. Domestic disturbances quickly defused. Fights broken up without blood or guts. Piece of cake.

Those successes had been mostly Zach. His special skills made her ordinary ones redundant. Until it came to taking blows, bullets or any other manner of ass-saving.

She'd done her job. She'd kept him alive. Number one on her to-do list. It wasn't always easy—the man could be so frickin' irritating. A few times she'd considered killing him herself.

Even with their successes—or maybe because of them—he could be reassigned. And she sensed he was ready for that. Not that he was getting bored, but that mentally he was somewhere else. Looking beyond the job and their partnership. Zach Harris wasn't a day-to-day grind kind of guy.

Action. Adventure. Attention. That's what made him tick.

A sound came from the front of the house. The creak of the front screen door. A footfall. A muffled voice. *Male.* How many? She strained to hear. *More than one.*

The comforting weight of her service weapon in her hand, she slid out of bed wearing a battered Crescent City Classic T-shirt and gym shorts. She crossed to her bedroom door, eased it open and peered out.

A figure at the end of the dark hall. Tall. Broad shouldered. Something in his hand. A weapon?

Game time, Mad Dog.

She swung into the doorway, gun out, aimed at the intruder's chest. "Stop where you are, motherfucker! Hands in the air!"

"Wait! There's been—"

"Hands up!"

His hands shot up. "—a mistake."

"You bet your ass there's been a mistake. You. In my house. Big, fucking mistake—"

"Micki—" Angel darted from the living room into the hall "—no! He's with me!"

Micki didn't alter her aim. "What do you mean he's *with* you?"

"We were just talking. On the porch."

"This doesn't look like the porch to me."

"He had to use the bathroom."

With her elbow, Micki flipped the light switch and looked him over. Too old for Angel, she decided. Too good-looking. Too . . . everything. Maybe she should shoot him anyway, she thought, firming her grip on the gun.

"Ma'am, if you don't mind, I never did use the bathroom and you pointing that gun at me that way, well, it's not doing anything to help the situation, if you know what I mean?"

She lowered the Glock, but scowled. "Bathroom's there. Make it quick, then you're out of here."

Angel made a sound of outrage. "Micki!"

"It's cool, Angel." He looked back at her. "I apologize for the intrusion. I'll be out of your hair in two minutes."

He ducked into the bathroom. The moment, the door snapped shut, Angel spun to face her. "You had no right to talk to him that way."

"I had every right. This is my house, and as far as I'm concerned he's an uninvited guest."

"You're so unreasonable!"

"Angel, it's almost two in the morning."

"So?"

"You broke the rules. Unless you tell me otherwise, you come straight home after work. It's for your own safety."

"It's bullshit, that's what it is."

"I need to know you're safe. I made the rules for your protection—"

"I'm eighteen years old."

"And how old is he?"

"Twenty-two," he answered, stepping out of the restroom. He looked at Angel. "You told her, right?"

"Told me what?"

She folded her arms across her chest. "Nothing."

Micki turned to the young man. "What?"

His gaze was on Angel. "You need to tell her yourself."

She hesitated a moment, then released her breath in a huff. "Two guys jumped me on my way home. Seth came to my rescue."

Micki's heart dropped. "Wait, you were attacked?"

"Yes."

"Are you okay?"

"I'm fine. It was nothing."

"Bullshit. Obviously, if Seth hadn't come along, it would have been something."

"I'm fine," she said again.

"Where was Ginger? She was supposed to drive you home."

"It's not her fault. She had a date, I told her she could go."

"Brilliant."

"Look," Seth said, "she's fine. And I'm sure she'll be more careful next time."

"Thank you for your help . . . Seth. But I think you should go now."

Angel drew a sharp breath. "That makes no sense! Why?"

"That it's two in the morning isn't enough? That I need to take your statement and make a report isn't enough?"

"She's right, Angel." He walked over and kissed her cheek. "I'm glad you're okay."

Angel looked about to faint. "I had fun."

"Me too. See you around."

As the door shut behind him, Micki turned to Angel. "Did you just tell him you had *fun?*"

⚜ ⚜ ⚜

An hour and a half later, Micki had taken Angel's statement and called it in. Angel had given a detailed description of the two guys, including one of their names, but even so, Micki doubted they'd be picked up. She was waiting for a call back about the hoodie.

They sat at the kitchen table; Angel had her hands curled around a cup of warm milk. "You could have been raped," Micki said softly.

"I know." She hung her head for a moment, then looked back up at Micki. "I'm sorry about before. I don't know what came over me."

Micki did. An older, super-hot guy she had been trying to impress. Micki didn't tell her that her oppositional attitude had made her look younger, not older. She figured the girl had dealt with enough tonight.

"Don't worry about that," she said. "You didn't have your mace?"

"It was in my purse. Stupid, huh?"

"Sometimes it takes something bad happening to make us realize we're vulnerable."

"He was nice. Seth, I mean."

"Seemed so."

"If those guys hadn't attacked me, we wouldn't have met."

"I thought he came into the coffeehouse?"

"He did. But we wouldn't have *really* met."

Micki started to say he was too old for her, but decided not to press her luck. She remembered being that age and how much that kind of comment from an adult would've pissed her off.

Her cell buzzed. "Dare," she answered.

"Detective, Officer Collins. No sweatshirt. Either the perps came back for it or somebody else snatched it."

"Thanks," she said. "Let me know if anything turns up."

She ended the call and turned back to Angel. "Sweatshirt's gone."

"Figured." She curved her arms around her middle. "Why were you up?"

"What?"

"When I pointed Seth in the direction of the bathroom, I saw your bedroom light was on."

"I was thinking about that night."

Angel didn't have to ask which one. All nights seemed to point back to that one.

"Having a nightmare again, you mean."

"Why would you say that?"

Angel cocked an eyebrow. "I heard you the other night. You shouted."

"I did?" Micki frowned. "What'd I shout?"

"'No!' and 'Don't go.'" Angel took a swallow of the milk. "I've heard you call out before. For Hank."

Best friend and mentor. She still missed him every day. Micki swallowed hard, feeling exposed. "Why didn't you say something before?"

"That wouldn't be sort of rude?"

Angel said it bluntly, in that way of hers. Angel, Micki had learned, didn't have the patience for niceties. And Micki supposed it *would* have been rude, considering their relationship: they were connected by neither blood nor history. They barely knew each other, but were bound together by something much stronger—the dark force that had tried to kill them both.

"You look tired. Why don't you go to bed?"

Angel nodded and stood. "How about you?"

"I think I'm going to stay up awhile."

"'kay." She carried her empty mug to the sink, rinsed it and set it in the dishwasher.

"Angel?"

She looked back and was silhouetted by the night behind her and the light before her.

Light and dark. Good and evil. Two sides of the same coin.

Angel straightened and the trick of light evaporated. "Can I ask you something?"

"Duh, sure."

"Did you tell me everything about that night? Everything that happened?"

"Everything I remember."

"Tell me again."

Angel frowned. "Micki, I blacked out. I don't—"

"I need to hear it again. What do you remember?"

"Putnam and Miller screaming. Kicking in the door to save them. Being attacked from behind. Knocked to the ground. Pain. Fear. Zach saving us." She crossed her arms. "That Dark Bearer, in my head. Taunting me."

"What did he say?"

"That I was going to die."

She'd hesitated before answering. And blinked--twice. There was something Angel wasn't ready to share. Something worse than being threatened with death.

"Okay, thanks. Night, Angel."

"Night." She crossed to the door, then stopped and looked back. "Ask Zach. About that night. I'm sure he knows more than I do."

Micki frowned at the wording. Her oh-so-casual tone. "Do you think there's something he's not telling me?"

"Didn't say that. But unlike you and me, he was fully conscious the whole time."

CHAPTER THREE

Saturday, October 17
6:15 A.M.

MICKI LOWERED THE DRIVER'S SIDE window to let in the chilly fall morning. The breaking sun painted the horizon a brilliant pink and orange; the day's forecast was pure glory. October in New Orleans was a gift. Sort of a *"Congratulations, people, you made it through another summer."*

This morning she needed the snap of the cold air against her face to wake her up. After Angel had gone to bed, she'd pored over the events of that night, reliving each moment, then had brooded over her dream and its meaning.

She'd kept circling back to what Angel had said before she'd gone off to bed. *Ask Zach about that night. I'm sure he knows more than I do.*

The wording of that irritated the way some scabs did. She kept wanting to pick at it. Her right eye began to twitch. Something . . . there was something her subconscious wanted her to remember.

The facts didn't add up, because she didn't have them all.

But she, Zach and Angel weren't the only ones who had been at the scene. Which was the reason for this morning's pre-dawn excursion.

The paramedics had been there. She'd called the service and as luck would have it, one of the pair who had attended to her had left the company, but the other's shift was ending now. She'd asked them to have him wait, she needed to speak with him and was on her way over.

Micki reached the New Orleans Emergency Medical Services facility, parked and checked in at the front desk. "Paul just clocked out," the dispatcher said. "That's him, over there by the water cooler." She pointed to a man in a Saints cap. "You made it just in time."

Micki hurried across the room. "Paul Cleary?" she asked.

He turned. Judging by the deep creases around his eyes and mouth, it'd been a busy night. "Micki Dare, NOPD. You responded to—"

"I remember you." He smiled. "You look well, Detective. Sure as hell a lot better than last time I saw you. Congratulations on your recovery."

"Thanks. People keep telling me it's nothing short of miraculous."

His expression became wary. "What can I do for you today?"

"I was hoping you could answer a couple questions for me, about that night."

He glanced at his watch. "I'm really beat, Detective. It was one of those nights."

"I'll be quick. Promise."

He nodded. "But just so you know, scenes run together in my head. Though that night has stuck better than most."

"My partner said he heard you arriving and left me to go free the captives. You didn't see him?"

"Nope."

She frowned. "He said he called out to you."

"Didn't hear him. Sorry."

"Was there anyone else there?"

"Other than the guy who didn't make it? Not that I saw."

"What did you see?"

"Two victims. One male. One female—you. Both shot." He paused a moment as if in thought. "Knew right away the male victim was dead. Checked his pulse anyway, which confirmed it."

"How did you know I wasn't dead?"

He looked surprised. "Excuse me?"

"You said you knew right away the male victim was dead, which suggests you knew I wasn't. How?"

He hesitated. "You had a pulse. You were breathing, though labored."

"So, you knew after you physically confirmed it."

He rolled his shoulders, expression uncomfortable. "Yeah, that's right."

She frowned. He wasn't telling her something. "I saw the crime scene photos. I lost a lot of blood."

"You did."

"Doctor told me the bullet punctured my lung."

"Yes. Ascertained that immediately by the sound of your breathing."

"A sucking chest wound."

"Yes. We patched the chest wall with an Asherman Seal. It's always a choice between load-and-go and stay-and-play. With you I was worried, because of your breathing, that your condition would worsen with travel. Needle decompression was indicated, followed by insertion of a chest tube."

"How long did it take you and your partner to get to the scene?"

"Longer than usual. Because of the location. I'd say twenty or twenty-five minutes."

"Long time. In a situation like that." He didn't comment, so she went on. "Considering everything you did, how long were you at the scene?"

"Ten minutes. Another eight to get to the trauma center." He tugged on the bill of his cap. "Everything's in the log, Detective."

"I don't think what I'm looking for is. I'm looking for what you're not telling me."

He blinked. "What reason would I have for keeping something from you?"

"You tell me." When he didn't respond, she looked him in the eyes. "I'm trying to figure out why I'm alive."

"How about you're one of the lucky ones? Be thankful and walk away."

He sounded like Zach. She knew they were both right, but she couldn't let go. Not yet. "How did you know I was alive and the other guy wasn't?"

For a moment, he looked like he was going to blow her off. Then he shrugged. "I see things sometimes. It doesn't mean anything."

"What do you mean, see things?"

"You were surrounded by light. The guy wasn't."

Like in her dream. Her heart sped up. "Surrounded by light?"

"Yeah." The word came out as a challenge.

"Did your partner—"

"No, she never did. We stopped talking about it."

"Was it like some sort of a force field or—"

"I'm done." He stood up.

"Wait!" She jumped to her feet. "I'm not making fun of you. I want to know. I *need* to."

"It's something I see sometimes. A glow. I don't know if it's the person's energy, their aura or life force I pick up on, but it's about me. I see it. I haven't run across anyone else who does."

"Sometimes, you said. How often?"

"Once a month maybe. Why does it matter, Detective?"

He suddenly looked exhausted. Out on his feet. She felt guilty about keeping him. She lowered her voice.

"I dreamed about that night. I was cocooned in light. It was bright, but not harsh. Does that describe what you saw?"

He nodded.

"I have this feeling that glow is why I'm alive. That there's something about it I need to know."

"Maybe it just wasn't your time to go? Have you thought about that?"

"That doesn't sound very scientific."

"It's not. I see all sorts of miraculous shit every day, Detective. Stuff that doesn't make one bit of scientific sense, but there it is. Can't explain it. Stopped trying."

"Miraculous?"

"Yeah. It's made a believer out of me."

"A believer. Like in a divine force?"

"Something beyond what we know. Like I said, unexplainable."

"And when you see this light, the person is always alive?"

"Yeah. Look, like I said, I'm dead on my feet. We done here?"

She nodded and held out her hand. "Thanks for this. And for saving my life."

He started off then stopped, glanced back. "Detective Dare?"

She met his serious gaze.

"Maybe you're asking the wrong questions? Instead of wondering how it is you survived, you should ask why it wasn't your turn to die."

"Like I have some unfinished business?"

"Or a greater purpose. Think about it."

"Paul?"

"Yeah?"

"You ever see anything else? Besides the light?"

"Like what?"

How did she ask? The grim reaper or the boogeyman? Evil incarnate, darkness itself?

She was already on thin ice. "Good point. What else could there be?"

CHAPTER FOUR

Monday, October 19
8:20 P.M.

JUGGLING A LOADED BEVERAGE CADDY, Zach bounded up the stairs and into the NOPD Eighth District station. The neoclassical building, at Royal and Conti Streets in the heart of the French Quarter, had been repurposed to house the Eighth. Because so many visitors made their way inside for a photo op—or to visit the Cops 8 vending machines—the first floor had been all spiffed up, clean and classy.

The building's second floor told the real story: crumbling walls and peeling paint, mold and overburdened AC units. Zach had learned that here in New Orleans, they called that "atmosphere."

Zach worked the coolest gig on the force. Officially, that was the Eighth District Investigative Unit, the most happening real estate in The Big Easy: French Quarter, Marigny, and Central Business District. Unofficially he was part of Sixers, an undercover, FBI initiative that placed specially "gifted" recruits with local P.Ds.

His particular gifts were a mixed bag. A little psychometry, a little clairvoyance and telepathy, all sweetened by retrocognition. Lots of fancy words to describe his freak gene. Which made him really good at this cop thing.

So yeah, super-secret, special agent—coolest gig on the force.

As long as he didn't focus on pulsing shadows with the ability to kill. Or the fact these Dark Bearers wanted to kill him because his gumbo of abilities made him able to not only see them, but track them by their energy.

Took a little bit of the shine off the whole deal.

The desk sergeant was deep in conversation with a group of agitated tourists. They were getting loud and she looked ready to blow. Some people you didn't push. Especially before noon on a Monday.

She caught sight of him and her scowl melted. "What you got there, Hollywood?"

"Something to make this morning a little more palatable."

She glared at the group. "Move aside, people. Let the detective through."

He set the white chocolate mocha on the desk; she grabbed it like a lifeline and leaned forward. "You might have just saved somebody's life. You know that, right?"

He winked at her and headed up to the Investigative Unit. He stopped at the receptionist's desk, deposited her drink and gathered up his messages. "Mad Dog make it in yet?"

Sue fluffed her teased-up do. "Been here awhile. And she's in a mood."

He laughed. "Isn't she always?"

"I'd tell you to watch your ass this morning, but I'm happy to watch it for you."

He grinned. "You're just bad, you know that?"

"You don't know the half of it, baby." She winked. "If you give me a chance, I'll show you."

He teased her right back. "You're way too hot for me, Sue. Besides, that boyfriend of yours is crazy."

Her phone rang before she could respond and he went in search of Mick. He found her where he knew she'd be, at her desk, studying the contents of a folder in front of her. Her head was lowered, strands of her shoulder-length hair had escaped her ponytail and she absently twirled them while she read.

Zach cocked his head, studying her. Sometimes she was just Mick. Partner, kick-ass, take-no-prisoners Mad Dog Dare.

And sometimes, like now, he'd look at her and she'd be the woman from the club that night, moving to the thundering music, drawing the hungry gaze of every man near her—including his.

The woman whose mouth had set his blood on fire. He could recall the way she'd felt pressed against him, the feel of her heartbeat against his chest, her breath against his ear.

That woman didn't really exist. The moment had been make-believe, part of the undercover operation that had nearly cost her life.

As if sensing his gaze, she glanced up. And typical Mick, frowned. "What?"

The memory evaporated. He smiled and closed the distance between them. "Morning, partner." He set the drink caddy on the desk in front of her along with a white paper bag. "I brought you breakfast."

She eyed the bag suspiciously. "What is it?"

"Coffee cake. Cinnamon."

"Sounds good. What's the catch?"

"Why would you think there's a catch?"

She snorted. "You know why. The last 'treat' you brought me tasted like dirt."

"Leave it to you to know what dirt tastes like. But this time it won't, I promise."

She slid the pastry out and sniffed it. "What's in it?"

"If I tell you that, it'll ruin all the fun."

When she just looked at him, he said, "You scared, Mad Dog?"

"Hell, yeah. You're a whack job."

She slid it back into the bag. "Tell me the thermal cup's for me. Tell me it's my favorite three-shot latté with just the right amount of vanilla syrup."

"Nope. The other one's yours."

"It's the color of vomit."

"It's a green drink. Kale and mango and—"

"Fuck no, I'm not drinking that. Besides, I've already had breakfast."

"Cheese crackers? Or powdered donuts?"

"Both. Asshole."

He laughed, pulled up a chair and helped himself to the green drink and coffee cake. "Figured you'd say that, which is why I haven't had breakfast. Take the coffee."

She did, sipped and sighed. He took a bite of the whole grain, gluten-free confection. "Sue said you got here early. What's up?"

"Couldn't sleep."

"How come?" he asked around a slurp of the drink.

"Something's bothering me."

"Shocker."

She opened the folder on her desk. Scene photos, he saw. From that night. She fanned them out.

He had a hard time looking at them. The first, Kenny, sprawled on his back. Covered in his own blood. And Mick's.

The second, a photo of the spot where she'd lain. Bleeding out.

Even as Zach told himself to look away, he stared at the image. It all rushed back: the sound of the gun going off, once, then again. She and Kenny going down, then him rolling her onto her back, seeing how bad it was; knowing that he was losing her.

He sensed her scrutiny and returned his gaze to hers. "Not my favorite memories," he said lightly. "I can't imagine they're yours. You have a reason for paying them a visit?"

"That's exactly it. Memories." She shifted her attention to the desk, and the fan of grisly images. "I lost a lot of blood."

"That you did, Mick."

"It's a miracle I'm alive. That's what everyone says."

He suspected where this was going but hoped he was wrong. "It is."

"How?" she asked, looking him straight in the eyes.

He wasn't wrong. But he didn't look away. "What do you mean?"

"How did you save me?"

"It wasn't me. The paramedics—"

"You called them."

"Yes."

"Did you stay with me until they got there?"

"Mick—"

"My chest wound." Her voice deepened ever-so-slightly. "You applied pressure?"

He didn't want to lie to her and would do whatever he could to avoid it. "I don't understand what you're getting at."

"It's standard procedure. Apply continual pressure to stem the flow of blood."

"You're alive, Mick. Why isn't that good enough?"

"Keep the victim warm," she continued. "Make certain they keep breathing. If they stop, begin artificial breathing. Did you do that?"

"Mick," he said softly, reaching across the desk and covering her hand with his, "when the paramedics arrived I went to help Angel and the other two."

"They didn't see you."

"Who?"

"The paramedics. I talked to one of them. Paul."

"When?"

"This morning." Her expression softened with vulnerability. "So, you were with me when they arrived?"

He wouldn't lie to her. She didn't deserve that. "No. I heard them arriving, and went to help Angel. They were screaming, Mick. I'm sorry I left you. I felt like I had to."

"That's not it, I—" She slid her hand from beneath his. "How long did it take for the paramedics to arrive?"

"I don't know. I wasn't watching the clock."

"More than an hour?"

"From the time you were shot?"

"Yes."

"Might have been. Like I said, I wasn't watching a clock." He searched her gaze, troubled. "What's going on, Mick?"

"Maybe nothing, I just . . . Ever heard of the Golden Hour?" He shook his head. "Basically, this doctor recognized that if trauma patients arrived at a hospital within sixty minutes of being injured, their survival rate spiked. He called it the Golden Hour."

"Okay. And?"

"I was wondering if I did."

"Why does it matter, Mick? You made it."

"Was someone else with you?"

His mouth went dry.

"You go, Zach. I'll take care of her."

She wasn't supposed to remember. They had assured him she wouldn't. Just as they had convinced him it wasn't time for Mick to know everything. For her own well-being.

"Like who?"

"I've had this dream, a couple of times . . ."

"And?" He held his breath.

"There was someone with you. He took care of me. He's the reason I'm alive. Not the paramedics."

"What did he look like?"

"I didn't see," she began, "I—" She shook her head. "Never mind, it was just a dream, right?"

"Right."

"Yo, Hollywood!"

They both turned in the direction of the voice. Sue, tottering across the squad room in her ridiculously high wedges, looked completely put out. "You didn't hear your desk phone ringing?"

"I'm not at my desk."

"Good thing you're so hot, because you're a major pain in the ass."

"He's been told that before," Micki said, grinning. "By everyone."

"Everyone?" He looked at her. "So, you think I'm hot?"

"No, I think you're a pain in the ass." She turned back to Sue. "What's up?"

"Major wants you both in his office. Now."

CHAPTER FIVE

Monday, October 19
9:01 P.M.

A FORMER LSU FOOTBALL PLAYER, MAJOR Nichols towered over them both. It didn't matter that his middle had turned soft and his hair gray, his very presence commanded respect.

"Take a seat."

He handed them each an envelope. "You're aware of the rash of home invasions across the city in the past few weeks? Another one occurred last night, this time in the Lake Vista neighborhood."

Micki thrummed her fingers on her thigh. "That makes four. All in different neighborhoods." She read the list. "The first in Gert Town. Then Treme, followed by Hollygrove."

"And now," Zach added, "Lake Vista. What's the connection?"

"There doesn't seem to be one. The four neighborhoods, the homes invaded and the families who live in them don't seem to have much in common."

Micki flipped through, quickly assessing. She lifted her gaze. "They all had kids." She had his attention. "It's something they have in common. Different ages and number of 'em, but all four families have kids."

Zach spoke up. "Between the ages of four and twelve."

"It's something," Nichols said.

"What about the perpetrators?" Zach asked. "Do we believe the same ones carried out each incident?"

"We're not clear on that either. The first crime was committed by three masked males, two of them armed. The second by four, again two armed. The third by six men, two armed. Last night, six again. Whether the same two armed men were at every scene is also uncertain."

"But highly probable," Micki said.

"Yes, that's the theory."

"All males?"

"Yes. And young."

Micki looked up. "I thought their identities were concealed."

"They were. Both by hoodies and masks of some sort. But they couldn't conceal their voices or their builds which, except for the armed two, were slight. In interviews, every victim described them as young. They pinned their ages between fourteen and twenty-two."

"Fourteen?" Zach shook his head. "Wow, that is young."

Micki shuffled through the report once more. "Victims of home invasions are usually targeted because they're seen driving an expensive car or wearing flashy jewelry, something like that. Not one of these families seem to fit that profile."

"Indeed," Nichols said. "And nothing's been taken from any of the scenes, so robbery's not the motive."

"Then what is?"

"That's what the Chief wants you two to figure out." He moved his gaze between them. "Here's the other thing, until last night nobody had been hurt. Terrorized, property destroyed, but left physically unharmed."

"That's the worry, isn't it?" Micki muttered. "When do these assholes get bored with terrorizing and move on to torture, rape and murder? Last night they took a step in that direction."

He folded his hands on the desk in front of him. "Exactly."

"None of these fell in our jurisdiction," Micki said. "We're gonna step on toes."

"Not like you haven't done *that* before." A smile pulled at his mouth. "Congratulations, you two. You know your roles. Dare, you take the investigative lead. Harris, for God's sake keep your abilities to yourself. Let Dare figure out how to filter your leads, or how you came by them, to the media community. Any questions?"

Zach jumped to his feet. "On it, Major. Nothing better than fresh energy at a crime scene."

Micki rolled her eyes and stood. "These victims have names?"

"Rick and Margie Fowler and their two kids. Here's the address."

He tore a sheet from the notepad by his phone and handed it to Micki. "After you've interviewed the Fowlers and reviewed all the other detectives' case notes, check in with me on how you plan to proceed."

She got to her feet. "Timeframe?"

"Fast. Chief wants a press conference by the end of the day."

Micki cocked an eyebrow. "You can't be serious? A press conference? Today?"

"As serious as a level ten first-degree felony."

Zach grinned. "No worries, Major. If all goes well, we'll have solid suspects by then. That's just the way I roll."

When they'd cleared Major Nichols' office, Micki looked archly at Zack. "That's just the way *you* roll?"

"I said we."

"No, you didn't."

"I meant we."

She stopped, turned to him. "Look, I don't care about that. What I do care about is your over-confidence. It'll get somebody and if history repeats, that somebody'll be me."

"C'mon, Mick—" His bright blue eyes crinkled at the corners. "I haven't gotten you hurt in three months."

Charming, Micki thought, irritated. Borderline irresistible. It just wasn't fair. "One month of which I was on medical leave. From being shot, because of you."

"That month still counts. We talked every day."

She rolled her eyes and grabbed her jacket off the back of her chair. "Whatever." They headed downstairs and outside.

"Which ride are you feeling today," he asked, "my POS or the Nova?"

The Nova, classic American muscle machine, circa 1971. Her pride and joy. Just sitting behind the wheel revved her engine.

"You even have to ask, Hollywood? I'm driving."

CHAPTER SIX

Monday, October 19
1:00 P.M.

"THIS DOESN'T EVEN LOOK LIKE New Orleans," Zach said, taking in the low-slung, angular homes they passed on their way to the Fowler scene.

Micki agreed as she turned onto Marconi Drive. "I remember the first time I saw this neighborhood, I thought I'd been magically transported to some other time and place.

"The bird streets," Micki went on. "Heron, Gull, Flamingo. They're all part of Lake Vista, but New Orleanians often call 'em the Bird Streets. Just past the Birds are the Jewels."

He glanced over at her. "What's the story?"

"This whole area was a mid-twentieth-century planned community. Like the current New Urbanism trend, it was supposed to have a town center with a school, shopping, and post office."

"There it is," he said, "Thrasher."

Moments later she had expertly squeezed the Nova between a cruiser and the crime scene van. They climbed out and headed up the walk.

The scene officer, whose bored expression suggested he'd not only seen it all but was totally over it, held out the log. "Names and credentials."

Micki stepped in. "Detectives Micki Dare and Zach Harris, Eighth District."

"Harris?" he said, eyes lighting up. "Hollywood Harris?"

Zach grinned. "The one and only."

"Hot damn. I had twenty bucks riding on you showing up today.

Figured with four of these, they'd call in the cavalry." He pursed his lips, obviously pleased. "Gibson's gonna be hot."

"Gibson?" Zach asked.

"Officer in charge. You'll recognize him by his bald head. Be sure to tell him he owes me twenty bucks."

"Wow," she muttered as they walked away, "you're so young to be so famous."

"Sour grapes?"

They stepped into the home's foyer. "Hardly. You—"

Zach lost what she said as a buzz filled his head. Like a colony of bees had descended upon him. He moved deeper into the room. The buzz intensified, becoming as chaotic as the scene before him. Furniture was toppled, pillows ripped open, foam guts strewn wildly about. Lamps smashed. Mirror broken.

Zach bent to pick up a piece of the shattered lamp. A memory. Wild laughter. Delight in destruction.

"What?" Micki asked softly.

"It's good. Lots of energy, fresh. You go find Gibson. I'm going to do my thing."

She nodded and moved on. No comment, not even an eye roll. Total acceptance of what he brought to the party. He watched her a moment, amazed at how far they had come as a team.

He carefully replaced the piece of lamp, moving on to the kitchen. Food had been smeared across stainless steel appliances, glassware broken. He squatted down and closed his eyes.

Flashes of light and sound. Images darting forward, then evaporating. Music. Heavy metal. Metallica maybe. Never was his genre. A kid. Young. Too young. Giggling as he smashed one plate after another.

He? Zach stopped, attempted to slow, focus on the image. Hoodie, bandana covering everything but the eyes. Yes, male. Those eyes, brown yet bright. In a way they shouldn't be, he thought. What did it mean?

From the kitchen, he went back to the bedrooms. The first, obviously a guest room, was untouched. From there he moved across the hall. A kid's room. Girls, judging by the tsunami of pink. He took a cautious step inside, waiting for the psychic terror to hit him.

Instead, children singing. Playing a children's game. *Ring around the rosie, a pocket-full posies…*

He moved his gaze over the interior, confused. It was messy, toys strewn about, bed a jumble. But not the destruction of the rest of the house. More like the Fowler girls had had a play date.

He made his way through the room, just to be certain he wasn't missing anything. Kid energy was different. Faster moving. Mercurial. He felt tears and joy, fear and elation, all tangled together in a crazy mix.

Zach frowned. They must have heard the chaos, raised voices and shattering glass. Why weren't they frightened?

"You done here?"

Zach glanced at the CSI tech in the doorway. "Yeah, it's all yours."

He slipped past him and out the door. The master bedroom was at the other end of the hallway. As he neared it, a heavy sensation settled over him, slowing his steps, making each one an effort. His heart rate accelerated and sweat broke out on his upper lip.

He drew in a deep breath and closed the distance between him and the bedroom. There it hit him—energy, in an angry wave. He felt it in his chest first, then his gut. And light. So bright it burned. Then dark. Deep as pitch. Like a strobe: dark, light, dark, light, faster and faster. His stomach lurched, his knees started to buckle and he grabbed the door frame for support.

Ride the wave, Zach. Breathe into it.

In. And out. In . . . out. In—

Light, dark. On . . . off. On—

His vision cleared and then was suffused with the wreckage before him. The same as the living room and kitchen. Yet different, as well. Somehow he saw more purpose here. His gaze settled on a dark stain on the light carpet. Smaller stains surrounded it. Like a spill. Blood.

He let go of the door frame and spied several lengths of rope. And caught the strong smell of urine.

But sensed a different energy--older and more organized.

He knew this energy, but didn't. Strange. Like a reflection of the real deal.

Zach crossed to one of the lengths of rope and gazed down at it. Hopelessness and helplessness. But not that of the victim.

The perpetrator.

An image formed in his head. A figure. Male. Zach squatted down, reaching for the rope.

As he closed his hand over it, a howl filled his head, the sound was one of agony. Of a soul in distress. The contents of his stomach lurched to his throat. He jumped to his feet and hurried to the door, darting out of the bedroom, through the crush of officers and under the crime tape. He made it to the bushes and threw up violently.

"It's back, isn't it? Our Dark Bearer?"

He turned. Micki, with a bottle of water. He held out his hand for it. "Maybe."

She handed him the sweating plastic bottle, watching as he rinsed his mouth, spit, then repeated.

"Maybe," she said, "What does that mean?"

"This is different."

"How so?"

"I'm not certain yet."

She cocked an eyebrow. "Maybe you should try dialing your freak-o-meter up a notch?"

Sarcasm. Mick wouldn't be Mick without it. "Thanks for the tip. I'll give that a whirl."

She motioned to the house. "Getting ready to interview the Fowlers. Figured you'd want in."

"I do. Thanks."

"Think you can handle it?"

"I'm freaking Hollywood Harris. Of course I can."

Coming from the guy who had just puked in the bushes, it should have been funny. At the minimum, absurd.

Neither of them cracked a smile. This shit had just gotten real.

Again.

CHAPTER SEVEN

Monday, October 19
1:35 P.M.

ZACH FELL INTO STEP WITH Micki. A tingling sensation skittered randomly over him, like an electrical current touching one place, then skipping over to another. Damn weird.

He'd never encountered a scene like this before--one that combined numerous perpetrators and victims of so many varying ages.

Mick was uneasy as well. Edgy. Readying for battle, totally focused. He felt the emotion rolling off her in waves.

He had the absurd urge to take her hand. Curve his fingers through hers. Show her she wasn't alone in this and prove to himself *he* wasn't.

If he tried something like that, she'd deck him.

"Gibson was not happy to see me," she said suddenly. "Rightly figured he'd just wasted two hours of his day."

"He give you anything?"

"Besides a dirty look? Apparently, party began around two a.m. Victims awakened to a strobe light and—"

"Wait, did you say a strobe light?"

"Yeah, why?"

"I picked that up. And blaring music."

"They had a boom box." She indicated the walkway around to the back of the house. "Fowlers are outside."

"What about the kids?"

"At Grandma's."

They rounded the house. The husband and wife huddled together on a bench in the sun, staring blankly at the park beyond. She wore a floral, wrap robe, and a sunny yellow gown peeked out from around her knees. He wore a T-shirt and sweats. His head had been bandaged and his face was bruised.

Zach let Micki take the lead.

"Mr. and Mrs. Fowler," she said as they reached them. They turned. Both had the hollow-eyed look of people who had been traumatized. "I'm Detective Dare. This is my partner, Detective Harris."

They didn't respond, even with a blink.

"We need to ask you some questions."

The woman nodded and Micki grabbed a chair and brought it around. Zach noted that the man didn't look at either of them.

"Tell me what happened," Micki said gently.

"We were sleeping," the woman began, voice shaking. "Then we were awake. You know, suddenly. There was this bright, flashing light. And this music battering at me. I was so . . . disoriented."

She curved her arms around her middle, so tightly Zach wondered how she could breathe. "And then I heard screaming. It was—" her voice lowered to a whisper, "—the kids."

Zach frowned. He hadn't gotten that. If it was true, why hadn't he picked that up? If it wasn't true, why would Marjorie Fowler lie?

The woman glanced quickly at her husband, then back at Micki. Her eyes welled with tears. "They were screaming for us."

"Excuse me, Mrs. Fowler," Zach said. "Just for clarity, were they calling for you or were they screaming?"

She started at him, looking startled. "I don't know, I— I'm not sure now." The tears spilled over and her husband put his arm around her, expression stony.

"Take your time, Mrs. Fowler," Micki said. "We know how traumatic this must have been for you."

"Then they . . . stopped. We panicked and when Rick tried to go to them … they hit him. The sound—" She shuddered. "I thought they'd crushed his skull. He went down and—"

Her throat closed over the words. "They tied him up, then made him watch."

"Watch what, Mrs. Fowler?" Mick pressed.

The woman hung her head. The tears rolled off her nose, dropped and splattered on that patch of sunny yellow fabric.

"How many of them were there?" Micki asked, changing her approach.

"Six."

"So, when you awakened, there were six strange men in your bedroom."

"No. At first just two. The others joined them later. There may have been more but . . . that's all I ever saw."

"Did you see their faces?"

She shook her head. "They were wearing ski masks and hoodies. All black."

"Were they wearing gloves?"

"No."

"That's good," Micki said. "There'll be prints all over this place. You saw their hands. Could you tell their race?"

She shook her head again. "No . . . I think I was so disoriented by the strobe . . ."

"How about other identifying characteristics?"

"Like what?"

"Their voices. Their body types. A tattoo, ponytail . . . anything."

"Enough!" Rick Fowler leapt to his feet, shaking with fury. "We've been asked all this already! Just leave us be!"

The outburst gave Zach his opportunity. He laid a hand on Fowler's arm. His hand tingled at the connection point, then grew hot. An image overcame him. The scene through Fowler's eyes. The strobe light. The perpetrators being revealed, then hidden, dancing around his wife on the bed, touching her—her hair, her face, with their hands and the guns.

Then Fowler's rage and shame and hopelessness. A terrible, punishing mix. Debilitating and destructive.

"It's okay, man," Zach said quietly, releasing his arm. "I get it."

"Do you? Have you ever had to watch your family be tortured? And been able to do nothing? Do you have children? Have you had to listen as they screamed to their daddy for help and you could do nothing?" His voice rose, then deepened. "Have you?"

Of course he hadn't, Zach knew. Until he laid his hand on Fowler's arm, and lived it through him. Now he understood. A man protected his family. It's what made him a man, in as primitive a way as there was. It was ingrained in the DNA.

In one night, Rick Fowler had been stripped of it.

Fowler sank back onto the bench. He dropped his face to his hands, shoulders shaking with the effort of holding back his sobs.

His wife tried to put her arms around him but he pushed her away. "Don't . . . I'm so ashamed."

"What could you do!" she cried. "They had guns! They could have killed you—"

"My job, Margie. You and the kids . . . what good am I . . . I can't even—"

Zach squatted in front of him. "Look at me, Rick." He said it with the cadence he had refined over the years, testing and adjusting until he'd found the one that worked best. Micki called it his super-mojo vision, part of his freak gene.

He'd thought of it that way at first. Now it was as natural to him as breathing.

Fowler looked at him. Zach felt the connection and held his gaze. "It's going to okay," he said. "You did what you had to do. A man does protect his family, to the best of his ability. You did that."

Fowler didn't blink. "I did what I could. I would have killed them if I'd been able."

"You're lucky to be alive. And that's what matters."

"It is. I'm alive."

"Your family needs you. Now more than ever."

"They could have been taken from me."

"But they weren't. They're safe. All of you are safe."

"Yes. Thank God." He looked at his wife. She caught his hand and clutched it tightly.

"Rick?" Fowler turned, meeting his gaze again. "Detective Dare and I need your help. You're going to help us catch the animals who did this."

"Yes, I am." He squared his shoulders, and drew his wife to his side, arm curved protectively around her. "At first," he began, voice steady, "it was just the two of them. They both had guns. They both wore jeans and dark hoodies. Bandanas over their faces. But I realized there must be others because of the music and the kids."

"They were both male?"

"Definitely. Deep voices, strong builds. And the way the one hit me, he knew what he was doing. No hesitation."

"What happened then?"

"I was out cold. When I came to, I was hogtied. Completely immobilized. That's the first thing I became aware of. Then it was of Margie." His voice deepened, as if with resolution. "Crying."

"Why was she crying?"

"It was a bizarre scene. Like something out of Peter Pan."

"Peter Pan? What do you mean?"

"Remember the Disney version? When the Lost Boys are playing Indians, dancing around the fire?" Zach nodded. "These six were dancing around Margie. Whooping it up. Having the time of their lives."

"What about your kids?"

"I don't know. Didn't hear them. They were quiet as mice. I was so afraid they'd been—" He couldn't bring himself to say it and shook his head. "But they're fine. Safe."

"That's right," Margie Fowler agreed. "They're safe."

"Tell me about your captors."

Fowler frowned at the term. Maybe he hadn't thought of himself in that way until now. A captive.

He cleared his throat. "What do you want to know?"

"Their ages. Who was in charge. Anything else that might have jumped out at you."

"The two with the guns were the leaders. No doubt about that."

"Was there one in particular?"

He drew his eyebrows together. "Yeah," he said after a moment.

"The one who hit you?"

"No, the other one."

Zach frowned, surprised. "Anything specifically make you think that?"

"He just . . . a guy just knows who the head guy is." He looked at his wife, as if for confirmation. "You agree?"

She nodded. "It was almost like the one who hit Rick was . . . trying to impress the other one."

"Gotcha. What about their ages?"

"Twenties. Early, I'd guess. But maybe twenty-five or six."

"How about the others?"

"Not men yet."

"Did any of them seem really young?"

He thought for a minute. "One of them. A teenager, voice cracked a couple times. He giggled. Where the hell are their parents?"

He'd picked up the giggling.

But he'd also picked up fear and shame.

"Did the young one act frightened? Any of them, did you pick up that they were being coerced or held against their will? Forced to carry out the act?"

"The only ones being held against their will and terrorized were us. Like I said, they seemed to be having the time of their lives." Bitterness colored his tone, and deep anger.

"Do you have a security system?" Micki asked, redirecting.

"Yes. It didn't go off."

"You sure you set it?"

"I always do."

"Could one of your kids have disarmed—"

"They're five and seven! Whoever this gang was, they must have disabled it."

"It's not tied in to your phone line?"

"It is." He frowned and glanced at his wife. "We still have a monitoring service, don't we?"

She nodded. "If the alarm is messed with, it's supposed to automatically trigger a call to the police."

Micki stood. Zach followed. "That's it for now. You've been a lot of help. Thank you."

"You're going to catch them, right?"

"Yeah," Zach said, "we are." He handed them both a card. "My cell number's on there. Call anytime. Day or night."

They started off, but Micki stopped, glancing back. "I noticed a dog bowl in the kitchen. You have a dog?"

Fowler's face went blank. He nodded. "A golden retriever. Roxanne. That was the weirdest thing."

"What?"

"She slept through the whole thing. They must have drugged her or something."

"Where is she now?"

"We sent her with the kids. So she wouldn't get in the way of the investigators."

"We'd like to question the kids," Micki said. "Or arrange to have someone from the juvenile division—"

"Absolutely not," Margie Fowler said. "I want this to be over for them. They've already endured too much."

"They may have noticed something you missed."

"They're so young! Terrified out of their minds. What could they tell you?"

She started to sob again. Zach thought they might be able to tell him a lot, but he kept that to himself. He and Mick had gotten all they would from the Fowlers for now.

⚜ ⚜ ⚜

Zach's cell rang as they were leaving the scene. Parker, he saw. "Harris," he answered.

"It's me."

"I know. What do you want?"

"You're going to get tired of that grudge eventually."

"Don't count on it."

"Heard you and Dare pulled the home invasions."

"Good news travels fast. Leaving the scene now."

"Dare's with you?"

"She sends her love, too."

Beside him, Micki snorted.

"Call me when you can talk freely," Parker said, then hung up.

Zach re-holstered his phone.

Micki looked at him. "What's going on with the two of you?"

"What do you mean?"

She arched an eyebrow. "I'm not deaf, dumb or blind, dude. Things haven't been right between you two in months."

Three to be exact. "The guy's a douche."

"Well, yeah. But he never made a secret of that."

Zach laughed. "Ain't that the truth."

They reached the Nova; Micki unlocked it and they climbed in. She fired up the engine, but didn't shift into gear. All humor gone, she looked at him. "So, what do you think? Earlier you said you weren't sure, you know, whether it was back. How about now?"

He squinted out the windshield, reviewing. "It wasn't our Dark Bearer. The power was different . . . but still . . . it's something twisted. Bad twisted."

She shifted into drive and pulled away from the curb. "Explain."

He frowned in thought. "It was chaotic. Gleeful."

She took a corner fast. "What do you mean, gleeful?"

"Joy in destruction. Chaos for chaos's sake."

"You asked Fowler if any of the perps seemed like they were being coerced. Or were there against their will. It seemed an odd question." She gunned the engine and roared through a changing light. "What prompted it?"

"When I . . . touched the rope used to bind Fowler, I picked up something that didn't make sense to me."

"Okay. What?"

"This deep sadness. Regret and shame."

"Fowler's," she said. "Had to be."

"I don't think so."

"Then whose? The perp's?"

"Yeah, that's what I'm thinking."

"First off, if you're right—which you may not be—there are many not so weird explanations. Gang mentality turns right and wrong upside down. The gang provides support, courage and bravado. It rationalizes, even legitimizes, the acts of the group. But there's shame involved. Fear of being caught. Especially if the perp is new to the group."

He nodded. "You're right."

"Wait, whoa, hold the fuck up, Hollywood. You just told me I'm right."

"Yeah, so?"

"Just give me a moment, you know, to breathe it in."

He laughed. "Okay. Just don't get used to it."

She slid into a parking spot beside the Eighth, and cut the engine. "Nichols was going to have all the case files delivered to us. We've got a lot of ground to make up."

"Reviewing case notes isn't my thing, Mad Dog. You know that."

"Necessary evil, dude. Sorry."

"I'm going a different direction. Major's orders."

She unsnapped her safety belt. "How do you figure that?"

"Said each of us should concentrate on our own unique abilities."

"And yours are hocus-pocus bullshit?"

He grinned. "Pretty much."

"Lucky me. You want to be just a little more specific?"

"Got a hunch. About the kids. You know their kids' terrified screaming the Fowlers described? I didn't pick that up, not at all. Everything else lined up, hit all the right notes."

"I wonder why?"

"That's what I want to find out." Zach popped open his door. "Gonna use my mojo to get permission to talk to them."

"That sounds right."

They climbed out of the vehicle. Zach started toward his car, she into the building.

But she stopped, calling back to him. "Press conference at six. We meet with Nichols first. Five-thirty."

"Got it."

"And, Hollywood? For the love of God, be there on time. You're our frontman."

CHAPTER EIGHT

Monday, October 19
3:10 P.M.

GERT TOWN. A FORGOTTEN NEIGHBORHOOD. Not by those who lived there, but by prosperity. Run-down shotgun homes, badly in need of fresh paint and a carpenter. Overgrown yards and gardens overrun with weeds. Yet there were pockets of hope--flowers blooming in the cracked planters, tidy porches, windows so clean they sparkled.

The house number Zach was looking for was one of the beacons. A young boy sat on the porch steps, playing with plastic dinosaurs. Zach parked the Taurus and climbed out, but when he started up the walk, the boy jumped up and ran to the door. A moment later, the screen door slapped shut behind him and Zach heard the boy calling his grandma.

He sounded scared.

A moment later a woman appeared at the door. She was large-framed, with skin like burnished mahogany and hair the color of snow. She wore an apron; a cross hung from around her neck.

"Mrs. Cole?"

She nodded, her gaze suspicious. "That's right."

"Detective Harris." He held up his shield. "NOPD Eighth District."

She squinted at the badge, taking a long moment to look it over. "Okay. What do you want?"

"May I come in?"

"Whatever you've got to say to me you can say from there."

Somebody was less than impressed with cops. "I'm investigating your home invasion—"

"Is this a joke?"

"No, ma'am. Why would it be?"

"Police don't care about crimes against folks like me in this kind of neighborhood.

"Folks like you? What does that mean?"

She scoffed. "Don't play dumb. It means poor and black."

"I'm sorry you've been made to feel that way, ma'am, but I promise you I do care."

She looked him up and down. "Been three weeks since those animals came in here with their guns and trash talk. Pretendin' to be all gangsta and street-wise. Smashin' my stuff and raisin' hell. That's the last time I saw them or the police."

"Until now," he said. "I want to hear what you have to say."

She squinted at him. "I may not be college-educated, but I ain't stupid. You're here 'cause those hoods are botherin' the rich folks now. I watch the news."

Zach wished he could argue with that, but he couldn't. It made him damn uncomfortable with the status quo.

"Don't know what they were doing around this neighborhood anyway," she went on. "Nothin' worth stealing. Lucky for them I don't keep a gun. They would've gotten their butts shot."

"You said the perpetrators were pretending to be gangster. Why?"

She folded her arms across her chest and just looked at him. He had to admit, it'd been a dumb question. He went in another direction. "The others we've interviewed said they couldn't tell the perpetrators' race because of the hoodies and bandanas. You're saying you could?"

"Theo," she said, nudging the boy. "You tell the policeman what you told me."

Zach glanced down. The boy clung to his grandmother's legs. He looked dutifully up at Zach. "They was white."

"Mrs. Cole, is it all right if I ask your grandson some questions?"

She studied him for a moment, then agreed and looked at her grandson. "You tell him everything you told me. And scream loud if he tries anything funny. I'll be right here, tending supper."

Zach squatted to be face-to-face with the child. "So, your name's Theo. That's a nice name."

"It's really Theodore," he said proudly. "Like the president."

"My name's Zachary. Like a president, too."

The boy smiled. "Did you see my dinosaurs?"

"I did. They're very cool."

He smiled and trotted over to the steps and his figures. Zach followed. "Which one is your favorite?"

"Stegs."

"The stegosaurus?" Theo nodded. "Not T. rex?"

"Rex is too mean."

"I think so, too."

"You want to talk to me about those bad guys, don't you?"

"I do, Theo. You think you can do that? I don't want you to be scared."

"I won't be scared. Me-Maw tol' me they was just trash."

"She's a smart lady, isn't she?"

"Yup." He picked up his figures and engaged them in mortal combat, complete with sound effects.

"So tell me about those bad guys, when they came in your house."

He paused a moment, then the prehistoric life-or-death scenario started up again. "First I was real scared. They shined a light in my eyes an' it stung bad."

Zach frowned. "Do you know why they did that?"

He shook his head.

"How many of them were there?"

He held up four fingers.

Zach frowned. If he recalled correctly, Major Nichols had said the first crime had included three perpetrators.

"One was real nice," Theo went on. "He played with me."

"He played with you?"

"Yeah. He was supposed to watch me. But I was cryin' and it made him sad."

"He didn't want you to cry?"

He shook his head. The dinosaur figures banded together against the T. rex. "So he lifted up his scarf. To show me he was nice."

That's how he had known the perps were white, Zach realized. "What did you two play?"

"We was superheroes. I got to wear a cape."

"That does sound fun."

"He's my friend. Me-Maw says that ain't true." Theo looked up to meet Zach's eyes. "But he is."

"Tell me more about him. What was his name?"

"Bear." He nodded. "Like a grizzly." Theo lowered his voice. "He didn't like the other ones."

"The other men who were there?"

He nodded. "He told me they were mean to him. He tol' me to do what he did."

"And what was that Theo?"

"Just to do what he said and everything would be okay."

"You know how old he was, Theo?"

"Eight."

The other victims had guessed the youngest to be fourteen. "That's what he told you?"

"Yup."

"And how old are you, Theo?"

"Six."

"Where's your mom?"

"School. She's gonna be a nurse."

Again, pride.

"What about your dad?"

"Don't have one. Never did."

"Theodore! Time to wash for dinner. And put your toys up."

He didn't hesitate, scooping up his dino figures and hurrying toward the door. He paused there, looked back and smiled. "Bye, Mr. Policeman."

"Bye, Theo. Thanks for talking to me."

"Yup," he said and ducked through the door and past his grandmother.

"It's time for you to go, Detective."

Zach stood. "Thank you for allowing me to talk with Theo. He's a good kid."

"I know that."

"His mother—"

"Is none of your business."

He'd hit a nerve. "Does she live here?"

The woman folded her arms across her chest.

"Was she here the night of the invasion?"

"She works nights."

"Have I offended you somehow, Mrs. Cole? If so, I apologize."

"We don't want him asking about his daddy. As far as he's concerned, he doesn't have one. And never did."

Zach frowned. "With all due respect, Mrs. Cole, Theo's six now, but in a few years it won't be so easy to brush off his questions."

"My daughter was raped, Detective." She curved her hand around the cross at her chest. "He was a bad man. But Theo's a good boy. And he's gonna stay that way."

CHAPTER NINE

Monday, October 19
5:20 P.M.

ZACH CHECKED HIS WATCH AND realized Mick was going to have his head—no way he was going to make the meeting with Nichols. Truth was, he was going to be lucky if he made the press conference on time. But he was on a roll—and not stopping now.

He'd left Theo's home in Gert Town and headed to the second victimized family in Treme, from there to the third location in Hollygrove. Their stories had been the same: waking up to flashing lights, blaring music and strangers in their bedroom.

He'd done what the other investigators had not—talked to the young children. Really talked to them.

They, too, had all shared a similar story—of flashlights being shone in their eyes. Of one of the perpetrators being young, and nice, and making friends with them.

Zach decided to leave the Fowlers for last. Because the event was still so fresh, he figured they'd be the least likely to acquiesce to his request.

He was been right. He stood before Margie Fowler, uncomfortable with her anguished expression. "Mrs. Fowler, I've questioned all the other children and it's really important I question your girls as well."

"Why? I just don't understand. We've told you everything—"

"Everything *you* know. The other children's stories contained some important differences from their parents, but match each other's. It's important to discover if your daughters' experiences are the same."

"I don't know." She nervously flexed and relaxed her fingers. "I just don't feel good about this."

He was going to have to use his special powers of persuasion, and he felt really bad about it. A parent should be able to decide what was best for their child—and he was about to take that away from them. Another invasion, just one done in secret.

"Mrs. Fowler, Margie, please—"

She met his eyes and he had her. He lowered his voice. "You can trust me."

"I can, can't I?" She seemed still hesitant and unconvinced.

He went on. "Yes. Absolutely, you can. You know it's the right thing to do and that I only have your girls' best interests at heart. You and Rick can be right there with us."

"That would make me feel so much better."

"Of course it would." He smiled. "Why don't you go get them now?"

A couple minutes later, they were all in the living room. He could tell by Rick Fowler's expression that he was confused by his wife's sudden change of heart. Feeling more than a little bit guilty, Zach sat across from the couple, who held a daughter perched on each lap. The girls were adorable. Asian, with matching haircuts and bright, curious eyes.

And they were fascinated with his. They stared at him. Finally Jada, the five-year-old, said, "Your eyes are like his."

"Whose, baby?" her mother asked.

Big sister Lexie scowled. "We weren't supposed to tell."

"Weren't supposed to tell what?"

Margie Fowler's voice had risen slightly in alarm. Zach stepped in. "Hi Lexie, Jada, I'm Detective Zach Harris. Do you know what a detective is?"

The five-year-old shook her head. Lexie rolled her eyes at her sister's ignorance. "It means you're the police."

"That's right." He smiled and looked her in the eyes. "You know what police do?"

She thought a moment. "Catch bad guys?"

He smiled. "That's right." He turned his gaze to Jada. "Because police are the good guys."

The little girl nodded, eyes wide.

"You know how we get the bad guys? We find the truth. Because the truth is never wrong."

Lexie sat up a bit straighter. "The big kids who came in our house were bad."

Big kids. He took note of the description. "Yes, they were."

"E'cept for Bear. He was good."

Both her mother and father opened their mouths to comment; Zach quelled them with a glance.

He went on. "Bear, was he one of the big kids?"

She thought a moment. "Not as big."

"Is he the one with eyes like mine?"

Both girls nodded.

"And he was nice?" Again they nodded. "If he was nice, why weren't you supposed to tell us about him?"

Lexie hung her head and Jada popped her thumb into her mouth. Zach leaned toward them, lowering his voice.

"You can tell me. I'm one of the good guys. That's my job."

The two exchanged furtive glances, then Lexie straightened, big sister taking charge. Zach figured she'd be doing that the rest of her life, whether little sister liked it or not.

"Bear was our friend. He was afraid of the big boys."

"He told you that?"

She nodded, then Jada spoke up. "He tol' us to do what they said and everything would be a'right."

"All right," her sister corrected. "Everything would be all right."

Jada stuck her thumb back into her mouth, expression hurt. Her mother cradled her.

Rick Fowler stepped in. "Sweetheart, why didn't you tell us this? We wouldn't have been mad."

She tipped her face up to her father's. "Bear was afraid the others would find out."

"And that would be bad?"

"He said . . . he—"

Her chin began to quiver; Zach intervened. "Lexie, when did you find out Bear was nice?"

"Right after."

"Right after what?"

"They pointed the light in our . . . in our—"

From the way her parents were hanging on every word, this was the first time they had heard this.

"What, baby?" Fowler coaxed his daughter. "You can tell daddy."

Her chin began quivering again. "Eyes," she managed before her tears began. Once they did, they turned to sobs. Jada joined in and

Zach stood. "Thank you," he said softly. "We'll find those who did this, I promise you."

"You gotta help Bear," Lexie whimpered. "He's a good boy. They want him to be bad, but he's not."

A good boy. Just the way Theo's grandma had described her grandson.

"I will." Zach said, then squatted down and laid a hand on her arm, preparing himself for the onslaught of emotions and memories. They came, fast and furious, a deafening cry for help.

But not Lexie's or her sister's.

Bear's.

CHAPTER TEN

Monday, October 19
6:02 P.M.

MICKI CALLED ZACH FOR THE fourth time. Finally, he picked up. "Where the hell are you?" she asked, glancing at the clock on the wall directly across from the dais. "The press conference was supposed to have started two minutes ago!"

"I'm on my way. Get started without me."

"I can't get started without you!" She lowered her voice even more. "You're the frontman, remember?"

"Hold 'em off. I'm ten minutes out."

"Ten minutes! But—"

Her exclamation did no good, since he'd already hung up. She had to resist the urge to throw her phone across the room and shout something inappropriate—or a string of somethings.

The Chief strode her way, expression a thundercloud. "Detective Dare, what are we waiting for?"

"Detective Harris, sir."

"Where the hell is he?"

"I just got off the phone with him, he's only a couple minutes away."

"Looks like you're going to have to handle this rodeo yourself, Detective."

She didn't like the limelight. She didn't like talking to a crowd and she certainly didn't enjoy questions being thrown at her. Not these kinds of questions. These required diplomacy, not honesty.

"Chief," she said, "I think Major Nichols is much more suited to—"

"Handle it." He started toward the mic, stopped and looked back.

"And try not to be yourself, Detective."

Cranky. Surly. To-the-point in a rude sort of way. That was the only way she knew how to be.

From beside her came a muffled chuckle. She glanced over. Major Nichols, looking way too pleased. He met her eyes. "You've got this."

And then he was gone and she was joining Chief Howard at the podium. He introduced her, then stepped aside so she could take the mic. She realized she was scowling and tried to look at least pleasant.

It felt completely unnatural.

"Thank you, Chief Howard," she said, then turned to the audience. "Good evening. As you know, last night at approximately two a.m., a home invasion occurred in the Lake Vista neighborhood. It was the fourth such crime in less than a month. Along with my partner, Detective Zachary Harris—"

"Where is Detective Harris?"

The question, called out from the Fox affiliate, caught her off guard. "Excuse me?"

"Detective Harris," the reporter repeated. "Where is he?"

"Following some leads. As I was saying—"

"Leads pertaining to this case?" shouted another reporter.

"Yes, but I can't discuss—"

"You must have a working theory you could share?"

"Again, it's premature to discuss any theory at this point."

"At least share what you do know so far..."

"I know what you know. This gang appears to be—"

"So these crimes are the work of a gang?"

"Group," she corrected, acknowledging that she was sinking fast. And that what she really wanted to do was tell them all to shut the fuck up and let them do their jobs. She imagined doing just that, but suspected that wasn't quite what Chief Howard meant when he'd told her to "handle it."

The Fox reporter jumped back in. "You have an impressive record, Detective Dare. Even so, since partnering with Detective Harris, you've tripled your case close rate. To what do you owe your success?"

Sweat beaded her upper lip. Her pits were a mess. She wished she'd worn white instead of blue.

She cleared her throat. "We make a good team—"

"No, we don't." Every head in the rooms swiveled toward the doorway. Zach, striding up to the dais. "We make a *great* team." He bounded onto the stage. "Good evening, I'm Zach Harris. And, obviously, I'm late."

He smiled. Mr. Charming. Affable and confident. Handsome.

Irritating as hell.

"My friends call me Hollywood. Consider yourselves my friends."

Laughter rippled through the assembled group. It was all Micki could do not to roll her eyes. How could she be one hundred percent grateful for his arrival and one hundred percent annoyed as well?

Micki watched him woo the assembled group of sharks and snake oil salesmen.

"What's your take on your success, Detective Harris?"

"The ultimate good cop, bad cop scenario." He leaned forward. "I think we know who the good cop is."

Laughter. Again.

Spell cast, hook set, reeling them in.

"You," he said, indicating a gorgeous redhead from the ABC affiliate. Her expression lit up so brightly, you'd have thought she just won the freakin' Powerball.

"Casey Daniels, WGNO. What can you tell us about the crimes so far?"

Micki listened as he expertly recounted everything that had already been made public. The crimes had been committed by a group of young adults and teens. Two of the perpetrators had been armed. The families had been terrorized, their property vandalized.

"What's their motivation?" she asked

"We can't share everything just yet, darlin'. But rest assured we're already following up on leads and will quickly put an end to these disturbing crimes. The public can rest well tonight knowing that we're totally on this."

His politically correct version of 'Shut the fuck up and let us do our jobs,' she realized. Why hadn't she thought of that?

"You sound awfully confident," the Fox reporter called.

"Because I am. We'll have these punks busted and booked very soon."

Micki's gaze strayed. It landed on a tall, blond man toward the back of the room. Strikingly handsome. Somehow familiar. She knew him from somewhere. They'd met . . . it was there, at the edge of consciousness.

As if he sensed her studying him, he looked at her. And smiled. A feeling washed over her. Warmth. Safety. An almost visceral connection to the man.

"Detective Dare? Any final thoughts?"

She jerked her attention to Zach. She couldn't be sure, but his expression suggested he had asked the question more than once. She stepped back up to the mic. "No more questions. We'll keep you apprised of our progress. Thank you."

When Micki looked back, the blond man was exiting the room. "Excuse me," she said to Zach, "there's someone I have to speak to."

She hurried after the man, her heart pounding wildly. A strange urgency pushed her to pursue him. She made the doorway, stepped into the hallway, looked left, then right. Folks were dispersing, but no tall blond. Maybe he wasn't as tall as she'd thought? Or as blond? Or as—

From the corner of her eye, she saw the elevator doors slide closed. She ran for the stairs, and reached the main floor in time to see the elevator doors open.

The gorgeous reporter from ABC stepped off. "Excuse me," Micki said, "did this elevator stop at any floors before this one?"

"Nope."

Micki stopped her again. "Did you happen to notice a blond man around the elevator? Tall, really handsome?"

"I wish." She made a face. "Sorry."

Micki frowned as she watched the woman walk away. She'd lost him. She didn't know how, but she had.

She made her way back to the conference room. There she found Zach and the Chief deep in conversation.

As she approached, Chief Howard clearly changed the subject and slapped Zach on the back. "Good job, Detective. Excellent."

He turned to Micki. "I have great confidence in you both."

"Thank you, Chief."

"I want daily updates." He looked back at Zach. "On everything."

As he cleared earshot, Micki cocked an eyebrow. "What was that all about?"

"I could ask you the same thing. You rushed off like you were about to miss the last bus to paradise."

"I'm not sure. One of the reporters looked—"

She stopped. Was he a reporter? She didn't recall him asking a question or taking notes. Why else would he have come to the press conference?

She drew her eyebrows together. "When you were up there, did you happen to notice a tall male, blond hair, sitting toward the very back?"

"Did not."

"I was sure I knew him, but couldn't place from where."

"That happens, Mick."

"But this guy—" She bit back what she was about to say. But this one made her feel all warm and fuzzy? And by the way, did she mention he was Greek god handsome? Or that he had the most beautiful blue eyes.

Like Zach's.

His voice. *Not yet, Michaela. Not yet.* She knew it . . . but from where? She shook her head to clear it. "You and the Chief looked awful cozy."

"He was offering advice."

"That so?"

"Mmm hmm. Thought I should tone down my confidence next time around."

"And what'd you say?"

"That next time I'd be explaining how we nailed the punks."

She laughed. "Okay then. Is there anything else I need to know?"

"Only about this case."

"Hit me up."

"I managed to question all the kids, even the Fowlers' girls. Which, by the way, is the reason I was late. Apparently, there's a very young member of the gang. One none of the children had told their parents about."

"Wait, how young?"

"Eight."

"Holy shit."

"The children told me his name is Bear, and that he was really nice. They called him their friend."

"Their friend?"

"The weirdness doesn't stop there. All of the children were awakened by a flashlight being shone in their eyes. Directly in their eyes. Not just aimed at their faces."

"To what purpose?" she wondered aloud. "Intimidation, maybe? Or as a way to unbalance and subdue them?"

"That's what I thought. Remember what I told you about the energy in the kids' room not matching the Fowlers' description of their daughters' reactions?"

"Yeah. Why?"

"It's because of Bear. He played with them. Told them he was scared of the 'big kids' and if they did what he told them, everything would be okay. They were determined to protect him. In fact, the Fowler girls are afraid *for* him."

"You see what they're doing? It's good cop, bad cop, only the home invasion version."

"Nice bad guy, scary bad guy." He nodded. "It works with us, why not with them?"

"Effing brilliant." She thought a moment. "Maybe he's a relative of one of the older two? A little brother or a cousin? Maybe he's being groomed, but obviously he's being used to control the kids."

"I think so, too. It's smart. Give the kids something to focus on besides their own fear. One problem." He looked away for a moment, then back at her. "Why keep the kids quiet? This group is there to terrorize. Why not the kids, too?"

He had a point. "I don't know. A soft spot for kids, maybe?"

"Maybe, but probably not. But here's another thing. Bear wasn't lying."

"What do you mean?"

"He's terrified of the others. I picked it up. He's in trouble, Mick. We've got to find him."

She drew her eyebrows together, absorbing what he was saying. "Wait a minute. Our job is to find and arrest these perps. If there are juveniles involved, the juvenile division will make certain they're safe and treated fairly. That's *their* job."

"That's just semantics."

"No." Micki shook her head for emphasis. "No, it's not at all. Our focus needs to be—"

"We find Bear, he leads us to them all. And he *wants* to be found."

"So?"

"I think he's going to leave me a trail."

"An energy trail?"

"Yeah. Maybe."

She hated maybes and muttered an oath. Fact was, Bear was the best lead they had. "I've got a friend in J.D.. I'll see what she can find out about Bear, have her run the name. Could be a runaway, a kid in the system."

He grinned. "I knew you'd see it my way."

"No, I don't. And you're aggravating as hell."

He laughed. "It's my specialty."

"I've figured that out. Lucky me."

CHAPTER ELEVEN

Monday, October 19
8:15 P.M.

ANGEL SAT AT ONE OF Sacred Grounds' corner tables. She'd finished her shift at six, snagged the table, a coffee and croissant, and brought out her sketch pad and pencil box. Since Friday night, her dreams had been particularly vivid. Light and dark, glimpses of Seth, Micki and others whom she didn't recognize. Numbers, swirling. For the first time in a while, she'd felt compelled to capture the confusing chaotic mix on paper.

She studied the emerging image. A vortex-like shape, light at the top, swirling down to black. The suggestion of faces. Souls caught in the spinning rush. She tilted her head. It needed color, she decided, and added a slash of brilliant blue. Feeding into the vortex. A spot of green. Summer-bright. A shock of red. There, at the bottom. Bleeding out.

"Hey, Angel."

She jumped and the red pencil skittered across the drawing, leaving a faint red trail. "Oh, my God, you scared . . . Seth?"

"Last time I checked." He pulled out a chair, swung it around and straddled it. "You look surprised to see me."

"I am, I—" She had done almost nothing but fantasize about seeing him again. Now that her fantasy had come true, she didn't know what to say or how to act. "You startled me, that's all."

"Sorry about that."

He cocked his head, openly studying the drawing. Her cheeks burned and she closed her sketchbook. "What're you doing here?"

"I came to see you. I took the chance that you'd be working."

"To see me?"

He laughed again. "Is that so weird?"

As far as she was concerned it was off-the-charts weird, but she kept that to herself. "I guess not."

"What're you working on?"

"A couple sketches."

"Of what?"

"Just stuff I dream."

"Now I'm really curious. You dream stuff, then draw it?"

"Basically. But just sometimes."

"Can I see?"

She hesitated. "It's kind of personal."

He had the most beautiful smile, she thought, as he turned it on her. Mesmerizing.

"Seems to me, art is to be shared. That's what makes it art, right? Otherwise, it's just, I don't know, navel gazing?"

Angel laughed. "Navel gazing?"

He laughed, too. "Yeah. You never do that?"

Suddenly, they were gazing into one another's eyes, smiling at their secret joke, as if they had been a couple forever. She felt almost giddy.

"They're not finished," she said, opening the sketchbook.

He silently studied the contents, slowly flipping through. Her palms began to sweat.

"They're awesome," he finally said.

"You really think so?"

He looked back up at her. "Yeah, you're really good."

Her cheeks warmed with pleasure. "Thanks."

He tapped on the one she'd been working on when he walked up. "What does it mean?"

"I don't know yet."

"Not any of it?"

"Some." She indicated the areas of color she had just added. "Red, for violence. Green for earth, that physical connection. The blue—"

"For water and sky?" he guessed.

For his eyes, she realized, looking up at him. The blue she'd chosen was the exact shade of his irises. She shifted her gaze. "Yes. Water and sky."

"You want to go eat?"

"Eat?"

"You know, food. Spoon, fork, knife."

She laughed at her own awkwardness. "Sure. That sounds good."

They decided on sushi, so it ended up being chopsticks instead of spoon and fork. She fumbled with the sticks and he took her hand and showed her how to hold them. "See? Hold the top stick like a pencil. Like this."

"Got it," she said, feeling her color rise. "Just a little nervous, that's all."

"Nervous?" He popped a roll into his mouth. "Why?"

"You make me nervous." She silently groaned. Why had she said that? It opened the door—

"Me? Why?"

—For *that.* "Because you're so . . . so you."

He captured a crunchy roll and dipped it in the sauce. "That makes no sense."

It didn't. She already looked foolish; she might as well go all in. "Because you're so . . . so much cooler than I am."

He nearly choked on his sushi. He took a sip of water, then another, eyes watering. "Sorry, I didn't expect that."

"Really?"

"Really." He leaned forward, those beautiful eyes of his alight with amusement. "I don't think that. Obviously."

Or he wouldn't be here. Her cheeks went from warm to burning. "Oh."

He helped himself to another roll. "I saw your roommate on TV tonight."

"Micki? Really?"

"The news. Some press conference."

"Those home invasions, I bet."

"What's the story with you two?"

"No story."

He cocked an eyebrow. "Let's see, you call her a roommate but she's a lot older than you. She's a cop and acts like your mother."

"It's pretty crazy, huh?"

"Just a little." She watched as he expertly caught another roll with his sticks. "How'd you two end up together?"

She thought for a moment about what she wanted to say, how she wanted to frame it. "This past summer, I was in some trouble, had nowhere to live and Micki took me in."

"The abridged version." He sat back, studying her thoughtfully.

"What kind of trouble?"

"This crazy . . . dude was stalking me. I don't know if I'd be alive if it wasn't for Micki. And Zach."

"Who's Zach?"

"Her partner. I owe them everything."

"But you're still here with me, even knowing she disapproves."

"You picked up on that, huh?"

"Kind of hard not to."

"Being a cop and all, she worries too much."

"Or maybe she worries because you had some dangerous, crazy dude stalking you?"

A part of her was annoyed at his taking Micki's side, but the other part was secretly pleased. "I know, I get it." She took a sip of her water. "The thing is, I've been mostly on my own for years. Before that, I was in and out of foster care. It feels really weird to have someone worrying about me all the time."

"What happened to your folks?"

"My mom abandoned me as a baby." She lifted a shoulder. "No big deal."

He reached his hand across the table, palm up, inviting hers to join his. She reached toward him and he curled his fingers around hers. "Actually, I think it was a very big deal."

Tears stung her eyes and she looked quickly away. She hadn't cried over her mother's abandonment in years. She didn't care. Not anymore.

"I didn't mean to make you cry."

"I'm not crying." She cleared her throat. "What about you? Best family unit ever?"

He laughed so loudly the couple at the next table sent them a curious glance. "Hardly. My uncle took me in, raised me."

"What happened to your mom?"

"Killed herself." He said it with a bluntness that came with practice.

She tightened her hand in his. "How old were you?"

"Nine."

"I'm so sorry."

He released her hand. "I need to get you home."

"I don't want to go home."

"You're sure?"

She didn't hesitate. She wanted to be with him. "Yes."

His mouth curved up, the small, satisfied smile almost feline. An excited trill ran up her spine.

"Okay," he said. "Let's get out of here."

CHAPTER TWELVE

Monday, October 19
10:10 P.M.

ZACH CLIMBED THE STAIRS TO his Marigny apartment. The building was old, the stairs narrow. It smelled old as well, at least here, in the stairwell. Not bad. Just that recognizable hint of age and the history that went along with the French Quarter. It made his senses sing.

As he reached the second floor landing, he became aware of another energy, one he recognized. His mouth thinned. Parker. Waiting for him.

He let himself into the apartment. Parker looked up from his spot on the couch. "Comfy?" Zach asked.

"Very. Thank you."

Zach folded his arms across his chest. "What are you doing in my place, P?"

"My job."

"Get out."

"You've been avoiding me, Zach."

"Sure have, *Uncle* Parker."

Parker tossed aside the magazine he'd been reading and stood. "You hate my guts right now, but I'm your boss. Deal with it."

"Fine. Say what you have to say and get the hell out."

"I saw you on TV tonight. You put on quite a show. Maybe too much of a show."

"Just doing what comes naturally. Isn't that why you recruited me?"

"We recruited you for a number of reasons. Calling attention to yourself wasn't one of them."

"Screw you."

"We heard a story from a kid who came into LAM a couple weeks ago."

"What kind of a story?" Zach crossed to the refrigerator and pulled out a pitcher of tea. "Want a glass?"

"Got anything stronger?"

"Beer. Abita Amber."

"That'll do."

Zach tossed him a bottle. "Opener's in the top drawer."

"Seriously?" Cupping his hand over the top, he flicked his wrist and the cap popped off. He caught it and grinned. "I never get tired of that."

Zach didn't have the patience for Parker's nonsense, not tonight. "The story?"

"Told us this guy tried to recruit him for a gang. A different sort of gang."

Zach took a long swallow of the tea. "How so?"

"Promised him more fun than he'd had in his whole life. That he'd teach him 'tricks' that would get him whatever he wanted."

Zach set down his glass and looked at Parker. "The kid's a Half Light."

"Yup."

"Holy crap, the guy's recruiting us for crimes."

"That's what we suspect."

"I take it since he ended up at LAM, he turned the guy down."

"Yeah, he turned him down. He picked up something weird about this guy. Said it made his nerves twitch. Like they were reacting to the guy's very presence."

The way he reacted to Dark Bearer energy, Zach thought. It was one of his own gifts, perhaps the most valuable of all. It gave him the ability to track Dark Bearers.

"The kid's like me," Zach said. "A tracker."

"We think so. And, maybe, First Gen like you, too."

First generation. That meant at least one of his parents had been a Full Light, another rarity, as the worldwide number of Full Lights had become alarmingly small. At least, according to the professor.

Zach processed that. "Who's the guy who tried to recruit him?"

"He didn't know him." Parker took a swallow of the beer. "Similar situation to how I recruited you. Came up to him in a bar."

He thought a minute. "If he can find this guy, I could maybe get close, read him."

"Kid's too scared. Besides, if what we're thinking is correct, you won't get anywhere near this guy."

"You're thinking they know who I am."

"Yeah. And if they didn't, they will after tonight's little show. Or should I say showboating?" He rolled the bottle between his palms. "Here's the thing. We believe the group this guy was recruiting for is the same one behind the home invasions."

Zach nodded. "That'd mean the perps are Half Lights."

"Being trained to use their abilities to hurt humanity."

Legions of people had varying degrees of Lightkeeper in them, some aware of their abilities, but most not. He thought of how he'd been before being enlightened, using his powers like a spoiled child.

"This explains the energy at the scene."

"Describe it to me."

"At first I wondered if it was our Dark Bearer, because the energy was so strong. But it was really different. Chaotic. Destructive but . . . gleeful. The delight surprised me, but now it makes sense."

Parker agreed. "The perps are young. The kids being recruited are not the most stable to begin with. Then they're handed what's essentially a loaded weapon."

"Clever."

"This Dark Bearer is working through someone. Someone charismatic, powerful and most probably wealthy."

"Why the home invasions?"

"We're not certain yet. Tell me more about the scene."

"There's a really young member of the group. Eight, if he told the children I interviewed the truth. His name's Bear and he's afraid of the others. He doesn't want to be there. I picked up that energy; the victims' children confirmed it."

Parker frowned in thought. "Anything else jump out as weird?"

Zach finished his tea and set the glass in the sink. "A couple things."

"Such as?"

"Three of the four families had dogs. They slept through the entire event. We assumed they must have been drugged but—"

Parker cut him off. "It's a form of telepathy—the user can control and manipulate animals."

"You're not kidding?"

He shook his head. "Obviously, then, one of the group has that ability. What was the other odd thing?"

"All of the kids told me that they awakened by a flashlight beam being directed into their eyes."

"Right in their eyes?"

"Yeah. You know what they were looking for?" Parker shook his head and Zach frowned. "More of your need-to-know bullshit?"

Parker drained his beer, found the trash and tossed the bottle. "That's just the way I roll. Deal with it."

"Time for you to go, P. I've had enough."

"Not quite. There's something we need to talk about."

Zach cocked an eyebrow. "You think? You and me, talk?"

"I appreciate the sarcasm. I even suppose I deserve it." He held out his hand. "Take it, Zach."

"Your hand? Why?"

"There's something I need to share with you. It's something I should have done a long time ago."

He folded his arms across his chest. "Yes, and what's that?"

"Your mother."

Zach grasped Parker's hand. He felt the familiar heat, the tingling at the contact point, the rush of the energy.

But this time the energy flow reversed, rushing into him, not from him.

Suddenly his senses were filled with his mother and Parker. As young children, brother and sister. Holding hands. Whispering and giggling together. The smell of a spring day all around him.

Zach's knees went weak. He would have fallen if not for Parker's energy; it kept him on his feet.

The images continued to roll out. He was spellbound, transfixed. All his life he had wondered about her-- what she looked like, if he had gotten his coloring from her. Her smile or eyes.

He had. All of them.

Memories, the feelings associated with them, flowed between them. As real as if he was a third child, there with them. No, even more, a part of them. Sharing heart and spirit and childhood secrets. Playing together.

Zach was there as brother and sister simultaneously came into their abilities. Living that time with them. They'd been siblings and best friends. Confidants.

Their lives progressed; Truebell recruited them to be a part of his newly formed Lost Angel Ministries.

The bond between the brother and sister grew stronger than ever.

Then not. A shudder moved over Zach, along with something cold. He wanted the warmth back. He called out her name—Arianna— and begged her to come back.

But something had changed. Arianna was secretive. Avoiding her brother, Truebell, their friends. Parker confronting her. Pregnant, she told him. She was pregnant.

He was the baby she carried, Zach knew.

The child she carried was the result of a love affair with a human.

Parker had been hurt. Angry and disillusioned. The pair argued bitterly, said things that made him cringe.

The energy transfer stopped, the connection broke. Zach stumbled backward, grabbing the counter to keep from falling. He didn't want it to stop. Didn't want to lose his connection to her or the overwhelming feeling of being loved.

"That's the last time I saw her," Parker said. "She left us, went into hiding."

"Hiding?" he repeated. "Why?"

"She'd broken the law. She would be punished, her child—you—taken from her."

"Whoa, back up. What law?"

"Full Lights mating with humans is not just discouraged, Zach. It's against the law. A Full Light mating with a human was outlawed thirty years ago.

"Outlawed by whom? You . . . Truebell—"

"No. God, no. We're the anti-judgment group."

"Then who?"

"The High Council."

"What's that? Like a Lightkeeper Executive Branch?"

He said it with sarcasm. Parker didn't blink an eye. "Yeah, basically. The High Council came into being with the second industrial revolution. The world was changing, small towns were giving way to big cities. Our local links were being broken, we needed a centralized group to be a touchstone for the Lightkeeper race."

"This High Council, who are they?"

"Full Lights from very traditional and influential families. At first, they dispatched information, kept far-flung Light Keepers abreast of news of anything pertinent to our kind. They also kept count of us.

Like the U.S. census, as a way to monitor our health. Keep a "Light meter", so to speak.

"The sixties, then seventies happened with their Age of Aquarius, if-it-feels-good-do-it mentalities. There had always been some mixing of human and Lightkeeper, but after that it snowballed. Our numbers were depleting so rapidly, the Council estimated Full Lights would be extinct by the turn of the twenty-first century."

"Which clearly didn't happen."

"Because of the law. The High Council did what they thought they had to to protect not only our people, but also our mission on this planet."

"Your mission? You mean the one about being guardians of the Light and protectors of all that's good? More like a governing body whose focus is protecting the purity of its race. Sounds an awful lot like Hitler's regime to me. And like you approve."

"Absolutely not. Their methods are—"

"Their methods?" Zach made a sound of disgust. "What about their ideology? I thought Lighkeepers were the good guys?"

"They were, once upon a time. Now *we're* the good guys." He made a circle with his index finger. "Us. LAM. The professor's followers." He grew silent. When he spoke again, his tone had become pensive. "The tragic truth is, the Dark Bearers and their forces attack us from without, and we attack ourselves from within."

Zach narrowed his eyes. "Why are you trusting me with this information? Frankly, it's out of character."

"Arianna went into hiding, then gave you up, to protect you. She wanted you to be safe. To have a chance at a good, happy life. Not because she didn't want or love you."

For a split second, Zach couldn't breathe. He turned his back to Parker, not wanting him to see his struggle for composure. She'd wanted him. Loved him.

He'd always known that, he realized. It'd been buried in a place deep within him. Just as he had known the woman's voice in his head, the one leading him to safety as he faced the Dark Bearer, had been hers.

"The day you told me about my mother, you said she was dead." He turned and looked Parker in the eyes. "How do you know?"

"I just do."

Zach shook his head. "That's not good enough, P."

"I *know.* Because of our connection. You felt it just now, in the transfer. You weren't just an observer, you were *of* us. We're connected by our light. She and I, brother and sister, we're connected by our light."

He *had* felt it. It had been a magical feeling of belonging. Of history and of being. "You're saying that if you died, I would know it."

"Yes, you'd feel it. Same as I would if you died. Like a part of you has been ripped away. She's gone, Zach."

"Then why don't I feel that?"

"Maybe you just don't recognize it. Because you never knew her."

He was angry. Not at Parker. At his own helplessness. The truth was, he'd always said one thing, but hoped for another. That she was alive and they would be reunited. As a kid, he'd imagined that day so many times, it had become real to him. Something in his future that *would* happen.

He felt as if she was being ripped from him now.

He cleared his throat. "How'd she die?"

"I don't know for certain, but I suspect at the hands of a Dark Bearer."

"How can I find out?"

"You can't."

Zach curved his hands into fists. "Someone knows."

"Needle in a haystack. You don't think I've tried? I'm FBI. I've used every database accessible to law enforcement. Nothing."

"There'd be a death certificate—"

"She could have changed her name. Or be a Jane Doe on some file folder."

"No."

"I'm sorry."

"No," Zach said again, balling his hands into fists. "I'm not going to accept that. I refuse to."

Parker sighed. "I can't change what is. I wish to hell I could."

"Leave," Zach managed, voice thick. "Now. I want you to go."

Parker nodded and started for the door. He stopped when he reached it and looked back at Zach. "I should have shared her with you a long time ago. I'm sorry, Zach."

CHAPTER THIRTEEN

Tuesday, October 20
3:50 A.M.

ZACH SAT IN THE DARK. He couldn't sleep even if he wanted to. He kept going over the things Parker had shared with him, reliving those moments with his mother. He didn't want to lose the clarity of them, the way he'd felt connected. Connected in a way he'd never felt with anyone.

He fought to hold onto it. Even so, he felt it muting, growing fuzzy around the edges. Soon all that would be left was the memory itself.

Parker said they had been connected by their light, that he knew his sister was dead because he *felt* it. But he didn't. She'd spoken to him. He felt certain it had been her voice in his head.

If not hers, whose?

His phone went off. Mick, he saw.

He thought about letting it roll over to voicemail, but a call from her in the middle of the night only meant one thing.

"Yo," he answered, feeling his connection with the young Arianna snapping.

Micki hesitated a moment before answering, as if just the tone of his voice had alerted her that something was wrong.

"Time to rise and shine, partner. They hit again."

"Crap. Where?"

"Your neighborhood."

"The Marigny?"

"Not just the neighborhood, the block. The folks two buildings down. Your side of the street."

The bookstore, he realized. The couple who lived above it.

"If you're not dressed," she went on, "I suggest you hustle. I'm almost at the scene now."

Within moments of hanging up, he heard the growl of the Nova's powerful engine passing his building. He let himself out and jogged down the stairs to the street. The air slapped him, cold and damp. He hunched into his jacket and started toward the bookstore, lit up like a pinball machine in a dark bar. The visual was all flashing lights and whistles.

Mick parked behind the cruiser and climbed out. When Zach strolled over to meet her, she eyed him. "You okay, Hollywood? You look a little rough this morning."

"Tired, that's all." He didn't meet her eyes. "Couldn't sleep."

"Welcome to my frickin' world."

"What's your excuse?"

"Angel. Coming in all hours."

He jammed his hands deep into his pockets. "You call her on it?"

"Yeah. It didn't go over well."

"You're not her mom."

"Believe me, she pointed that out."

They reached the crime scene tape, ducked under it and crossed to the Officer manning the log. When he looked up at them, his eyes lit up. "You're Hollywood Harris."

Zach eyed his badge. "That I am, Officer Neely. This is my partner—"

"I know Dare. Hi ya, Mad Dog." He glanced at her, then back at Zach. "I've heard about you. Quite a press conference last night."

Zach heard Micki sigh and he smiled. "I thought so myself. What do we have here, Neely?"

"Call came in to my unit around three. Home invasion at this address. I arrived, secured the scene and called it in. Couple awakened to armed intruders in their bedroom. They were tied up and terrorized, their place is trashed."

"Alarm system?"

"Thought they'd set it, but if they did, it failed."

"They don't recall?"

"Not one hundred percent, but they think so." He held out the log book for her to sign. "One of the perps took a big, steaming crap on their velvet couch."

"Man, that's low."

"I know, right? The worst."

Micki stepped in. "Tell us about the victims?"

"Own the bookstore. Couldn't bear to be in their apartment, so they're over there. Officer Jenkins is with them."

"Names?"

"Stephen Benson and Carl Fiorenza."

"No kids in the home?" Neely shook his head and Micki went on. "Are they in need of medical assistance?"

"For psychological trauma. But I called a unit anyway, 'cause I ain't no M.D. Crossing t's and dotting i's? Got to do it, right?"

No sooner were the words out than Zach heard the squeal of sirens in the distance. "Right," he agreed. "Keep us posted."

Zach followed Micki inside. Chaos, similar to the Fowler scene and the photos of the others he'd studied. Awful smell, thanks to Mr. Poops-a-lot.

They made their way past the desecrated sofa and into the living room. Destruction. Books, knickknacks, lamps, throw pillows—nothing left untouched or unspoiled.

He stopped to take it in. The energy tripped over him like a snicker.

"You're frowning," she said. "Your mojo on?"

"Yeah."

"And?"

"This is different from the others. The energy. Way different."

"How so?"

He stopped, moved his gaze over the room. "Deliberate."

"The others weren't deliberate?"

"Yes, but in a different way. Delight in destruction. A kind of child-like glee."

"And here?"

"You're going to think it's crazy."

"Really?" She cocked an eyebrow. "When *don't* I think it's crazy?"

She had a point. Zach turned in a slow circle, absorbing, opening the pathways, as if his very pores were sucking it all in. His nerve endings began to tingle. His mouth went dry, his heartbeat quickened.

"It's unemotional. Like they were proving a point."

"To who?"

He met her eyes. "To us."

She frowned, internalizing, Zach knew. "Why?"

He didn't answer. The couple owned a bookstore and obviously loved and collected books. An entire wall had been devoted to shelving them. Most had been yanked from the shelves and flung. Helter-skelter. Except for one neat stack of six volumes.

Zach gazed at the stack; it seemed to beckon him. He took a pair of gloves from his pocket, fitted them on and crossed to the small tower. He floated his hand over and alongside. Laughter echoed in his head. Not delighted or joyful.

Sly.

He scanned the titles. Mysteries series, all of them. From Arthur Conan Doyle's Sherlock Holmes to Agatha Christie's Hercule Poirot and Sue Grafton's Kinsey Millhone.

Micki came to stand beside him. "Detective novels?"

He nodded. "Whodunits."

"They're challenging us."

"And mocking us."

"I might be wrong, partner, but I think they caught last night's news conference."

He thought she was probably right but didn't comment, and started instead for the kitchen. There, more destruction. Another neatly arranged stack of six. Donuts this time.

"Very funny," Micki muttered. "Assholes."

Zach laughed. "Sorry," he said. "You've got to admit that is sort of funny."

"Detective Harris?"

They turned. Officer Neely was holding out what looked like a lunch sack. "Jenkins brought this up. Apparently the perps wanted you to have it."

"Me?" Zach said. "You're sure?"

"Your name's on it." From the other room came the sound of the crime techs arriving. Neely looked over his shoulder.

"I'll take it," Micki said.

Neely handed it to her. "I didn't check the contents."

"We've got it," Zach said. "Thanks."

He watched as Mick, holding the bag at arm's length, carefully opened it. She waited a moment, then peeked inside.

She looked at him. "A cigarette lighter."

"That's it?" She nodded, crossed to the café-style table and gently shook it out onto the tile top.

A metal Zippo. Screen printed with the NYC skyline, Statue of Liberty, and the words, *The Big Apple.*

Energy pulsed from it. Energy he recognized.

She frowned. "What?"

He shook his head, not wanting to speak just yet. Not wanting to break the flow of energy. It seemed to be drawing him across the room. He stopped at the table, reaching out. The pull intensified. A jolt of energy shot up his arm; his body jerked with the force of it.

A sensation like electrical sparks hit his palm. He smelled smoke. Heavy and acrid. He and Micki, together in a room he didn't recognize. Smoke was filling it.

Zach couldn't breathe. His eyes began to water. Heat rose from the lighter, burning his palm. Then, suddenly, the image of fire surrounding them. He frantically searched for an exit, a clear path through the flames. There was none.

No way out. They were trapped.

In moments they would be engulfed by the fire. Burned alive.

"Partner, you sure you want—"

The lighter burst into flames. Like fingers, they stretched up to snatch his hand.

"Whoa—" Micki grabbed his arm, jerking it back.

The flame coiled up, hissing like a furious snake before turning on him. He told himself to look away but couldn't.

In the next instant, he was going down. He hit the tile floor, the breath knocked out of him. Micki landed on top of him.

Over her shoulder, the fire grew bigger, brighter, then, suddenly, extinguished. The air cleared. The pulsing energy vanished too.

"What the fuck . . . was that?" Micki asked, rolling off him, grimacing as she pushed herself up.

"You're hurt," he said, indicating her arm. An angry red mark, snakelike, coiled from her wrist up her forearm.

"Holy crap." She held her arm out. "I thought I imagined . . . that it was a trick of the eye . . . not actually a—"

They both turned their gaze to the tabletop, the paper bag and lighter. Both looked untouched.

Zach swallowed hard. Looked at her. "Not a what, Mick. A who."

A *Dark Bearer.*

And he had just sent them a message.

CHAPTER FOURTEEN

Tuesday, October 20
5:46 A.M.

THE PARAMEDICS TENDED HER BURN. Micki now sported a non-adhesive bandage curling up her forearm, which stung like hell. The medic had commented he'd never seen a burn pattern quite like hers before.

She hoped he never did again.

They left the scene, stepping onto the street. They'd interviewed the vics; their experience varied little from the experiences of the other victims. Two big disparities between last night's invasion and the previous ones—one everyone could evaluate--no kids involved, and the other one only she and Zach would know--that the energy had been completely different.

"How about breakfast?" Zach asked. "I'll buy."

"Sounds good. I'm starving."

They walked down to a little hole-in-the-wall all-day breakfast joint. The owner recognized Zach and called out a greeting.

"You saved my butt again," Zach said lightly when they'd seated themselves at a corner table. "Thanks, Partner."

"I take my job seriously."

"And you do it well." He was quiet a moment. "Is that it? It's just a job?"

The question took her totally by surprise, as did his serious tone. She wasn't comfortable with either. Or with his intense gaze on hers. Suddenly, the memory of their kiss filled her head. The way her body had heated and her pulse had raced. It was a memory she didn't allow herself often.

She quickly looked away. "We're partners; I cover your ass, you cover mine. No big deal."

"Right."

The waitress brought them coffee and menus. She seemed to hover over Zach for a moment more than was necessary, then to melt when he smiled at her. Micki wondered what that kind of power over the opposite sex felt like. It was so every day to him, he didn't seem to even notice it.

Micki added milk to her coffee. "What was that thing?"

"You know."

She did, though she wished she could deny it. "A Dark Bearer, sending us a message."

"Yeah." He took a swallow of the coffee. "And whatever this group is up to, he's controlling them."

She thought about that a moment. "Why?"

"We have an idea."

"We?"

"Parker and I."

"You've talked to him about this?"

"He talked to me." He paused; she saw a muscle jump in his jaw. "He talked to me about this and some other things. Personal things."

She told herself to play it cool, let him tell her on his own terms.

So, she waited. Tension rolled off him in waves. No, not tension, she decided. Something much more complicated.

"Parker's my uncle," he said suddenly, flatly.

That wasn't what she had expected, nor could she have foreseen, not in a million years.

"How long have you known?" she asked finally.

"He told me . . . recently."

"The bad blood between you—"

"Yes."

The waitress delivered their eggs. They dug in, though Micki sensed he was as uninterested in it now as she was; she ate because she needed fuel.

They finished their plates without speaking. The waitress cleared them. And Zach cleared his throat. "My mother was his sister. His only sibling."

"Was?"

"She's dead. Or so he tells me."

"You don't believe him?"

"Should I?"

He had a point. A good one. "What was . . . is her name?"

"Arianna."

"That's beautiful."

"She was beautiful. A good person."

His voice thickened and she reached across the table. But he didn't take her hand and looked away.

It hurt that he'd rejected her support.

"That's why Parker and I can . . . communicate the way we do."

"Because you're blood."

He paused. "Yes, because we're . . . blood."

The pause told her there was something he wasn't telling her. She wondered what it was.

"I always wanted to know—" When he shook his head, his expression changed, shifted slightly. No longer personal, she thought but now about their case.

"There's more. Something I got from Parker."

"Go on."

He hesitated. "Bureau's thinking the kids in this group might have psychic abilities."

"Like you and Parker? Why?"

"A kid came in. Claimed someone tried to recruit him for a gang, promised him more fun than he'd ever had and he'd learn really neat tricks. Ones that would get him anything he wanted."

"Oh, shit."

"My sentiments exactly."

"Not just anybody," she said. "The Dark Bearer."

"Or one of his followers."

They fell silent as the waitress brought their check. When they'd drained their coffee, Zach paid the bill. They stepped out onto the French Quarter street, which had come fully to life in the time they had been eating.

They started toward the bookstore and apartment above. "The Bureau recruited me and the others to help fight crime. It seems somebody thought that was a pretty good idea and we've got us a copycat."

Micki mulled over that a moment. "I've got a question. You special folk, how many of you are there?"

He hesitated. "Quite a lot, I'm learning."

What did she do with that? Micki wondered. Special folk battling special folk?

He gave her a sidelong glance. "That's why the dogs didn't bark during the home invasions. Apparently, some of us possess the ability to control animals."

She stopped to look fully at him. "You're freaking kidding me, right?"

He only looked at her. She shook her head, and started walking again. "When did Parker tell you all this?"

"Last night. He was waiting in my apartment when I got home." His mouth thinned. "He likes to do that."

Micki started to tell him he should have called her immediately, then stopped and changed the subject. "I think we may be in luck with this one," she said, referring to the home invasion. "With all these businesses around, I'll bet several of them have video surveillance. I know for a fact that parking lot does." She indicated the cameras mounted atop the light poles. "So unless the group transported telepathically, I think we may be able to make them from a piece of tape."

He nodded. "We might score a traffic cam or two as well. Capture a plate number."

Good, old-fashioned police work. Now *that* she was comfortable with.

"I'll call the major, bring him up to speed. You get Neely and Jenkins started on a door-to-door. It's going to be a long day."

He nodded, and started toward the bookstore. "Hey, Mick?"

"Yeah?"

"Thanks."

"For what?"

"Everything," he said simply.

She watched him walk away, an unfamiliar catch in her chest.

CHAPTER FIFTEEN

Tuesday, October 20
5:40 P.M.

MICKI BATTLED RUSH HOUR TRAFFIC, cursing her decision to dart home for a quick shower, a bite to eat and to check in with Angel. She should have realized there was no such thing as "darting" this time of day.

As she came to a dead stop, she resisted the urge to lean on the horn. Like that was going to do anything but raise her—and everyone else's around her—blood pressure. She'd bet hers was pretty high already.

After spending the rest of the day reviewing video, it had become obvious their perps had known where the cameras were by how adeptly they had avoided them. She had identified a group of probable suspects. Three males, close in height and build, backs to every camera, all dressed in dark hoodies and jeans.

Micki inched the Nova forward, then stopped again. She drummed her fingers on the steering wheel, anxious, thoughts shifting.

"Apparently, some of us possess the ability to control animals."

Un-effing-believable. Just about the time she grew accustomed to the freak-show boundaries, they changed.

Control animals. So what, besides being able to make then sleep through a home invasion, did *that* mean? She was pretty damn certain she didn't want to find out.

As traffic started moving forward again, her thoughts shifted back to the surveillance videos. She rolled past the Rouses Market and turned onto Carrollton Avenue heading uptown. Piecing together several sequences from different videos, she had a partial plate number. Maybe.

She cleared Willow Street and the character of the Avenue began to change. Shotgun cottages and multi-family units gave way to grand, old, single-family homes. Oak trees lined the Avenue, their branches so thick in places they created canopies.

Moments later, she reached her street and turned onto it. Parked in front of her cottage was Jacqui's battered Honda Civic. Micki smiled. It'd been a while since she'd seen her friend or her son, Alexander. She'd missed them.

She parked and hopped out. Jacqui met her on the front porch.

"I heard that monster of yours from a block away," Jacqui said and hugged her.

Micki laughed and hugged her back. "What are you doing here?"

"Zander saw you on the news last night and has been beside himself to see you. I held him off as long as I could."

"I'm glad you're here." She started to link her arm through Jacqui's, then remembered her bandage and thought better of it.

Jacqui noticed and frowned. "What happened?"

"A burn. Nothing serious. Alexander's inside?"

"Playing a game with Angel. Honestly, those two are thick as thieves."

The moment Zander caught sight of her, he squealed with delight. "Auntie Mouse!"

She scooped him up and twirled him around. "You, sir," she said, setting him back on his feet, "have grown. What do you weigh now, three thousand pounds?"

He laughed. "You're silly, Auntie Mouse. Then how could you pick me up?"

"You're still getting awfully big."

He grew serious. "Eli says when I get really big I'll have lots of 'portant things to do."

Micki frowned. "Eli? Who's—"

"Zander!" Angel called, "C'mon, it's your turn!"

He scampered off and Micki looked at Jacqui. "Who's Eli?"

"His imaginary friend."

"When did this start?"

"The last couple months. It's the name of one of our neighbors. Actually the man who saw him at the bus stop and brought him home, that night he tried to find Angel."

Micki glanced over at him. Angel was whispering something in his ear. He had his super-serious, super-hero face on.

"You ever see that guy again?"

"Nope. I asked a couple other neighbors, they didn't know him. Why?"

Eli. The name of Professor Truebell's assistant. Eli, the name of the guy who had come to Angel's aid, now also Alexander's imaginary friend. It couldn't be a coincidence.

"You're certain the friend's imaginary?"

Jacqui paled. "Of course I'm . . . why would you say that?"

"Because I'm a cop." She lowered her voice. "And I know there're bad people who prey on kids."

"There's no way. Alexander's never out of my sight!"

Her hands were shaking, Micki saw, and backed off. "I'm not trying to upset you."

"Well, you are. Angel," she said, turning toward the girl, "when that game's finished, send Alexander over."

"Sure," she said. "We're finishing now."

Moments later, Zander trotted over. Jacqui lifted him and propped him on her hip. "Auntie Mouse wants to ask you about Eli."

His face lit up. "He's really nice. He tells me I'm a good boy and to always do what my mom says."

"He plays with you?"

He looked at her like he wondered if she was dealing with a full deck. "How's he 'posed to do that?"

"Don't friends play together?"

"Kid friends. He's a grown-up friend."

Micki glanced at Jacqui; she could all but feel the tension rolling off of her.

"He watches me sometimes."

Jacqui sucked in a sharp breath. "What did you—"

Micki cut her off. "You see him watching you?"

"Auntie Mouse, you're so funny. I hear him. Here—" He pointed to his head. "He talks to me."

Jacqui smiled. "See Aunt Mouse, I told you. Eli is Zander's imaginary friend."

He let out a huff of disgust and wriggled free of his mother's hold. "Eli's my *real* friend! I told you before."

"I know, Sweetie. Sorry." She ruffled his curls. "Go find Angel and see if she wants to get pizza with us."

"'Kay!" All smiles, he darted off, then stopped suddenly and looked back at them. "Eli's Angel's friend, too. Ask her 'bout him!"

CHAPTER SIXTEEN

Wednesday, October 21
6:50 P.M.

MICKI OFFERED TO DRIVE ANGEL to work. She pulled into the only available spot in front of the coffeehouse, then cut the engine. "Angel—"

"Thanks," Angel said, starting to open the door. "I work until midnight. I'll call you when I—"

"Wait. I want to talk to you about something."

She frowned. "What?"

Micki noted the caution in her tone. As if the last thing she wanted to do was talk to her. Secrets, Micki thought. Too damn many secrets.

"You know about Zander's imaginary friend?"

"Yes." She drew the word out. "What about him?"

"His name's Eli."

"So what?"

"Zander said Eli was your friend, too."

She looked at her phone. "I've got to get into work."

"You have a couple minutes."

"They like us to clock in a few minutes early."

She laid a hand on her arm. "You seem nervous."

"I'm not." She glanced toward the coffee shop, then back at Micki. "I don't know what you're asking."

Micki counted to five, then started again. "The night Zander ran away, trying to find you, a man named Eli brought him home. Was it the same Eli who rescued you?"

"I don't know, Micki. I wasn't there."

But Zach was, she realized. Zach had gone to help Jacqui that night.

Which meant that Zach had met Eli.

And he hadn't told her.

"Can I go?"

"What about your Eli?"

"What about him?"

"Maybe they're one and the same?"

"Maybe, but that'd be weird. And like I said, I wasn't there so I don't know. Can I go now?"

"Wait. Zander says he hears Eli in his head. That he talks to him that way. How would that be possible?" When Angel didn't respond, she pressed harder. "Didn't you say that you and Eli—"

Angel glanced nervously at the shop, then back at Micki. "Now *you're* being weird. I've got to go."

Maybe so, but Angel was as well. Repeatedly glancing at the coffeehouse, checking the time. As if she wanted to be rid of Micki as soon as possible. The hair on the back of her neck prickled.

Micki looked toward Sacred Grounds, at a group leaving the shop, then back at Angel. "That Seth, have you seen him again?"

Her cheeks flamed. "He comes into the shop. He's a nice guy."

"Angel, look, you're young and sometimes it's hard to—"

"You're not my mom."

"And I'm not trying to be."

"Then what are you trying to be?"

Micki stopped on that. If not a mother, what was she to Angel? A friend? She was too old, had seen too much, to truly be just a friend. A mentor, maybe? Offering up sage, worldly-wise advice? The thought made her feel slightly squeamish. Or her guardian and protector? Keeping her safe from those who would ruin her?

God, it all seemed overwrought and ridiculous.

"I don't know," she said again. "I just . . . I don't want to see you hurt."

Angel looked at her with those mysterious dark eyes, eyes that had seen so much in her eighteen years. Too much.

"What is life but pain?" Angel said softly.

The words were like a kick to the stomach. "Joy," Micki answered, surprising herself. "Moments of it. For some more than others."

Angel stared at her as if she had suddenly sprouted a halo. She had reason to, Micki acknowledged. That bit of optimism from the woman who angrily fought everything and everyone, all the time?

"I know, he's too old for me. Too cool, too good-looking. Too . . . everything for me." She popped open the car door but didn't climb out. "But what if he makes me happy? What if, when I'm with him, I get one of those joy moments?"

"Last night, you were with him, weren't you?"

"I don't know what you're talking about."

"I heard you sneaking in late."

Angel bristled. "Did you really just say that? Sneaking?"

"Okay, how would you describe your tiptoeing past my door?"

"Considerate? You hardly sleep, Micki. The last thing I wanted to do was wake you if you were finally getting some rest. Next time I won't bother."

The acid in her tone stung. "Angel, I'm sorry, but when it's after the time you're supposed to be home—"

"So now I have a curfew?"

"No. We didn't set a curfew. But we have an understanding. All you have to do is let me know when—"

"Whatever. Fine."

Angel swung her legs out of the car, then stopped and looked angrily back at Micki. "And your question about Zander? About how it's possible? You already know the answer to it."

She exited the vehicle, slamming the door behind her. Without a glance back, she darted into the coffee shop.

For a long time Micki just sat, hands on the steering wheel, gazing blankly ahead, thoughts churning with the things Angel had said about Seth. And conversely, what those things said about her opinion of herself.

Angel didn't think she was good enough for him.

They were seeing each other, Micki acknowledged. More than once, she'd bet. And yeah, last night had been one of those times.

"And your question about Zander? About how it's possible? You already know the answer to it."

In fact, she could have tripped over the truth if it had been any more obvious: Zander was special. The way Zach and Angel were. And, obviously, Eli.

Her cell went off. She didn't recognize the number and picked up. "Detective Dare."

"Detective, it's Paul Cleary from New Orleans Emergency Medical

Services."

The EMT who had treated her. "Yes, Paul. What can I do for you?"

"I've remembered something, from the night you were shot. When we were stabilizing you, you said a name. Several times."

She felt her heartbeat quicken. "What was it?"

"You couldn't speak clearly and I had to strain to hear, so I've got to tell you up front I could be wrong."

"What was it?" she asked again, although she knew, deep in her gut what he was going to say. Already she felt betrayed. She prayed she was wrong.

"Eli. You said Eli."

CHAPTER SEVENTEEN

Wednesday, October 21
7:16 P.M.

MICKI'S HANDS SHOOK. SHE'D ASKED Zach, point blank. Was anyone else there that night? No, he'd said. She told him about her dream. He'd passed it off as due to blood loss, or a near-death experience. Every single thing she'd shared—basically opening a vein and bleeding—he'd brushed off.

Liar. He was a liar. She didn't know whose team he was on, but it wasn't hers.

Her cell went off again. *Zach this time.* She almost didn't answer. Almost took the way he would, the coward's way. Dodge and hide.

Mad Dog didn't play that way.

"Dare," she answered.

"Mick?" A pause. "It's me. You okay?"

"Why wouldn't I be?"

"I thought you'd be back by now. I wanted to make sure you hadn't run into trouble. Especially now that we know Mr. Big and Bad Ass is out there."

"I just had an interesting phone call."

"About the case?"

"Paul Cleary. The paramedic who treated me the night I was shot."

The slightest pause. "What'd he want?"

"He remembered something about that night. Something important."

He didn't respond; his silence was damning. He'd been caught and he knew it.

"I know, you son-of-a-bitch. I know."

"Know what, Mick?"

"About Eli. He was there that night; I said his name to the paramedic. And don't you fucking dare try to deny it."

"Okay, yes, he was there. I kept it from you because—"

"You didn't just keep it from me. You *lied*. At every turn."

"I didn't want to, Mick. I promise you—"

"Your promises don't mean a thing to me. Not anymore."

"I get it. I'm sorry, I really am."

"I am too."

She hung up and tossed the phone onto the passenger seat.

Micki drove aimlessly up and down streets for a while. Some she didn't know, some she knew like the back of her hand. She handled the powerful car expertly, comforted by her control of it, fighting for control of her emotions over the way this cut, deep and scorching.

She had been lied to before. Duped, betrayed. She'd get over it; that's what she did. Move on, learn from it that the only safe place to put her trust was in herself. Everybody else had an agenda.

She'd started to believe that Zach had her back. The way that Hank used to. Hank, her friend and mentor. Her savior.

Stupid. Zach wasn't like Hank. Nobody was. And Hank was gone.

The light ahead turned red; Micki pulled to a stop. A Dark Bearer was attacking them; she had the burn to prove it. But she wasn't a quitter. She'd close this case, then she was out. If the Chief wouldn't release her from Sixers, she'd resign. Join another force in a new city, far from here and all this crazy-other-world bullshit.

Screw 'em all.

A honk came from the car behind. Her street ahead, she realized belatedly. She rolled forward, then turned onto it. As she neared her house, she noticed the silhouette of a man standing on her dark porch.

At first, she thought was it was Zach, then she rejected the thought. This man was taller and held himself differently than Zach did.

She eased her gun from its holster, laid it on her lap, and parked, choosing the point that would put her in the best position to defend herself: a clear shot for her; the Nova between her and his line of fire.

As she opened the car door and stepped out, her hands curved around the weapon's grip. "You," she called, "hands up! Step into the light."

He lifted his hands and moved to the far side of the porch, where the light from her neighbor's flood lamp spilled across him.

The blond man, from the night of the press conference.

She made her way cautiously forward. "Who are you and what are you doing on my property?"

"You know who I am, Micki."

"How do you know my name?" Micki kept the gun trained on his chest. "And why were you at the press conference the other night?"

"I'm the one you've been looking for."

"Enough with the bullshit. I want to see ID. *Now.*"

"Okay. I'm going for my license." He retrieved his wallet, opened it.

"Hold it up, where I can see it. Slowly."

He did as she asked, expression eerily unfazed. As if he didn't have a gun trained on his chest and a woman on the other end who wouldn't hesitate to use it. As if she had the gun but he had something more powerful.

He held out the license. "I'm Eli."

According to the license, he was telling the truth. "What are you doing on my front porch, Eli?"

"I told you. I heard you were looking for me. Figured I'd come to you, help you out."

"Heard from who?"

"Alexander. And Angel. Can I put my ID away?"

She nodded, watched as he did, then said, "Hands against the wall."

"You're serious?"

"Dead serious, asshole."

He did as she asked. She ran her hands quickly over him, torso, arms, and legs. He was clean. She holstered her Glock and stepped back. "You can lower your hands and turn around."

He did. "It must be difficult," he said, "not to be able to trust."

"Comes with the badge." She motioned towards the two folding lawn chairs perched in the corner. "Sit."

He opened his and she followed suit, placing her chair directly in front of his, interrogation style.

He smiled slightly. "You're a tough case, Michaela Dare."

She ignored the comment. "Why are you messing with Alexander?"

"Messing with him? We're friends."

"He's a minor. You have no right."

"He's my brother."

"Like you're Angel's brother?"

He seemed not to notice her sarcasm. "That's right."

"Tell me what happened that night, the night I was shot. You were there?"

"Yes."

"And?"

"And I used my light to keep you alive."

"Your light? What the hell's that?"

"It's not just Zach who can accomplish the remarkable."

"A cryptic answer. Why am I not surprised?"

He smiled slightly at her sarcasm. "Here's the deal, Michaela. I'm a healer. That's what I do-- it's my gift."

She arched her eyebrows in exaggerated disbelief. "You heal people. With your *light* force."

"Basically. Plus a few other things." He leaned toward her. "May I?"

"May you what?"

"Heal you."

"I'm not sick." She shook her head. "And I have strict rules about mumbo-jumbo bullshit being used on me."

"There are more kinds of illnesses than physical ones. Emotional. Spiritual."

"It's a sick fucking world. So, since you're this super healer dude, maybe you need to be out there, helping people."

"Instead of wasting my time here with you?"

"Exactly. Because *I'm*—" she tapped her chest, making certain she didn't meet his eyes "—fine."

"Why won't you look me in the eyes?"

"You know why. I'm onto your little tricks, and I refuse to be manipulated."

"Always in control," he murmured. "Afraid to let go."

"Damn right. In my line of work, letting go is dangerous. Being in control is a means of staying alive."

He cocked his head, studying her. "What about all that anger? Is that keeping you alive as well? Or is it killing you?"

Her neck and head hurt. She was angry and felt betrayed. Now this? No, thank you. Not tonight.

She jumped to her feet. "It's late, I'm tired and—"

He caught her hand, curled his fingers around it, warm and snug. She looked down at him, the order to back off dying on her lips. His eyes were like an endless summer sky with clouds moving lazily across.

"Sit, Michaela," Eli said, "Let me help you."

She told herself to fight, to look away, refuse. He wouldn't hold her against her will, she knew that. Felt it deep in her being, with a part of her she hadn't felt in a very long time. Since Hank, she realized.

She sank back to the chair. He brought his fingertips to her forehead and temples. Each fingertip became a point of warmth and light. A feeling of peace rolled over her, like a river of well-being.

Her anger evaporated. Exhaustion and tension melted away along with their physical manifestations. His eyes . . . a summer sky. The cry of a seagull. The sound of a child's laughter. Her toes curling into warm, white sand.

Her head filled with the memory. She looked down at her feet. Small and pudgy. How old was she? Four?

Yes, she thought, hearing the sound of her own giggles. Her squeals of laughter as she was scooped up and twirled around. Free, she thought. Pure and deliriously content with herself and her place in the world.

Eli dropped his hands. The connection to the memory was broken. But the feeling of pure and utter peace remained.

"Feel better?"

She did. Fatigue, headache and heartbreak had all slipped away. "How'd you do that?" she asked.

"I told you, it's what I do. It's my gift."

"Can we bottle it, sell it at Walgreens? We'd make a fortune."

"We would at that." He smiled and rested his forehead against hers. *"But the truth is, we don't have to bottle it. It's already in you. It's in everyone."*

Micki heard the words as clearly as if he had said them out loud. But his mouth hadn't moved.

"You're communicating with me telepathically. The way you do with Angel. And Alexander."

"Cool, huh? By the way, you are, too."

She was, she realized. *"How is this possible?"*

"I'm not entirely sure, but I have an idea."

She felt lightheaded, giddy. *"It's fun."*

"We need to talk."

"I thought we were." She drank him in. *"You're so pretty."*

"Thank you, although I thought guys were handsome and girls were pretty."

"You're both."

He laughed. Not at her. She knew that. But with affection. Like a parent might have for a child. Or an older cousin for a younger one.

"It's my light."

"Your light?" she repeated.

"Don't be mad at Zach."

She'd forgotten all about Zach. About why she had been so angry and hurt. *"I can't trust him. He keeps things from me."*

"We asked him to. We made him promise."

"You and Professor Truebell?"

"And Parker. Yes."

She digested that. *"Parker's a dick."*

He laughed. *"Sometimes. You weren't supposed to remember, Micki. That night. Me or what happened. I thought I took care of that."*

"But I did remember. A little anyway."

"Yes. Zach told me you were asking questions. It bothered him a lot. He hated not being honest with you. It would have been so much easier for him if you hadn't recalled even a glimmer of it."

She frowned. *"Why didn't you want me to remember?"*

"We didn't know if we could trust you."

"I haven't proved myself? I've saved Zach's life. I've kept his secret. What could be so important I couldn't be trusted with it?"

"I see that now. You're one of the most trustworthy people I've ever met. When you believe in someone or something, you're all in."

He lifted his head, breaking the connection. She felt suddenly bereft. Abandoned.

"You're not alone, Michaela. You're one of us now."

"One of you? What does that mean? That you finally trust me?"

"You've been given a gift. One I didn't know about until now."

"I don't know what you mean. What gift?"

"You have to wait, just a little longer."

"I don't like secrets."

"But there are secrets that change you once you know them. Once you know, you can't go back."

"I don't care. It's always better to know."

He smiled. "I like you, Micki Dare. Prickly parts and all." He laid his fingertips on her forehead once more. "Are you sure about this? Your

view of the world will never be the same. Once shared, I can't take it back."

"Yes, I want to know."

CHAPTER EIGHTEEN

Wednesday, October 21
11:10 P.M.

ANGEL AND SETH SAT ON a Moon Walk bench facing the Mississippi River. She rested her head on his shoulder, liking the snug feeling of his arm around her and being cradled to his side.

She'd never had this before. Hadn't believed it was possible to feel this way-- like she belonged. Like she was . . . worthy. Of attention and affection. Not possible for her--strange, unwanted Angel Gomez. The one who had never fit in. Who had always been different. A barge, being guided in by a tug boat, crossed her line of vision, their lights like diamonds glistening on the black water.

From the French Quarter behind them came the music of a saxophonist playing on the Square, the melody beautiful, but so sad, she thought, feeling anything but. Sadness couldn't exist now, not with Seth's arm around her.

She sighed.

"What's wrong?" he asked softly.

"Nothing," she answered. "Not now anyway."

He threaded his fingers through her hair. The sensation was almost hypnotic.

"Which means that earlier, something was?"

"This dweeb friend of mine shared something I'd asked him to keep a secret."

"He?" Seth's fingers stilled. "Should I be jealous?"

She tipped her face up to his. "Hardly. Zander just turned four."

She liked the way his laughter rumbled in his chest and nestled closer.

"I didn't know four-year-olds could keep secrets."

"Apparently, they can't."

"What secret could you have shared with a preschooler that would matter?"

He was right—for normal people. But she was anything but normal. A fact she wasn't about to share with him.

"His mom, Jacqui, is Micki's best friend. I babysit for him sometimes. Because of his big mouth, Micki and I argued."

"About us?" She nodded. "And you admitted we were seeing each other?"

"No. She guessed it and I couldn't deny it."

"Why would you?" He rested his forehead on hers. "Embarrassed by me?"

"No! God, no. It's just—" She bit the words back, not wanting to put thoughts in his head. Not wanting him to look at her that way—like she was too young, too inexperienced.

"Come on, Angel. What?"

"She thinks you're too old for me. And that you're going to hurt me."

He held her gaze for a long moment. "And what do you think?"

"That you make me happy." Even as she murmured the words, she acknowledged it was so much more than that. It was like being near him ignited a part of her that had been dead or sleeping. Like he was the other part of her and together they could do anything.

"I felt sort of bad, you know, acting that way toward her. She's helped me so much, but—"

"She just doesn't understand."

Angel rested her head against his shoulder. "Exactly."

"She's not your mom."

"That's what I told her."

They fell silent a moment. He broke it. "So, I have a question," he said.

"What is it?"

"We've seen each almost every day since we met, but I haven't kissed you. Have you wondered why?"

It was embarrassing, but she had wondered constantly. "Yes."

"I didn't know if you wanted me to." He leaned closer. "Do you? Want me to kiss you?"

"Yes."

"You're certain?"

He was laughing at her. "Jerk." She started to her feet. He grabbed her hand and pulled her back down. She landed on his lap.

"Tell me the truth."

"I already did. You're a jerk."

He took her mouth on a laugh. She'd been kissed before. But it hadn't been like this. Like the fourth of July, New Year's Eve and running with the wind all in one. Electric and brilliant, fuzzy-headed and tingly.

Something, some switch, flipped inside her. Like she was finally, fully alive.

He deepened the kiss. Pulled her closer to tangle his fingers in her hair. Said her name, throaty and deep.

Then he ended the kiss. Too soon, she thought. She had wanted it to go on forever.

He trailed his thumb across her bottom lip. "You should tell Micki about us. What's the worst that could happen?"

"She could kick me out."

"You think she'd do that?"

Angel bit her lower lip. "I don't know. Maybe."

Maybe if she found out she'd lied to her. That the reason she'd wanted out of the car wasn't because she needed to clock in, but because she wasn't even working tonight. She'd been meeting Seth.

"If that happened, you could come live with me," he said.

She straightened and drew away from him. "Are you serious? We hardly know each other."

He looked hurt. "That's not the way I feel, Angel. It's weird because I feel like I've known you all my life."

A knot of tears stuck in her throat. "I can't believe you said that."

"Too much? Too fast?" He searched her gaze. "I'll back off."

"No. It's . . . that's the way I feel, too. And, like somehow, you're a part of me."

He curved his arms back around her. The feel of his embrace was at once soothing and invigorating, almost agitating. But in a good way. Like she could burst into song or flight or whatever.

"I want you to meet my uncle."

His uncle? It was one thing for Seth—for some crazy reason—to like her. But his uncle? The thought of it caused a knot to form in the pit of her stomach.

When she didn't comment, he went on. "Uncle Will. He'll like you,

I know it."

"What if he doesn't?"

"Of course he will. Why wouldn't he?"

"I don't know. Maybe he'll think I'm too young?"

"Just because Micki has trust issues, doesn't mean he will."

"Why do you think she has trust issues?"

"Seriously? She sleeps with a gun."

"Because she's a cop. Because she's seen a lot of really bad stuff and—"

"Has trust issues," he finished. "I read it all over her. But that doesn't mean she's not a good person, okay? I didn't mean that."

"So do I."

"What?"

"Have a hard time trusting. It comes from being hurt so often."

He drew her close, tucking her head under his chin. "You trust me, don't you?"

"You're special. I don't know why."

He laughed. "Uncle Will is going to adore you. I've already told him all about you."

"Really?" She couldn't quite believe it. "About me?"

"About *us*, Angel. That's what we are now, right?"

It was, she thought dizzily. The two of them, together.

"So, you'll meet him, won't you?"

"Can I think about it?"

"Sure. If that's what you want."

Was that hurt or annoyance she heard in his voice? Either made her doubt herself. "Tell me more about him. Then I won't be so nervous about meeting him. I'm guessing he doesn't sleep with a gun?"

He smiled. "I don't think he even owns one. He's an art collector and has an amazing collection."

"Really?"

He nodded. "You'll love it. And you should show him your art. I bet he'd like it. He might even buy a piece."

"I'm not going to show him my drawings."

"Why not?"

"I'm not a professional. I'm just a student."

"Aren't we all just students of life?"

She laughed at that. "Okay, I'll meet him. He sounds really cool."

But instead of commenting, he fell silent. The moment stretched out uncomfortably. Angel wanted to break it, ask him what was wrong or if she'd said something to upset him, but she didn't want to look too anxious.

He checked the time. "We better head back."

She didn't want to, but after her confrontation with Micki earlier, coming in late wasn't an option. Micki thought she was working until midnight, so if she made it home by the regular time, she should be golden.

She scooted off his lap. He caught her hand, lacing his fingers through hers. She liked the connection, the solid feel of his hand. Something to hold onto, she thought. No, better—*someone* to hold onto.

CHAPTER NINETEEN

Thursday, October 22
7:10 A.M.

MICKI OPENED HER EYES. SHE lay on the couch. How had she ended up here? She blinked, confused. The last thing she remembered, it had been Wednesday night. She'd been angry about something. Or at . . . wait, someone . . . waiting on her porch. Eli. His fingertips on her forehead. Light and warmth and a memory--of her, as a little girl.

The memory came rushing back. The beach. The sound of the surf and the salty smell of the ocean. A seagull swooping overhead. Her bare feet and giddy laughter. She'd been as free as that bird, sure of herself and her world.

Sure that she was loved.

Micki massaged the lines that formed between her eyebrows. Whose hands had been holding her? Whose laughter had that been, joyously mingling with hers? She had trusted that person wholly. Had trusted in their love.

Before Uncle Beau, Micki thought. Before mother checked out.

She hadn't wanted the memory to end. No, not a memory. She'd been dreaming. A crazy-real dream.

"Morning."

Angel stood in the kitchen doorway, dressed for class in jeans and a T-shirt, one of the flannels she loved over the tee. Micki sat up and pushed her hair away from her face. "Morning."

Angel held a glass of orange juice in one hand, a piece of toast in the other. She took a big bite of the toast. Micki smelled peanut butter. And cinnamon.

"You okay?" Angel asked.

"I had the weirdest dream last night."

She took another bite. "What about?"

"That I met Eli."

"My Eli?"

"Yes. He came to see me."

"Why?"

"Because I was looking for him, he said. And to tell me not to be mad at Zach."

"You're mad at Zach?"

"Yes, I—" Why came tumbling back. His lying to her. Letting her down, breaking trust. Again.

How angry she'd been.

Past tense. No, she was still angry.

Wasn't she?

"I need some coffee." She stood. Her legs felt weak, rubbery. What the hell was wrong with her this morning? She prayed she wasn't getting sick, no way she had time for that.

Angel trailed her into the kitchen. "Why're you mad at Zach?"

"Typical Zach." Micki sensed Angel's frown at the non-answer. She fitted a coffee pod into her machine and hit the button. "What time did you get home?"

"Regular. Twelve-fifteen or so. You were completely out, even though I coughed, cleared my throat and made a snack. I didn't want to be accused of *sneaking*."

Micki winced. "About that, I'm sorry. This whole thing is new to me and— You're eighteen. I guess I need to lighten up."

Angel finished her juice and rinsed her glass. "Don't worry about it."

Micki added some milk to her cup and sipped. All that activity and she didn't wake up? That wasn't like her. "I must have been out cold."

"How's your arm?" Angel asked.

Micki looked at her bandaged arm. She'd forgotten all about it. How could that . . . she should be in pain, bad enough to be unable to sleep without medication.

Maybe that was it, she thought. The reason for her deep sleep, the lethargy she felt now—even the wild dream. She'd taken pain medication. She frowned. But wouldn't she remember that?

With a strange feeling in the pit of her stomach, she unrolled the gauze. She expected to see an angry red stripe curling up her arm.

Expected the skin of her arm to be swollen, to see some blistering.

Instead there was . . . nothing. Her arm looked like it always did, freckled but otherwise unmarred.

She stared at it, confused. "Oh, my God."

"What?"

Micki found a chair and sat down hard. It had really happened.

"Zach isn't the only one who can do special things."

"I'm a healer."

Eli *had* been here. He had drawn that beautiful memory out of her deep subconscious, stripping her of the anger and hurt that had held her in its grip. Obviously, before he left, he had healed her arm.

Micki brought a hand to her mouth, her thoughts racing. Real. It was all real. She and Eli had communicated telepathically. She'd told him he was pretty, for God's sake.

"You're one of us now."

There was more, but she couldn't quite grasp it.

"Micki, say something. You're scaring me."

She looked at Angel. "Eli."

"What?"

"It wasn't a dream, Angel. Eli was here."

Angel looked unconvinced.

Micki's phone went off in the living room. She knew without answering that it was Eli calling. She ran to grab it and answered.

She was right.

"How are you this morning?"

"Confused and groggy. Wondering if you drugged me."

He laughed. "That happens sometimes. You're not used to the energy transfer."

"The energy transfer," she repeated. "Could you be more specific?"

"Not right now, sorry. How's your arm?"

"You know how it is. Healed. Completely."

"Excellent." He sounded pleased with himself. "Professor Truebell wants to see you."

"Me? About what?"

"The home invasions. What you're up against."

"I know what I'm up against. I faced it before--a Dark Bearer."

"Yes. Bring Angel along. Tell her we're meeting at LAM. She'll give you directions."

"Wait. Will Zach be there?"

"Of course, Michaela. Let's say thirty minutes."

CHAPTER TWENTY

Thursday, October 22
8:30 A.M.

"IT'S RIGHT THERE," ANGEL SAID. "On the left."

Micki found a parking spot in front of the repurposed Mid-City Victorian. The sign out front announced *Lost Angel Ministries.*

She and Angel had spoken little on the drive here. Angel had been lost in her phone; Micki with her own thoughts. She wasn't sure what to expect from this meeting or how she was going to react to seeing Zach.

She didn't have long to wait to learn the latter. Zach arrived almost simultaneously, coming from the other direction. He met her at her car. Something had changed between them, Micki realized. She wasn't angry, not anymore. She wasn't even hurt, she didn't feel betrayed. She remembered the feelings, but they'd lost the power to sting.

In an odd way it was almost as if she was looking at a stranger.

Angel squealed and ran to give him a hug. He hugged her back, his gaze finding hers over Angel's shoulder.

"Hey," he said.

"Hey."

"I guess they're letting you into the fold."

"I guess they are. I say it's about frickin' time."

"Micki, I—"

"I'm not mad. Not anymore. It wasn't all on you, I know that now."

"But?"

"No buts."

His brow furrowed. He didn't understand, she knew. She supposed there was no way he could.

"Come on, you two!" Angel had hurried ahead and was waiting at the front door.

As they reached the porch, Angel pushed the buzzer and looked into the camera. "It's us."

Eli let them in. Angel hugged him and darted inside. Eli clapped Zach on the back in greeting, then turned to her. He smiled. "I'm really glad you're here."

"Me too."

Professor Truebell emerged from what she assumed was an office at the top of the stairs.

"Professor!" Angel called and ran up the stairs to greet him.

He hugged her and they descended, arm-in-arm, Angel chattering excitedly. When they reached the landing, Truebell crossed to her, his hand out. "The lovely Detective Dare," he said. "Welcome to LAM."

She took his hand. It was smooth and soft. Definitely not the hand of a cop. "What is this place?"

"A not-for-profit I created a number of years ago to help our young people. So many have lost their way."

He indicated she should follow him. "So many problems, so few services to help. There was no place for them to fit in, to feel like they belong."

"That's what this place is, then? A kind of counseling center?"

"And more. Here we are," he said, stopping at the doorway to a conference room. "Everyone, find a seat."

Micki did and looked at Truebell. "Let me guess," she said. "These lost and hurting young people you're talking about are—" she made air quotes, "—'special.'"

A small smile curved his mouth, all but hidden under his beard. "All people, young and old, are special, Detective."

"What a fat load of crap," she said lightly. "Because, obviously, you only provide services to the particularly unique. Like Angel, Zach and Parker. And you and Eli here."

"Perceptive and lovely."

She snorted. "So, you find these gifted young people in order to help them?"

"Yes."

"Why?"

"Because it's my purpose and my passion."

She narrowed her eyes. "I'll give you that, Professor, because you—and Eli here—seem like touchy-feely sort of guys. But Parker and Zach? Not so much."

Truebell laughed. "You're right. Helping the lost I would do even if we didn't have another, even greater, purpose." He turned to Angel. "There's a small class upstairs, newcomers to LAM. I think hearing your story would be a wonderful encouragement for them."

"Okay." She got to her feet. "Can I come back when I've finished?"

"Of course. You're always welcome with us, Angel."

The door shut behind her; Eli looked at Professor Truebell. "Should I call him now?"

"One minute." The professor folded his hands on the table in front of him. "I understand that last night you and Eli got to know each other."

"Actually, I already knew Eli. That night at the church, he saved my life. You wanted me to forget, but I didn't. Not really."

"That was quite a surprise. More of one after last night. I promise you, had we known we wouldn't have asked Zach to keep the whole story from you."

"Lie," she corrected. "You asked him to lie. Which he did to protect you—" she made a sweeping gesture, "—and this place."

"Actually to protect much more than that."

She felt Zach's gaze on her, but she didn't look his way. She didn't trust herself to. "What?"

He ignored her question, choosing another direction. "Eli wasn't the only one of us there that night. I was there. Parker. Others. There were fourteen in all. We were there to battle the Dark One."

"Battle the Dark—" She did look at Zach then, in accusation, then back at the professor. "I thought Zach had—"

She bit the words back. That had never added up. That Zach could have saved Angel and the other two women *and* dispatched the Dark Bearer. She never bought it, not really.

She turned to look him straight in the eyes. "More untruths, Zach?"

"Not untruths," Eli interjected. "Unexplainables."

"That's such bullshit."

"Unexplainable until now," Truebell said. "Eli's convinced me that you can be trusted with our secret."

She shifted her accusing gaze to Eli. "But you didn't trust me either. You put me to sleep and when I woke up I sure as hell didn't recall any super secrets."

"I didn't put you to sleep, Michaela. I imparted the information but I put a lock on it. Just in case."

"Just in case what?"

"The professor disagreed."

"But I didn't," Truebell said. "I'm authorizing him to unlock it now. If you still want to know."

A part of her wanted to tell them all to go to hell. But another part had to know. She set her jaw. "I do."

Eli swiveled his chair around to face hers. He smiled. "Ready?"

As he had the night before, he placed his fingertips against her forehead. And the same as then, she felt warmth, then light spilling over her. A connection happening, between the two of them, but something larger as well.

The something grew, expanded, then exploded inside her. Images filled her head, playing on the back of her eyelids like a film on crack. Neurons fired, synapses ignited, pathways opened. Expanding, collecting, learning.

The creation of the world. Ancient peoples, light beings. Angels, not as depicted in popular culture, but human, with faults and foibles and weaknesses. Centuries passing, love and loss, procreation with humans. Then an explosion of all types of humanity—and all that went with it. Poverty and despair. Man's inhumanity to man.

The shit she saw and shoveled every day.

The emergence of the Dark One--the ancient of evils. Turning the weakest away from the light and feeding on the light of those who remained. Feasting as a vampire feasted. Creating the army they now called Dark Bearers.

The world's host of light growing smaller, weaker. The formation of a governing body; a law forbidding the mating of Lightkeeper with human.

The images came faster, racing forward. The night she was shot, the bullet tearing into her, then a second, going down with the shooter . . . an explosion of another kind inside her, bright and white . . . Angel suspended above the ground by a dark pulsing energy. The Dark Bearer, frightening in his power. The one Zach had seen, and she never could.

And Zach standing up to him, the way a candle stood up to the wind. She saw him growing weaker, his strength and light ebbing. The end of him near. She reached out, calling his name.

Suddenly a circle of figures, a circle of light, growing brighter--so bright she couldn't bear to look any longer. A howl as if straight from the abyss. The splitting of the night.

Then absolute quiet.

CHAPTER TWENTY-ONE

Thursday, October 22
9:50 P.M.

ZACH COULDN'T TAKE HIS EYES off Micki. She sat erectly, her eyes closed, but lids twitching as if she were viewing or processing something behind those closed lids.

Astounded, he watched the information transfer, like ribbons of light, from Eli to her. He hadn't known such a thing was possible.

And earlier he'd seen the tender way Eli looked at her. And the way her eyes had sought him out, noting the way her smile for him lit up her face.

He was damn sure she never smiled at him that way.

Suddenly her eyes popped open. A cry ripping from her lips, she launched to her feet, then seemed to simply crumble.

Zach caught her before she hit the ground. "Dammit, Eli!" he said, cradling her in his arms and carrying her to the waiting room couch. "You hit her with too much, too fast."

"I've got her," Eli said. "Just let me—"

"No, *I've* got her."

"She'll be fine, Zach," Truebell said, laying a hand on his arm. "Let Eli revive her. It was a lot to take in so quickly."

Zach hesitated, not wanting the other man close to her. As if by relinquishing this moment, he was allowing Eli to stake his claim.

It was irrational, he knew. He had no claim on her at all.

Zach looked at Eli, holding his gaze a long moment in warning, then stepped aside.

Eli took Zach's place, bent his face close to Micki's, and breathed his light into her. Like some freaky form of mouth-to-mouth, Zach thought. It set his teeth on edge.

But it worked. Micki opened her eyes, then looked past him to Eli. "You're here," she said.

"And so am I, Mick." Zach squeezed her hand. "How're you feeling?"

Her gaze shifted to him and lingered a moment, as if seeing him for the first time, then moved on to Truebell. "Why am I lying down?"

"You fainted."

She frowned slightly. "I don't faint."

Typical Mick. Zach held back a smile. "Feel strong enough to sit up?"

She bristled. "I'm fine. I just need y'all to back up and give me a little room to work with."

They did and she started to stand, wobbled and Zach caught her arm. "You've got this, Mad Dog."

"Of course I do." She shook her head, as if to clear it, then freed her arm from his grasp. "We have work to do."

Zach looked at Truebell. "Give us five minutes."

"I don't need—"

Zach cut her off. "But I do."

"Zach's right," Truebell said. "You two need to talk. Take the conference room." He paused. "And all the time you need."

Moments later they sat across the conference room table from each other.

Micki wouldn't quite meet his eyes. "So, you *are* a Half Light? I remember you've been called that before."

"Yes. My mother, Parker's sister, mated with a human and I was the result."

"They're light beings," she said. "Dressed as humans."

He smiled at the description. "You're handling this all much better than I did."

"Don't be so sure. My mind's completely blown."

"But you buy it all?"

"Yeah." She shrugged. "I don't see how Eli could have engineered what I just experienced if it wasn't the real deal. Besides, I bought into you and Parker and the whole Dark Bearer thing. Why not this?"

"Like I said, you're taking this way better than I did."

She looked down at her hands, folded on the table in front of her, then finally directly at him. "That's why you almost quit before, isn't it?

They laid all this on you?"

"Yes. But not the way Eli did you. Seems to me you got a much cooler version." She didn't smile and he went on. "I was furious that Parker lied, that he—that they all—kept the truth from me. Ironic, considering."

When she didn't comment, he asked, "What are you thinking?"

"There's so much to . . . think about. It's like, everything I took for granted as being the absolute truth . . . isn't. A different race of beings? The battle of good against evil being real, not just a metaphor? Learning that the world is even more of a fucked-up mess than I thought?"

She fell silent for a beat, then continued, softly, "I get it. Why you lied to me. Why you felt you had to."

Emotion knotted in his throat. "You know I didn't want to."

"Yes. But it doesn't . . . Never mind."

"No, what?"

"Like I said, I get it, Zach. They asked you to keep the truth from me. You felt you had to choose a side."

"But?"

She hesitated a moment, then said, "But I wish it would have been mine. I wish you could have believed in me enough to trust me."

He felt the truth of her words like a fist to his chest, knocking the wind out of him. She wasn't angry anymore, he knew. Like she said, she got the why. But it was still there between them: that he hadn't trusted her, that she couldn't trust him because of it. It always would be between them.

"Still partners?" he asked.

She nodded. "Can't do this without you. And you know how much I hate admitting that."

Neither of them laughed. For his part, he couldn't. The feeling of loss in the pit of his gut was too strong. He wondered if she felt the same way.

He stood, went to the door and called the others in. Within a moment they were all reassembled around the table.

"Do you have any questions?" Truebell asked, looking at Mick. "Anything you need some clarity on?"

"You're called Lightkeepers?"

"We are."

"And your job was supposed to be spreading love, joy and goodwill among all men?"

"Was supposed to be, yes. Although that sounded a little like a soft drink advertisement at Christmastime."

"But somewhere along the line, y'all fucked things up as bad as us ordinary humans."

"Pretty much."

"I've got to say, I'm a little pissed off. Y'all were supposed to be the good guys."

"Afraid so. But I promise you, we're trying to turn things around now."

"Nothing like waiting until the last frickin' minute." She let out a long breath. "So you created this place, this ministry, to help the kids your people threw away—basically because they're half-breeds."

Micki folded her hands on the table in front of her. "But at the same time you're also recruiting them—and preparing them for battle against the Dark One and his forces."

"His army of Dark Bearers," Truebell said. "Yes."

"Okay, I think I'm up to speed on my history lesson. Now, what does all this have to do with me and my investigation?"

CHAPTER TWENTY-TWO

Thursday, October 22
10:30 P.M.

MICKI STRUGGLED TO FOCUS ON exactly what Professor Truebell was saying. She couldn't let her mind wander, not for a second, or she would become mired in a freak-storm of "no ways" and "how can this be happenings."

When she told Zach her mind was blown, she meant it. All she had left was her police training. She was a cop, it's what she did. What she was good at.

"Tell us what you know so far about the home invasions, Detective Dare. What you saw."

"There have been five. All but one, the last, very similar."

"What was different?"

Zach answered, "The energy for one. It was deliberate, yes. But not gleeful. Last night they were proving a point."

Micki stepped back in. "The other big difference is this last family didn't have children. At the other four invasions, the children were awakened by flashlights being shone into their eyes."

Truebell glanced at Eli. Something in his expression suggested that had more significance to him than anything said before.

"Interesting," he said. "Go on."

"What made the most impact on me," Zach said, "was the youngest of the perpetrators, Bear. According to the children in all four cases, he kept them company, played with them. And he told them he was afraid of the others in the group." Zach moved his gaze from Truebell to Eli. "He was telling them the truth. I picked up his cry for help."

"You need to find him," Eli said. "He may be the key."

"I think so too."

Micki took over. "The last invasion was a definite message to Zach from whatever Dark Bearer is behind the group and their crimes."

Truebell looked at her. "And I understand you were injured?"

"Yes, my arm."

Micki felt a twinge and looked down. She didn't know if her memory was playing tricks on her but she thought she could see a shadow of the serpentine burn on her arm. She frowned.

"Is something wrong, Michaela?"

"No." She shook her head. "Eli healed it."

"The lighter spontaneously combusted," Zach said. "It was as if the fire came to life and went after me."

"I tried to take it down and it got me instead."

Truebell look at Eli. "Could you call Angel now?"

He nodded but did not move or go for a phone. Micki realized he was calling her telepathically. Sure enough, a minute later Angel came into the conference room, a young man Micki didn't recognize with her. He had dark hair, fashionably cut, short on the sides, longer on the top. Attractive stubble, easy smile. His green eyes were his most mesmerizing feature. She pegged him to be in his early to mid-twenties.

Truebell invited the two to sit, then went around the table with introductions. "And this is Tommy Mason. A couple weeks ago, he came to us with a very interesting story. Zach, I know Parker mentioned it to you already, but I wanted Tommy to tell his story to you in his own words."

"I was downtown at a club called Metro. It's a pretty cool scene. And this guy comes up to me. I'd noticed him before, at other clubs. He makes the rounds, knows people."

Micki noticed some part of Tommy's body was always moving. Fingers tapping, knee popping, just constant nervous energy. Like he was juiced.

"He was always buying rounds. Lots of girls hanging around, everybody's buddy. You know the kind of guy."

She did know. "Go on."

"So this one night, he comes up to me, starts a conversation. We hang out, he buys drinks. We start hanging out like that pretty regular."

Tommy rolled his shoulders. "There's something about this dude, I don't know . . . he made my nerves twitch. Cool guy, super nice, just—"

"Made your skin crawl?" Zach offered.

"That's cold, man, but yeah. Sorta like that. So we're getting tight, right? We're buds."

He flexed his fingers, then cracked his knuckles. "So he tells me he's part of this exclusive group. 'What kind of group,' I ask. 'Wicked awesome,' he says again. 'Dope.' So he asks me if I want to join."

"How did you respond?"

"I'm intrigued, right? He tells me shit like I'll have more fun than I've had in my entire life. That I'll learn tricks, ways to do things, that will get me whatever I want."

"Did you wonder what the catch was?" Micki asked.

"There's always a catch, right?" He rubbed his palms on his thighs. "But I'm thinking this is some sort of sex thing. Maybe some drugs involved. Not that I wanted any part of that."

"So, you told him no."

If he heard the edge of sarcasm in her voice, he didn't let on. "I told him it sounded interesting and that I was in. The thing is, Kyle—that's his name—he didn't strike me as the kind of guy who took kindly to a 'no thanks.'"

"Did you feel threatened?"

"Not really."

"Did the group have a name?"

"Six Cubed. You know, big six, little three."

"Six to the third power?"

"Yeah. He said that. Whatever the fuck that means."

"So, what happened?" Zach asked. "How'd you end up here?"

"We were supposed to meet the next night. I didn't show."

"Why not?"

He looked uncomfortable. "I had this thing happen."

"What sort of thing?"

Angel piped up. "He's kind of like me, he sees things. But he doesn't draw them."

"Things," Micki repeated. "Like what?"

"Visions, like. It's stuff that happens. I've always had it. Like, I see a drink spilled, then it happens. Or I see this girl in the bar, I don't know her from Adam, right? But I just know what she's going to do or say next."

"I get it," Zach said. "A precognition thing. And you had one of these precogs about Kyle?"

"Yeah. I saw him—" Tommy stopped; the poor guy looked like he might jump out of his own skin.

"You can tell them," Angel said. "I've told them crazier stuff than that. I promise."

"Okay." He rubbed his palms on his jeans again. "I saw Kyle, he was standing there smirking at me . . . then this thing stepped out from behind him—"

"Thing?" Micki prodded.

"A monster."

The table went quiet. Tommy darted his gaze around the table, not looking at any one person for more than a second, then stopping on Angel.

"It freaked me the fuck out. So I came here."

"I drew it," Angel said. "He described it and drew it. Look—"

She flipped open her sketch pad. Dark and light. A twisting, swirling cloud. Something dragon-like emerging from it. Micki heard the breath hiss past Zach's lips and looked at him. He was staring at the drawing; he'd gone white.

"That's it," he said. "The Dark Bearer we battled last time."

CHAPTER TWENTY-THREE

Thursday, October 22
10:55 P.M.

MICKI LET THE CONVERSATION SWIRL around her. The group was discussing having Tommy describe Kyle to Angel so she could draw his likeness. Once they had his likeness, they had many more opportunities to I.D. him. Micki only partially tuned in, thinking instead about the home invasions, Tommy's story and how all the pieces fit together. This was clearly so much more than a string of home invasions, but she kept coming back to the whys: why these crimes, these families, why New Orleans, why now?

"What do you think, Mick?"

She blinked, startled, and focused on Zach. "About what?"

"Angel doing a composite of Tommy's Kyle, then have her meet the kids who interacted with Bear, see if she can get enough to get a likeness of him too?"

"I really want to," Angel said, gaze earnest. "I want to help and this is the only way I know how."

"Good idea," Micki said. "I vote yes."

Angel smiled. "Cool." She turned to Professor Truebell. "Should we go back upstairs, where we were before?"

Truebell agreed they should, then turned to Micki. "You have a question?"

"Several, actually. And they all begin with why."

He nodded and stood. "How about I give you a tour of our facility. I think you'll find it interesting."

Micki bit back a loud, rather colorful response. A tour? Really? When the Dark Bearer was out there doing whatever? Maybe they should make some popcorn and settle in for an all-day Netflix binge?

Zach covered a chuckle by clearing his throat. "I'll call in, let Major Nichols know we're following leads."

Eli nodded and followed him to his feet. "I'll check in with our groups, see if anybody needs anything."

Truebell motioned toward the door. "Shall we?"

The first floor consisted of a kitchen, the conference room, parlor-turned-waiting room and offices. "The building," he said, "was constructed at the turn of the nineteenth century. There were many big old homes like this along the Boulevard. Sadly, many were destroyed to make way for more modern office and commercial space. This one, like many up and down this stretch of Canal Boulevard, was saved."

"Did you flood during Hurricane Katrina?" she asked, as they started up the grand old staircase.

"We did. The storm wasn't kind to Mid-City, but like most of New Orleans, we've bounded back." They reached the second floor landing. "In all, including our third floor, we have just over five thousand square feet."

They started down the hall. "How do Half Lights find you?" she asked. "They certainly can't Google you."

He laughed. "Actually, we are searchable. But we have a wide network of social workers, therapists, adoption agencies, teachers, the full gamut of people who work with youth. They refer them to us."

"This 'wide network' is made up of Lightkeepers?"

"And Half Lights, yes. Besides our network, some youth find us on their own, it's a word of mouth thing. And some Rachel and Daniel find for us."

"Rachel and Daniel?"

"You'll meet them. They're trackers. Light trackers, to be specific."

She narrowed her eyes. "They're sensitive to a person's light, the way Zach's sensitive to the dark?"

"Yes. Excellent, Detective. I can see why you're so good at your job."

"Okay, so a new kid enters your program. What happens then? You start training them to find and develop their gifts? Or tricks, as Tommy called them?"

"First, we do an evaluation. If a particular young person has no Lightkeeper in them, we refer them to a different facility."

He stopped at the second floor landing.

"For those we decide to treat, the first thing we do is stabilize them. The kids who come here haven't had it easy. They're troubled, some addicted to drugs. Some facing jail time. We intervene. We use traditional therapeutic techniques, and prescribe pharmaceutical stabilizers when necessary, but few of our youth need them long term."

"I have a question about that."

"I'd hoped you would." He smiled. "Shoot."

"So the kids you treat, for lack of a better word, are all part Lightkeeper?" He nodded and she went on. "Then why so troubled? It seems like having that light force would predispose them toward being good little boys and girls."

He leaned forward, expression animated. "It is a *force*, Detective. And it's at odds with the rest of their being. It causes psychic discomfort, even turmoil. It causes them to feel odd, as if they somehow don't belong."

"Sounds like every teenager I ever met."

"Amplify that. Throw in adoption and abandonment issues, the lack of proper psychological care, all of which by the way, predisposes them to self-medicate, and you have a recipe for a troubled kid becoming a troubled adult."

"That's where you and LAM step in."

"Yes. First and foremost, they are life, beautiful and sanctified. We honor that."

They reached a back office and stepped inside. There was a small but lovely stained glass window depicting hovering angels, seeming to look down to the room below, watching over its occupant. Light streamed through, creating patches of watery color on the floor and desk.

"This is your office," she said.

"It is." He motioned to the small settee. "Sit. We'll visit some more."

They did and he began. "We don't teach these kids how to develop and use their gifts—if they even have them—until we're convinced they will use them for good."

"But don't some of them already know they can do things other people can't? The way Zach did?"

"Some, sure. But Zach's a first generation Half Light, truly a 'Half' light."

He glanced up at the angel window, then returned his gaze directly to hers. She didn't flinch or look away—Lester Truebell had total control of, and confidence in, himself and his supernatural abilities.

"Most of the kids who come through these doors will never even know what you now know. Yes, they are Half Lights, but we use the term loosely. They have a tiny fraction of Lightkeeper in them. Not enough to do more with than to feel as if they don't belong. Like there's something inside of them that doesn't fit."

"No special powers at all?"

He leaned forward and light from the stained glass fell across his elfin face. "But we all have a special power, Detective. The power to love."

She cocked an eyebrow. "Professor, isn't that a bit gooey, even coming from you?"

"Do you deny it, Detective? That love can move mountains? That it can transform lives or topple regimes?"

"In literature. As a wishful notion, like in that John Lennon song *Imagine.*"

"Love is nonsense, you think. Notions of its power is goody-two-shoes thinking from people who don't have a clue about real life. Because *you* know real life."

She shifted slightly under his penetrating gaze. "You have me pegged, Doc. Now, this place, that window—" she motioned to the angels, "—your cotton-candy views, it's like I've fallen down the rabbit hole into this trippy, feel-good, all-we-need-is-love universe."

He smiled. "That you have."

"So, any minute I'm going to wake up and see the men in white coats?"

He tipped his head back and laughed. "You are who you are, Detective Dare, and that's *your* gift. And it's one of the reasons why we need you."

"There's more than one? I can't imagine what that would—"

"Professor!" Tommy charged into the office, expression panicked. "Come quick! Something's wrong with Angel!"

CHAPTER TWENTY-FOUR

Thursday, October 22
12:01 P.M.

"I DON'T KNOW WHAT HAPPENED!" TOMMY said as they raced up to the third floor. "I was describing Kyle, she was having some difficulty and suddenly she said she didn't feel well. Then—"

They stopped in the doorway. Micki's heart leapt to her throat at the sight of Angel on the floor, writhing in pain.

"—this!" he finished.

"Angel? Oh my God!" Micki ran to her side, knelt beside her, alarmed as the girl's face twisted in pain. "Somebody, call 9-1-1!"

"It wasn't my fault, I swear—"

"Everyone stay calm," Truebell said. "Eli's on his way."

As the words passed his lips, Eli arrived, Zach right behind him. Truebell caught Micki's hand and led her away from Angel's side.

"She needs a doctor," Micki said, resisting. "We need to call an ambu—"

"Eli can handle this," Truebell said softly.

"But—"

"I promise."

Heart in her throat, Micki watched as Eli knelt beside Angel, then folded himself over her, cradling his body around hers. She watched a soft glow bloom between them, then grow larger and brighter until it encased them both in a cocoon of light.

The way Eli had cocooned her. She recalled its warmth, the feeling of peace and total serenity she had experienced in those moments.

But it didn't appear to be having the same effect on Angel. She arched and kicked and clawed. Almost as if she was rejecting the light, fighting its healing.

"It's making it worse!" Micki cried, watching as Angel's body stiffened, then jerked as a shudder rolled over her. "Tell him to stop. He has to stop!"

"Trust me." Professor Truebell laid a hand on her shoulder. "Let's give Eli some time."

They waited. And watched. The seconds seemed like forever, but finally Angel's violent shudders began to ease, absorbed into the light, transferred to Eli. With each transfer, Eli jerked, as if receiving a blow. His muscles tensed, his features twisted. But he didn't cry out.

Micki wondered at his pain, what stabilizing Angel was costing him. She rubbed her forearm, wondering if in healing her burn he had absorbed it, pain and all.

Angel began to still, the tremors coming farther apart. Eventually both she and Eli were still, their breathing deep and even, the bubble of light dimming.

Eli drew away from her. Angel's eyes flew open. "Seth!"

"It's Eli. The professor and Zach and Micki."

"Oh," she murmured, eyes closing again.

"I'll take her downstairs," Eli said softly. "Get her set up on the couch."

Micki wasn't convinced. "Maybe I should get her to the doctor or an emergency room—"

"She's fine now," Eli murmured. "Go on to the conference room. I'll meet you there."

Ten minutes later, Eli entered the conference room. He looked tired, his perfectly featured face drawn. He looked as if the process had aged him five years.

"How is she?" Zach asked.

"Fine. Resting. Tommy's sitting with her."

Micki frowned. "Are you sure leaving the two of them together is a good idea? I mean, Tommy was the only one with her when she had that attack. What do we really know about him?"

Truebell met her eyes. "He's one of us, Micki."

"But what if he's a . . . plant? A Trojan horse?"

"He checked out," Truebell said softly. "Eli and I both scanned him. His story checked out."

"Scanned? What is that? Some sort of super-mojo MRI?"

"Yeah, pretty much."

"And it never fails?"

"I stay away from words like never and always. Absolutes are dangerous."

Micki fisted her fingers, suddenly fed up with it. "Enough philosophical mumbo-fucking-jumbo! What the hell happened to her? How'd she go from fine to writhing pain?"

Eli spoke up. "Best guess—"

"I don't want to hear guesses! I want answers."

"Best guess," he continued calmly, "she was being blocked from drawing by an outside force. My best description would be a snake, like a python, inside her, coiling around her organs and squeezing. The harder she tried to focus on bringing Tommy's description of Kyle to life, the tighter it squeezed. Until the pain became unbearable."

Micki brought her hand to her arm, remembering the night before, the way the flame from the lighter had transformed. The way it had curled up her arm like a snake, searing her skin.

But that was different. She shook her head. "Back up. Angel had just drawn that monster, which Zach identified as the Dark Bearer he saw, no problem. She tries again and is made violently ill?"

Truebell stepped in. "Detective, do you have databases with photographs of monsters to cross reference? No. This Dark Bearer doesn't care about his true nature being revealed to us, but the identity of one of his human lieutenants? That's a different story."

"How?" she asked. "How'd he get inside her that way?"

"I'm not sure. A portal of some sort or an invitation. Angel's ability is rare."

She's a prophet," Truebell went on. "She dreams the future. Not the way, say Tommy, described. Big picture."

"Which means she's not safe?"

"The Dark One would love to have her in his stable."

"She's not an animal."

"To him, there is nothing more than his agenda. Nothing else matters."

"How do we protect her?"

"I thought keeping her out of our inner workings would, but I was wrong. We need to keep her close."

Zach looked at her. "She said a name when she first woke up. Seth.

Who is that?"

"A guy she met through work. I think they're seeing each other, but she denied it."

"Has her personality changed at all?"

Micki thought a moment. "She seems more secretive. Nervous, not wanting to spend time with me. Blowing me off."

"You've met him?"

"Yes. He said all the right things, but—" She thought a moment, wanting to be fair. "There was something about him that bothered me, but the circumstances of our meeting could have prejudiced me."

Zach grinned. "You, Mick, suspicious? No way."

He had her there, no doubt about that. "He's in his twenties. I told her he was too old for her. It just made her mad."

"Tell us about him."

"I don't know much more. His name's Seth. Twenty-something. Very handsome. Dark hair, beautiful—"

"—eyes," Eli finished for her. "What color?"

"I can't say for certain. I just remember them being striking."

Truebell turned to Zach. "You're going to need to get Angel to introduce him to you. When she does, shake his hand, see if you can get a read on him."

"I'm better at picking up dark energy—" He drew his eyebrows together. "You don't think Seth could be one of them?"

"Anything's possible, isn't it? But I hope not."

"I can definitely get a bead on whether he's being truthful or not."

Truebell looked back at Micki. "Does she show you her drawings, talk about her art at all?"

"A little. That her classes are going well. Once in a while she'll be working on something and I'll get a peek. She's pretty private about it."

"I need you to find the opportunity to look at her sketchbook."

"You think she's hiding something in there?"

"Not purposely, no. She might not even understand what she has yet. Looking at her sketches is a way to look at the future. Maybe her own."

Truebell cleared his throat. "Until today I thought the Dark One and his army were simply recruiting Half Lights and training them to further their agenda of misery and hate. But something you said today changed that. Something you said about the home invasions. Can you guess what it was?"

"The flashlight being shone in the kids' eyes," Micki said. "It's the one thing that seems totally out of context."

"Exactly."

Zach jumped in. "If they're looking for Half Lights, what are they doing?"

"I fear the Dark One is looking for a certain Half Light. A very important one."

Zach drew his eyebrows together. Micki saw by his expression he was as clueless as she was.

"Lightkeeper pupils react differently than human pupils to sudden, intense light change," Eli offered. "Where the human pupil expands or contracts, ours for a lightning fast moment absorb and reflect the light, making the irises glow."

"Like a cat's in the dark?" she asked.

"Think a swimming pool at night with the pool lights on. Or when the sun hits the ocean just so." Truebell turned to Zach. "Tell me about the children you interviewed."

"Sweet kids, all of 'em. Little Theo was super-serious. The Fowler girls bright and curious. And the Carlson and Greene children were silly and active."

"Those aren't the qualities I'm wondering about." Truebell shifted in his seat. "What about their personal histories?"

"Personal histories," Zach repeated, drawing his eyebrows together. "I'm not sure what you—"

But then he did. Micki saw the realization cross his features. "The Fowler girls were Asian, both adopted. Theo's grandma told me her daughter was raped and Theo was the result. And both the Carlsons and Greenes are foster parents."

"Similar profiles to the kids who come into LAM."

"The law," Micki murmured.

Truebell agreed. "The High Council thought they were protecting our race. They were wrong. Many Lightkeepers have been forced to give up or abandon their children. Some have gone into hiding to protect them. Now, when we most need their light."

Eli stepped in. "The High Council believes the Half Light children are an abomination. We think Half Lights will be our salvation. That's what the prophecy says as well."

Zach's eyebrows shot up. "Prophecy? First I've heard of that."

"An ancient prophecy tells of one who will be born half light and half dark and will have the power to bring peace and balance to our world.

Or—" he paused, "—bring about the end."

"As in kaboom?"

"The end of days. Whether that means total destruction or the end of life as we now know it, no one knows for sure."

Gooseflesh raced up her arms. "That's who the Dark Bearers are looking for?"

"The Chosen One, yes. He wants to find him or her, and gain control of them. And if he can't control them, he'll kill them."

Eli nodded. "There are signs not only that The Chosen One has been born, but that he—or she—is from the American South." He paused. "A city by water. A place heavily populated by both dark and light."

"New Orleans," Zach murmured. "The other five Sixers, what cities were they assigned to?"

"Charleston, Savannah, Memphis, Mobile, and Los Angeles."

"Los Angeles?"

"Covering our bases, right? It is the City of Angels."

"Back to the home invasions," Micki said, "and the flashlights being shone into the children's eyes. You described the reaction in a Lightkeeper's eyes. What about in a Dark Bearer's?"

"The sudden bright light makes them go dark, but just for a split second."

Micki's cell went off. She excused herself to answer. "This is Dare."

"Detective, this is Baker from the lab. Got some good news for you."

"I could use some good news. Talk to me."

"We got a hit on a print from the Marigny scene. Ex-con. Reggie Bhear. Twenty-eight years old, in and out of jail since he was seventeen. Stupid, small time raps: possession, robbery, assault, but enough to finally earn him a short stint in Angola. Out on parole. I'm emailing the report now."

"We're on our way."

CHAPTER TWENTY-FIVE

Thursday, October 22
1:25 P.M.

AFTER STUDYING REGGIE 'BAM BAM' Bhear's file, Micki pegged Reggie as one of the group's weapon-wielding leaders, which meant she was taking no chances: she'd arranged backup, insisted on Kevlar, and laid in extra rounds.

Micki glanced at Zach, in the passenger seat next to her. "You're quiet."

"Thinking about Little Bear."

"The kid from the home invasions?"

"Yeah. Can't be a coincidence that his name's the same as Reggie's."

"Agreed. This fits our theory that he was somebody's little brother."

"He might be there."

"Might be."

Zach frowned. "I don't want to scare him. He's a good kid."

"First off, you don't know him. All that stuff he told the other kids about being scared might have been scripted bullshit."

"It wasn't."

She made a sound of frustration. "Second, you're afraid of scaring him, after what he's been part of? That's nuts, dude."

He didn't respond and she pursed her lips. "Speaking of script, you're not going to go off ours, right?"

"Right."

She frowned slightly. He'd said it automatically, as if his thoughts were a million miles away. He probably hadn't even heard what she said.

She tried to make her point again. "Unless you want to get shot, you do exactly as I say. Dude's armed, he's done time. Nine and a half times out of ten, they put up a fight."

"Got it."

She let out a frustrated breath. "Do you?"

He looked her way. "It's just... I have this feeling. If I could just talk to—"

"No," she said. "No feelings, no talking. You can have all the feelings and do all the talking you want later, when we have our suspect safely in custody."

"Our suspect has a name, Mick."

"I know that. And I'm sure he has a million reasons why he's involved in this shit, but I don't care. It's my job—our job—to bring him into custody."

"Okay, fine. We play it your way, but—"

"No buts. You're in my backyard now." She paused. "I don't want to get shot, Hollywood. I really, really don't."

"I get it, but—" he held up a hand to stop another protest, "—what I was going to say is, be careful, Bhear might have some special tricks up his sleeve."

He might. But how special could his tricks be? He'd not only been arrested a couple dozen times, but incarcerated. "I'll cross that bridge when I come to it."

"S'okay with me, Mick. Though you usually like to be more prepared than that."

Luckily, they'd reached Bam Bam's place, making a response impossible. Lucky because taking her hands off the wheel to strangle him would have been really dangerous.

Micki parked in front of the small two-story home while the back-up cruisers slid into place behind her, one of them blocking Bhear's driveway and possible escape. This Holy Cross neighborhood, named after the Catholic school that sat square in the middle of it, was one in transition. Hit hard by Katrina, it'd roared back because of the school and proximity to downtown.

She looked at Zach. "Pretty nice place for a part-time grease monkey."

"Corner lot. School playground in sight. Location, location, location."

They climbed out, joined the back-up officers. "Let's split up," Micki said. "Harris and I will take the front, you two cover the back. He's gonna know why we're here, so be prepared for a fight. Expect him to be armed."

They took their positions. Micki rang the bell, then knocked. "Mr. Bhear, NOPD. We need to ask you a few questions."

When she got no response, she tried again. "Mr. Bhear, we need to speak with you! If you don't allow us in, we're prepared to—"

At the sound of the deadbolt turning, Micki nodded at Zach. They stepped out of the line of fire. Her heart beat accelerated as she counted to five. The door eased open.

Neither Bhear—nor anyone else—appeared.

"We're armed, Mr. Bhear. Step out where we can see you, hands up."

Still nothing. The hackles on the back of her neck rose. "We're going in," she said softly into the mic. "Hold your position."

She motioned Zach to follow her and she stepped inside, weapon out. She swung right, then left.

No sign of life. She glanced at Zach. He stopped, lifted his face as if intently listening. "They're both here. Reggie and Little Bear."

They did a quick check of the lower level. "Lower level clear," she said. "Heading upstairs."

They started up. A sound came from the room directly in front of them. The door was partially open and Micki nudged it the rest of the way. The room appeared empty. She stepped inside, motioning for Zach to follow. He crossed to check under the bed, she to check the closet.

The door slammed shut behind them.

"What the—" Micki ran for the door, grabbed the knob. It wouldn't budge. "Son of a bitch, it's locked!"

At the sound of feet pounding on the stairs, she shouted into her mic, "Suspect on the move! I repeat, suspect is on the move!"

"Don't be mad at me! I had to do it."

At the child's voice, Micki wheeled around. Zach held a small boy by the scruff of his neck. He had a mop of curly brown hair, fat cheeks and a mouth full of teeth he hadn't grown into.

He was completely adorable.

And she wanted to kill him.

"I had to do it! He made me!"

"Who did? Your brother?"

He nodded; his curls bobbled with the movement. "Or else he would've been real mad at me."

"Well, I'm real mad," she said. "Let go of the damn door!"

"It too late." His cherubic face puckered with regret. "I'm sorry."

A deep rumble came from the front of the house. Like a mother who knows the sound of her own baby's cry, Micki lifted her head, turned toward the window.

"Oh, hell no."

A moment later came a roar, a squeal of burning rubber. She ran to the window in time to see the back of the Nova disappear from sight.

Son of a bitch had just stolen her car!

CHAPTER TWENTY-SIX

Thursday, October 22
2:05 P.M.

ZACH SAT ACROSS THE EIGHTH'S break room table from Lil' Bear. They were sharing a bag of peanut M&Ms that Zach had nabbed from vending.

Lil' Bear popped one into his mouth. "I like the plain ones better. But these are good."

"Glad you like 'em."

He sucked on it a moment, rolling it around in his mouth, then bit down on it. "You don't think she's going to shoot me, do you?"

"Who, Mick? Nah, she's okay. Besides, I'd stop her if she tried."

Lil' Bear giggled. "She really loves that car, doesn't she?"

"You picked up on that, did you?"

"Wasn't hard. Some things are, but not that."

"What do you mean by somethings are hard to pick up?" Lil' Bear shrugged and popped another candy into his mouth.

Zach gave him a moment. "Why'd your brother take it?"

"He said it was really hot. And that he had nothing to lose."

"Why'd he say that, Bear? That he had nothing to lose?" Zach bit down on an M&M.

Bear scrunched up his forehead in thought. "Not sure. But he knew you guys were coming."

"He knew we were coming? How?"

"Don't know that either. Maybe somebody told him?"

Zach frowned. "You're sure he knew?"

He nodded, sucking on another candy. "So we planned what to do."

"All of it?" He nodded. "Even the car?"

"Yup. He wasn't sure it'd work, but he was gonna try anyway." He looked over his shoulder at the door. "Uh-oh. Here she comes."

"Mick?"

"She's real mad." He turned back to Zach. "Promise she won't shoot me?"

"I promise, buddy."

Mick appeared in the doorway. "Hey."

"Hey." He glanced at Lil' Bear, who had slumped lower in his seat. "Any word on Reggie?"

"He's in custody."

"And the Nova?"

"Wet."

He didn't like the sound of that. Neither did Bear, judging by the way he inched even lower.

"Bear here's a little worried you might shoot him. I promised him you wouldn't."

Lil' Bear peeked over his shoulder. "I'm real sorry about your car."

She let out a long breath. "I'm not angry with you, kiddo. But I am angry with your brother."

"Yeah, you're angry with me. I can tell."

She pursed her lips. "Okay, I am a little. Not enough to shoot you, though."

Bear seemed to relax and straightened up. "You can come sit with us. I'll even share my M&Ms with you."

"I will, too," said Zach and grinned.

She crossed to them and sat, choosing the seat next to Bear's. They each passed her half their candies. She chose a blue one and Zach wondered if it was in honor of the Nova.

"A nice lady is coming to take care of you," she said around the candy.

Bear looked deflated. "Reggie's going back to jail, isn't he?"

"I don't know for sure, but I think so."

He put a candy in his mouth and sucked on it for a minute before speaking. "He's not bad."

"No?"

He shook his head. "He's just real sad."

A lump formed in Zach's throat. From Micki's expression, the child's simple honesty had affected her as well.

"Why's he sad?" Micki asked.

"Don't know that. He just is. Kind of like you."

Mick looked surprised, then uncomfortable. "I'm not sad except about my car. I'm super unhappy about that."

Without saying a word, Bear reached over and curled his hand around hers. She seemed to freeze, then melt.

Zach cleared his throat. "I know you didn't like what your brother was doing and that you were afraid of his friends."

He nodded. "I don't like being mean. And I didn't want to scare all those kids. They were nice."

"That's what the kids told us."

"You talked to them?"

"Uh-huh. They were worried about you."

"Are they okay?"

"They're fine. And I promised them I'd make certain you were, too." He smiled encouragingly. "Do you know why your brother and his friends were there, at those homes?"

He shook his head. "They just told me what to do. Play with the kids, keep 'em from making a bunch of noise." He sighed. "Reggie made me go."

"Like he made you help him today?" Micki asked. He nodded and she went on. "What about my car? Did you—"

He shook his head with an emphatically "That was Reggie. He does that kind of stuff."

"What do you do?"

"I just know things."

"What kind of things?"

"How people feel."

That made sense, Zach thought. He'd known how much Micki loved her car and that she was sad, despite her disclaimer.

"Have you been living with your brother, Bear?"

"Yeah."

"What about your parents?"

"Don't have a mom or dad. I lived with my grandma until Reggie took me."

"Was that okay with your grandma?"

He shook his head. "She didn't want him to. They had a big fight about it."

Zach's cell went off. It was the desk sergeant telling him that Rachel Adams from child protective services was on her way up.

A couple minutes later, he greeted her at the elevator. "Rachel Adams?" he said, holding out his hand, "Zach Harris."

She took his hand. He immediately felt the connection, a tingle and warm rush.

She smiled. "We have a mutual friend, Detective. Lester Truebell. I'm a big fan of his organization. They help a lot of kids."

"I agree." He motioned down the hallway. "My partner and the boy are this way."

They reached the break room. Both Micki and Lil' Bear looked their way. After introducing herself to Micki, she crossed to Bear and squatted in front of him so she could look him directly in the eyes. "Hi, buddy," she said. "I'm Rachel. Are you okay?"

"I locked the door for him," he said. "It's my fault."

"No it wasn't, Bear. You were just helping out somebody you love. That's what we're supposed to do, right?"

"But I knew it was wrong." He hung his head. "I was afraid, though."

She nodded and held out her hand. Bear took it and stood. "How about we hang out for a while?"

"Until my grandma comes and gets me?"

"Yup. But we've got to make sure she's okay."

"She is."

"You've talked to her?"

He nodded. "She's been worried about me. I wanted to go back but Reggie wouldn't let me."

"Is that where you'd like to live? With your grandma?"

"She doesn't make me do bad things. I like that." He sighed. "But I'm gonna miss Reggie. He loves me a lot."

Rachel squeezed his hand. "I know, buddy. And I'm going to make certain you're safe and happy. You trust me?"

He nodded and looked back at Zach and Micki. "Bye. And I'm really sorry about your car."

Micki watched him leave with Rachel, then looked at Zach. "She's part of the professor's team, isn't she? He mentioned a Rachel to me."

"Yeah, she is." He sent her a sympathetic glance. "Where's the Nova?"

"In Bayou St. John. Or—" she checked her watch, "—being hauled out of it."

"Oh, man, Mick . . . that—"

"Sucks," she finished for him. "But I don't want to talk about it."

"You don't?"

"Nope. What I really want to do is have a conversation with my new best buddy, Bam Bam."

"And lower the Boom Boom?"

She smiled grimly. "That's the plan, Partner. Finally, my day is looking up."

CHAPTER TWENTY-SEVEN

Thursday, October 22
3:10 P.M.

GOOD NEWS TRAVELED FAST; THE mood in the Eighth's Detective Unit was celebratory. She and Zach both took a bow, though Micki admitted hers was bittersweet—she'd received word the Nova had been hauled out of the bayou and towed to the shop. Wounded in the line of fire, she thought. She would've rather it had been her.

Fricking hocus-pocus. None of them were safe.

As they made their way past their colleagues heading toward Major Nichols' office, J.B. called out, "Hey, Mad Dog, maybe take your car keys next time."

The room went expectantly silent. Micki stopped, turned, and met the man's eyes. "Hey, J.B.—" She flipped him the bird. "Oh, and by the way, you're a complete asshole."

"Damn, he really is," Zach muttered, grabbing the case file off his desk.

"I'm so excited to get a crack at Bam Bam, I don't even care. Let's close this thing."

When they reached Major Nichols' office, they saw he was on the phone. He waved them in, then, in the next moment, hung up and smiled broadly. "That was Chief Howard. He's very happy. He's calling a press conference for five o'clock."

He paused, his expression as pleased as a parent's who'd just seen a report card with all 'A's. "He wants you both there. Harris, you'll do the talking. The Chief's request."

Micki wasn't going to argue with that part, but the one about a press conference before they'd even interrogated the perp was making her eye twitch. "Maybe we should hold off? See what he has to say first?"

Nichols frowned. "Is there any question he's a part of the group behind the home invasions?"

"No. But once the press knows we have him, they'll want details and—"

"Two words, partner," Zach said with a grin. "No comment."

Micki rolled her eyes. "I know how it works. But I also know the media can be like a pack of starving dogs when they want something. I suggest we question Bhear first. Let's see how cooperative he is, maybe get a sense of how open he might be to making a deal in exchange for names."

Major Nichols pushed his phone toward her. "Go ahead."

She frowned. "Major?"

"Call Chief Howard and tell him to hold off, explain that in *your* opinion he's being hasty."

Beside her, Zach stifled a chuckle. The traitor. "I see your point, sir."

"Good. Press conference, five o'clock." He leaned forward. "Play this smart. Get the information you need. Do whatever it takes—within reason. Now get out of here."

"It's a mistake," Micki said, once they were out of earshot.

Zach shrugged. "You worry too much. Besides, we don't have a choice, so let's just do it."

They made their way to the interview room, stopping outside the door when they reached it. Zach looked at her. "How do you want to play this?"

"He trashed the Nova. How do you think I want to play it?"

He nodded. "Okay. Give me five minutes with him. If I'm not making progress, bring in the heavy artillery."

Although chomping at the bit to get a crack at Bam Bam, Micki knew Zach was right. A moment later, she was in the viewing room, watching as Zach greeted Bhear.

"Hello Reggie," he said.

The man barely glanced his way. "Fuck you. Not talking without a lawyer."

"Sure, no problem." Zach pulled out the chair across from Bhear and sat. "Pretty neat trick, starting my partner's car that way."

"Thanks."

"She's pretty pissed about it."

He shrugged, still not looking directly at Zach. "I'm not worried."

"Maybe you should be. She can get a little crazy. I'm not sure I can hold her back."

He snorted dismissively, and Micki narrowed her eyes. To the very limit of the law, she thought. The absolute tip-top.

Zach shifted direction. "Why won't you look at me, Bam Bam?"

"That against the law?"

"I know what you are."

"Really? And what's that?"

Zach leaned forward. Lowered his voice. "Special."

"Aren't we all? Isn't that what people like *you* always say? That we're all special and beautiful in God's eyes?"

"People like me?

Bhear had obviously been schooled in Zach's powers: what he could do, that looking him in the eyes could be dangerous.

His lips curled into a snarl. "*Special.*"

"You know you're being used, right? *He's* using you."

"I don't know what you're talking about."

"Bullshit." Zach rapped his knuckles on the table. "The Dark Bearer."

"The dark what? You're crazy, man."

He didn't know, Zach gathered. Whoever was head honcho of the operation hadn't clued him in.

"The one in charge, he have a name?"

"I told you, I'm not talking without a lawyer."

"This is just between you and me." He indicated the video camera. "No green light. Not recording."

"I could change that. Without even getting up."

"You're the one who took care of all the alarm systems, am I right? Pretty slick."

He winked, obviously proud of himself. "No comment."

"How about the dogs? Who did that?"

He opened his mouth as if to respond, then shut it. "Don't know what you're talking about, dude."

Micki couldn't sit back another moment. Grabbing a phone book from a desk outside the interrogation room, she entered, locking the door behind her. "Well, if it isn't the dumb-ass, carjacking Bam Bam."

She crossed to the table and dropped the phone book on it. It landed with a thud.

He looked way too pleased with himself and she felt her blood pressure rise. "Go ahead, asshole, enjoy the moment. That little joyride earned you a ticket back to Angola. I hope it was worth it."

"It was." He smirked. "Kind of like being on an amusement park water flume ride. That moment you hit the water is the best."

"Hollywood, do me a favor, cuff our dumb-ass friend here."

"Mick," Zach intoned, "I don't think this is a good idea."

"We're just going to have a nice, little chat. Do it."

"Sorry, man." He snapped on the cuffs. "They don't call her Mad Dog for nothing."

For the first time, Bam Bam looked queasy. "You won't get away with it."

"I don't care. I'm sick of this job. Sick of having to deal with stupid fucks like you. Here's what I want to know. Who's in charge of your little gang? Because I sure as hell know it isn't you."

"I want a lawyer."

"We know the name of your gang of home crashers, Six Cubed." She smiled. "I see you're surprised by that."

"I don't know anything."

"Your fingerprint was found at the scene. You were there. Who was with you?" She paused. "Besides your brother."

"Leave Lil' Bear out of this."

"Sorry, Bam Bam, but I can't. He admitted he was there. That you forced him to come along. Such a shame. He seems like a great kid."

Something like regret crossed his expression. His soft spot, she realized. She might not need the phone book after all.

"Deserves a lot better than a loser like you for a big brother. What kind of scum gets an eight-year-old to help him commit crimes?"

"He'll be fine."

"My guess is he's going to juvie. He seems kinda soft for a place like that. Those kids are hard, you know what I mean?" She widened her eyes in mock surprise. "Yeah, you know about that. You spent time in juvie, didn't you?"

He'd gone from looking queasy to downright sick. "Leave him alone! He didn't do nothin'."

"Oh, but he did. Just being there, keeping the kids occupied so you could do your thing . . . What you won't tell us, he will."

"He doesn't know anything. I made sure of that."

"He was there. He's seen faces, heard names. He'll be easy to scare. He'll do the right thing."

His hands began to shake. "You have no idea what you're messing with."

"You're wrong. I have a better idea than you do." Micki laid her palms on the table and leaned in to look him dead in the eyes. "Come to think of it, since we've got him, we don't even need you."

She straightened up and smiled at him. "We don't need you to talk, so you don't get a deal."

She stepped away from the table, started toward the door. "Undo the cuffs, Hollywood. We're done here."

"Wait."

She stopped and glanced back.

"I changed my mind. I want a lawyer and a deal. I'm ready to talk."

CHAPTER TWENTY-EIGHT

Thursday, October 22
5:02 P.M.

THE PRESS HAD ASSEMBLED. A beaming Chief Howard greeted the group. "Thank you for coming. We have good news to report. A suspect in the recent series of home invasions is in custody. We owe this arrest to the excellent investigative work of two of the NOPD's finest, Detective Michaela Dare and Detective Zach Harris. I'll turn the mic over to Detective Harris and let him fill you in."

Micki watched as Zach stepped up, shook the chief's hand, then turned and smiled at the reporters. "Thank you, Chief Howard. Just a few days ago, Detective Dare and I promised you results, and today we give them to you. Reggie Bhear was apprehended—"

On Micki's hip, her cell phone vibrated. She stepped away from the dais to take it. "Dare here."

"Detective, it's Rachel Adams, Child Protective—"

"I remember. Is Bear all right?"

"He's fine. He just . . . he's worried about his brother."

"His brother's fine. We were with him thirty minutes ago."

"He's pretty upset. Keeps saying Reggie's . . . gone."

She glanced at Zach; he was expertly fielding questions while the Chief looked on like a proud father.

Something like a chill moved over her. "Gone where?"

"Dead, Detective. He says his brother is dead."

⚜ ⚜ ⚜

Micki left the press conference immediately, texting Zach an explanation and catching a ride with a patrol unit. She hadn't alerted anyone at the Eighth, had wanted to see for herself first if it was true. And if it was, she wanted the first look at the scene.

Now, she stared at the bloody mess that had been Reggie Bhear. It looked as if somebody had beaten the hell out him. A pen stuck out the side of his neck. The floor and table had been sprayed with blood when the pen punctured his carotid artery.

"Holy shit," said Peterson, who'd unlocked the door for her.

"Since I left, who's been here?"

"Just his lawyer."

"He sign in?"

"Yeah. Of course." Peterson dragged a hand through his hair. It shook. "I unlocked the door, waited, then relocked it when he left."

"At that time, you checked on Bhear?"

"Yeah. He was staring at the wall. His mouth was moving like he was talking to himself."

"The lawyer say anything?"

"Nada."

"Get me that attorney's name and number. And inform Major Nichols of what's happened."

The kid looked like he'd rather call the devil himself, but nodded and darted to his desk, passing the elevator as Zach stepped off.

"What's up?" Zach asked as he reached her. "You flew out of there like a bat out of—"

The words died on his lips. His eyes widened. "That's not—"

"Bam Bam? I'm afraid it is."

"Son of a bitch."

"Yeah, my sentiments exactly."

Major Nichols arrived. He took one look into the room and bellowed for Peterson. "How the hell did this happen? He was in our custody, dammit! He should have been safe!"

"He was fine, I swear. I stood right outside the door while he conferred with his lawyer, and glanced in when the lawyer left. Like I told Detective Dare, he was fine. In the chair, staring at the wall. Looked like he was talking to himself."

Micki picked her way carefully closer to the body. Cuts, bruises, contusions. "He took a battering," she said, and looked at Peterson. "You didn't hear a thing?"

"I wasn't outside the door the whole time, but I wasn't ordered to be. It was locked."

Micki confirmed that fact for the major. "It was locked when I arrived. I heard the lock turn over."

Zach hadn't said anything since he'd first arrived. She looked at him. His expression was strangely intent, as if his every cell was fully engaged and on alert.

No, she prayed. Not the Dark Bearer. She'd rather a dirty cop than that.

She glanced up at the video camera. Its green light blinked at her. "It's recording," she said. "The camera, it's on."

They headed to the viewing room and everyone crowded around the monitor. For the first several moments, Bhear did nothing, just stared blankly at what seemed like a place off in space, muttering to himself, occasionally twitching.

Then, suddenly, a shudder racked his body and he launched to his feet. The muttering became bursts of garbled speech, his twitching more intense.

"Stop . . . no . . .no go no me . . .stop don't can't hurt—" He bounced into the back wall, then, like a ping-pong ball, rebounded, hitting the side wall, the table, then back to the original wall.

Major Nichols sucked in a sharp breath. "What the hell?"

A knot of anxiety settled in Micki's chest. She realized she was fisting her fingers so tightly, they'd gone numb. They were witnessing the mental and emotional deconstruction of a human being.

Bhear stopped moving, frozen for a second.

Micki took a breath, hoping he was coming out of the schizophrenic state, but knowing the worst was to come. Its result lay on the floor in the next room.

He opened his mouth and a stream of sounds came out—words, or an attempt at them. Micki couldn't be sure, but it sounded like he was saying stop, over and over, without pause.

But he didn't stop. Instead, he slapped his face. Hard enough that everyone in the room jumped at the sound of his palm connecting with his cheek. He did it again and again, faster and faster, until he was weaving and stumbling about.

A howl or growl spilled past his mouth as he threw himself against the table, continually beating his head against the top. Blood poured from his wounds, smeared his face and hands.

The room was silent. Micki realized she had her lips pressed together to hold back a cry of horror. It was a brutal, vicious attack. The worst she'd ever witnessed. And Bhear was perpetrating it upon himself.

The growling became a pleading wail. "Lveimalone . . . Lveimalone!"

It seemed that they all saw it the same time Bhear did. An ink pen. Like a Bic. The lawyer must have left it; neither she nor Zach had had one. With a grunt, he grabbed it and stabbed himself in the throat.

He struck the carotid, blood sprayed. He stood for a moment, mouth still moving, then crumpled, hitting the floor with a thud.

The room went morgue-at-midnight quiet. Several seconds ticked past before Nichols broke it by clearing his throat. "As unfortunate and as . . . shocking as that was, the good news is that we now know what happened. We have proof that the NOPD is blameless in this man's tragic death."

The others murmured their agreement.

"What was he saying?" Micki asked. "At the end there? Back it up."

Peterson did. They listened again.

"Lveimalone . . . Lveimalone . . ."

"Leave me alone," Nichols said. "That's it. Classic schizophrenic event. Poor bastard was hearing voices in his head."

"One more time," she said, unconvinced. He did and she listened intently. "Leave him alone." She met Zach's eyes. "It's leave *him* alone."

She knew by Zach's expression he understood the distinction. Little Bear. Reggie was pleading to the Dark Bearer to leave his brother alone.

Zach turned to Major Nichols. "I'm no shrink, but isn't referring to yourself in the third person classic dissociative behavior?"

The major nodded. "I've got to update Chief Howard. I'm sure he's going to want to see the video. Make damn sure nothing happens to it. And for the love of God get something we can use from the kid. He's all we've got left."

CHAPTER TWENTY-NINE

Thursday, October 22
7:15 P.M.

ANGEL SAT IN HER BEDROOM. The only light, one from a small desk lamp, was trained at her sketchpad, laying open on the bed before her. She trembled.

The pain had been unlike anything she had ever experienced. It had felt as if her organs were being crushed, the life being choked out of her—from the inside. Before Eli had wrapped himself around her, the pressure in her head had become so intense, she was certain her eyes were going to pop out of their sockets, her brain from her skull.

Eli had saved her. Tears stung her eyes and she swallowed past the lump in her throat. *Thank you, my brother.*

She glanced at the sketch pad. The almost blank page. A few lines. The outline of a chin and the beginning of an eye looking out from the page at her.

Smirking.

He'd won. She shook her head and looked away. Tommy had described Kyle to her, but as hard as she'd tried to grasp the image with her mind's eye to recreate it, she'd been unable to.

Her head had begun to hurt, her vision to blur. She should have stopped trying, but she'd known how important it'd been to Professor Truebell and the rest of the team. So she'd pressed on.

She ripped the nearly empty page from the sketchbook, crumpled it into a ball and threw it at the trash can.

Blocked, Eli had told her. Most likely by the Dark Bearer. To keep her from revealing the identity of one of his soldiers. Gooseflesh ran up her arms and she shuddered. Could it be someone she'd been in contact with? Someone close to them?

Her phone went off. She saw it was Seth and picked up, wishing she could talk to him about it. How would he respond? If he even believed her. He might decide she was crazy and be done with her.

"Babe," he said, "you there?"

"I am. Sorry, I'm a little distracted tonight."

"What's up?"

"Nothing. I didn't feel well today, that's all."

"That sucks. You okay now?"

She said she was and he went on. "Good, because I have a surprise."

"What is it?"

My uncle's back in town and he wants to meet you."

"Cool. When?"

"You have tomorrow off work, right?"

"The whole day."

"I was thinking lunch."

"Lunch would be awesome."

"You okay now? Or do you want to talk some more?"

"Would you mind?" He said he wouldn't and she scooted down in her bed, phone cradled to her ear. He started to talk about his day, and as she listened she acknowledged that he had become the most important person in her life.

CHAPTER THIRTY

Thursday, October 22
8:50 P.M.

REGGIE BHEAR'S MOTHER, MARY JANE Stevens, lived in Algiers Point, a small family-oriented community across the Mississippi River Bridge on New Orleans' West Bank.

Zach parked in front of the house but didn't make a move to get out. He flexed his fingers on the steering wheel and took a deep breath. He'd never had to do this before, never had to look a mother in the eye and tell her that her son was dead. And having relived that death at the scene, he flat didn't know if he could do it without transmitting that horror.

Micki angled toward him, laying a hand on his arm. "You've hardly said a word since we left the Eighth. You okay?"

How did he answer that? he wondered. Yeah, he was alive. He would make it through this. Was he okay? Hell, no.

"The energy in that room . . . I—" He took a deep breath, then released it. "Let's just say I experienced Bhear's murder with him, in every way but physically."

She said nothing. Her hand, on his arm, trembled. He looked at her—and saw a world of understanding in her eyes.

She squeezed his arm. "Let's do this."

They climbed out of the car and crossed to the front door. The home was small and neat, same as the woman who answered the doorbell.

"Mrs. Stevens?" Zach asked, holding up his shield. "Detectives Harris and Dare, NOPD."

She didn't even glance at their badges. Her faded blue eyes looked sad.

"You've come about Reggie?"

"Yes, Ma'am. May we come in?"

"Of course."

She stepped away from the door. Zach entered first. The only thing he picked up was the sound of the TV in the other room—The Weather Channel. "You're not surprised we're here."

It wasn't a question, but she answered anyway. "My Reggie's always been in and out of trouble, Detective. You two are not the first police officers to show up at my door looking for him."

"We're not looking for him, Mrs. Stevens," Micki said quietly. "I'm afraid we have bad news."

"He's dead, isn't he?"

"Yes, he is," Micki answered. "I'm sorry for your loss."

Stevens brought a shaking hand to her mouth, visibly working to get control. "Do you mind . . . I think I need to sit down."

They followed her to the small living room. She sank onto the couch. Micki took the chair opposite her, Zach took the other end of the couch.

"I had a feeling, since this morning, that something was wrong." She clasped her hands together. "Silly old woman with her premonitions."

No, Zach thought, her Lightkeeper heritage.

"How did he—" She stopped, looked down at her hands, then back up at him. "Was he murdered?"

Zach wasn't sure how to answer. Yes, he believed he was murdered, but that certainly wasn't what the media would report. "He . . . took his own life. He was in custody, Mrs. Stevens."

"Did your son have a history of mental illness?" Micki asked. "Schizophrenia? Bi-polar disorder? Depression? Was he on any psychotropic medications?"

"No." She shook her head. "When he was a teen, we took him to doctors and counselors. One would diagnose this, another would prescribe that. We did everything we knew to do."

"We're not blaming you," Zach said softly.

She met his eyes, hers blue pools of regret. "I'm blaming myself, Detective. I was his mother."

She seemed to pull herself together. "But our Little Bear is safe, thank God."

"Is that another of your premonitions?" Micki asked.

"No. A nice young woman named Rachel called me this afternoon. She said R.J. was with her and safe. And that I'd be seeing him soon."

"And that's all she told you?"

She nodded, eyes brimming with tears. "Only thing Reggie ever did right was love that boy."

"There's nearly twenty years between them. Any sisters or brothers in between?"

She looked at them strangely. "What do you mean?"

"For brothers, they're spaced so far apart, I just wondered—"

"R.J. is Reggie's son. Not his brother."

The name, Zach thought, of course. Reggie Junior, Little Bear. The twenty-year difference in their ages.

"That's not what Reggie told us. And Little Bear—R.J.—didn't correct us when we called Reggie his brother. Do you know why he would tell people that?"

"To protect R.J. maybe. Or to ease his own conscience."

"Why would that ease his conscience?"

"Reggie promised he'd never be the kind of father his was. Absent, in and out of jail."

"What happened to him?" Zach asked.

"We divorced and he disappeared from Reggie's life."

"What about R.J.'s mother?"

"I didn't know her. And Reggie didn't talk about her. He came home with a baby and asked if I'd help him out. Of course I said yes."

Micki leaned forward, obviously anxious to move on. "Reggie had gotten himself mixed up in a serious situation, Mrs. Stevens."

"The home invasions."

Micki looked almost comically surprised. Stevens must have thought so too, because her eyes crinkled at the corners. "It's not magic. I saw you both on the news and put two and two together."

"Then you know how serious this is. We're hoping you can help us."

"I'll try."

"When was the last time you talked to your son?"

"During the summer. When he came to collect R.J."

"Came to collect him?"

"He was out on parole. He wanted Little Bear with him."

"And you were okay with that?"

She shook her head. "But he . . . promised me he'd changed. His time in prison had changed him. His parole officer would be checking on him. He had a real job."

"And where was that, Mrs. Stevens?"

She thought a moment. "A-1 Motorsports. An engine repair shop."

Zach made a note. "What about friends? Associates? He introduce you to anyone?"

She shook her head.

"What about a girlfriend? Anyone he was seeing?"

"Not that I'm aware of. R.J. would know better than me."

"How about a friend from the old days? Someone he kept in contact with?"

"There must be someone, but I can't—" Her voice began to shake, as if the reality of what had happened was fully seeping in. "Will R.J. be coming back to me?"

"Do you think he'd be safe here? Zach asked.

"Why wouldn't he be?"

"R.J.'s different from other kids his age, isn't he?"

Her expression turned guarded. "I don't know what you mean. He's just a regular little boy."

Zach tried another tack. "You have a close bond with him, don't you?"

"I'm his grandmother. I love him very, very much."

He tried again. "Did Reggie have any particular talents, things that he could do exceptionally well or easily?"

"He was always mechanical. Engines, electronics. He could always figure out how to make them work. I always thought that someday he'd go into that line of work. That's why, when he told me about this job, I was so optimistic."

"What about your grandson. What's he especially good at?"

"He's just a nice boy," she said almost fiercely. "Just like he's supposed to be."

Zach handed her his card. "If you recall a name or anything else comes to you, or if you and R.J. need anything, anytime, you call me."

As she took the card he curved his fingers around hers for a moment, then let go.

"Well?" Micki asked as they headed to his car.

"Nice lady. Feels bad about all this. Like she let Reggie down."

"Anything that might help us?"

"She really couldn't recall any names. She was experiencing a lot of different emotions, which could have blocked her memory."

"Pick up anything she deliberately didn't share?"

"Only one. That she knows Bear has extrasensory abilities and she does, too."

"She's a Lightkeeper?"

"I'm guessing she has some small slice from a relative somewhere down the line. All she knows is her premonitions often come true and that she and her grandson communicate telepathically."

"And she really believed Reggie would do anything to protect his son?"

"You didn't. I saw it on your face."

"Look at the danger he was putting him in! The lifestyle he was exposing him to. If he'd really wanted to protect him, he would have left him with his grandmother."

"What if he didn't have a choice?"

"What do you mean?"

"I don't know for sure. Just . . . something . . ."

She stopped, turned toward him, searched his gaze. "You withholding, Hollywood?"

"No. Trying to formulate."

"Then do it out loud, dammit."

"He knew we were coming. That's what Bear said."

"Okay. So?"

"How?"

"You're the one formulating. You tell me."

"No need to get testy," he said easily. They reached his car and stopped. "Maybe he purposely got caught?"

"Deliberately left a print? Knowing we'd lift it and find him in the system?"

"Yes."

"Again, partner, why?"

"To protect his kid. He got himself—and Bear—into something bigger and badder than he expected. And he couldn't get out."

"I don't know." She shook her head. "Reggie was a bad guy. A lifelong loser. Suddenly, he makes himself the sacrificial lamb."

"Plus he stole your car?"

"And took it for a swim. Why not just put his hands up and say 'you got me?'"

Zach unlocked the Taurus. "Make a show for whoever's in charge. Think about what he was saying on that video—leave him alone."

"If that was his plan, it didn't work out so well."

"That doesn't mean it wasn't his plan." He paused. "Remember how at the Fowler scene, I zeroed in on the emotional resonance—fear and regret. And I said I was sure it wasn't the victims, but one of the perpetrators?"

"Yeah, that must have been Little Bear's."

"No. This was in the master bedroom. R.J. was never in there. He was with the kids the whole time."

She frowned. "You're sure?"

"Positive. When their girls told me about Bear, their parents were shocked."

"Great." She went around the vehicle and climbed in. He slid behind the wheel, then looked over at her. "What?"

"Bam Bam gets to trash the Nova *and* be a hero-martyr? That fucking sucks."

CHAPTER THIRTY-ONE

Friday, October 23
8:36 A.M.

MICKI STOOD UNDER THE SHOWER'S stinging hot spray. The way it prickled as it hit her skin, then streamed over her, that was real. That she recognized. Everything else about the past twenty-four hours had been surreal.

Eli had been right to say that knowing all the secrets would change her, that there would be no going back, and to ask if she was certain she wanted to know.

She should have taken him more seriously. Always wanting to know, to be in control, it'd bitten her in the ass this time. Her world had been turned up-freaking-side down.

She'd hardly slept and felt every minute of the tossing and turning. How did she wrap her mind around this? How did she go on with her everyday life? Thinking that her gun and badge made her all big and bad? Or that her little problems amounted to more than mouse turds?

She shut off the water and climbed out. Her cell went off and she quickly dried enough to hit speaker. "Dare."

"Morning partner. You okay?"

She towel-dried her hair. "Why wouldn't I be?"

He paused. "I don't know, you just learned that we're not alone. That's some pretty deep shit. And the Nova's dead, which is definitely not cool."

That was one way to put it, Micki thought, tossing the towel toward her hamper. "So, what's up?"

"You in the mood for some crazy irony this morning?"

She dusted her pits with deodorant. "No, but lay it on me anyway."

"Take a guess where the Nova was towed?

"A-1 Motorsports? No fricking way."

"Yes, ma'am. You know what that means?"

"Two birds, one stone. Hot damn." She snatched up the phone and ran for the bedroom. She slipped into her panties, then bra and grabbed her navy trousers off the chair and rifled through her closet for a clean white button-down.

"You talk to Nichols yet?"

"Waiting on you, partner."

She got into her shirt, grabbed her socks and boots. "I'll be ready in five."

"I'll see you then. I'm pulling up in front of your place now."

⚜ ⚜ ⚜

A-1 Motorsports was located in part of a Central City warehouse. It didn't look like much—one of those pre-fab metal jobs, garage doors on three sides, parking all around, not so much as a single shrub to green it up.

The wrecker had deposited the Nova around back. Micki took it in. Muddy front end, slimy looking crap hanging off the bumper. Sludge line marking where the progression of water had stopped. Like the ones that had marked everything after Katrina.

Tears stung her eyes. Not an option, she told herself, blinking furiously. Mad Dog Dare did *not* cry.

"I'm sorry, Mick."

"It'll be okay. It's just a—"

She couldn't say it. Because it was more than a car—it was her connection to Hank. When she was in the Nova, she felt like he was with her.

"Howdy, folks."

Micki tore her gaze away from the Nova. Middle-aged guy, blue jeans, standard paunch protruding over his belt, not-so-standard Rolex on his wrist. A 'Motor Doctor' ball cap protecting his no-doubt-balding head.

"Name's Ed. They call me The Motor Doctor. This your car?"

"Yeah," Micki answered. "It is."

"Beautiful machine. You have my sympathy."

"Appreciate that. What's the prognosis?"

He tugged on the brim of his ball cap. "Come on in, we'll talk."

They followed him into the shop. A half-dozen vehicles were being worked on, several of them high end. That comforted.

He motioned them into his office. They took a seat. "Got you some good news and some bad news."

She looked at him. "I've got eyes. It all sucks. So give me the best of the bad first."

"On the bright side, the car was only partially submerged. Interior was dry as a bone. Unfortunately, the engine compartment was swamped."

"Which means?"

"We need to dry her out. See how much we can save."

"Him," she corrected.

"Pardon?"

"The car. It's a he."

He eyed her speculatively a moment, then inclined his head. "Bet there's a story that goes with that."

"There is," Zach offered. "Maybe she'll tell you someday."

The same as she's told him on several occasions. She appreciated his making it easier for her.

"Gotcha." Ed nodded and went on. "We're going to start taking it apart this morning. Check for moisture everywhere, inside doors and seals, in the oil and fuel, blow out the lines. Anywhere there's water, there's corrosion—and it begins immediately."

"Do whatever you have to," she said, voice tight. "Whatever it takes."

"There's another option, depending on what we find. These classic engine parts are hard to come by. And they're not cheap. We could replace this baby with a brand new—"

"No."

He paused. "I understand your feelings—"

"No, you don't. This car isn't just a means of transportation, it's kin. And that'd be like giving him a lobotomy. He'd be a shell, like the Tin Man and Cowardly Lion rolled into one. No heart and no guts."

"You're certain?" She nodded and he agreed. "Okay, it's your baby."

"Yeah, it is. Exactly that."

"Okay then." Ed started to stand. "We'll get right to—"

"There's another reason we're here," Zach said. "A rather weird coincidence."

Micki took over. "I'm Detective Dare and this is my partner Detective Harris, Eighth District, NOPD. We're investigating—"

"Those home invasions. That's it." He looked at Zach. "I knew I recognized you. From the news."

"You got me."

"Hot damn." Ed slapped his thigh. "And my wife says I'm oblivious, hah! Wait 'til I tell her. So how can I help you this morning, Detective Harris?"

The amazing, invisible girl, Micki thought. And who knew so many folks still watched the evening news?

"You catch those guys yet?"

"One of 'em." Zach smiled, smooth as silk. "That's why we're here."

"No kidding?"

"No kidding," Zach agreed. "It just so happens that the guy we caught is one of your employees."

His eyebrows shot up. "No way."

"And the one who trashed my car," Micki said.

Her comment earned her a surprised glance. Yup, he'd definitely forgotten she was there. Micki had to bite her cheek to keep from snorting.

Zach handed the man a photograph of Reggie. "Is this one of your employees?"

"Was. Not anymore." He handed the photo back. "Had to fire him."

"What happened?"

"He started off great. Hard worker. And he had a way with engines, like magic. Then, same as I've seen again and again with guys like him, he started slacking off. Coming in late, missing altogether. Always some excuse. Finally, magic or no, I had to let him go."

"Guys like him," she asked. "What do you mean?"

"Ex-cons. Guys who've always taken the easy way. To guys like that, a hard day's work doesn't appeal in the long run, no matter how much they want it to."

"He pal up with anybody here?"

He thought a moment, then nodded. "Yeah, he and Troy seemed to hit it off."

"Troy here today?"

"He is." He pushed away from his desk and stood. "Seems to me he's about due a break."

"Thanks, Ed," Zach said, sticking out his hand. "Appreciate your help."

"You betcha." He took it and pumped it enthusiastically. "I'm calling my wife now. Shows what she knows. Oblivious, indeed." He stepped through the doorway. "Yo, Troy! There's some detectives here who need to ask you a couple questions."

A tall black man unfolded himself from under the hood of a Porsche Carrera. He wiped his hands on a towel and crossed to them. "What's up?"

"Need to ask you a couple questions about Reggie Bhear."

"Bam Bam? I haven't heard from him in weeks, not since Ed had to let him go. Reggie got himself back in trouble, didn't he?"

"Yeah," Micki said, "the worst kind. He's dead."

"Oh damn. Man, I'm sorry." He shook his head. "Dude wasn't interested in my good advice."

"Which was?"

"Drop those friends of his like a bad habit and keep his eyes on the real prize."

"And what was that?"

"Eternal life." He lifted his eyes and pointed upward. "He wasn't gonna get there scamming."

"His friends. That's what we wanted to ask you about. You meet any of them?"

"Yeah, a couple times, when he and I went out. They were all bad news. I didn't want to have anything to do with 'em."

"Remember any names?"

"Only one. Kyle. Dude made the hair on my arms stand straight up. Got the hell out of there as soon as I could."

Micki glanced at Zach. She could see he was trying to keep his excitement in check. "Could you describe him to us?"

"Handsome. You know, one of those guys that are too handsome? Dark hair, creepy eyes."

"In what way?"

"They seemed to change color."

Before Zach, she would've thought the man was exaggerating or playing with a short deck. Now she knew exactly what he meant. Because she'd seen eyes like those before.

Micki looked at her notes. "Bam Bam have a girlfriend?"

"Nah. Too busy chasin' the devil and all his empty promises."

"So, you two were friends?"

"I was tryin' to minister to him. I'd been where he was. It's a bad, sad place."

"You an ex-con."

He nodded. "Been out for years. Turned my life around."

"Know where this Kyle lived?"

"No way, Detective. Wouldn't have wanted to know."

"What about the name of the place you went?"

"Evolution." He let out a long, unhappy-sounding breath. "Shame about Reggie. He had mad skills with a motor. That term, gear head, that was Reggie. He could've had his own place one day."

Zach thanked him, slipped him a card and shook his hand. "Call us if you remember anything else."

Troy stopped them on their way out. "He had a little brother he was taking care of. He okay?"

"Yeah, he's good. He's safe."

"Praise God for that, brother."

CHAPTER THIRTY-TWO

Friday, October 23
10:40 A.M.

SETH HAD BROUGHT HER FLOWERS. A small pot of bright gold mums. Angel worked to keep from crying. No one had ever given her flowers, not in her whole life.

"What's this for?" she asked.

"I felt bad that you had such a crappy day yesterday. I thought they might make you feel better."

Angel trailed her finger along a blossom's ruffly edge. "Thank you, but I already felt better. You made me feel better."

He reached across his car's console and caught her hand. "I'm glad."

They drove that way for several blocks, until he jumped on the interstate, heading west, toward Metairie.

"Tell me more about your uncle."

"Well, he's excited to meet you."

"He is?" He heard the doubt in her voice and shot her an exasperated smile.

"Because you're important to me."

She felt herself flush and hated it.

"Uncle Will, William really, but no one calls him that. Not anybody who really knows him. He's a great guy. Very cool. Super successful."

"What does he do—besides collect art, I mean?"

"He's a lawyer."

"What kind?"

"Corporate. He's on the staff of a multi-national company. He travels all over the world. I watch his place."

"Where does he live?"

"In Chateau Estates. He wanted to be near the airport, since he travels so much. It's massive, really impressive."

She hung on every word, fascinated. He was obviously very attached to his uncle.

Her cell chirped an incoming call. "It's Zach," she said to him, "I better take it. Hi, Zach!"

"Hey Angel. I'm calling to see how you're feeling today."

She angled a glance towards Seth, but he seemed not to be paying any attention to her conversation. "I'm fine now."

"That was pretty intense yesterday. Any clue what caused it?"

"Not really. I think maybe I just tried too hard."

"I thought if you were free, I'd come pick you up and we could go to lunch."

"Oh, I can't. I'm going to lunch with a friend."

"Anybody I know?"

"I don't think so."

He was silent a moment, as if giving her an opportunity to offer more. When she didn't, he went on. "It wouldn't be Seth, would it?"

"What do you . . . I mean, how do you—" She glanced at Seth. He was frowning and she lowered her voice. "How do you know about Seth?"

"You said his name yesterday."

"I did?"

"In fact, it was the first thing you said when you opened your eyes."

"I don't even remember that." She bit her lip. "Did Micki—"

"Yeah she did."

"Crap." Seth's frown had deepened. "Please don't say anything to her."

"What's the deal, Angel? You're seeing this guy, so what? Why do you want to keep it from her?"

"She doesn't get it. She thinks he's too old for me. Please, please don't say anything."

"I tell you what, you introduce me to him, and I won't say a word. After all, I've got to make sure he's good enough for you."

She rolled her eyes. "Zach, I swear you're as crazy as she is. But yeah, okay. I think *you'll* like him a lot."

A moment later, she ended the call. "That was Zach."

"So you said. He's Micki's partner?"

"Yes."

"And you really think he won't tell her?"

She thought a moment, then nodded. "He's lots cooler than Micki. I know he's on my side."

"You're sure he doesn't have feelings for you?"

"Positive. We're just friends."

"Cool." He smiled. "We're almost there. You excited?"

"Totally. You're sure he'll like me?"

"Positive."

He turned into the country club community. Large houses on estate-sized lots. All bright, shiny and perfectly tended.

"Here we are."

He pulled up to a massive home that resembled an Italian villa. Though the mansion was surrounded by a brick wall, its columns and arches were revealed through the wrought iron gate.

As Seth pulled up to the gate, it magically opened. A circular drive with a fountain in the center. Like the ones she was studying in her Art of the Renaissance class.

Seth turned in, cut the motor. She could tell he was as anxious for her to meet his uncle as she was. It was so sweet.

He came around to her side of the car to open the door for her but she'd already climbed out. He caught her hand just as the front door opened and a man dressed in jeans, a button-down shirt and jacket stepped out.

Her first thought was that Seth didn't look anything like him. In fact, his uncle looked a little like the actor Don Johnson. With that older, cool guy swagger.

"Seth!" He came down the stairs to meet them. After hugging Seth, he grabbed her hands. "So, you're the famous Angel."

She felt herself flush. "Hello," she said, sounding as awkward as she felt. "It's good to meet you."

"I hear you're an artist. Art is my passion. Seth said you were bringing some drawings to show me."

"She brought them but she's too shy to show you."

He looked her in the eyes. "Never hide your gifts, my dear. So few truly have them. Now, come, lunch is ready. And I'm sorry to say I have to cut this visit shorter than I'd like, so viewing your art may have to wait. I've been called away."

"Uncle Will—"

"I know, Seth. I'm sorry. But you two stay. The pool's heated if you'd like to swim, or use the hot tub."

"I don't have a suit," Angel said.

"I keep extras on hand."

They ate a delicious lunch of lobster salad on tiny, flaky croissants and drank champagne from long-stemmed glasses. Angel took a few sips, even though she typically didn't drink and the bubbles went straight to her head--though she wasn't sure whether it was the bubbles making her dizzy or the whole experience, being here, in this luxurious place with Seth.

In what seemed like no time at all, they'd finished lunch and she and Seth were alone.

"C'mon," he said, grabbing her hand, "I'll give you a tour."

From the dining room, they walked through to the kitchen with its shiny appliances and stone counters, to the formal living room outfitted with silk drapes and rugs so thick her feet sank into them, then to a movie room complete with theater seating and motorized curtains. Using the remote, Seth showed her how, with a hum, the red velvet curtains opened to reveal a wall-sized screen.

"It's just you two living here?"

"Full-time. We have guests and parties. But day-to-day, yeah, just us."

They moved on to the master suite. "This is the biggest bedroom I've ever seen." Angel turned in a slow circle, taking it all in. "Oh my God, that bed is huge!"

"It's a California king," he said, tugging on her hand. "Wait until you see the master bath."

When she did, she looked at him. "People live like this? The bathtub is as big as a pond!"

He laughed. "I know, right?"

"How do you keep this all clean?"

"We pay people to do that. I'll show you the upstairs."

Five more bedrooms, she saw. Each with its own bathroom. The last they visited was his.

"It smells like you," she said.

He laughed. "I hope that's in a good way."

"It is." She wandered across to the dresser. Two framed photos sat on its top, the first of a pretty young woman holding a toddler that looked like Seth in her arms. Angel studied his solemn expression and smiled.

"You were so serious."

He came up behind her, circled his arms around her and rested his head on hers. "Still am."

"That's your mom?"

"Yeah."

"She was pretty."

"She was. Very."

"How old were you there?"

"I don't remember. I would think around two."

Angel turned her attention to the other photo, this one of a teenage Seth standing beside a shiny, white pick-up truck and smiling broadly. "The day I got my driver's license."

"You look really happy."

"I was. I always planned— Never mind."

"No. What did you plan?"

He shook his head. "One day I'll tell you."

She turned in his arms and looped hers around his neck. "Now would the perfect time for you to kiss me."

But he didn't, just studied her, looking for all the world like that serious little boy in the photograph.

"I'm thinking this is a really dangerous time to kiss you. And if we're smart, I won't."

She frowned. "Why?"

"Because I won't want to stop."

Then she understood. That he'd want more, he might even want . . . it. But she wanted it too. She pressed herself to him. "I'm not as young and silly as I seem."

"You don't seem either. I just . . . I want to do this right."

"Then kiss me."

He bent his head and brushed his mouth against hers. Once, then again, almost as if teasing her. Brush, taste, nibble. Like a bee or butterfly at a flower. Then, just when she thought she would go crazy wanting his mouth, he deepened the kiss. Deeper and longer, his tongue mating with hers, hers with his.

"Tell me to stop and I'll stop."

"I don't want you to stop. Don't . . . stop."

She threaded her fingers in his hair and arched against him. He made a sound that went straight to her head. He drew her to the bed, going slow, treating her like she was the most important thing in the whole world.

She'd never been the most important thing to anyone. Tears stung her eyes, then rolled down her cheeks as he entered her. She wrapped her arms and legs around him, wanting him even closer.

Afterward, he wiped the tears from her cheeks, expression full of regret. "I'm sorry, I shouldn't have—"

"It's okay, I wanted you to. More than anything."

"I didn't want to hurt you."

"You didn't."

"But . . . you were crying."

"Because you made me so happy." She fell silent a moment. "I never had . . . this, but I wasn't a— I was raped, Seth. So being with you this way and knowing how wonderful it can—"

She choked up and he cradled her against him. "Who," he asked tightly.

"A foster brother." She paused. "After the first time, I didn't even fight him. 'Cause I knew I wasn't strong enough and nobody would come to help."

He just held her. She could feel the way her story affected him in the way he trembled, as if fighting to hold a strong emotion back.

"I would just lie there and plan how I would kill him." He rubbed her back while she spoke, ever-so-softly. "I finally told the social worker, I guess when I realized I didn't have the guts to kill him. And like I knew would happen, I was moved to another foster home."

"That wasn't a good thing?"

"Except for him, I was happy there. I had a nice room and I liked the school. I had friends."

"What about your foster mom?"

"They took her license away. I felt bad about that. She was good to me. Just . . . overwhelmed."

"You're too nice," he said, voice tight. "What about him?"

"Last I heard he was in jail."

"How old were you?"

"Thirteen. The next home they sent me to, I ran away. And the next. And next. I was on my own by my fifteenth birthday."

"Thank you," he murmured.

"For what?"

"Trusting me." He searched her gaze. "There's something I have to tell you, and I hope you're not mad."

She propped herself on an elbow and looked down at him, her dark hair pooling on his chest. "What?"

"Will's not my uncle. He's not family at all." She waited for him to go on. "He took me in when I was twelve. I was angry at the world and showing it. I'd been hauled in and out of juvie several times already."

"How did you meet?"

"He caught me breaking into his car. Felt sorry for me. I was a mess." He paused. "I told everyone he was my uncle. It made things easier. People think it's weird when a single guy lives with a male non-family member."

"Why are you telling me this now?"

"It seemed like the right thing to do."

"I love you."

She felt him stiffen and she knew she'd made a mistake--come on too hard and too strong, way too soon.

So she said it again. "I'm in love with you."

"No. You can't be."

"But I am."

"You don't even know me. Not really."

"I think I do."

"I don't know what to say."

"As long as you don't say goodbye."

He gazed silently at her. Moments ticked painfully past and Angel wondered if that was exactly what he meant to do. Say goodbye. Break her heart.

Instead, he drew her close and buried his face in her hair. "I can't," he whispered. "Even if I wanted to."

CHAPTER THIRTY-THREE

Friday, October 23
6:50 P.M.

"ANGEL, WAKE UP."

Angel opened her eyes. She'd been dreaming. Of her and Seth. And here he was.

She smiled sleepily. "Hey."

"Baby, Will's home."

She gazed at him, the remnants of the dream evaporating. "Wait . . . what did you—"

"Will's home. It's almost seven."

"At night? Oh my God."

"It's okay. We fell asleep."

"It's not okay." She pulled the covers tightly to her chin, realizing she was naked under them. Naked! "What am I going to do? He's going to hate me."

"He won't. He's chill."

She shook her head. "He can't know. I'm so embarrassed."

"Don't worry." He climbed out of bed and into his clothes. "I'll tell him we just got out of the pool and you're changing."

"You think it'll work?"

"Yes, hurry."

She remembered her hair wasn't wet. Neither was his. "Wait!"

He stopped, looked back. "I'm rinsing off. Because of the chlorine. And your hair's not wet."

"Got it."

Angel was out of the shower and into her clothes in record time.

Carrying her shoes, she tiptoed down the stairs. When she reached the landing, she followed the sound of their voices.

They stood across from each other at the kitchen island.

"I want to tell her," Seth said.

She froze. Her? Was she the one they were talking about?

"That's not a good idea," Will responded. "She could react badly. Very."

She told herself that eavesdropping was rude, but couldn't bring herself to stop. They had to be talking about her. What might she react badly to?

"I trust Angel. Completely."

He trusted her completely and here she stood *spying* on him. She didn't deserve his trust. Angel stepped out from the doorway, fully into the hall, a greeting on her lips.

She stopped. Her sketch book. Open on the counter between them.

She felt as if the greeting had lodged in her throat. As if it might choke her. Her heart hurt. Seth knew how she felt about his uncle seeing her drawings, but he'd shown them to him anyway? It was a slap in the face, a complete violation after the intimacy they'd just shared.

Before she could say so, Seth did it for her. "Uncle Will, you had no right to look at her drawings without permission. I told you how she felt."

Not Seth. His uncle. Relief took her breath.

"They're good. Really good. Just like you said."

"That doesn't change the fact that you violated her trust by—"

"It's okay, Seth," she said, stepping into the kitchen. They both turned her way and she forced a comfortable smile. "If I didn't want anyone to look at it I shouldn't have left it out."

"No," Will said, "Seth's right. I apologize. It was an intrusion. But I don't regret it."

"Uncle Will!"

"Because they're too good." He crossed to her, took her hands in his and looked her in the eyes. She experienced the strangest sensation. Of warmth and connection—but cold and distant as well. As if she was both drawn to and repelled by his touch.

It was strange. And dangerous and uncomfortable.

But somehow, oddly, satisfying. Delicious.

"They're meant to be seen. And admired, Angel."

She felt herself flush. "I'm just a student. Really, until now I've had no formal training and I—"

"More reason to admire you. Come—"

Still holding one of her hands, he led her to the open sketchbook. "Untrained and you can create this?" He flipped to the drawing of Seth. The one she had done in a frenzy. "And this? You've given him such a dark angst. It's so powerful."

She looked at it, as if for the first time. It was true. There was power in the drawing. It smoldered with a deep anger.

This wasn't the Seth she knew. It was the one whose mother had committed suicide and left him to find his way on his own, to be taken in by a stranger.

"And this one," Will said, turning to another.

One from her recent dreams. The one with the vortex, the swirling numbers and faces of lost souls.

"Tell me about this one."

"It's not finished," she said.

"What's it about?"

"I don't know."

"Really?"

She nodded. "Really."

Will was quiet a moment, then began. "I'm no artist and can't even imagine having a talent as great as yours. But one thing I do know is that all great artists understand what drives their art."

"I didn't know that. I just . . . the images, they just come to me."

Seth brought Will a drink, some cocktail whose ice cubes made a lovely clicking sound in the glass. He brought himself a beer and her a wine cooler.

She eyed it. "Thanks, but I don't care for—"

"I knew you didn't like beer, I thought you might enjoy this." He smiled. "It's like Kool Aid."

She took it. The bottle was cold and damp between her palms. She recalled the old saying *Don't drink the Kool Aid* and wondered if that admonition would apply here.

The beverage was light and sweet. She liked it way more than beer—or Kool Aid, for that matter.

"Tell me about this process of the images just coming to you."

"I dream the images. When I wake up, I get them on paper as soon as possible."

He looked almost startled. "That's it?"

"No . . . I dream them in pieces. And little by little, I build them."

"How do you know when they're finished?"

"I'm not sure. I've never given it any thought."

"Maybe you should?"

Angel caught her bottom lip between her teeth. "Here's the thing. Sometimes my drawings are just drawings. Like this one of Seth. But. . ."

"What?"

"But sometimes they're stories."

"About what?" Seth asked.

"Stories about things going on in my life. In the world, even."

"All great art is narrative," Will said. "Even this sketch of Seth is narrative. It tells a story about *him*. Do you understand?"

She did and nodded, amazed. Not one of her UNO instructors had said that, or had said it in a way she understood.

"What makes an artist special," Will went on, "is not just what they put on the paper or canvas...it's what they're *saying* through their art."

"I'm taking an art history class and the professor has talked about the styles as a reflection of the culture of the time, but I didn't really get it." She smiled at him. "Until now."

He leaned forward. "As an artist you need to be in control of your gift. Can you do that?"

"I don't understand."

"You have to learn to develop your gift. And I don't mean shading light and dark, or improving composition. You have all that, no matter what your *professors* might tell you. But you need to control it." He paused a moment. "Right now, it seems as if it's controlling you."

She frowned, suddenly uncomfortable. "I don't think that's true."

"Of course it is, Angel. Do you want your subconscious to deliver the imagery? To supply the story?"

She felt herself flush. "That's just . . . I mean, it's always been that way and I thought—"

"You want to show someday? Sell your work?"

"Yes! I'd love to be able to do that, but I always thought it was too much to hope for."

"I don't ever want to hear you say something like that again!"

She was taken aback by his ferocity. By the fervor in his eyes.

"You're that good, Angel. In a few years you could be the hot, new artist everyone's buzzing about."

She wanted that. Wanted it so badly, the hair on the back of her neck stood up. "How do I do that?"

"That's what *you* have to figure out."

Angel glanced up at Seth for reassurance, but he was looking past them both, expression bored. Hurt, she turned back to Will. "But I don't know where to start."

"You say you dream the images?" She nodded. "Those nights, do you go to bed thinking about something in particular? Are you happy and fulfilled? Anxious about the next day? Or stewing over something that already happened?"

"I don't remember."

"Think, Angel." He let go of her hands. "What kind of artist you become depends on it."

She dropped her gaze to her sketchbook, then curious, began slowly flipping the pages, remembering.

"Worry," she said. "Anxiety. Fear." She stopped to look up at him. "Despair."

"You don't make happy art, Angel. That's not where it comes from."

"But it's more than that. I—"

She bit the last back. About how her art not only told stories but depicted future events.

"What?" he asked her, his voice coaxing, drawing her gaze back to his. She felt for a moment as if she were drowning in his dark eyes. "Angel, you can tell me. You can tell us."

She blinked, breaking the connection. "It's late, I really need to go. I have homework and I work all day tomorrow." She looked at Seth. "Can you take me home?"

If he noticed her voice shaking, he didn't comment. He set down his half-finished beer. "Sure."

"Don't forget your drawings." Will held out her sketchpad.

"Thank you." She took it, slipped into her shoes and grabbed her purse.

"Think about it, Angel," he called after her. "You could be art's new It Girl. You just have to want it bad enough."

A minute later they were in Seth's BMW and heading for the highway. Her thoughts raced with the things Will had said about her art, about what her future could be.

And the things she had learned about herself.

She rubbed her arms, suddenly chilled.

Without commenting, Seth flipped on the heat. In that moment, she realized she had been so caught up in herself she hadn't noticed he'd hardly spoken a word. Not since they'd climbed into the car, and not before.

She glanced at him. "What's wrong?"

"Nothing."

She folded her hands in her lap. "Do you think he's right? About my talent?"

He gunned the engine and changed lanes. "Why should my opinion matter? I'm not the art expert."

"Oh." She looked away, hurt. "Okay."

"You sure seemed to suck up the compliments."

"What?"

"You were taken with him, no doubt." He yanked the wheel right, and they flew down an exit.

She grabbed the door handle, heart jumping to her throat. "Slow down, Seth! You're scaring me."

He eased up on the accelerator. "Interesting, you're not even trying to deny it."

"Deny what? I don't understand."

"That you were completely, I don't know . . . charmed by Uncle Will. Under his spell and . . . thirsty."

She sucked in a shocked breath. "Thirsty? You're going to accuse me of having the hots for your *uncle*? After what you and I . . ."

A knot of tears formed in her throat and her words came out thick. "You don't know me at all."

A muscle jumped in his jaw. "But I know *him*."

"What does that mean? You sang his praises, but now you're saying he's a bad guy?"

"What I'm saying is, I know how people respond to him. The power he exudes, especially over women. I've seen it a million times—the way they hang on his every word, the way they can't take their eyes off him."

"You're jealous?"

"I didn't say that."

"You said everything but. And yes, I was hanging on every word. Because of *what* he was saying . . . not because I think he's—" she made a face, "—hot."

He pulled to the side of the road, threw the car into park and turned to her. "You're going to sit there and tell me he's not handsome and charming and—"

"For an old guy."

A smile tugged at his mouth. "He's not that old."

"I'm eighteen. He's what, in his thirties?"

He unsnapped his seat belt and leaned across the seat to rest his forehead against hers. "I was jealous. Watching you with him, the way you seemed to light up. As if you'd forgotten I was even there. I guess—" he paused, "—I want you to light up that way for me."

"You think I don't? Are you crazy?" She wound her arms around his neck. "What I said earlier? I meant it. I love you."

He stiffened, though she could tell he tried to hide it. "As much as I'm enjoying this—" he eased free of her arms "—I'd better get you home."

CHAPTER THIRTY-FOUR

Saturday, October 24
7:36 P.M.

ANGEL SILENCED HER PHONE'S ALARM and climbed out of bed. Her legs were rubbery and she grabbed the headboard for support. Parts of her body that had never ached before ached now. Muscles complained. Her head hurt and her stomach pinched.

She hadn't eaten anything since lunch with Seth and Will. No wonder she felt wobbly and headachy.

She made her way to the bathroom. She'd fallen asleep thinking of Seth, recalling their every moment together. How it had felt to have him inside her. How they had joined--not just bodies, but as if their souls had come together.

She loved him. And even if he hadn't said it back, she felt as if she were floating on top of the world. And she'd slept deeply and dreamlessly because of it--no dark images to hurry and record.

What if Will was right? That her art came from a dark place? Would she ever be able to draw again? If she had to choose right now, she would choose Seth.

After cleaning up, Angel headed out to the kitchen. Micki stood at the sink, gazing out at the morning. Ready for work, even though it was a Saturday. Angel had learned that when a detective worked a case, they worked it until they closed it—or were forced to move on. No rest. No days off.

Angel's gaze settled on Micki's gun, tucked securely in a shoulder holster. She wondered how heavy it was. She'd never even held one before. Had never been interested. But now, for some reason, it intrigued her.

Maybe Micki would give her shooting lessons?

As if becoming aware of Angel's presence, she looked over her shoulder. "Morning."

"Hey." Angel crossed to the fridge and grabbed the carton of orange juice. "What's going on?"

"This case."

"Always is." She poured herself a glass of juice. "I was just thinking about how much being a cop must suck."

"Some days suck more than others." Micki rinsed her cup. "Zach's picking me up this morning, if you want to say hello."

"Cool. You're not taking the Nova?"

"Out of commission. Suspect stole it and drove it into Bayou St. John."

Angel experienced the strangest urge to laugh but she bit it back. "I'm sorry."

"Yeah, me, too."

"Hey, guess what?"

"Hmm?"

"I met an art collector yesterday. And you know what he said?"

Micki grabbed her jacket from the back of a chair and shrugged it on. "What?"

"That I was really good."

"Where'd you meet him?" she asked, glancing at her phone.

Angel frowned, annoyed. That was it? Not even a 'that's awesome' or 'good for you, Angel?'

"Out at school. The studio."

"He was there looking at student work?"

The comment rankled. Student work? Just lump her with the others, as if she wasn't special enough to be singled out for praise.

"No," she snapped, "he was just there, visiting, and he saw *my* drawings." She paused; Micki didn't look her way. "He said I'm *really* good. Like I could be a big deal someday."

Micki blinked and looked up from her phone. "What? I'm sorry, I—"

"Never mind." Angry heat stung her cheeks. She'd never had anyone who really gave a shit about her. Including Micki.

Until now. Until Seth. And Will.

"Hey, Angel? I was wondering . . . what do you think about trying again?"

She downed the juice and poured some more. "Trying what again?"

"Drawing the guy who approached Tommy."

"You're kidding, right? You saw what happened to me."

"This time would be different. There's this kid. He's only eight and I—"

"This is such bullshit. You realize you haven't even asked how I am?"

Micki looked surprised, then guilty. "I'm sorry. You're right . . . it's just that so much has already happened since—"

"And now you still haven't."

"I'm sorry," she said again. "How do you feel?"

"Not great, okay. That was the worst . . . I thought I was going to die. And you want me to try again?"

"We had a suspect in custody. He was going to talk in exchange for a deal."

"But?"

"The Dark Bearer we're up against killed him. Now we've got nothing. Again."

"No. The department must have sketch artists for this."

"But I trust you. I know how special you—"

"All you care about is this case. That's all you ever care about!"

"That's not true. But right now there's so much at stake."

"What about me? What about my life, what I want?" Hearing the words coming out of her own mouth was like listening to someone else's voice. Someone she didn't recognize. "I could be *somebody*."

"You are someone, Angel. Someone special."

"Maybe I don't want to be your weird little prophet girl!"

"What's gotten into you? I don't—"

At the thump against the window behind her head, Micki jumped and whirled around. "What was—"

"A bird. I saw it hit. Poor thing."

Angel crossed to the window and peered down. Not a sparrow, she saw. A crow. A big one. "It looks like it broke its neck."

"I'll go see if it's still alive."

"You do that."

Micki drew her eyebrows together. "What's going on with you this morning, Angel? Did something happen that—"

"Mick! You ready?"

Zach appeared at the kitchen door. "Hey, nobody answered so I let myself in." He moved his gaze between them. "Am I interrupting something?"

"Nothing important," Angel said. "Just Micki being a complete asshole."

CHAPTER THIRTY-FIVE

Saturday, October 24
8:05 P.M.

ZACH WATCHED ANGEL STORM OUT of the room and turned to Micki. "Wow. She discovered the real you?"

"Not amused, Hollywood. Something's going on with her."

"She may be our world-wise, little Yoda, but she's still a teenager."

Micki frowned, shook her head. He noticed the way the bridge of her nose crinkled and fought a grin. When, he wondered, had he decided she was cute when she was grumpy?

He looked quickly away, afraid she'd see him fighting the smile. Cute was for puppies, she'd told him once. Not for tough cops, and certainly not for the likes of Mad Dog Dare. He'd bet her opinion on that hadn't changed.

"Just two days ago she wanted to help. Now, she wants nothing to do with the case, the Lightkeepers or me, for that matter."

"I think you're overreacting."

She placed her fists on her hips and stared him down. "Overreacting? Were you here? No."

"C'mon, she's young and she's a girl."

"What the hell does *that* mean?"

"Umm . . . PMS?"

"You're an idiot."

"So that time of the month *doesn't* turn you into a lunatic?"

"This is different. I don't know how, but I wonder—"

She bit back whatever she was about to say, turned away from him and started to gather up her things.

"You wonder what, Mick?"

"If our Dark Bearer . . ." She looked over her shoulder at him. "Could he be doing something to her? Like infecting her or something?"

Zach wanted to brush it off with a laugh, but he couldn't. "Maybe I should talk to her? If she's been in contact with the Dark Bearer, I'll pick up its energy."

"I don't know. Look at me." She held up her hands. They trembled. "Mad Dog faces monsters but shakes after a fight with an irrational eighteen-year-old?"

"Maybe you're the one with PMS?"

She sent him a withering look. "Go talk to her. I'll wait in the car."

He tossed her the keys. "If I'm not out in ten minutes, call in reinforcements."

Zach made his way down the hall and tapped on Angel's bedroom door. "It's Zach. Can I come in?"

"Whatever."

He eased the door open and peeked into the room. She sat cross-legged on her bed, sketchbook open in front of her.

"Hey," he said.

She glanced up. "Hey."

He stepped into the room. "What's going on?"

"I'm super-pissed right now."

"So I hear." He grabbed the desk chair and pulled it over to the side of the bed. "Want to talk about it?"

"Nope."

"Mick's a little on the intense side."

She looked up. "You think?"

"Nah. I know."

She smiled a little and returned to her drawing. He tipped his head, looking at it. A drawing of a dark-haired guy. Good looking, piercing gaze.

"That's him, isn't it? Seth?"

She shut her book. "Yes."

Defiance in her tone, in the tilt of her chin. For this guy, she would go to battle. "He's nice?"

"Very."

"You're certain?"

"Not you, too?"

"Hey, this is Zach." He held up his hands in surrender. "No judgment. I care about you, kiddo. That's all."

"Yes, I'm sure. He makes me happy."

"Then it's all good with me."

She visibly relaxed. Even smiled slightly. "Look—" she motioned to a flowering plant on her bedside table, "—he gave me this yesterday, because I told him I was sick. And Micki didn't even ask how I was feeling. What kind of friend is that?"

"She cares about you, Angel. A lot."

She fiddled a moment with the edge of her sketchpad. "Seth introduced me to his uncle."

"That seems like a serious move on his part."

"I know. I mean, we haven't even known each other that long, but there's just something about him . . . I don't usually, you know, trust people right off. But Seth is different."

"How so?"

"I don't know, it's just the way we are together. We fit." She paused a moment. "Like he's a missing piece of me. It's weird."

He thought of Mick. How clearly they *didn't* fit. "Well, I'm happy for you, kiddo. That's hard to find. Now since I see you're okay, I've got to go."

"Got to catch the bad guys?"

"That's the plan. Remember--you, me and your fella, lunch, coffee whatever."

"I won't forget." She jumped up and gave him a hug. "Tell Micki I'm sorry. I was kind of a brat."

He nodded and started for the door.

She stopped him. "Zach?"

He turned, met her eyes.

"His uncle, he's an art collector."

"Yeah?"

"He thinks I'm really good."

Zach saw the pride in her expression—she all but glowed with it.

"He thinks I could be an important artist."

"I think so, too," he said softly. "Always have. If that's what you want."

"It is," she said, tone fierce. "But I never thought it could happen."

Moments later, he slid behind the wheel of his car and looked at Micki. "She's fine."

Micki frowned slightly. "Fine? You're sure?"

"Yeah. She even hugged me before I left. Plus, no dark energy at all."

"Freaking wonderful. She hugs you, but *I'm* an asshole?"

He grinned. "We each have our roles, right?"

He backed out of her driveway, pretending not to notice her fuming. After letting her stew for a moment, he added, "I almost forgot, she asked me to tell you she's sorry for acting like a brat."

"She said that? Really?"

"Really." He took a left at the end of her street. "But I'm worried we have a bigger problem than her thinking you're a jerk."

"And what would that be?"

"She's in love with this guy. Or thinks she is."

"She told you that?"

"She didn't have to."

"Lord help us." Mick let out a long breath. "She's still going to introduce you to him?"

"She said she was."

"Good. Because I really don't like him now."

"Why's that, partner?"

"Simple. She didn't start acting this way until he came into her life."

CHAPTER THIRTY-SIX

Saturday, October 24
10:50 A.M.

ANGEL'S FINGERS CRAMPED FROM GRIPPING the charcoal pencil. They were stained black from the material, as were the sides of her hands. She worked quickly, feverishly. She had the sense that her art was being sucked forcefully out of her. She couldn't resist, couldn't move fast enough, couldn't give enough.

It was as if she *had* to get it out of her. Expel it the way one expelled spoiled meat. Violently. Painfully.

Then, suddenly, she was done. The creative disgorging was complete. With a cry, Angel dropped the pencil, shoved aside the sketchbook, and climbed off the bed.

Or tried to. Her legs buckled, she stumbled, fell to her knees. Over two hours, she realized, looking at her watch in disbelief. That's how long she been cross-legged on the bed, bent over in a creative frenzy.

She moaned and stretched. Her muscles protested at having been in one position so long. She'd been unaware of time passing, unaware of her body seizing up.

Crazy.

Now she hurt. Her hands and legs shook. She felt light-headed, both exhilarated and enervated. She rolled her shoulders, flexed her fingers and tipped her head from side to side, then made her way to the bathroom.

She stood in front of the mirror. A stranger stared back at her. No, she thought, tilting her head, not a stranger—a strange version of herself. Her face was smeared with black--cheeks, forehead, chin. Her hair was a tangled mess, her lips bright and swollen from gnawing at them.

But it was her eyes that seemed most different. Darker, but at the same time, more luminous.

Angel leaned toward the mirror to get a closer look, but the effect was gone. The eyes reflected back at her were the same as they had always been.

She was losing her freaking mind.

She clipped her hair back, grabbed her sketchbook from the bedroom, then headed to the kitchen. Though she laid the pad on the table, she was purposely averting her gaze. She'd worked automatically, as if she'd been in some sort of altered state, so she wasn't quite ready to see what she'd drawn.

Angel poured herself a glass of milk and grabbed an apple. While she enjoyed her snack, she checked her email, Facebook page and Instagram.

Finally, she couldn't hold off another moment and looked down at her drawing. It was dark, with figures emerging from areas of soft swirling black. Dreamlike, she thought. Ironic, considering. A figure near the center of the drawing drew her scrutiny. A boy. It was Zander. Surrounded by a bubble of light.

Angel smiled. She'd portrayed the expression he so often wore, at once stoic and impish.

She moved her gaze to the left corner. A bear cub, stretching, reaching for the boy. But despite the claws, not vicious. Reaching for a hug, Angel thought. She tipped her head. Or to protect Alexander.

She shifted her attention again. She and Seth, twined together, in a passionate embrace, their lower bodies like gnarled vines, rising up from the black earth as one.

Joined at the hip, she thought, for that was where they split into two torsos. His and hers, together and apart. And, curiously, she had drawn a zipper on Seth, one that traveled up his side all the way to the top of his head. There, instead of a pull tab was a padlock.

The roots appeared again on the left of the drawing, snaking in and out of the dark fog, tying the piece together.

Angel realized she was holding her breath and released it. She brought a hand to her chest, felt the wild beating of her heart.

It was good. Really good. Better than anything she'd done before.

Maybe Seth's uncle had been right. Maybe she could learn to be more in control her of art. She didn't need to wait for sleep and hope she dreamed up something good.

Tilting her head, she frowned, studying it. So, where had it come from? And what did it mean?

Her cell phone went off. She saw it was Seth and snatched it up. "The most amazing thing just happened!"

"What's that, babe?"

"I just created the most amazing drawing while I was awake."

He laughed. "You know how messed up that sounds?"

"I guess it does, doesn't it?" She smiled, thoughts of the day before, of their lovemaking, flooding her mind. With the memory, heat surged through her body.

"We're in the drawing," she said softly. "Together."

"So it's *that* kind of art."

She laughed. "Not together like *that*." She looked at the drawing, the joining of their roots. "Not explicitly, anyway."

"I've been thinking," he said softly. "About what you said last night, and about the way I responded."

That she loved him. "Pretty awkward, huh?"

"No, it's not that. It's just . . . growing up the way I did, there wasn't a lot of . . . love." His voice thickened on the last word and he cleared his throat. "It's hard for me, you know, to accept that."

"There wasn't any of that for me, either. I guess that's why I'm so certain now."

For a long moment, he was silent. She closed her eyes. *Say it, Seth. Please. Tell me you love me, too.*

"I don't want to hurt you, Angel," he said instead.

But it did hurt. Like crazy.

"I said it, Seth. It's true and I can't take it back."

"I don't want you to."

"You don't?"

"Just don't give up on me, okay?"

How could she, she wondered a short time later, as they ended the call. They were connected, just like in her drawing. Tangled together, for better or for worse.

CHAPTER THIRTY-SEVEN

Saturday, October 24
Noon

MICKI AND ZACH SAT ACROSS from Major Nichols, waiting for him to finish his call with the chief. From the side of the conversation she could hear—and Nichols' expression—it wasn't going well.

She and Zach had spent the morning observing Bhear's autopsy. They'd learned little that was new. He'd been a fairly healthy man. A few old scars, an irritated stomach lining and a liver that looked like it had been ridden hard. The only thing of note was the small tattoo at the base of his skull—three sixes in a cube.

Six-Cubed. The name of the gang behind the home invasions. Part of Team Dark Bearer, she thought.

Major Nichols hung up the phone and looked directly at her. "Chief Howard watched the video."

"And?"

"He's not a happy camper."

"And we are?"

He ignored her sarcasm. "Bhear was an important witness. He wonders why we didn't have an officer with him?"

"The door was locked. We can't babysit every witness on the very bizarre and remote chance they'll kill themselves."

"The press is having a field day with this suicide. The Public Integrity Bureau's asked for a copy of the video. They've been getting calls."

"I'm not surprised," Zach said. "It looks shady as shit."

"Thank you that for that colorful confirmation, Detective Harris. I feel so much better now." He folded his hands on the desk in front of him. "What's your game plan?"

Micki jumped in. "Three-pronged, Major. We've got Bhear's phone."

Zack took over. "And we're certain digital forensics on the device will reveal something we can use. Then we plan—"

"To do a thorough search of his apartment this afternoon," Micki finished for him. "From there, we'll—"

"Follow up on any leads extracted from both."

Major looked from one to the other, eyebrow cocked. "You realize you're finishing each other's sentences? That's either weird as hell or you're up to something."

"Neither, Major," she said. "Just working long hours."

"Feeling a bit punch drunk." Zach added.

"I'm certain that's just bullshit, but maybe I don't want to know." Nichols shook his head. "Talk to me about the kid."

"Safe with Social Services. He claims to not know the names of any of the others involved in the home invasions."

"Seems unlikely."

"Agreed. We plan on interviewing him again as well as having him describe the others to a sketch artist."

Zach stepped in. "But there's a chance he never clearly saw their faces, since they covered them."

"C'mon," Nichols said. "That would mean they kept them covered out on the street, in the car, whatever. I don't buy that."

"Bhear seemed to be set on protecting his son."

"By involving him in a string of home invasions?"

"What if he didn't have a choice?" Micki said.

"What do you know?"

"Nothing specific. Talked to Bhear's mother, the kid's grandmother. She said Reggie was very protective."

"What mother ever thinks her kid's a bad apple?" He changed topics. "You sat in on the autopsy this morning?"

"Yes. Only one thing of note. Tattoo, on the back of his neck." She slid a photo of it across the desk.

He looked at it, frowning. "This was his only tattoo?"

"No, he had a half dozen. This is the only one of interest to us."

Zach took over. "We interviewed a witness who claims someone from the group tried to recruit him. Called themselves Six Cubed."

"As in six to the third power?"

"Or, as we see here, three sixes in a cube. So, maybe, we have the name of the gang."

"Assign someone to scour the Internet and social media sites, see if we get a hit."

"Done."

"Good work. Keep me posted."

Micki's cell went off as they exited the major's office. She saw it was the pathologist's office. "Dare," she answered.

"Detective, the tox report is back on Reggie Bhear."

"And?"

"And nothing."

"Nothing," she repeated.

"Not even any OTCs. Guy's blood was clean. Squeaky clean."

She ended the call and shared the news with Zach. He shrugged. "You're surprised?"

"Hell, yeah, I'm surprised. Guys like Bhear don't come back squeaky clean."

"What does it matter? We both know what killed him."

They stopped at Sue's desk, signed out, then headed downstairs.

He was right. And it didn't undermine the most obvious version of his death—a psychotic break. Dude was completely off his meds.

"What now?" Zach asked.

"Somehow, we find this Kyle. Something's gonna turn up—"

Her phone sounded again. This time it was the crime lab. "Detective Dare, there's something on Bhear's phone I think you're going to want to take a look at."

Deleted photos, she discovered ten minutes later. Retrieved from Bhear's cell phone's memory card. Micki scrolled through the first few, a knot forming in the pit of her gut. Her neighborhood. Her street.

Her house. A picture of her mailbox, address boldly displayed.

She heard Zach's sharply in-drawn breath and muttered "What the hell," but didn't take her eyes from the computer screen.

More photos. Angel, leaving the house. Waiting at the bus stop with her backpack. Another of her on the UNO campus. Arriving, leaving. The same with Sacred Grounds. Arriving for a shift, leaving after. Often alone.

"Son of a bitch," she said, dragging her gaze from the images to look at Zach. "Why was he following her?"

"I think we know why."

The Dark One. Truebell had said the Dark One would love to get his hands on her. Bring her over to his side. And if he couldn't bring her over, he'd kill her.

Because of her gift. Her ability to predict his next move and warn Truebell's people.

When, she wondered, was the last time she'd checked in with Angel? "Oh my God."

"What?" Zach asked.

"I haven't talked to Angel all day."

"She's fine. If someone was messing with her she would have tried to contact me, but it's been completely quiet."

Not good enough, Micki thought. Not after seeing those pictures. "I'm going to check on her."

Micki stood and went beyond earshot of the technician. She dialed Angel. Nothing. No answer. She tried again. Answer, she thought with each ring. After five it went to voicemail. Again.

Micki took a deep, careful breath, trying to recall Angel's work schedule. She had been scheduled to close today. That meant she would clock in at four, clock out at midnight. It wasn't even one yet. Maybe her schedule had changed?

Micki called up the coffeehouse's number and dialed. She almost wept with relief when Angel answered. "It's me," she said. "Are you okay?"

"Of course. Why wouldn't I be?"

"I thought you were working the late shift?"

"I am. Ginger didn't show so they called me in." She made a sound of exasperation. "I've gotta go—"

"Listen to me, this is more important than your job. You're being followed, Angel. Your schedule and movements. We found photographic records of it on a perp's phone."

"Oh my God," she said, voice rising with alarm. "It's that Dark Bearer, isn't it?"

"Maybe, yes."

"What should I do?"

"Stay there. Work your shift, but don't leave the shop, even for a moment. What time do you get off?"

"Midnight." Her voice shook slightly. "Ginger closes with me."

"Zach and I will come get you. If anything feels wrong to you, call us. Do you understand?"

She said she did and hung up.

Micki returned to the computer. Zach glanced up. "How'd she take it?"

"She's scared."

"Good. It'll keep her from doing anything stupid." He motioned toward the computer display. "Take a look."

More images extracted from Bam Bam's phone. Party shots from clubs around town, several on Fulton Street. The guy liked to party, no doubt about it.

"Stop on that one. See anyone you know?" Zach asked.

The hair on the back of her neck stood up. Troy, Bhear's co-worker from A-1 Motor Sports. "Holy shit, this is it. The break we've needed."

She turned to Meyer. "Can you print these out?"

"All of them? There's over five hundred."

"Yeah, but start with these." She tapped all the ones that appeared to have been taken that same night. "Email a file with the rest."

Within five minutes, she had an envelope of the copies and they were on the road, lights and siren screaming.

"We've got Kyle," she said, excited. "He's in one of these pictures, I know it."

"What if Troy can't I.D. him?"

"The guy made his skin crawl--you don't forget that face."

"Good point," Zach agreed, then switched the subject. "Why do you think Bhear was following Angel?"

"Maybe he wasn't?"

"What do you mean?"

"Subtle difference I know, but I think he might have been doing recon. He wasn't following her—"

"He was learning her daily patterns for someone else."

Their eyes met. They both knew who that someone else would be. "So, what does the Dark Bearer want with her?"

"You heard Truebell and Eli. She's special. He'd love to get his hooks into her."

They reached the repair shop, cut the siren but not the light. The owner met them at the shop's entrance, expression alarmed. "Detectives? Can I help you?"

"We need to speak with Troy."

"Troy? Why—"

"It's urgent. Is he here?"

"No." He shifted his gaze between them. "He doesn't work Saturdays. Is something wrong?"

"We hope not. Zach," she said, turning to him, "call for back-up. Ed, I need an address. Now."

CHAPTER THIRTY-EIGHT

Saturday, October 24
2:00 P.M.

TROY WILSON WAS DEAD. HE lay on his back, just inside his front door. He'd been shot in the chest, in the vicinity of his heart. It had been game over nearly instantly. It looked as if he'd had time to recoil and stumble back a couple steps, and for his hand to go to his chest and clutch at the spot. The hand was stained red from his blood.

Zach watched as Micki picked her way around the pool of blood to squat beside the body. Though there was no doubt he was dead, she pressed gloved fingers to his throat.

Zach swallowed past the metallic taste in his mouth. His pulse beat so heavily in his head, it felt like a native drum.

Thump thump . . . thump thump . . .

Was it warning him away or welcoming him in?

Zach closed his eyes, breathed deeply though his nose. The energy swirled on the small front porch. Crazy bad. Angry, like a trapped animal. And also—somehow—fractured.

Zach stopped on that. Night and day. Two sides of the same coin.

Micki looked up at him. "You comin' through that door?"

He blinked; his thoughts cleared. "Yeah. Can't rush the master."

The words sounded hollow to his own ears; she seemed not to notice and rolled her eyes in response. He prepared himself and stepped across the threshold.

The dark energy fell away in a trail behind him.

Surprised, he looked over his shoulder.

"What?" she asked.

"The perpetrator was never inside. Energy stops cold at the door."

"You're sure?"

"Really, Mick? You're going to ask me that? Yeah, I'm sure." He fitted on his gloves and joined her beside the body.

"Judging by rigor mortis and lividity, he's been dead—"

"Don't talk." Zach hovered his right hand over Wilson's chest. The impressions came lightning fast. The sound of the doorbell; swinging the door open. Recognition. Zach didn't pick up fear. A sort of surprise. Resignation without the regret.

Troy Wilson had been ready to die.

The crack of the gun firing rang in Zach's head; he experienced the shock with Wilson, body jerking on impact, stumbling back, hand to chest.

Red. Warm and thick, seeping through his fingers.

Zach's eyes popped open. "I saw him."

"The perp?"

"Yeah. It was Kyle. Through Wilson's eyes, the moment he shot him."

"Don't let it go. Hold on—"

"It's gone. It was too fast."

"Son of a bitch!"

The scream of a siren announced the paramedics. A moment later, the ambulance's lights bounced crazily off the neighboring homes.

"Quick," she said, "absorb whatever you can."

Whatever had remained evaporated with the rush of the paramedics. The crime scene van followed and Zach gave up any attempt to read the energy.

While Micki spoke to the scene techs, Zach made his way through the house. Neat. Everything had a place and everything was in its place. Lamps burned, casting a soft, comfortable glow. In the kitchen, the remnants of roasted chicken had been scraped into the garbage; under that, the deli box the meal had come home in. The plate, utensils, and glass sat in the sink waiting to be washed.

He'd been killed the night before, sometime after dinner.

Mick came up behind him. "What are you thinking?"

He told her, pointing out the lights being on, the dishes from an evening meal and the fact the remnants of the food had long since dried out.

She agreed. "Body temp should give us close estimation of the time."

He nodded and crossed to the small, scarred kitchen table. A well-worn Bible lay open on its top. He floated his hand over the book. A soothing energy emanated up, warming his hand. Wilson's energy. His love of this book. His gratitude for life.

"He was a good man," Zach said. "He didn't deserve for this to happen to him."

"No," she said, "he didn't."

Zach looked back at the Bible, his gaze landing on a highlighted passage. The highlighter rested on the table beside the book. Not the typical yellow but a bright orange.

He bent and read the passage out loud, gooseflesh running up his arms. "Beware your enemy, the devil, prowls around like a roaring lion, looking for someone to devour. First Peter, chapter five, verse eight."

Zach lifted his gaze to Mick's. "He knew this was coming and left us a message."

"That seems like a reach to me, partner."

"He highlighted it last night, maybe only moments before the doorbell rang."

"So, the guy was religious? My grandma used to do the same thing. I'm gonna check the—"

"No, wait, I want to try something."

He started to take off his right glove. "Whoa, Hollywood—"

"Chill. You really think the Dark Bearer was messing with this book?"

Zach picked up the highlighter; Wilson's energy clung to it, the quiet moments he had been spending here with his Lord. Deeply spiritual moments, calming. Zach replaced the pen, then brought his hand to the book, and trailed his fingers slowly along the edges of the pages.

"Hollywood," she said, "time, dude."

He ignored her, tuned her—and everything else—out. Everything but the vibration, like a song, against his fingertips.

The vibration intensified; he stopped, carefully slipping the pages apart. Orange highlighter.

Mick came to stand beside him, reading over his shoulder. *Walk as children of light . . .* Then another: *We are not of the night or of the darkness . . .* And another: *Light shines in the darkness, and the darkness has not overcome it . . .*

The crime scene techs came in; Micki stopped them. "Give us a minute, please."

"It's okay," he said, closing the book. "That was the last."

She nodded and turned to the waiting techs. "Bag the Bible," she instructed them. "Be careful, the pages are delicate."

She looked at Zach. He saw by the expression in her eyes that she was deeply shaken.

When she spoke, however, she was all business. Typical Mick. "You search the bedroom yet?"

"Didn't get past the kitchen."

She nodded and pointed at his hand. "Glove."

Zach fitted the glove back on as they headed down the hall. "Four verses. Each mentioned both the light and the dark. All four he highlighted last night, shortly before he took a bullet to his heart. I don't think it was a coincidence. He had Lightkeeper in him. He must have."

"I don't know what I believe, Hollywood. There's not enough evidence to support either conclusion with certainty and—"

"And there may never be."

She didn't respond. They reached the first bedroom. There were two, one slightly larger than the other. A bathroom occupied the space between the two. Interestingly, Wilson had chosen the smaller of the two as his.

They stepped into the room. "Do you feel that?" Zach asked.

"What?"

"Peace."

"Peace? Here?" She shook her head. "You're losing it, Hollywood."

Maybe he was, he thought. But whatever he was picking up, he'd never experienced it before. Not even in the presence of Eli or Truebell. There had been something very special about Troy Wilson.

Simple furniture. Double bed, nightstand, small dresser. A lamp burning on the nightstand. Some framed photographs. Children. A family.

They'd have to be notified. Zach grimaced at the thought.

His gaze landed on an envelope there on the bedside table. Across the front in a sure-handed scrawl: *Detectives Harris and Dare*

"What the hell?" Micki muttered.

Zach opened the envelope, pulled out the folded sheet of lined paper.

Detectives,

The Lord whispered in my ear and told me tonight would be my last on earth. The darkness comes for me. It takes many forms, its purpose is always destruction. Destruction of all that is good: of beauty and joy, peace and prosperity. And love, the greatest of all.

Brace yourself, Detectives. Arm yourself in The Light. The war is only just begun.

God bless you and keep you,

Troy Wilson

Zach swallowed past the lump in his throat, shaken not by the other man's warning but—oddly—by his complete and utter peace with what had been about to happen.

"Do you think God really whispered in his ear?" he asked.

"Of course not." Her voice shook slightly.

"Then how did he know?"

"Intuition, Hollywood. Like you said, maybe he had Lightkeeper in him?"

"Dare? Harris?"

They turned. Hollister, the coroner's investigator.

"We're getting ready to bag the body. You need a final look?"

"I've seen enough," Micki said. She looked at Zach. "You?"

"I'm good."

Hollister frowned slightly. "Any questions?"

"Not from me," she said.

Zach seconded her. "Nope."

Hollister's frown deepened. "You okay, Detective Dare?"

"Fine. Why do you ask?"

"You're usually a lot bossier than this."

She looked at him blankly, as if he were speaking in tongues. "Cause and manner of death look pretty cut-and-dried. It doesn't appear the perp entered the house."

"Right." Hollister cleared his throat, obviously nonplussed. "Looks that way to me, but you never know what blood work and autopsy will turn up. Might help you with the why."

Zach watched the man walk away and turned to Micki. He saw by her expression she was thinking the same thing he was. They already knew the why: Troy Wilson had been a loose end; the one person they knew of who could have identified Kyle.

CHAPTER THIRTY-NINE

Saturday, October 24
11:40 P.M.

ZACH NAVIGATED THE QUIET CITY streets, heading uptown on St. Charles Avenue. Beside him, Mick sat staring straight ahead, lost in her own thoughts. They had said little since leaving the Wilson scene, their usual banter replaced by a heavy silence.

It'd been a long, frustrating day, spinning their wheels, encountering one closed door after another. They'd gotten nothing from Reggie's apartment, nothing of consequence from the numbers in his phone—just a bunch of restaurants and bars, pay phones and disposable cell numbers.

Autopsy turned up zip, just as showing the photos to Little Bear had. He hadn't recognized any of the faces. As for Tommy, turned out after what went down with Angel, he'd bolted.

Then, later, Rachel had called from Social Services with more bad news: the law stated that Little Bear had to go to his next of kin, and Rachel was running out of red tape for the grandmother to wade through. Fact was, sometime in the next twenty-four hours he would leave the Social Services' safe house and go back to his grandma's.

Where he'd be completely vulnerable to the Dark Bearer and his Six-Cubed crew. He wasn't going to let that happen, Zach thought. Somehow he'd find a way to keep the kid out of the Dark Bearer's hands.

"I'll have a car tomorrow," Micki said suddenly. "I would've had one already but I didn't put the request in."

"And here I was enjoying playing chauffeur." His attempt at humor came off flat.

She glanced at him. "Do you ever wonder— Never mind, it doesn't matter."

"Sure, it does. Wonder what?"

"If you're strong enough? Or if you should just admit defeat, pack up your toys and move on?"

"C'mon, Mick, me? Only at least once an hour."

"And here I am, a mere mortal." She pursed her lips. "Problem is, I don't know where I'd move on to."

He reached across the seat and squeezed her hand. "You're the strongest person I've ever met."

A corner of her mouth lifted in a half smile. "But what's the point? The bad's gonna always win out over the good, no matter how hard I fight."

"That's not true. There's still so much good in the world."

"Not in my world."

Zach sensed she wasn't referring to only the world at large, but her personal one. The one where her very own demons lived. "You're just tired."

"That I am." She laid her head back against the rest, face turned toward the window. They fell silent once more. The blocks passed. The famous landmarks: Loyola University, Audubon Park, Tulane University. They passed Broadway and its row of frat houses; Zach glanced that way, saw one of their famous parties underway.

"It's almost midnight," she said. "Swing by Sacred Grounds, we'll pick up Angel."

"She's still going to have to clean up," he said. "And she promised not to leave alone. How about I drop you off first, then go pick her up?"

She started to protest, he stopped her. "I wanted some time with her anyway, and let's face it, right now I've got a better relationship with her than you do."

She hesitated a moment, then sighed. "You know what you have to do, right? Until we know for certain he's not one of them?"

Tell her she couldn't see Seth. "Yeah," he said. "I know."

Ten minutes later, Zach pulled up in front of Sacred Grounds. Midnight on the button. The neon Open sign was dark, but the lights were on inside.

He parked, went to the door and peeked inside. Angel was behind the bar cleaning, Ginger was in front mopping, and a dark-haired guy was keeping them both company.

Not any guy. Angel's Seth. He'd bet his badge on it.

He tapped on the glass. They all turned his way, but he only had eyes for Angel. She looked like the kid who'd just been caught with her hand in the candy bowl. And not just any candy, the forbidden stuff.

He smiled and lifted his hand in greeting. In the next instant Ginger let him in, all smiles. "Zach!" She gave him a big hug. "What're you doing here?"

"Just dropped Mick off, came to give Angel her lift home."

He walked over to the guy and held out his hand. "I'm Zach."

The kid hesitated a moment, then clasped it. "Seth."

"The Seth I've heard so much about." He tightened his fingers, absorbing. "Finally."

Lightning quick, a series of images popped into his head. A woman, bleeding out in a bathtub. A soul-deep howl of pain. Seth and Angel together—the moment, like a quickly expelled breath of peace. Then—

A chest, like a strongbox. Strapped and padlocked. The box bowed, groaning. There was something inside. Something confined, that wanted to get out.

Zach released his hand and smiled easily. "I've been looking forward to meeting you."

"Back at you, dude."

"Hey, Zach," Angel said, coming over, wiping her hands on a towel, "no Micki, huh?"

"Nope, just me."

"Well, Seth stopped by and offered to drive me home, so—"

Before Zach could respond, Seth stepped in. "It's chill, babe. I've got an early day tomorrow anyway."

She looked disappointed. "But you came all this way."

"And I've been here a couple hours. Go with Zach." He bent and kissed her, not deeply, but lingering just long enough that Zach wanted to throttle him.

"You'll call me later?" she said, when he ended the kiss.

"I will." He turned back to Zach. "Good to meet you, man."

A short while later, he and Angel were on their way to Mick's. They rode in silence. She sat with her arms around herself, her face turned toward the window, gnawing at her bottom lip.

"You okay?" he asked.

She shrugged. "I guess."

"Pretty scary, about those photos."

"Did you see them?"

He frowned slightly. "Yeah, I did."

"Are you sure they—"

"Yes. Pictures of you leaving for work, at the bus stop, leaving work at night."

"Oh." She hunched deeper into her seat. "Why me? It doesn't make any sense."

Zach considered his words carefully. What to say, what to leave out. He decided to be blunt. "The professor and Eli believe Dark Bearers are recruiting Half Lights to fight for his side. You're a powerful prophet, so he wants you."

"Well, he can't have me," she said fiercely. "I'll never fight for him. Never."

Spoken like an all-powerful eighteen-year-old, Zach thought, turning onto Mick's street. Up ahead, the light on her front porch burned brightly. He saw the neighborhood stray cat—the one Micki had imaginatively named Kitty—cleaning itself on the top step.

He parked; they both climbed out. "You're staying?" she asked, obviously surprised.

"Let's sit and talk awhile. Okay?"

She nodded and plopped down on the porch step. Kitty came over and climbed into her lap.

"I see she's taken to you as well."

"She'll still ditch me in a heartbeat for you." Sure enough, he sat and the cat immediately abandoned Angel. "See."

The cat was rubbing herself against him and purring so loudly it was like the rumble of an engine.

Zach again pondered what to say. Angel was head-over-heels in love with the guy—and the two were having sex. Even a hint of criticism would fall flat.

"The Dark Bearer—or one of his followers—killed a man last night. A good man." Her eyes widened and he went on. "Mick took it really hard."

She twisted her fingers together. "How come?"

"Good question," he said. "One I'm not completely sure of the answer to, but I think she's afraid the Dark Bearer's winning. Like she's helpless to stop him."

"It's not true, is it?"

"This man, this good man, was killed because he might have been able to put a face to Kyle."

She frowned in thought a moment. "The guy Tommy told us about?"

"Yes."

"The one I tried to draw but couldn't." Her expression puckered with regret. "I'm sorry."

"It's not your fault."

"But if I'd been able to draw him—" She looked away. "I really did try."

"I know, kiddo."

They fell silent. Zach sensed there was something she wasn't saying. Something she wanted to share but was afraid to.

He angled toward her, found her hands and laced their fingers. "You can trust me. Angel. With anything. You know that, right?"

She lifted her gaze, met his eyes. Her hands trembled slightly and she slipped them from his grasp.

"Sure. Of course."

"What aren't you telling me?"

"Nothing."

Secretive. Dishonest. That wasn't the Angel he knew.

"It's something about Seth, isn't it?"

She flushed. "Why would you say that?"

"Because I picked up on something when we shook hands—"

"You were spying on him?"

"No." He shook his head. "You know what my abilities are, it just happened."

"That's such . . . crap. You can shut it off." She jumped to her feet. "You just didn't want to!"

He stood, faced her. "Can you turn off your dreams?"

"That's different."

"Why?"

"It just is."

"Angel, listen to me."

"Micki sent you, didn't she? To poison my mind against him?"

"Why would you even think that? She's frightened for you. We all are." He caught her arm. "Angel, there's something . . . I'm afraid Seth's not a good guy."

She yanked free of his grasp. "I thought you were my friend." Her voice shook. "I thought you were on my side."

"I am. I promise. Look, I know you're sleeping together. You think you love him, but—"

"Oh my God. You spied on . . . *that?*"

"No, God no. I picked it up, but—"

"That's my private business! *Mine.*"

"You need to stop seeing him, only for a—"

"What? You can't tell me what to do!"

"Only for a little while. It's too dangerous. Until we know he's—"

"I know! Doesn't that mean anything? He would protect me, I know he would."

"You're only eighteen. What you feel for him is powerful, I know. But it's not love." You don't know what love is. Angel, you're only—"

Something in her expression changed, like a subtle ripple across the water's surface. "Like *you* know what love is?" She all but spat the words at him. "Please. Have you ever loved anyone but yourself?"

He flinched. "That's not fair. And what I do know is, love isn't sex. And sex isn't love."

Kitty jumped up on the porch rail and meowed, the sound plaintive. "Eli and the professor believe the reason you couldn't draw that day is because you were being blocked. Who would do that, Angel? Why would they?"

"Leave me alone. I don't—"

He cut her off. "The Dark Bearer. It's the Dark Bearer who's behind the home invasions—"

"That has nothing to do with me!" she cried. "With me or Seth!"

"Then why couldn't you draw a picture of the person who approached Tommy? Maybe because you know him. Maybe he's insinuated himself into your life? Gained your trust—"

"Shut up!" she screamed. "I got sick that day. People get sick. It doesn't mean anything."

She started past him, but he caught her by the shoulders and forced her to look at him. "When I shook Seth's hand, this image—"

"Stop it! I won't listen!"

"A strongbox, Angel. Padlocked."

"No."

"Something was in it, trying to get out."

"No!" she shouted, the sound as if coming from the very bowels of her being. She jerked free of his grasp. "Shut up! Just shut—"

Suddenly, Kitty screeched, the noise like a battle cry. Zach swung to look at the cat, turning just in time to see her leap at him, claws out. He raised his hands to protect his face; her claws sank into his arms.

With a shout of pain he shook her off; but she came at him again, this time sinking her claws into his leg.

The door flew open. Micki. The look on her face would have been comical if he didn't have a mad cat attached to his leg. "What are you two—"

"I hate you both!" Angel yelled and stormed into the house, nearly knocking Micki over.

"What the—"

"Get this cat off—"

He didn't finish, but he didn't need to. As suddenly as she had attacked, Kitty retreated, darting under the porch railing and into the bushes.

Zach stared after her, then looked down at his cut up forearms. Blood ran down them and dripped from his elbows.

"C'mon in," Micki said. "Let's get that cleaned up."

Her voice shook. He silently agreed and followed her in. She led him to the kitchen.

"Sit," she said, pulling out a chair. He did, pushing his shirt sleeves higher and watching silently as she got a first aid kit out of her pantry.

"I can do it," he said as she swung a chair to face his.

"I've got it." She soaked a sterile pad with antiseptic. "This is going to hurt."

"Of course it is," he muttered, gritting his teeth, waiting for the burn of the antiseptic meeting the open wound.

It came, but her touch was surprisingly gentle as she carefully cleaned and bandaged the right forearm, then moved on to the left.

He gazed down at her, mesmerized by the way her lashes brushed her cheeks, the rose of her mouth and slope of her neck.

The soft curve of her breast against the clinging white tee.

His heart rate accelerated. He shifted his gaze, working to get the image of the clinging tee out of his head. Another replaced it, of her on the dance floor, moving erotically to the music. Then, the memory of her mouth against his, her body melting into his.

"Kitty did a good job of messing you up," she said. "What the hell did you do to her? Step on her tail?"

He didn't reply and she looked up at him, frowned slightly. "What?"

"Do you ever think about that night? At Kudzu?"

He saw the memory creep into her eyes; felt the energy change between them, crackling like static electricity.

"How could I not? I almost died that night."

"That's not what I'm talking about." His voice thickened. "I'm talking about you and me."

"We were working. We—"

"I think about it."

"You need to stop this now. We'll both—"

He bent his head to hers and kissed her. He felt her surprise. A brief moment of resistance, then response.

He deepened the kiss. Her hands went to his chest, her fingers curling into the cotton broadcloth. A small sound passed her lips, throaty with pleasure and surrender.

And then it was over.

She flattened her hands, pushed him away. "No, Zach. We're partners. We can't do this."

She was right and he knew it. If they took this to its conclusion, it wouldn't be just sex, enjoyed and forgotten. It would be more, the way it was supposed to be. Which made it dangerous.

He swallowed hard, straightened. "You're right. I'm sorry." He shifted his gaze away from her soft, red mouth. "I don't know what I was thinking."

"It's cool. Stuff happens."

"I should go."

"I haven't finished. Your leg—"

"Mick, really? I think the last thing I should do right now is take off my pants."

A smile tugged at her mouth. "You've got a point there, Hollywood."

"That isn't what I have. And you know it."

Her gaze dropped to his lap, then, as if realizing what she'd done, shot back up to his. Her cheeks turned red.

This time it was he who laughed. "I think I'll leave now, with the last shreds of my ego intact."

They both stood. She walked him to the door.

"Pick you up tomorrow?" he asked.

"Yeah. Text when you're on your way."

She closed the door behind him. He paused there, expelling a long breath. So that had been a mistake, he thought. A big one.

So why didn't he regret it in the least?

Kitty jumped out of the shrubs and onto the porch. He eyed her suspiciously. "Oh sure, now you want to be friends."

She mewed plaintively and crossed the porch. He watched her progress, ready to fend off an attack. Instead, she rubbed herself against his leg and mewed, as if asking for forgiveness. He hesitated a moment, then bent and scratched behind her ears.

Once again the feline he knew, she went spastic with delight, purring and rolling onto her back in a very un-catlike fashion.

His cell went off. He gave her a last stroke and straightened, heading for his car and going for his phone at the same time.

"This is Harris," he answered.

"It's me."

Parker. "Where the hell you been, P?"

"Quantico. Got a new group of recruits."

"God help 'em."

"Think you've got that backwards."

Zach climbed into his car, started it up. "Any relatives you want to tell me about? Brothers, this time? Cousins?"

"I guess I deserve that. And no, as far as I know, you're a one-and-only."

"Things are a little crazy here."

"Fill me in."

Zach did, sharing the events of the last few days, holding back the 'I've got the hots for my partner' part of the equation. Need-to-know that wasn't.

"There's something going on with Angel," Zach finished. "We're worried."

"Keep her close."

"Easier said than done." He explained about their argument over Seth, how she had stormed off. "She says she's in love with him."

"What do you know about him?"

"Not enough. What should I know?"

"If he's one of them, of course."

Parker hung up, and Zach was left with an uncomfortable feeling in the pit of his gut that he and Mick might have just sent Angel running into the arms of the enemy.

CHAPTER FORTY

Sunday, October 25
2:10 A.M.

MICKI SAT AT THE KITCHEN table, staring blankly at its scarred top. With everything that had happened in the past twenty-four hours—including two horrific murders—she was thinking about Zach—their kiss, her response to it, and wondering what would have happened if she hadn't gotten a grip and pushed him away.

That wasn't quite true. She knew what would have happened: they would have slept together. What she was really pondering was what it would have been like.

Dammit. That first day they'd met, he'd told her she'd wonder what he was like in bed. And now she had, prediction fulfilled.

With a caveat—it wouldn't have been good.

It would have been mind-blowing.

How long had it been since she'd had sex? Any kind, forget mind-blowing?

A couple years. There'd been a guy after Hank's death. A way to take her mind off her grief. After that a guy from the Jefferson Parish force. She'd met him at a training seminar. That relationship had burned out almost before it started.

Both had been nothing. Forgettable wastes of her time and soul.

She glanced toward the kitchen doorway, the hallway beyond. Were Angel and Seth sleeping together?

She hadn't considered it before, though she should have, considering their ages and the fact Angel seemed so smitten. It would explain Angel's sudden personality change, Micki thought. From easy-going and open, to defensive and secretive. She wasn't so old she couldn't remember that first flush of young, erotic love. Hell, a few hours ago, she'd been a kiss away from throwing caution to the winds and common sense out the window.

Poor Angel, she thought, standing and moving into the hallway. Soft light seeped from the bottom of her door. Micki tapped on it. "Angel, it's me. Are you awake?"

She didn't get a response but thought she heard a stirring on the other side of the door, so she tapped again. "I was hoping we could talk."

She waited a moment; when she still got no reply, she went on anyway. "I think I get it now, you and Seth. The way you're feeling. It's been a long time since—"

She bit the last of that back and started again. "I really care about you. And I'm . . . I'm really bad at caring, you know? It's not in my nature and—"

Micki took a deep breath, acknowledging that she was undoubtedly mangling this but that she didn't know what else to do, so she pressed on.

"—with this whole Dark Bearer thing going on, I'm . . . there's even more that's out of my control. I worry, you know? Not only about how I keep me alive, but you and Zach, too."

She waited for Angel to respond. When that didn't happen, she continued. "I always thought . . . if I just kept everything and everyone in a box, it wouldn't get messy. It'd all work out and life would continue just the way I wanted it to."

She thought of Zach, his mouth against hers, and how very close she'd been to letting go of control.

"I've made so many mistakes, Angel. Because I never . . . I never felt wanted. That can drive you, and I don't want that to happen to you."

Micki rested her forehead against the door. "I know you get that because I know you've been there." She paused a moment, feeling vulnerable and way too exposed, and wishing Angel would say something. "We'll work this out. If Seth's who you want, I'll stand by you."

Through the door she heard what sounded like the lid of a garbage can going over, clattering noisily to the pavement, then the sound of laughter.

That wasn't right. She glanced left, a straight shot down the hall, through the living room to the front door. It was shut tight.

She suddenly realized her bare feet were cold. That a cold breeze wafted from beneath Angel's bedroom door.

She tried the knob, found the door locked. She knocked. "Angel, open this door now."

When she got no response, she tried again. "Let me in, Angel. Right now or I'm going to kick the door in. And I really, really don't want to do that."

She counted to ten, backwards. When the door didn't open, she reared back and kicked. The lock, old and wobbly, gave easily. The door flew in.

The window stood open, curtains fluttering in the breeze. The bed was made, the room empty.

It took Micki a moment to process what had happened.

Angel had bolted.

Micki crossed the threshold and gazed quickly over the room. Angel's personal items were scattered about: a photograph of her and Ginger, tucked into the frame around the dresser mirror; on the desk, a tube of the organic hand lotion she used; her Sacred Grounds ball cap hanging off the back of the chair.

No purse, Micki noted. No backpack. No sketchbook.

With a knot in the pit of her stomach, she crossed to the closet, slid the door back. Angel's minimal wardrobe appeared intact. She owned two pairs of athletic-type shoes, flip flops, and a pair of hiking boots. The boots, flip flops and one pair of the Nikes were neatly lined up on the floor of the closet. Micki went to the dresser. A drawer of undergarments and socks, the shorts and T-shirt she slept in.

Micki released a breath she hadn't realized she was holding. She went to the open window and peered out. The drop was minimal; nothing for someone in as good of shape as Angel.

She'd been mad and hurt, so she'd done what a kid like Angel always did. Ducked out. Sought temporary refuge elsewhere.

The guy, Micki thought. Or Ginger.

Micki shut and latched the window. Angel had a key. When she came back, she could use the front door.

If she came back.

At the niggling doubt, she headed to the house's only bathroom. The door was closed but unlocked. She opened it slowly, just in case. This room, like the bedroom, was empty. And as in the bedroom, Angel had left her stuff behind. Even her toothbrush.

Micki let out a long, tired breath; truth was, she was out on her feet.

She retrieved her phone to dial Angel. The device went straight to voicemail. Of course, she'd turned it off—Micki was the last person Angel would want to talk to right now. Except, maybe, for Zach.

She left a quick message. No sooner had she hung up than her cell went off. "Angel?" she answered without looking at the display.

A moment of silence. "No, Zach."

"Oh. What's going on?"

"Seems I should be asking you that. Where's Angel?"

"Gone. Climbed out her bedroom window. As far as I can tell she didn't take anything but her purse, backpack and sketchbook."

"You tried calling her?"

"Went straight to voicemail."

"What do we do now?"

"There's nothing we can do."

"We're cops. We find her and—"

"How?"

"Issue a BOLO. Get some officers on the street—"

"She hasn't broken any law. She's of age and free to come and go as she pleases."

"You heard Eli and Truebell. The Dark Bearer's searching for people like her. C'mon, Mick, we have to do something!"

"Tell me what."

"She ran to the guy."

"Most likely." She made a sound of frustration. "I don't even know his last name."

"Ginger will."

"Maybe. And she might not tell us, even if she does."

He snorted. "I can find that out, easy."

"It'll have to wait until morning, unless you want to totally freak her out. I'm hoping she comes home before then."

"This is my fault," he said. "I forgot my role."

"What role is that?"

"The good cop. Her buddy." She heard the frustration in his voice. "I should've kept her confidence, just listened and agreed."

"Look, you were trying to do the right thing. You can't beat yourself up for that. You were trying to help her."

"Yeah," he muttered. "My bad."

"Stop it. I could've backed off, too. I should have remembered how it felt to be young and in love and how irrational that can make you."

"We could go to Eli and Truebell," he suggested. "They might be able to reach her."

"Let's wait. She might be home yet tonight."

"She'll come bopping back in like nothing happened." His voice deepened. "Grab some sleep. I'll see you in the morning."

Micki agreed and hung up, only realizing then that Zach had never said why he'd called.

CHAPTER FORTY-ONE

Monday, October 26
9:10 A.M.

ANGEL AWAKENED WITH A START. Her eyes flew open and for a moment she didn't know where she was. Huge four poster bed, dark wood, feather-stuffed pillows and comforter. French doors out to a balcony, sunlight streaming through.

"Morning, sleepy."

She turned her head. Seth, wearing running shorts and nothing else, brushing his teeth.

She drank him in, feeling light-headed, almost drunk. She smiled. "Hey."

"How do you feel today?"

"Amazing. I love it here."

He smiled. "You were asleep a really long time."

"I was?"

"Completely knocked out."

As he ducked back into the bathroom, she sat up, propping the pillow behind her, recalling the events of the night before. Calling Seth, asking him to come pick her up, asking if she could move in with him and Will, just until she got another place. She'd felt elated, as if she'd been freed from jail.

Will had been waiting for them. He'd welcomed her warmly, telling her she could stay as long as she liked.

Seth exited the bathroom and crossed to the bed, slipping in beside her. She snuggled up to him and laid her head on his shoulder. "Did I really throw my phone out the car window?"

He laughed and threaded his fingers through her hair. "Yup. So they couldn't track you."

"That was kind of stupid."

"They're cops, that's what cops do. We'll get you another one." He kissed her and climbed off the bed. "You hungry?"

"Starving."

"Great, I am too. I'll make us some breakfast-- come down when you're ready."

"Okay. I'm going to take a quick shower."

The minute he left the room, she jumped up and ran to the bathroom. A new toothbrush waited on the counter, along with a hairbrush, face cleanser, and moisturizer. Girl stuff.

When had Seth gotten these? The middle of the night?

She jumped into the shower; the hot spray felt amazing and as she stepped out and wrapped herself in one of the thick, fluffy towels, she wished she'd grabbed at least one clean shirt and pair of panties.

Dressed, she opened the door and stepped out of the bathroom, then stopped in surprise. On the bed sat a half dozen shopping bags from Abercrombie and Fitch.

Girls' things. All in her size.

With a squeal of excitement, she went through each bag. Everything she could need: jeans and khakis, shirts and tees, zip-up hoodie and a real jacket. Even socks, panties and PJs.

She held each one up and looked in the mirror. She used to pass the French Quarter Abercrombie on her way to work. She'd always linger a moment, admiring the clothes, wondering how it would feel to be one of those people who went in empty-handed and came out with bags and bags, all stuffed full.

Now she knew.

She tugged off her shabby jeans and shirt and slipped into her new ones. They felt different against her skin than her Target and Wal-Mart stuff—softer, more luxurious. And she looked different in them. Transformed, like Cinderella. Her eyes a deeper but brighter brown, her skin glowing, her cheeks rosy without blush.

Her? Cinderella? Rolling her eyes at the thought, she hurried downstairs for breakfast.

Seth had made them bacon, eggs and toast. Angel scraped the last of her second helping of eggs from her plate. She thought about getting a third, then decided it'd be too embarrassing—she'd already eaten more than he had.

Will ambled into the kitchen, smiling brightly when he saw her. "Good morning. I trust you slept well?"

"How could I not? That's the most comfortable bed ever."

"Good." He crossed to the coffeepot and poured a cup. "When you're done eating, I have a surprise for you."

"I already got it. The clothes are amazing, I love them. Thank you."

He smiled, obviously pleased. "That's not the surprise."

"No?" She looked at Seth, then back at his uncle.

"No. Close your eyes."

Angel did and Seth took her hand. He guided her outside—she smelled flowers on the breeze, heard the tinkling of a fountain. The patio, and the flagstone walkway around the pool and spa.

They stopped. "Okay, open your eyes."

The pool house. Only it wasn't anymore. The front porch was gone, the windows closed over. Her heart began to thump against the wall of her chest. Like a prison, she thought. Surrounded by flowers.

She took a step back. Seth held tight to her hand. "What's wrong?"

Her head began to pound, her mouth went dry.

"Angel," Will coaxed, "come dear. This is your surprise."

She took a step, then another, forcing herself to put one foot in front of the other. A strange sensation came over her, a twisted combination of fear and anticipation.

Will unlocked the door, eased it open and flipped on the lights.

Angel caught her breath. A studio. Outfitted with everything she could ever need. She stepped into the space, turning in a slow circle to take it all in. Skylights. Easels, tables and drying racks. Equipment cubbies. Pencils and charcoals and pastels. Paints and brushes. Paper. Good paper, the archival stuff with the rag edges. She trailed her fingers along them, loving the feel, then brought a piece to her nose. It smelled different than the cheap stuff she used. Earthy, like wood.

Finally, she looked at Seth; he smiled, eyes crinkling at the corners. She turned her gaze to Will. "Is this. . . this can't all be for . . . me?"

He beamed like a proud father. "All for you."

"Why?"

"Why not? Don't you think you deserve it?"

Of course she didn't. Not her--strange and unwanted Angel Gomez.

Will crossed to her, gathered her hands in his and looked her in the eyes. "This is how much I believe in you."

A lump formed in her throat. Had anyone ever believed in her this way? "This is too much."

"It's not enough," he countered. "Not nearly."

"But this all must have cost . . . so much."

"Remember, you're not to worry about money. I have so much. What better way to spend it than on nurturing a young artist?"

"How?" she asked. "I just got here last night."

"Night before last," Seth corrected.

"What? But I don't—"

"I wasn't kidding when I said you slept a long time."

She'd slept more than twenty-four hours? Angel looked around her again. "Even so, to do all this in that amount of time?"

"Angel, there's something you'll learn about me. I'm a man who makes things happen."

"But—" Her eyes widened. "Wait, today's Monday? What time is it? I'm scheduled for noon."

"Call in sick," Seth said.

"I can't do that."

"Why not? In fact, tell them you have mono or something and will be out all week." She opened her mouth to protest, but before she could, he added, "It's the first place Micki and Zach will look for you. This will give you all some time to cool down."

"Besides," Will said, voice smooth as silk, "wouldn't playing in here this week be so much more fun? And be honest, so much better a use of your time? A talent like you? Serving coffee?"

He said it like it was a fate worse than death. She wanted to tell him it wasn't so bad, but a part of her wanted to agree with him. Not with the worse than death part, but the part about her talent and her time being better spent here. It all felt rushed, yes. But thrilling, too.

"I've got to go." Will looked at Seth. "You'll take care of our young progeny?"

Seth put his arm protectively around her. "Of course, Uncle Will. I won't take my eyes off her."

When the door had clicked shut behind Will, Angel turned in Seth's arms, lifting her face to his. "How should I feel about this?"

"Wonderful."

"You're sure?"

"Yes. Of course."

She frowned. "Then why does it feel sort of . . . wrong? I mean, who does this? It's so much."

He smoothed the crease between her brows with his thumb. "To you, not him. This is a drop in the bucket for him. He's got more money than God. Why not spend it on you?"

Why not? she wondered. Didn't she deserve a big break? Someone who believed in her, her talent and her future, so much?

"It's just, I can't stop wondering . . . what does he want in return?"

Seth hesitated. She saw by his expression that her question bothered him.

When he answered, his tone was measured, thoughtful. "Respect, I guess. Someday, acknowledgment of his part in your success. You deserve this, Angel."

Pride swelled up in her. Hadn't she dreamed of being discovered someday? Now, it was happening.

"Respect doesn't seem like much measured against all . . . this."

He rubbed his nose playfully against hers. "Then, what's the problem? You're so suspicious."

"That's not the way the world works. Somebody gives you something, they want something in return."

He rested his forehead against hers and gazed into her eyes. "We're together, babe. You and me. What can be wrong with that?"

Nothing, she thought, standing on tiptoe to kiss him. Nothing at all.

CHAPTER FORTY-TWO

Monday, October 26
1:10 P.M.

MICKI PARKED HER NEWLY ACQUIRED crapmobile in front of LAM. Tommy had shown up again and had agreed to take a look at the pictures from Bam Bam's phone in an attempt to identify Kyle.

Micki cut the engine but didn't make a move to climb out of the car. Her stop at the coffee shop for information about Sethh had been a bust. Ginger hadn't seen or heard from Angel. She didn't know Seth's last name, or anything else useful. Just that he lived with his uncle in some kind of mansion and worked in sales. Nell, the shop's owner, had known even less.

Her phone pinged the arrival of a text. Zach, she saw. Wondering where she was.

Here now, she replied, then climbed out of the car and headed up the walk. Eli buzzed her in; she found him, the professor, Zach and Tommy waiting in the conference room. The young man looked thinner than the last time they'd been there together, hollow-eyed and pale.

"Sorry I'm late," she said and took a seat at the table.

"Perfect timing," Truebell said, "Tommy is just finishing lunch."

He was indeed, wolfing down a foot-long, roast beef po'boy. It smelled like heaven and her mouth began to water. She wished she'd picked something up at the coffeehouse, and dug in her bag for the pack of peanut butter crackers she'd tossed in on her way out of the house that morning.

She ripped them open and stuffed one into her mouth, grateful Zach didn't comment.

"Why'd you bolt, Tommy?" she asked, timing the question between bites.

He took a swallow of his Barq's root beer. "Why do you think?"

"Let me rephrase that. Why're you back?"

"Thinking I'm safer here than out there."

He took another bite; gravy oozed out and dripped onto the paper the sandwich had been wrapped in.

"Explain."

He looked at Eli in question. "It's okay, Tommy. Tell them everything."

He swallowed, took another swig of the root beer, then wiped his hands on the paper napkin. "You might think I'm crazy."

"Actually, I don't call much of anything crazy anymore."

"Cool." He hesitated again anyway, then began. "So, before, I took off thinking I'd be able to hide out, let all this shit blow over. But I felt them."

"What do you mean 'felt them'?"

"Around me. Watching, following. If I'd gone to the cops, they would've called the white coats to lock me up."

"You say they were following you? You saw them?"

"No, I only felt their presence. Everywhere. Like shadows with eyes. And sometimes—" he bit whatever he was about to say back, looking down at the remnants of his meal, "—never mind."

"Go on, Tommy." Zach said softly. "I've experienced these things--you're sensitive to them, the way I am. I get it, buddy."

Tommy nodded, then let out a shuddering breath. "Sometimes it's like they're trying to get inside me." He lifted his chin as if in challenge. "See, I told you you'd think I was nuts."

Six months ago, she would have. If he had told her this story then, she would have had him committed for a psych eval. A diagnosis of a psychotic disorder, most probably schizophrenia, would have come back. He'd have been labeled, drugged and back out on the street.

"I don't think you're crazy," she said. "Truthfully, I wish you were. It's a bitch knowing this is real."

She'd struck a nerve, Micki noticed, as he teared up and quickly looked away.

"The shadows with eyes, you don't feel them here?"

Before Tommy could reply, Truebell stepped in. "He wouldn't. This is a safe house, protected by our collective light. It's too bright for the dark to penetrate."

He turned to Tommy. "We'll do everything we can to protect you, but you have to help us, too."

He nodded. "The photographs."

"Yes." Micki slid them out of the manila envelope. "These were taken at several local bars by someone we believe was introduced to Kyle via a friend. We're hoping Kyle might be pictured in one of them."

"I'm ready," he said, the confident words belied by the quiver in his voice.

Micki laid them out in a row on the table in front of him. Tommy picked up the first, studied it carefully. She watched as he shifted his gaze from one face to another, fascinated with his eyes. Something about the irises was almost liquid. Like light on the ocean, but subtle. Had they been like that last time? She couldn't recall.

He shook his head, laid that photo down on the table, then went for the next. He repeated the process, each time with the same result. With each discarded photo, her hopes sank a little more. He came to the last, studied it.

"Sorry, I don't—" He stopped, cocking his head. "Wait." He squinted. "This guy." He tapped his finger. "This is him. The photo's really blurry, but . . . yeah, that's Kyle."

Tommy handed her the photo, pointed. "That guy."

A person in the background, slightly blurry, face partially obscured. But she recognized him anyway.

Zach leaned over to get a look. He swore under his breath. Obviously, he recognized him too.

Seth. The man in the photo was Seth.

Their worst fears, realized. And she and Zach had played right into the Dark Bearer's plans by sending Angel running straight to the arms of a monster.

"We've got a problem," she said. "A big one."

"Angel?"

That came from Eli. "Yes," she said. "This guy, it's her boyfriend, Seth. We believe she's with him right now."

"No way," Tommy said. "She wouldn't go with a guy like him."

"She thinks he's her knight in shining armor."

"Then we have to tell her," Tommy said. "We have to!"

"Tommy," Truebell said calmly, "could you give us a few minutes alone?"

He stood, though with obvious reluctance. He looked at Micki. "Angel, she's going to be okay. Right?"

If it was the last thing she did on this earth, Micki thought. "Yeah, she is. I'm going to make sure of it."

A ghost of a smile curved his mouth. "If you need me, I'm totally here."

"Thanks." She forced a smile. "You already helped a lot."

When the door snapped shut behind Tommy, Truebell turned to her. "Tell us exactly what happened."

Micki quickly explained the sequence of events leading up to discovering Angel had taken off.

"I screwed up," Zach said. "I shouldn't have pushed her away. She was so upset, she wouldn't even hear me. Then the cat attacked me and—"

Truebell sat up straighter. "What did you say? About the cat?"

"We were on the porch. The neighborhood stray, who's usually my best friend, turned vicious. While I was trying to pry her claws out of my leg, Angel ran inside."

Micki stepped in. "It was maybe an hour later, when I went to check on her and found she'd run off."

"And you're certain she left of her own volition?"

Truebell, normally the picture of philosophical calm, looked strangely tense.

Eli frowned. "What is it?"

"Not yet," he murmured. "I'm not sure how what I'm considering can even be."

"I'll see if I can reach her." Eli stood. "Excuse me."

Micki watched him go, then turned back to Professor Truebell. "She climbed out her window, not taking anything with her but her purse and backpack. I thought she'd be back. That maybe she'd called Seth to cry on his shoulder."

"Her backpack, you say. Was her sketchbook in it? Her drawing supplies?"

"Yes. I stopped by the coffeehouse this morning, to see if I could catch her. I learned she called in sick for the week. She told her boss she had mono."

"How did she and Seth meet?"

"He came into the coffee shop one night right before closing. She was attacked on her way home, and he saved her."

Zach looked at her. "Mick, the pictures on Reggie Bhear's phone. Of your house, of Angel coming and going. I bet that whole thing—"

"Was a set-up!" she finished for him, launching to her feet. "Son of a bitch, of course it was!"

Eli returned. "She's blocked me."

Micki swung toward him. "What does that mean? Like blocking a friend on Facebook?"

"Ironically, in a way it is. My telepathic call keeps bouncing back."

"What do we do now?" Zach asked.

Her cell vibrated and she checked the display. She didn't recognize the number but hoped it was Angel. She answered. "This is Dare."

"Detective, this is Rachel Adams."

Micki's heart sank. *No, not Bear. Not now.*

"I wanted to let you know, Bear was released into his grandmother's custody. I only just learned of it."

"When?" Micki asked, voice tight.

"Late yesterday. She went over my head, to my boss."

Son of a bitch. He could be anywhere, with anyone.

"I'd just spoken with her. I'd explained that for Bear's safety we wanted keep him in the state's care a little longer. She was on board, very agreeable."

"What happened?"

"I don't know!" Her voice rose. "Viv—that's my boss—said his grandma was furious over the delay and claimed I was acting inappropriately."

Micki looked over her shoulder at Zach, mouthed "we've got to go," and pointed to the door.

Zach nodded and got to his feet, expression wrinkling with concern.

"That doesn't sound like the woman we met. Is there any way your boss could have turned him over to someone other than his grandmother?"

"No way. We check the driver's license, then cross-reference that photo to the one we have online. No," she said again, "impossible. This doesn't feel right, but my hands are tied."

"Ours aren't. Zach and I will see what we can do."

CHAPTER FORTY-THREE

Monday, October 26
2:55 P.M.

MICKI FILLED ZACH IN AS they headed to the car. "Best case," she finished as they buckled up, "you use your blue-eyed mojo to convince granny that Bear's not safe with her."

"And worst case?"

She snapped on the siren and pulled into traffic. "I think you already know."

They fell silent. Micki drove, that worst-case scenario like a devil at her heels. She pictured Reggie Bhear's battered, bloody body, his tortured expression as he basically beat himself to death, and depressed the accelerator, pushing the seen-better-days sedan to its outer limits.

No, she thought, Little Bear wasn't dead. If Seth and his buddies had kidnapped him, they'd gone to a lot of trouble just to kill him. No, they orchestrated this because they needed him. For another home invasion? Or something else?

Zach angled in his seat to look at her. "There hasn't been another home invasion since we arrested Bam Bam and rescued Little Bear. They were on a pretty steady clip until then."

She glanced at him. "You reading my mind, partner?"

Zach looked surprised. "Just thinking aloud."

"Then I guess we're just starting to think alike." Micki roared onto the I-10 ramp doing fifty. "Scary."

"Speaking of scary . . ." Zach grabbed the arm rest to brace himself. "If this cop thing doesn't pan out, you'd have a big future in Nascar. Just saying."

She didn't smile. "Appreciate the love, Hollywood."

"So," he went on, "the question is why? Why'd they stop?"

"Too much pressure from us?"

"You might be giving us a little too much credit, Mick. I'm thinking, either they needed Bear to handle the kids—"

"A stretch."

"—or the invasions served their purpose?"

"They found The Chosen One? But none of those kids have gone missing."

"Yet."

She seemed to digest that; he saw her tighten her fingers on the wheel. "The kids liked Bear. They trusted him, he kept them calm. That's what they need him for."

"Yes," Zach said. "Once they have Little Bear in place to calm and control The Chosen One—"

"They abduct the child. Son of a bitch! Get Nichols on the phone. We need to get security on those kids."

Zach made the call, getting off just in time to grab the arm rest as she wove around a car that failed to yield. "Asshole!" she shouted as they flew past. "You're going to get someone killed!"

"Damn, Mick—" he sucked in a sharp breath, "—just so you know, my testicles now reside in my stomach."

She couldn't help but smile, though grimly. "I'm sure they'll be nice and comfy up there."

"Maybe I'll just shut up and pray now."

"Good idea. In fact, take a nap. I'll let you know if we get there alive."

Although she never had any doubt they would, Zach must have been uncertain because he all but leapt out of the car when they reached Mary Jane Stevens' home.

"You're a maniac, you know that?"

"Whatever." She slammed her door and went around the car to meet him. "I got us here, didn't I?"

Their anything-but-stealth arrival had drawn an audience—the elderly man across the street, puttering in his yard, the young woman on her cell as she pushed a stroller, and the woman next door, in Pepto-Bismol pink rollers and matching pink velour jogging suit—who all stopped what they were doing and stared.

Micki and Zach reached the front door. A package from a home shopping network sat propped up against it. It'd been there long enough to be wet from the sudden storm the day before.

Micki didn't like the looks of that. She saw by Zach's expression that he didn't either. She rang the bell, then knocked. "Mrs. Stevens! It's Detectives Dare and Harris, NOPD."

When there was no reply, she tried again. "Mrs. Stevens, it's urgent we speak with—"

"Yoo-hoo!" the woman in pink velour called to them, waving frantically as she wobbled her way toward them.

At first Micki wondered if the woman was drunk, then realized her extreme apple shape perched atop flimsy wedge-heeled shoes was unbalancing her.

She called out again and Micki lifted her hand in acknowledgement. Instead of slowing down, she seemed to speed up. Micki held her breath, afraid the woman might topple over.

She finally reached them. Out of breath, she fanned herself and batted her eyelashes at Zach. "Are you looking for Mary Jane?"

"We are," he said.

"Good. I'm Beatrice Quick. I know, I know . . . it's funny, since I'm so short and slow. My cross to bear."

"How can I help you, Mrs. Quick?" he asked.

"Beatrice, please." She smiled broadly at him. "My, you're handsome. Are you married?"

"No, ma'am."

"Engaged? In a committed relationship?"

"No ma'am. About Mrs.—"

"Gay?"

"Yes," Micki said, aggravated. "Very gay. Have you seen Mrs. Stevens recently?"

"Very gay? Drats, such a pity." She looked at Micki for the first time. "Oh, hello."

Micki held up her shield. "Detective Dare. My partner, Detective Harris."

Mary Jane looked ready to swoon. "I knew something was wrong."

"How's that, Mrs. Quick?" Micki asked, noticing the woman didn't insist that she call her by her first name.

"I haven't seen her in several days and I was worried. That's why I ran over here."

"She's usually out and about?"

"Oh yes." She beamed. "That's the kind of neighborhood this is.

Very friendly."

"Did you try calling her? Stop by and knock?"

"Called but didn't get an answer. Joe—" she turned and pointed to the man in his yard across the street, who waved in response, "—stopped by. Like you, he didn't get an answer."

"What about her grandson?" Zach asked. "Have you seen him?"

"Little Bear? Not in weeks and weeks." She made a clucking sound with her tongue. "Like I said, very troubling."

"Mrs. Quick . . . Beatrice, you didn't think to call the police?"

Her eyes widened. "Heavens, no! I'm no busybody."

Micki decided they'd wasted enough time. "Ma'am, for your safety and ours, I need you to move away from the home."

"Do I have to?" She sent Zach a pouty look. "This is so—"

"Yes!" Micki snapped. "Detective Harris, kindly escort Mrs. Quick home. If she resists, cuff her. I'm going to take a look around back."

Without a glance back, Micki rounded the corner of the house. A small patio, she saw. Glass sliders, small table and chair. The yard needed a mow.

She crossed to the sliders, peered inside. The family room looked much as it had the night they had been there, neat and tidy, with no sign of Stevens. She pulled on a Nitrile glove, but before she could even try the door, Zach was opening it from the inside.

"Beatrice had a key," he said. "And she told me you need to work on your manners."

"Of course she did," she muttered. "She have anything else to say?"

"Only that she had an unmarried daughter who could probably turn me, should I want to take a whack at it."

Micki nearly choked on a laugh. "She did not."

"Oh, yeah she did. Told her I'd keep it in mind."

Micki stepped into the family room. It felt empty. Like one of those staged, model homes. A faint, sour odor reached her nose and she prepared herself for what was most probably waiting.

Micki glanced at Zach, at his intent expression. She wanted to ask what he was picking up, but knew he would share when he was ready, so she made her way to the kitchen.

Food, strewn across the counter, the floor. Milk spilled. Some sort of stew—looked like dried vomit. She'd never eat gumbo again.

But no dead granny, thank God.

She had put up a fight, Micki thought, slowly circling. The place was a mess, but not the way the home invasions had been. Besides the spilled food, a chair was overturned, a vase lay on its side, silk posies askew. But little else.

"Yo, Hollywood," she called, "come take a look." When he didn't respond, she looked around the corner.

He hadn't moved. "What?' she asked.

"Weird. A box. Shut and sealed."

"What kind of box? A coffin?"

He shook his head. "It's more like I sense a box, the feeling of being trapped in it. There's a light inside, feeble, growing dimmer."

"Stevens?"

"I think so." He met her eyes. "She's alive. And she's here."

"Where?"

"I don't know. A closet maybe. Someplace close. Dark. She can't get out. If the dimming light means what I think it does, we don't have much time."

They went from room to room, checking inside closets and under beds. The kitchen turned out to be the only room disturbed in any way.

When none of those panned out, they located the attic. Zach ascended the pull-down ladder, but it proved a bust, too.

"I don't get it," he said. "I was sure she was—"

"Her car," Micki said. "That's it, the trunk. It's got to be."

They found the car keys in Stevens' purse, sitting untouched on the counter, and hurried out to the garage. An old Buick sedan. Big back end, roomy. Great body-carrying trunk.

"Mrs. Stevens," Micki said as Zach tried the first key, "if you're in there, we'll have you out in a flash. Just hold on."

The third key was the right one; the trunk lid popped open.

Empty. The trunk was empty.

"Dammit!" Micki made a sound of frustration. "I was so certain."

"Where, then? I was so sure." He looked back at the door into the house. "Let's see if I can still pick her up. Or maybe something else will come to me."

As they reentered the house, Micki heard a faint scratching sound. Like a cat pawing at its litter box or a branch against a window.

"You hear that?"

Zach stopped. "What?"

It came again; he nodded. "Where's it coming from?"

They followed the sound in the family room. Micki stopped, turning in a slow circle, taking in every detail.

"I've got the box again," he said. "She's here. In this room."

She surveyed the room again—the sofa and TV, tucked into the corner on a stand; a small recliner; the fireplace.

"She can't be," Micki said. "There's no place for her to be stashed."

Her gaze landed on the television, then lowered to the carpeting. Judging by the indentations, the stand had been moved recently. "Oh my God! Give me a hand."

Together they moved the TV and stand. Sure enough, there was a door to a crawl space, one of those little oddities old homes had.

And there, stuffed inside, was Mary Jane Stevens.

CHAPTER FORTY-FOUR

Monday, October 26
6:10 P.M.

ANGEL SAT ON A TALL stool facing an easel. On it sat a board with an eighteen-by-twenty-four piece of paper clipped to it. She hadn't known where to begin; Will had suggested to start with an existing sketch and enlarge it. Add detail. The images would make more of a statement, he said. They would command the viewer's attention.

That made sense. But it felt wrong. Every stroke and mark, every choice of shading. She'd told herself to just power through; every lift of her hand seemed an effort.

Maybe it was the drawing she'd chosen. The last one, with Bear and Zander and Seth. And the zipper.

She couldn't stop focusing on that zipper.

What did it mean? What was trying to break free?

"Hey."

She looked over her shoulder. Seth and Will. She was happy to see Seth, but his uncle always made her feel slightly uncomfortable. He shouldn't; he'd been so kind to her, so incredibly generous. "Hey."

"Mind some company?"

"I'd love it."

Seth crossed to her, bent and kissed her. Not a quick brush of his lips against hers, but a deep, passionate kiss. She stiffened, pressed her hands against chest, embarrassed with the public display of affection.

He jerked away as if stung. She hadn't meant to hurt his feelings and tried to catch his eye, to silently explain, but he refused to look at her.

Seeming oblivious, Will stopped in front of the easel. "How's the work going?"

"Good." She shifted, uncomfortable. "But the larger scale feels weird."

"That's to be expected." He cocked his head, studying. "Who is this?" he asked, indicating Alexander.

"That's Zander. I babysit him sometimes."

"How do you know him?"

"He's Micki's best friend's kid. Jacqui Clark. She's pretty cool."

He looked at her, his dark gaze seeming to penetrate to her core. "Let yourself go, Angel. Don't hold back."

She twisted her fingers together. "I'm trying."

"It's all new and unfamiliar," he said, patting her shoulder. "It'll get easier."

His attempt to reassure her left her feeling threatened instead. It was all she could do not to shudder. She called herself an idiot and shook the feeling off.

"I have a surprise for you," he said.

"Another one?"

He laughed. "Yes, *another* one. I've arranged for a friend of mine to pay you a visit here. He owns a gallery in the Warehouse District."

She glanced at Seth in question, then back at Will. "I don't understand. I don't have anything but sketches—"

"I want to introduce you, get you on his radar. You may not be ready for a show now, but you will be. I want him to be thinking about *you*, Angel."

"But . . . I don't know if I'm ready for this, Will."

Something passed over his expression. Like a cloud. In that instant, all resemblance to the kind and generous man she knew was gone.

"For God's sake, Angel! Look at me."

She responded automatically to the command. His gaze drew her in, like the depths of a dark sea.

"Don't you want it all? Everything this world has to offer?"

"I guess so. I just never believed—"

He cut her off, impatient. "Believe now. Dream big. For yourself, because no one's going to do it for you. Not even me. Do you understand?"

Suddenly, she did. Confidence surged up in her. With it came a desire to have it all, everything—money and fame and importance in the art community. To *be* somebody, just like he said. She did deserve it. She was that good.

"Do you understand?" he asked again.

"You're right. How can I expect good things to come to me if I don't grab them?"

"That's my girl." He kissed her forehead, then turned to Seth. "I have some things to do before our meeting. Give me thirty minutes, then meet me at the car."

"Fine."

The word was clipped. Angry sounding. Angel frowned and watched Will leave the studio, then made a sound of surprise when Seth grabbed her arm.

"What was that all about?"

"What?"

"When I kissed you? You pushed me away."

"I was embarrassed. Your uncle was right there—"

"He's not my uncle. Stop calling him that."

"You told me to!"

He grabbed her arm. "Well, I don't like it."

She narrowed her eyes. "You're jealous."

"What? That's ridiculous!"

"Because he believes in me." She jerked free of his grasp. "He thinks *I'm* an amazing talent."

"Good for you." He made a dismissive gesture. "Changing already, I see."

"What's *that* supposed to mean?"

"Figure it out." He started for the door.

"I don't know why I ever thought I loved you."

He stopped, looked back at her, the expression in his eyes anguished. "I don't either."

Regret swamped her. With a cry, she ran to him, threw her arms around him. "I'm so sorry, Seth. Forgive me . . . I don't know what came over me!"

He looped his arms around her, holding her tightly. "It's okay, baby. He has that effect on people."

She clung to him. "Is it wrong for me to believe in myself?"

He drew away from her and looked into her eyes. "Of course not, baby. Just don't start believing in him more than me."

"Never," she promised, tone fierce.

He let out a long, contented sounding breath. "This is the first time

I've felt right since kissing you goodbye this morning."

"What's wrong?"

"Just a rough day. Will can be . . . demanding." He paused. "Sometimes I think he likes to make me feel stupid."

His phone pinged the arrival of a text message. He looked at it and frowned. "It's Will. He's ready and impatiently waiting."

He kissed her, then started toward the door, stopping when he reached it, looking back at her. "I love you, Angel."

And then he was gone. She stared at the closed door, thoughts whirling. She shut her eyes and her head filled with her drawing—Seth, the zipper straining to lower.

And then it did. By two teeth.

Angel caught her breath. That was it, she realized. She was meant to free him. But from what? she wondered.

No, not what. Who.

Will. She was meant to free him from Will.

CHAPTER FORTY-FIVE

Monday, October 26
8:40 P.M.

MARY JANE STEVENS HAD BEEN wedged into that tiny crawl space like a baby in a womb. Zach could only imagine how painful that must have been. When he eased her out of the space, he worried she might break in half. She hadn't been able to stand, let alone walk, and slipped in and out of consciousness all the way to the hospital.

She'd been admitted, treated for shock, dehydration and physical trauma. But it could have been worse, Zach acknowledged. Much worse.

He and Micki stepped off the elevator and crossed to the information desk. The doctor had finally given them permission to question her—if they made it quick and kept it stress free.

"Detectives Harris and Dare," he said holding up his shield. "We're here to see Mary Jane Stevens."

The nurse directed them down the hall and in a matter of moments were tapping on Stevens' half-open door. Zach peeked inside. "Mrs. Stevens," he said softly. "It's Detectives Harris and Dare."

She turned her head their way and smiled weakly. "My saviors."

He crossed to the bed, pulled up a chair and sat. Micki held back and stood at the foot of the bed. "You gave us a scare."

Her eyes filled with tears as he reached across and curved his hand around hers.

Lingering terror. The remnants of panic. Gratitude.

"You're going to be okay," he said. "Look at me, Mary Jane. It's over. You're safe now."

She released a breath that to him seemed to come from the very depths of her being, as if she had been secreting it inside until this very moment. As she expelled it, that terror and panic softened around the edges.

"Do you think you could answer a few questions for us?" Micki asked.

"I would do anything for you." She moved her watery gaze between them. "Both of you. If you hadn't shown up when you did . . ."

Her chin began to tremble and Zach gave her hand a squeeze. "But we did show up and you're going to be fine."

She nodded, visibly gathering herself together. "They have him, don't they?"

"Who, Mrs. Stevens?"

"My Little Bear."

"Yes," Zach agreed, "they do. But we're going to get him back. That's why we're here."

Micki stepped in. "Can you tell us what happened? From beginning to end, Mrs. Stevens. Your words."

"I was in the kitchen. I'd made chicken gumbo and was preparing a bowl for supper. A young man came to the door. He seemed so nice. He asked if he could use the phone."

"So you let him in."

"Yes. Next thing I know he had his arm around my throat and was dragging me to the kitchen. There were others at the back door. He let them in."

"How many of them were there all together?"

"Four."

"Can you describe them?"

"They were young. One, the leader, was older than the other three. They all wore jeans and sweatshirts."

"Was there anything written on the sweatshirts? Any logo that you can remember?"

She narrowed her eyes in thought, then shook her head. "I don't remember. They were dark blue, I think. Maybe dark gray . . . it all happened so fast . . . it's jumbled up in my mind."

"What did they want?" Micki asked.

She looked down at her lap, then back up at them. "To know where Little Bear was. I wouldn't tell them. That's when they—" she cleared her throat and went on, "—started breaking things. One slapped my face. When I started to cry, it seemed to make them madder. I kept thinking, why are they doing this to me? What purpose did they have for it?"

"So you told them how to find Bear?"

She shook her head. "They checked my phone. Rachel had left me a message. I didn't erase it because . . . because I—" Tears rolled down her cheeks. "And now they have him."

"Mrs. Stevens," Micki said, "we're going to find him and bring him home to you. But we need your help. I have some photographs with me. I need you to take a look at them, see if one or more of the men who did this to you is pictured. Can you do that?"

She nodded. Mick handed her each of the photos, giving her a moment to study each one thoroughly before handing her another, and saving the one in which Seth was pictured for last.

Micki handed it to her. For a long time, the woman stared at the image. Then she nodded and pointed. "Him. I recognize him."

Seth. Micki glanced at Zach. He looked as devastated as she felt.

"The others were younger. He was definitely the one in charge."

"How did you know?"

"The others kept telling him to just shoot me."

"He had a gun?"

"I thought you knew that." She twisted her fingers together. "He didn't want to."

"Shoot you?"

"Yes."

"He said so?"

"No, I *felt* it. This distaste . . ." She moved her gaze between the two, as if for approval, then settled on Zach. "I almost felt sorry for him. You understand, don't you, Detective Harris? He wasn't bad."

Zach absorbed her words. Was that Lightkeeper in her, reading him? Or a traumatized old woman, desperate to find the good in someone?

Micki stepped in before Zach could respond. "Maybe he wasn't as vicious as the other three, but you could have died in that cabinet."

Zach took over. "So the other three said to shoot you?"

"Yes."

"How did you end up in the crawl space behind the TV.?"

"The one from the photo said he had a better idea, to put me in there."

Micki frowned. "How did he know that space was there? It's well hidden by the TV. and entertainment stand."

Her face went blank. She blinked at them, obviously not having thought of that before now.

"I don't . . . know. I was thinking about it, though. I always imagined hiding in there if someone broke in. I remember wishing I'd had a warning and time to hide. That's where I would have gone."

Seth read her thoughts, Zach realized.

"Can you tell us anything else, Mrs. Stevens?" Micki asked.

"I begged them to just go. I promised not to say anything to anyone." She paused. "I didn't fight them. An old woman like me. What could I have done against them? But they hurt me anyway, on purpose. They laughed about it."

Her eyes brimmed with tears; her voice shook. "I don't understand why. Why did they hurt me?"

The question of every innocent victim, perhaps from the beginning of time. Zach squeezed her hand and looked in her eyes. "I'm sorry they hurt you, Mary Jane."

"Thank you." She clung to his hand. "Find my Little Bear. Please, Detective Harris."

He leaned forward to pat her hand. "I'm going to try. I won't give up, I promise."

They took their leave of her then but she stopped them at the door. "Detectives?"

They turned back. "What's his name? That young man in the photo?"

"Kyle."

"Kyle," she repeated. "He didn't laugh. And when they . . . pushed me into the cubby, he turned his back. So he didn't have to see."

"Thank you, Mrs. Stevens," Micki said. "If you think of anything else, call us. Anytime."

Her eyes were closed before Micki had even finished the sentence. Zach gently shut the door behind them.

"Good cop, bad cop," Micki muttered, turning in the direction of the elevator.

"What?" he asked, falling in step with her.

"Seth, playing the good cop."

"Why would he?"

"To earn her trust."

"Why bother? He didn't need it."

She frowned. "So, what are you saying? You think he really does have a heart?"

Zach shrugged. "Maybe. Maybe not. What Stevens described is someone who's seriously conflicted over what he's gotten himself into."

She snorted. "And maybe true love is transforming him from a piece of shit into a hero?"

"Maybe."

They reached the elevator. It arrived and they stepped on with several others, then rode down in silence. Mick resumed their conversation the moment they were out of earshot.

"He's a bad guy, Hollywood. A really bad guy. Yeah, he didn't shoot her, but he no doubt thought she'd die in there. In that case, shooting her would have been the humane thing to do."

"I understand why you feel that way, Mick."

"You don't?"

"I didn't say that."

"He's attached to the Dark Bearer—"

"I don't think he is. I would have picked up the energy."

"Okay, so he's aligned with one," she went on, cranking the engine. "He was playing at having a heart just in case we reached Stevens in time. Covering his bases."

Zach angled to face her. "Stevens has Lightkeeper in her, I'm almost positive."

"So?"

"She felt sorry for Seth. She felt he didn't want to hurt her . . . that he found it distasteful. I think the Lightkeeper part of her was reading him."

She cocked an eyebrow. "Or she wasn't reading him and he was playing her, and quite successfully I might add."

A corner of his mouth lifted. "I take it that's what you're going with?"

"Hell, yes. All the way."

"So we'll agree to disagree?"

"I guess we will." They took the ramp onto Mississippi River Bridge. "I say we have another chat with Eli and Truebell. Bring them up to speed and see if they have any ideas."

Zach's phone went off. He looked at the display and smiled ruefully. "Speak of the Prof and up he pops. Professor," he answered, "Mick and I were just talking about coming over to see you."

"Not now. First thing in the morning."

He sounded different, anxious, and Zach frowned. "You talked to Rachel?"

"Yes. I know we've lost Bear."

"Lost? Not permanently. Mick and I are going to get him back.

Angel, too."

"We'll talk more in the morning."

"What's going on, Professor?"

"We'll talk then. Both of you, get some rest."

And then he was gone. Zach looked at Mick. "That was frickin' weird."

She glanced at him. "What?"

"Truebell. He didn't sound like himself."

"Who'd he sound like?"

"Like Parker. All business, to the point of terse."

"I wonder why?"

"He wants us to meet in the morning. I guess we'll find out then."

CHAPTER FORTY-SIX

Monday, October 26
9:56 P.M.

IT WAS NEARLY TEN BEFORE Angel left the studio. She was tired, hungry and at the same time, oddly elated. Her work had gone well. She'd felt inspired. Will was right. She had to believe in herself. Nobody else could do that for her, not even Seth. She wanted all that the world had to offer. She was going to dream big—for herself and her future.

But the truth was, she suspected her elation had more to do with Seth saying he loved her than with her new-found confidence.

He. Loved. Her.

Amazing. Mind-blowing.

Perfect.

Smiling to herself, she crossed the patio and slipped inside, anxious to find him. Hearing Seth and Will talking in the kitchen, she headed that way, her stomach rumbling. She hadn't taken a break for dinner and now she felt as if she could eat a whole pizza, with everything on it. Maybe she and Seth could order one? Even if he'd already eaten, he'd be hungry again by the time the pizza arrived—he could eat more than anyone she'd ever known.

The kitchen came into view, light spilling out into the dark hallway. She opened her mouth to call out a greeting, then shut it when she heard her name.

Will, his voice low. Then Seth. Angry.

Angel inched closer to the doorway, careful to stay out of their line of sight. She pressed herself close to the wall and when she angled her head just right, could see them reflected in one of the room's many windows.

The glow of the pendant lights cast strange shadows on their faces.

"Stay away from her," Seth said, voice tight.

She frowned. Her? No way could he be talking about—

"What's the matter? Worried I'll steal her away from you?"

Will's words were both sneer and challenge. Her heart lurched to her throat.

"Shut the fuck up, asshole."

"Maybe a threesome, Seth? You'd like that, I bet. I know I would."

Angel clapped a hand to her mouth to keep a gasp from spilling past her lips. He was awful, vile and disgusting.

"You go near her and I'll—"

"What, big man? You forget your place. You're here because *I* allow it. She's here because *I* allow it. I *own* you, both of you."

Angel pressed deeper into the shadow, heart thundering. There was no love or respect between Seth and Will, that was obvious. Will controlled Seth. And Seth hated him for it. So, why did he stay?

She thought of her drawing. The zipper, something fighting to get out.

Their raised voices drew her attention.

"You don't own me and you sure as hell don't own her! She and I will go. We don't need you or all this . . . stuff."

"Don't fuck with me, you little shit. I can make bad things happen—to both of you."

"She's mine." Seth all but spat the words. "I'll fight for her."

"What? Do you *love* her?"

"Yes."

Will laughed, the sound somehow obscene; it crawled along her nerve endings like a chill wind.

"Love? Please, there's no such thing. Not in our world."

She closed her eyes and wished to be gone. To be anywhere but here with this horrible . . .

Not a man. A monster.

A Dark Bearer.

Zach and Micki had tried to warn her . . . She could run now. They wouldn't realize she had left—

No, she wouldn't leave Seth. He may have aligned himself with a monster, but he wasn't one himself. She could save him. It's what she was meant to do.

She closed her eyes. *Eli . . . help me! I've made a terrible, terrible mistake.*

Her plea seemed to bounce back at her, echoing hollowly, as if Eli had rejected her call. Had Eli turned his back on her the way she'd turned her back on Micki and Zach?

"In our world," Will went on, "there's power and control. There's sex. But not love."

"You're wrong. I love her."

Will laughed again. "All I'd have to do is crook my finger in her direction and she'd be mine. She's half there already."

Angel bit her lip to keep from shouting that he was wrong. That she would never allow him to touch her. That what she and Seth felt for each was real, that it was pure.

She longed to charge out of her hiding place and into the kitchen. Stand up for what she believed in, stand by the man she loved.

But something primal held her back. Fear, she acknowledged. Of Will. His power.

For he was powerful, she knew. He could crush them both.

Angel backed away, moving as carefully and quietly as she could. Hoping, praying, they didn't choose now to leave the kitchen. She wouldn't be able to hide that she'd been eavesdropping or fake her feelings, and Will would know that he repulsed her.

She made it to the far side of the great room and the ornate staircase that led to the second floor, then, up and into the bedroom, and from there into her private bathroom, where she bent over the commode and vomited.

CHAPTER FORTY-SEVEN

Tuesday, October 27
3:36 A.M.

ANGEL SAT CROSS-LEGGED ON THE bed. She had thought this all through. While Will slept, she and Seth would gather up their things and go. They had each other; they didn't need anything else.

She heard Seth in the hallway outside the door. She closed her eyes and took a deep breath. After the vile things Will had said, he would see it her way. He had to.

He stopped when he saw her there, waiting for him. "Babe? What's wrong?"

For a moment she couldn't find her voice. When she did, it shook. "We need to talk."

Seth's expression went from worried to panicked. "Please, don't leave me."

She thought of his and Will's fight, of Will's claim that she would choose him over Seth. No wonder he had jumped to that conclusion first thing.

"I'm not leaving you." Angel held out her hand. He crossed to the bed and took it; she drew him down beside her.

He curled up next to her, cradling her body against to his. "I went to the studio and you weren't there. For a moment I thought I'd lost you."

She turned so she could look him in the eyes. "Do you love me? Really love me?"

"I do." He searched her gaze. "You're trembling. What's wrong?"

"There's something about me I haven't told you."

"What, babe?"

"It's about my drawings." She pressed her lips together a moment, second- guessing herself. But he needed to know who she really was. How could they have a life together if he didn't? "My drawings . . . sometimes they're . . . more than just drawings."

"What do you mean?"

"I dream the images, right?" He nodded and she went on, voice wobbly. "Then, when they're finished, they come true."

"Come true?" He drew his eyebrows together. "I don't get what you're saying."

"It's a special thing I can do. My drawings are prophetic; they predict the future."

He studied her a moment, expression intent. Then he smiled. "Maybe they seem that way, because your art's so personal. Sort of autobiographical, right?"

"It's more than that, Seth."

"So . . . that drawing you were working on today is prophetic."

She held his gaze. "Yes."

He blinked, his expression suddenly seeming vulnerable. "You know what's happening? You create these really cool drawings, using bits and pieces of things from your life, some more symbolic than others." When she didn't respond, he went on, "Think about it, babe. You make them prophetic *after the fact*. How can it be predicting the future when you don't know about it until after whatever it is happens? You see what I'm saying?"

"It's more than that," she said again. "I'm sorry I didn't tell you sooner."

He didn't reply, and she took a deep breath, then let it out slowly. "I can't stay here, in this house with him anymore. We . . . you and I, we need to go."

"What are you talking about? Why can't you . . . Go where?"

"Away from here." She straddled his lap so she could look him in the eyes. She cupped his face in her hands. "Let's just go. Please."

"That's not a destination, babe. Tell me where you want to go and we will."

"Away from *him*, Seth. Micki would take us in."

His expression hardened. "The Micki who didn't want us to be together? The one who told you I was too old for you? The one you said you hated? *That* Micki?"

Her cheeks burned. He was right. Not that many days ago, she'd been crying about how awful Micki was. How Micki didn't understand anything—and certainly not true love.

"She would help us," Angel said, knowing in her heart it was true. "She would, I'd stake my life on it."

"Why do we need help?" he asked. "We have everything *and* each other."

"I heard you and Will in the kitchen. I heard what he said."

"You were spying on us?"

"No . . . I was coming inside to get something to eat and there you two were. You know what I heard, Seth. You know how sick it was."

He shifted his gaze. "Look at me," she said.

He did. The shame in his eyes made her want to weep.

"We were fighting," he said. "Big deal."

"You and Will are supposed to be a family. Families don't fight like that."

"So you're an expert in how families should and shouldn't behave?"

She climbed off his lap, stung. "I know right from wrong. Do you, Seth?"

"C'mon, Angel." This time it was he who held out his hand. "It was an argument. That's all."

"Do you really believe the things he said were okay? Or that beat-down was a simple argument?"

"Give me your hand." He flexed his fingers. "Please, sweetheart."

She shook her head. "I don't think so."

He lowered his arm. "Look, Will plays to win. You don't get to be as important or as powerful as he is by not playing that way. I pissed him off and he went in for the kill.

"Those ugly things about you and him, he didn't mean them. He wanted to hurt me. And he knew exactly how to trip my switch."

"Me."

"Yes, you. Because you're everything to me."

"He said he owns you."

"He doesn't." The words came out ferociously. "Nobody does."

"So we could go? Just pick up and leave?"

"Of course." He tilted his head to meet her eyes. "But, Angel, why would we?"

"You know why. It's not right . . . the way he treated you. The things he said."

"He's done so much for me, taking me in and raising me. Giving me a home, family, and an education."

The strings, Angel thought. The ones that tied him to Will. She saw them now. Why didn't he?

"He lets us be together," Seth went on. "He doesn't judge us. And he believes in you. Your talent. So much that he created that beautiful studio. And the gallery contact, who's coming to see you. *You*, babe. Who else believes in your art that way?"

"There's something else, Seth, about my drawing, the one you looked at today. You're trying to get away from him."

"Why do you . . . what makes you think that?"

"The zipper, Seth. I wondered about it at first, but understood today what it represented."

"And what's that?"

"Your spirit's trying to get free. Or get out. I think you're trying to break the hold he has on you and I'm supposed to help."

He went white. "I don't know . . . what to say or how to . . . respond."

Angel knelt beside him on the bed, clutching his hands in hers, trying as hard as she could to transmit the urgency she felt. "I got the zipper to lower, just a little. I know I'm right about this and we might not have much time. Please, Seth, let's just go."

He stared at her a moment, a shudder moving over him. "It's a big step . . . I need to . . . think it all through. Figure out how we're going to . . . do it."

"We could just go, while he's sleeping!" She heard the hopefulness in her voice. "Or when he goes out."

"Come here." He drew her down to him, so they lay side by side, facing each other. "Let me take care of this, Angel. I promise, I'll do what I have to."

Tears of joy stung her eyes and she kissed him. "I knew you'd understand," she said. "I knew it."

CHAPTER FORTY-EIGHT

Tuesday, October 27
8:03 A.M.

THE NEXT MORNING MICKI AND Zach met at LAM. She'd slept little of the precious few hours she'd allotted herself; from the look of Zach, he hadn't slept either. She clutched her coffee cup—a quad latte, no less—like a lifeline.

Eli had been waiting for them but other than a greeting, he'd said little. She wasn't sure if his reticence was in deference to their obvious fatigue or because he wasn't cleared to speak until Truebell arrived.

Which he finally did, ten minutes behind them. Micki saw from his expression that she was not going to like what he had to say.

"Sorry I'm late," he said and smiled, although the smile didn't reach his eyes. "I had a conference call."

He sat, reached for the carafe and poured himself a cup of coffee. Micki noted it was the first time she'd seen him drink the beverage.

"You called the meeting," she said watching him sip. "What's on your mind?"

"There's something . . . It's troubling news. About Angel."

Her stomach tightened; she waited, though the waiting was agony.

"We think we've lost her."

Her heart seemed to jump to her throat. "What do you mean?" She looked at Zach, then back at Truebell. "She's not . . . you don't mean—"

"Dead? No, not physically. Dead to us? Very possibly."

"You think she's turned?" Zach said, sounding as incredulous as she felt. "Then you don't know Angel."

"Zach's right," Micki said. "There's no way. Not Angel, not possible."

"Hear us out," Truebell said. "But I'm warning you, it's not pleasant."

His gaze lingered on Zach. It seemed to say "prepare yourself." Why? Would this information affect Zach more than her?

"For quite some time we've heard rumors, troubling rumors . . . about experiments the Dark One's been carrying out."

"For years, actually," Eli added. "But always unsubstantiated. Until recently."

"What sort of experiments?" she asked.

"Attempts to create the Chosen One."

Zach sat up straighter. "What do you mean, *create* the Chosen One? Like Frankenstein?"

"A disturbing but morally accurate analogy, Zachary. To refresh your memory, the prophecy foretells the birth of one who is half—"

"Half light and half dark—" Micki said, cutting him off, wanting him to get to it, "—and will either save humanity or bring its final destruction. Some things you don't forget."

"Yes, Michaela," Truebell went on in his infuriatingly unhurried way. "A being that is half light and half dark. Exactly half of each."

Micki moved her gaze between Truebell and Eli. "Is that even possible?"

"If we're to believe the ancient writings, yes."

"*If* we're to believe?" She looked at him in surprise. "You don't, do you?"

"That's not easy to answer. The text conveys philosophical truths about balance, survival and—"

"I'm not one of your students, Professor, so don't give me a lecture. Yes or no? Real simple."

"The fact is, what I believe doesn't matter. The Dark One believes it and he's taking steps to ensure the scale tips in his favor."

"Spit it out, Professor," Zach said, voice tight. "What kind of experiments? Test tube babies? In vitro fertilization?"

"Nothing so clinical." Truebell didn't blink, but Micki saw emotion flicker in his eyes. "Abduction, rape. In some cases, imprisonment at breeding compounds."

It took her a moment to process the scope of what he was saying. She shook her head. "And you've just . . . sat back and let this happen?"

She saw the emotion again. This time she was able to put a name to it—guilt. She didn't need to condemn him; he condemned himself.

"Like I said, these were rumors. We had no proof."

"I don't understand." She frowned. "These are reportable crimes. Family members report their loved ones missing. Rape victims give statements, investigations are begun."

"How many rapes occur in this city alone, Detective? In a calendar year? Over a hundred?"

"Unfortunately, yes. At least.

"And how many go unreported? I'm sure you have some sort of reliable statistic on that."

"The most recent estimate is about fifty percent."

"And those stats are for the general population, yes? What happens when you factor in the ages of the victims? Their economic status and support system—or lack of one?"

"The number goes up. Dramatically."

"What about runaways? How many of those, nationwide?" He didn't wait for a response. "A couple million, give or take. And what, Detective Dare, is your department's call-to-action for a reported runaway?"

"Unless we know the individual's in imminent danger—"

"You do nothing. No Amber Alert, searches or task force teams. It's considered a family problem."

Eli stepped in. "Factor in what we know about Half Lights, especially young—"

"Whoa, wait." Frowning, Zach glanced from one to the other. "Why Half Lights?"

"They're especially vulnerable." Eli turned to Zach. "They're disenfranchised, often troubled. Less likely to report. And yes, they provide an appropriate vessel because they're already—"

"Mutations?"

"No, Zachary," Truebell said, tone chiding, "genetically predisposed."

Micki snorted. "Seems to me, the best bet for creating this Chosen One would be for a Full Light and a Dark Bearer to mate."

"Impossible, Michaela. The sex act between Lightkeepers is . . . different."

"How so?"

"It involves not just these bodies we inhabit, but our light force as well. And darkness cannot exist in the light."

"And vice versa," Zach said.

Eli folded his hands on the table in front of him. "Actually, light, however feeble, can exist in the dark. Until it's deliberately snuffed out."

Micki thought of the night she was shot, of watching the bartender's metamorphosis, his writhing in pain, begging for the last of his light to be ripped from him.

"How many children?" she asked. "How many products of these unions are out there?"

"We have no idea. Hundreds, maybe thousands. It's a big planet."

"How can that . . . Where are they?"

"All over. With their biological mothers, adopted or in foster care—"

"Little Theo," Zach said, tersely. "The Fowler sisters and the Carlson boys."

Truebell agreed. "We'd thought this Dark Bearer was searching for the Chosen One, and we were right. What we didn't realize is that these aren't random children he's searching for, these are ones he considers his."

Micki recoiled from the idea. His? Rape was a violent, angry and soul-shattering act. And rape with the intent to . . . create life? To create a monster? And then for the ultimate perpetrator to call himself father?

Angry, she balled her hands into fists. Her fury was directed toward the perpetrators, yes. But also at Truebell and Eli, who could sit there and calmly share this information, showing as much emotion as T.V. newscasters. Maybe less. To suspect for years, and to do . . . nothing. Hundreds, he'd said. Hundreds of women, lives broken. Hundreds of children, conceived not in love, or even in lust, but in violence. With the intent to corrupt nature.

"What could we have done?"

Eli, in her head. She looked at him. *"Something. Anything."*

"You don't understand."

"I think I do. Get the fuck out of my head."

"What does this have to do with Angel?" Zach asked.

"We believe she's a product of one of these experiments—"

"No." Zach's vehemence left no room for argument. "Absolutely untrue."

Micki stepped in. "I've seen her light. When Zach clasped her hand the first time, the connection glowed."

"She's definitely a strong Half Light. And especially gifted." Truebell paused. "But she also has Dark Bearer in her."

"You're full of shit," Zach said. "She's one of us and she needs our help. Instead, you sit here and malign her?" He pushed away from the table. "I'm out of here."

"Hear me out, Zach. It came to me when you told me about the cat attacking you. Dark Bearers can control animals."

"And Lightkeepers can't?"

He shook his head. "We can't usurp the free will of any creature. Nor can we use our light force against nature."

"The cat went a little nuts," he said. "Big deal. She wouldn't be the first feline to do that. It happens."

"No, it doesn't. Not like that. You and Angel were arguing; she turned the animal against you—"

"She wouldn't do that."

"She most probably wasn't even aware she was doing it. She has abilities that extend far beyond what she knows. And she is now in the company of those who would love to expose and exploit those gifts."

"No," Micki said. "She wouldn't turn against us."

"Hasn't she already? She ran away without a word. She hasn't contacted any of us for help, either traditionally or telepathically. In fact, Eli has repeatedly reached out to her, hoping to break through, but has gotten nothing but a psychic wall. She's obviously blocked him."

Eli stepped in. "It's a seduction, Michaela. They bring her dark nature forward subtly. The Dark One knows our hopes, dreams and desires. Our hurts, where we thirst for vengeance, who we long to strike down for hurting us."

"It feels right," Truebell went on, "so natural, so *deserved.* What we long for most on this earth . . . suddenly ours. He plays to our human weaknesses, be it pride, envy, greed—"

"Gluttony, anger, lust or sloth," Micki finished for him, recalling the list she'd been made to memorize in Sunday school.

"Think about it, Michaela." Eli leaned forward. "What did Angel long for most? To fit in, to be loved." He looked at Zach. "And to be a recognized artist. You know that's true."

All the pieces fit, she acknowledged, a sinking sensation in her gut. "And Seth and his uncle gave her both," she said.

"Yes. Angel and Seth meeting was a set-up. Her falling in love with him was the most important part of their plan. It's how they manipulated her."

Micki felt sick at the thought of Angel being used that way, of their using love to create evil. She flexed her fingers. "Son of a bitch was in my home. Right under my nose."

Zach spoke up. "Angel told me how being with him felt right, like he was the other piece of her. How did they accomplish that? How do you fake that?"

"It wasn't faked, Zachary. Her immediate connection to him was probably biological. Her dark side was reacting to his. It'd be like a part of her coming to life for the very first time. They built from there."

"You said you have proof now," Zach said, tone icy. "Surely you're not pinning all this speculation on a cat taking a sudden dislike to me."

"No." He shifted his gaze slightly. "We have a victim. She escaped a breeding farm and found us."

"We need to talk to her," Micki said.

"Parker's debriefing her."

"Debriefing? In Washington, you mean?" Zach frowned. "Is she one of ours?"

Truebell hesitated a moment. "Yes."

"So, you're just washing your hands of Angel?"

"We will if we have to. These experiments—"

"Don't," Zach said, all but spitting out the word. "These aren't *experiments.* They're crimes. With victims. A lot of them." He looked at her. "I've had enough, I'll be in the car."

She watched him go, then turned back to Truebell. "He's right. All those victims? You don't seem very concerned about them."

"We are, Michaela, I promise you that. But we have to look beyond the individuals, at the bigger picture. We need to cut off the head of the snake."

She stood, disgusted. "Crimes against individuals? There isn't a bigger picture."

"Obviously, we're going to disagree on this. Talk to him, Michaela. Calm him down. We need him."

"I'll talk to him. But not because *you* need him, because Angel and Little Bear do."

Micki found Zach leaning against the car, looking as relaxed as a coiled snake. He faced away from LAM and didn't look at her when she approached.

"This is bullshit," he said tightly. "Sanctimonious assholes."

"Why are you so angry?"

"Aren't you?"

"Hell, yeah, I'm pissed. Bastard has Angel and Bear. And I mean to get them back."

"That's not what I'm talking about. All those kids, *experiments?* What's a life worth? Not much, obviously. And the life of a Half Light? Even less than that."

This was personal for him, she saw. Because of what he was, because it could have been him.

"I get it, partner. It's an abomination. But I can't focus on that right now. I—we—need to put all our energy toward finding Angel and Bear."

He drew a deep breath, let it out slowly as if using the extra moments to compose what he wanted to say. "Have you considered they could be right, about Angel?"

"Of course. And rejected it."

"Why hasn't she called or sent a text? Why's she blocking Eli?"

"I don't know. Maybe it's not her choice. Maybe she's being held against her will?"

"She chose to leave. Kyle didn't abduct her, the way Bear was abducted. The way . . . others have been abducted."

"No, she was seduced, manipulated by someone she trusted. I know—" her throat tightened over the words, "—what that's like. She's a victim, Zach."

He dragged a hand through his hair. Sunlight caught on the lightest strands, making them shimmer. "What's the point of any of it? I used to think the *human* race was screwed up. What a frickin' joke."

He still hadn't looked at her. She laid her hand on his arm. "Zach?"

He met her eyes; she saw anguish in his.

"We can't give up. *You* can't give up."

"Maybe it was over before it even started? Maybe the light never had a chance?"

"Stop it."

"If Angel can be turned, any of us can. Even Eli or Truebell."

"I can't do this without you, Hollywood. I'm going to drag your sorry ass around with me all day. And we're gonna figure this thing out."

He looked as if he meant to argue, so she took a step closer, almost nose-to-nose. "Y'all invited me to *your* party. I was happy busting bad guys and thinking I was all that. So you're stuck with me, you're stuck with *this,* and we're gonna do every *earthly* thing we can to find Angel and Bear and this Kyle, Seth or whatever the hell his name really is—"

She stopped. "Oh, my God. His name."

"What?"

"What are the chances Kyle and Seth are both his names?"

"I don't follow."

"Maybe one's a first name and one's a middle name? Or a first name and a last name? Criminals do it all the time, use some form of their name in their new identity. Because it's familiar."

"That doesn't seem real smart."

"It's not. It's human nature." As she said the words, Micki recognized the irony. She wasn't even certain Seth was human.

She yanked open the passenger side door, then hurried around to the driver's side. "C'mon, Hollywood. We're burning daylight here."

CHAPTER FORTY-NINE

Tuesday, October 27
10:36 P.M.

UNABLE TO QUIET HIS THOUGHTS, Zach paced. Behind him, Micki worked the magic of the database. Totally focused on the job at hand. Locate Seth. Rescue Angel and Little Bear.

Instead, Zach kept replaying those minutes at LAM. Not just the things Eli and Truebell had said, but the way they'd looked at him while they'd said it; their tone, body language, eye contact. They'd both been anxious not to reveal too much.

They were keeping something from him. Something about *him*.

But what?

Parker. Zach stopped pacing. Debriefing the victim, Truebell said. One of them.

What did that really mean? Lightkeeper? Half Light? Then why Parker? Another agent? A Sixer?

Zach unclipped his phone and dialed the man. "'P," he said, keeping his voice low, "it's me. We need to talk. Call me."

"Hot damn!" Micki clapped her hands. "Got a hit! Come see."

Zach holstered the phone and went to stand behind her. He looked over her shoulder at the screen. An image of a much younger Seth dominated it.

"Andrew Seth Kyles," she said. "That's Kyles with an 's'. Half dozen arrests in twenty-four months, starting six years ago. Simple burglary, public intoxication, threw a punch at a bouncer, resisted arrest. Nothing stuck."

"Then what?"

"Nada. Not even a ticket."

"What's he been doing?"

"That's the thing. He dropped completely off the grid. No paper trail. Dude didn't even renew his driver's license."

"He was recruited by a Dark Bearer," Zach said. "Or his envoy."

"That's what I'm thinking."

Zach skimmed the profile, frowning. "He drove a BMW. I saw it. Pretty nice wheels for a guy who didn't even file a tax return. Where'd he get it?"

"I think we both know the answer to that."

"What next?"

"Kyles was in the foster care system from six until he turned eighteen. The majority of that time he lived with the Dominick family, Fran and Joe." Mick looked at him. "I say we pay them a visit, see what they have to say about Andrew Seth Kyles."

⚜ ⚜ ⚜

The woman who answered the door of the Holy Cross neighborhood two-story had kind eyes and a warm smile. "Mrs. Dominick?"

"Yes?"

Zach held up his shield. "Detectives Harris and Dare. NOPD."

She frowned. The kind eyes turned worried. "Yes?"

"We need to ask you a few questions about Andrew Kyles."

"Drew?" She looked from him to Mick, then back at him. "Is he all right?"

Her concern was a surprise. "Yes. May we come in?"

"Of course." She stepped aside. "Excuse the mess. It's not easy staying on top of six kids." She shook her head. "Or maybe I'm just getting old."

"Are you still fostering, Mrs. Dominick?"

"Call me Fran, please." She relocated a stack of coloring books from the couch to the coffee table. "Oh, yes. So many kids need a family to love them."

"Like Drew?" Zach said, using the nickname she'd called Seth.

"Yes." She motioned towards the couch. "Please, sit."

She took the armchair across from the couch. Unless someone else in the house knitted, it was her regular seat. A big basket of yarn sat on the floor beside it, knitting needles sticking out of a periwinkle blue ball of the fiber.

She folded her hands in her lap. "What's going on with Drew?"

Micki took the lead. "We believe he's become involved with someone very dangerous. We're concerned for his well-being and need to talk to him as soon as possible."

Fran Dominick looked at Zach and frowned. "Wait a minute. I know you. You're—" She stopped, eyes widening in recognition. "You're the detective working on the home invasion investigation. I saw you on TV."

"Yes, ma'am. We both are."

She shook her head. "You don't think . . . you can't suspect that Drew's involved?"

"I'm sorry, Mrs. Dominick, but we do."

"But he was doing so well. A good job and—" Her shoulders drooped. "I was sure he was past all that."

"All what, Mrs. Dominick?" Micki asked.

"That rebellion. All the anger."

"Where was he working?"

"In sales. A beverage distribution company. What was the name— Yes, Pelican Liquor. Making good money. Why would he jeopardize all that?"

"I don't know," Zach said softly, feeling sorry for her. She cared deeply for Kyles, that was evident—no sixth sense required. "When did you last seen him?"

"I talk to him every couple of weeks, but I saw him about a month ago."

"Anything seem wrong?"

She twisted her fingers together. "No."

"And the last time you talked to him?"

"He was doing well. Happy. He'd said he'd met someone. He promised he'd bring her to meet me. Is she the one who led him down the wrong—"

"No," Micki said sharply.

The woman looked confused by Mick's tone; Zach stepped back in. "Tell us about Drew."

"When he came to live with us?"

"Yes. How old was he?"

"Eight. He'd been with another family before us. It didn't work out."

"Do you know why?"

"No. Maybe they wanted more from him than he could give."

"What do you mean by that, Fran?"

She was quiet a moment, as if remembering. "Andrew was a sad little boy. He didn't talk much. Fostering isn't easy . . . these kids, a lot of them have been hurt terribly. Victimized by their parents, then by the system. You have to meet them where they are."

A remarkable woman, Zach thought. The kind the world needed more of. "Do you know where he's living?"

"In the area. I don't have an address, I . . . never needed one."

"Is he online? Twitter or Facebook? Anything like that?"

"I don't think so, but I don't know for sure. That's not my thing. I stay pretty busy."

"Six kids? I guess you do." Zach smiled encouragingly. "If there's an emergency, how do you reach him?"

"I have a number." She hesitated. "But he made me promise not to give it out to anyone."

"You don't find that odd?" Micki asked.

She bristled visibly at the suggestion. "He had several rough years. Fell in with a bad crowd, got in some trouble with the law. He doesn't want anyone from his past contacting him."

"We obviously don't fall into that category, Fran. You don't want him to get in any deeper than he already is, do you?"

"No." Her eyes filled with tears and she looked pleadingly at Zach. "But I promised."

"We understand, of course. A promise is a promise."

Micki started to protest; Zach cut her off and stood. "Thank you for your time, Fran."

She followed him up, expression soft with relief. "I'll call him and have him get in contact with you. I'm sure there's some mistake here."

"We'd appreciate that," he said, handing her a card. "My number's on it."

She studied it a moment, then slipped it into the pocket of her housecoat.

"Thank you, Fran." He held out his hand. As she clasped it, a series of images played in his head. A young Kyles, curled into a protective ball; Fran Dominick drawing him out, loving him. Crying for him. And proud. His giving her a number; her writing it down. He held onto that image a moment, committing the number to memory.

"He must love you very much," he said softly. "Keeping in touch the way he does." He released her hand. "Stay safe, Fran."

Moments later, they were climbing into the sedan, buckling up. Micki looked at him. "You got it, didn't you?"

"Yeah." he muttered. "Like you always say, she had no idea she was being mind-fucked."

She started the car. "What's wrong with that? It's your job."

"I know. It's just . . . she was a really nice lady."

Micki pulled away from the curb. "Think of it this way, I wasn't going to leave without that number and the way I would have extracted it would have been much less pleasant for her. This way, everyone gets what they want."

"What are you going to do with it?"

"I'm going to call him."

"Just like that? Now?"

"Hell, yeah. As soon as we get down the road a bit and I pull over."

He frowned. "I'm still pretty new to this cop gig, but wouldn't it be better to get the phone's location and call history and track him down that way?"

"It'd be awesome." She turned into a school parking lot, the Catholic school the neighborhood had been named for. "But how do you propose we do that? Proper channels take time. They take a warrant, which takes just cause and a judge to buy into it. I've got a feeling we don't have that kind of time."

Zach cocked an eyebrow. "You turning psychic on me?"

She parked the sedan. "It's called intuition, Hollywood. And any cop worth a damn has it."

CHAPTER FIFTY

Tuesday, October 27
11:20 P.M.

IN THE SHADOW OF THE school's red brick facade, Micki punched in the number. Zach was right. This was a questionable move. Major Nichols, she was certain, wouldn't approve. But everything she'd told him was the truth. Waiting for a warrant was a waste of precious time, and they lost almost nothing if Kyles ditched the device.

The phone rang. Her heart rapping against the wall of her chest, she counted: one . . . two . . . three . . .

"Hello?"

Bingo. She recognized Seth's voice.

"Hi," she said brightly, "this is Sue, from Teddy's Po'boys. I was calling about your order."

Silence. She pressed on. "Our driver is having difficulty finding you. Could you give me that address again?"

"I didn't order anything. Goodbye—"

"Wait! Someone at your office must have used your phone. We have three roast beef and two fried shrimp."

"Sorry to hear that but I'm not at an office and I certainly didn't order five po'boys."

"Maybe I misdialed. Let me read the number back to—"

He ended the call and she looked at Zach. "It was definitely him."

"He hung up?"

Before she could answer, her phone sounded. "Dare here."

"Didn't you think I'd recognize your voice?"

"Hello Seth." She signaled Zach. "Or is it Kyle? Or Andrew?"

"Bravo. Too little, too late, but still, commendable."

"Let me talk to Angel."

"Sorry, she doesn't want to talk to you. She's with me now."

"If she tells me that herself, I'll totally back off."

"Bullshit. People like you don't back off."

"Talk to me about Little Bear. What do you want with him?"

"Aw, Micki, you don't want to mess with things that aren't your business. You'll regret it."

"Is that a threat?"

He laughed. "Of course. Is Mad Dog scared? If not, you should be."

"I'm coming for you, you son of a bitch."

"Knock yourself out. By the time you follow whatever trail of breadcrumbs you people follow, we'll be long gone."

"That's what people like *you* say, right before I bust your ass."

He laughed. "Just one more piece of the puzzle. That's all we need and we're so very close to getting it. As for where, let's just say somewhere you'll never find us."

"You think I'm going to let you get your hands on another child? Think again, asshole. Is it another Half Light? Another kid or something else—"

"I've got to go now, Micki. Tell my buddy, Zach, I send my regards. Have a good day."

He ended the call. Micki held the device to her ear, his words reverberating through her. *"One more piece of the puzzle . . . we'll be long gone . . . somewhere you'll never find us . . ."*

No, she promised herself and hit redial. She would not let the bastards win. His phone rang once, twice, then clicked over to an automated message—*The cellular customer you're trying to reach has a device that is turned off or no longer in service...*"

She thumped the steering wheel with her fist. "Shit!"

"Mick? What?"

She tossed her phone onto the console and shifted into drive. "We're on the clock. Unless Seth was just screwing with me, they've got something planned, then they're gone."

CHAPTER FIFTY-ONE

Wednesday, October 28
1:40 P.M.

MICKI SAT ON HER FRONT porch steps, a bottle of Abita Amber cradled in her hands. She and Zach had finished up so close to her place that it'd seemed stupid to head all the way back to the Eighth for Zach's car. He'd dropped her off with the plan to pick her up in the morning. She'd offered him a beer but he'd passed.

She gazed out at the dark street, the defeats of the day playing over in her mind. One dead end after another. The judge had denied their cell record warrant request. Apparently his idea of "just cause" and theirs didn't jibe. So she and Zach had followed every possible lead to Andrew Seth Kyles: the bouncer that had brought charges against him four years ago, associates, bartenders, and servers from places he'd been known to frequent, the public defender who had handled his case all those years ago. And Pelican Liquor Distributor, the company Fran Dominick told them he worked for? It didn't exist.

At least the kids were safe. She and Zach had convinced Major Nichols to authorize around-the-clock security for Theo, the Fowler girls and the Carlson and Greene kids. In addition, the professor had assigned each family an undercover Lightkeeper, one particularly sensitive to dark energy.

Micki brought the beer to her lips, took a long swallow. In terms of Angel and Little Bear, she feared they were beaten. Out-matched. If Seth had been telling her the truth, the clock would tick down and the two would be lost to them forever.

Micki rolled the cold, damp bottle between her palms and wished

Hank were alive, sitting beside her the way he used to. He'd talk her through it. Enclose her in one of his big squeeze-the-stuffing-outta-ya hugs.

And tell her everything was going to be okay.

A lump formed in her throat. She missed him. She missed *that.* Someone to hold her up, even if just for a minute.

Micki took another long sip. She was tired, so damn tired. Of being strong. Of fighting, always fighting.

Hank's voice filled her head. *"It's not you against the world, girl. You keep thinking that way, you won't recognize the real enemy when he shows up."*

Headlights cut across the porch as a car turned onto her street. It moved slowly, almost creeping toward her. Still wearing her shoulder holster, she instinctively brought her hand to her firearm, curving her fingers around the grip.

The vehicle passed under the streetlight and she frowned. Her crappy loaner, Zach at the wheel.

He climbed out of the vehicle and started toward her. She met him at the steps. "What's wrong?"

He stuffed his hands in his pockets. "I decided to take you up on that beer, if your offer's still open?"

She searched his expression, then nodded. "Sure. C'mon in."

He followed her inside, trailing her to the kitchen. She got a brew from the fridge, twisted off the cap and handed it to him.

"Thanks."

"You okay?"

"Yeah."

"Then why the beer? You don't drink."

"I don't." He sat on the couch, brought the bottle to his lips and took a swallow, proving himself a liar.

She sank into Hank's recliner, curling her legs under her, gaze on Zach. This felt weird. Different. Like he wanted to say something to her but couldn't bring himself to say it.

"Why'd you change your mind?" she asked. "About the beer?"

"Didn't want to be alone."

"Wow, that was honest."

"Yeah." He took another drink. "How about you? Why'd you offer?"

"Same. Figured my own company would suck. I was right--it did."

They fell silent, sipping their beers and gazing awkwardly past each other.

After several moments, Micki cleared her throat. "What're you thinking?"

"That I really don't know much about you. Tell me something."

"Like what?"

"Tell me about your family."

"They're crazy."

"Aren't all families?"

"Not like this."

"Try me."

"My dad left when I was little. I don't remember him at all."

Not quite true, she admitted, as the memory Eli had released from whatever deep, dark place she'd stashed it filled her head. *Strong sure hands. Her toes curling into the warm sand. Her squeals of delight as he swung her around.*

"And your mom?"

Micki blinked and the memory evaporated. "Mom," she said, hearing the edge in her own voice. "A narcissistic basket case. Drank too much. Was always looking for Mr. Right and dated a lot of Mr. Wrongs. She didn't have much left for an active little girl."

"And I bet you were a pip."

"Oh yeah, although pip doesn't even start to cover it. They wanted a perfect little doll, seen and not heard."

"Sounds just like you."

"Very funny." Her smile faded. "For a long time I tried."

"You said 'they' wanted you to be seen and not heard. It wasn't just you and your mom there in Mobile?"

She drained her beer and set aside the bottle. "We lived in my grandmother's house."

"The three of you?"

"No. My Mom's mom. Aunt Jo and—" she cleared her throat. "—Uncle Beau."

"A little manly influence."

"Depends on your definition of manly." She stood. "I'm getting another beer. Want one?"

"Nah. I won't even finish this one."

She retreated to the kitchen. Dropped her empty bottle into the trash and got out a cold one. She was beyond pissed to notice her hands shaking. She'd put Uncle Beau—and her entire family—in her rearview mirror and she wasn't looking back.

"What is it?"

Zach, in the doorway. He'd followed her. She schooled her expression. "Nothing."

"What'd he do to you, Mick?"

"I don't know what you're talking about."

"Your Uncle Beau. You said his name like it was poison."

She shrugged. "No love lost, that's all. You know me and authority figures."

She went to move past him; he stopped her, asked again, "What'd he do to you, Mick?"

"Nothing. I just hate him, that's all."

"Hate," he said, searching her eyes. "That's a really strong emotion."

She tipped up her chin. "So what?"

"Is he the reason for the chip? The story you were going to tell me someday?"

"It's time for you to go."

He took the beer from her hands, set it on the counter. "Talk to me."

"What makes you think you're entitled to my story? We're partners, let's leave it at that."

"Partners? Is that all we are?"

"Did I ever give you any indication we were more than that?"

"You know you did."

She knew what he was referring to. That night. Their kiss, her reaction to it. "Stop it."

"Stop what?"

"This. That night was work. We were undercover—"

"There was nothing professional about your reaction to me."

"Or *your* reaction to *me*."

"I know." He cupped her face in his hands. "I think about it. A lot. Do you?"

"Of course not," she lied.

He backed her up against the door jamb. "This is just how we were that night."

She laid her hands on his chest, but instead of pushing him away, she curled her fingers into his soft knit shirt. "This is a mistake."

"Yes." He bent his head, brushed his lips against hers, then found the side of her neck, the sensitive spot behind her ear. Her knees went weak, and she held back a moan.

He found her mouth. Kissed her deeply. She felt his body pressing against hers, hard and lean. Aroused.

Giving in, Micki slid her hands to his shoulders, then up, tangling her fingers in his hair. She'd forgotten the power of his lips against hers. Forgotten the power of her response.

How had she managed to live without this these past months? How would she manage tomorrow?

"Micki!"

She froze, her eyes searching over his shoulder. The sound of her name had been so clear, as if someone was right beside her.

But no one was there.

"What's wrong?"

She blinked. "I thought I heard—"

"I need you! Zander needs you! Hurry!"

"Oh, my God." She pushed him away.

"What? Talk to me—"

"It's Jacqui." Micki ran to collect her things. "I don't know how, but I heard her in my head. Calling me. Something's wrong. I have to go!"

CHAPTER FIFTY-TWO

Wednesday, October 28
2:50 A.M.

"SETH!"

The scream ripped from Angel's lips as she sat straight up in bed. It echoed off the bedroom walls. The empty bedroom, she now saw. Seth's side of the bed hadn't even been slept in.

Her heart began to thrum uncomfortably in her chest. Something was wrong. He was in trouble. In danger . . . Someone . . . But who?

Angel closed her eyes and worked to bring the dream back. He'd been writhing in pain. Fighting to save his own life.

She reached for her sketchbook; it wasn't there. The studio, she remembered, climbing out of bed. That's where she'd left it.

She slipped into her jeans and jacket, not even taking time for shoes. Seth needed her; she had to help him. Propelled by the frenzied beating of her heart, Angel ran—down the dark staircase, nearly tripping on the edge of the rug at the bottom, to the patio doors and out into the chill night.

The cold, damp air smacked her in the face, then began to seep through her inadequate clothing. She made her way to the studio, solar path lights weakly illuminating the way.

She punched in the lock code, then ducked through the door and into the cavernous studio. The safety light cast a reassuring glow, but at the same time made the dark places deeper and blacker. Places where anyone—or anything—could hide.

She retrieved her sketchbook and box of charcoal pencils and sank cross-legged to the floor.

Hurry. Hurry. Before it's too late.

The voice in her head was her own, as if a whole other Angel existed within herself. This Angel was serene, despite the urgency of the message.

She began to draw, hand and charcoal as one, racing across the page. Seth. And angry, swirling clouds. The zipper, its teeth. Wait . . . lowering. Peeling away to reveal—

She froze, suddenly unable to manipulate the pencil or guide it with her arm. Not stopped from within, but from without. As if someone—or something—had clapped their hand over hers, the weight pressing down on her arm. She strained. The harder she pushed, the harder it pushed back.

She felt sick. Nauseated, the way she had that day at LAM. Her head felt as if it might explode. She pictured it—like a balloon, stretching, stretching—

"No." Angel ground the word out. "Leave. Me. Be!"

Something inside her broke free. A strength, white hot, like lava. But it swirled up, circling, expanding. The room grew brighter; the light chasing away whatever had been stopping her from freeing Seth.

Her pencil began to move over the page again. Lines and marks, shadings and shapes.

A shape began to appear. Emerging from the image of Seth, transforming him.

A sound passed her lips. A cry of soul-deep distress, as if her heart had responded before her brain had had a chance to even register and name what she was looking at.

Some sort of animal. But somehow human as well. A hunter, carnivore. Cunning, deliberate. Vicious.

The charcoal pencil slipped from Angel's fingers, hitting the tablet and rolling off the side.

A beast. The thing fighting to get out of Seth was a beast.

A Dark Bearer.

She stood, legs rubbery, breath coming so fast, so painfully, she feared each might be her last. Seth had lied to her, tricked and manipulated her. His promise the other night, to take care of her . . . What was he planning? No, not just he, they—him and Will.

She wasn't safe. It had all been a beautiful illusion, created to bring her into the fold. They'd used her own weaknesses to do it. Her longing to be loved, to fit in, belong somewhere, with someone.

And there he'd been, like *magic.* Perfect Seth, handsome and kind, unbelievably head-over-heels for her.

All of it planned. Every glance, every brush of his hand, every shared secret. No doubt even the first time they'd made love had been perfectly orchestrated.

She choked back the bile that rose in her throat. Then along came Will, showering her with gifts and praises: she was a great talent, a master in the making. And she fell for it, every last compliment.

Shame and embarrassment threatened to swallow her. She wanted to curl up in a tight ball and die. As if they would allow her that! No, she had to go. Now. Get away from Seth and Will before they returned from wherever they were.

Whatever they were doing.

Her heart hurt. In a way it never had before—not even when she'd been bullied and rejected, not even that moment when she had fully understood what being abandoned meant, that the word's hateful definition applied to her.

Shoes, she thought. Her purse. Nothing else.

She left the studio and ran to the house, then stopped at the patio door and peered in. She eased it open, pausing again to listen intently. As dark and still as before.

Like a tomb. A beautifully decorated place of death.

Angel sprinted for the stairs and up them, not hesitating until she reached her closed bedroom door. Closed? She'd left it open, hadn't she?

She searched her memory but couldn't remember, not for certain.

Seth could be in there, waiting. The beast from her dream. A carnivore prepared to rip her to shreds if she resisted him.

She pressed her lips together to hold back a cry of fear. Will could be with him. Maybe they'd realized she had figured them out. Angel looked over her shoulder, then down at her bare feet.

If Seth had returned home and she hadn't been in bed, he would have come looking for her. He didn't know, couldn't know, what she was thinking. She must have closed the door; she couldn't remember because of her panic.

Angel grasped the knob and eased the door open. The room was empty, the bed looked just as she had left it— un-slept in.

She tiptoed anyway, as ridiculous as she knew it was. She slipped on socks and her running shoes and grabbed a hooded sweatshirt for extra warmth. She had to get to Micki, somehow. She'd depend on a ride from a stranger, find a business that was open and beg to use the phone, or just walk until she could walk no more.

She grabbed her purse, checked to make certain her wallet and ID were there. They were, though her wallet was empty. Not even a dollar or handful of change. It didn't matter. She'd had nothing before and found her way.

She heard them arriving home. The slam of car doors, the murmur of their voices. Her heart leapt to her throat.

Her sketchbook. She'd forgotten it in the studio.

She couldn't leave it behind.

She ran down the stairs, thoughts racing. Get to the studio, grab the sketchbook, go over the back wall, drop into the neighbor's yard and run. She could do it, use the vines to pull herself over. Wisteria vines, thick and gnarly.

She couldn't face Seth, she thought, panic rising up in her. She wouldn't be able to hide that she knew what he was.

Or that it had ripped her heart in two.

Angel reached the landing. A split second before her foot caught it, she remembered the edge of the rug. She tumbled forward, instinctively reaching out to catch herself, but she heard a sharp snap and hit the ground. Pain, shooting up her arm and into shoulder. Stars, like miniature, blinding strobes, exploding in her head.

Her world went black.

CHAPTER FIFTY-THREE

Wednesday, October 28
3:25 A.M.

ZACH DROVE. THEY DIDN'T SPEAK. Micki used the time to get hold of her runaway thoughts. To try to get a grip on her emotions and the horrific parade of *what ifs* accompanying those emotions. She needed to harness her terror and turn it into something cold and fierce. The way she always did.

Jacqui and Zander needed her.

All that control nearly flew out the window when she saw that Jacqui's front door stood ajar.

"I'll take lead," Zach said, as they neared the door.

"No," she managed, voice tight, "I've got this." She firmed her grip on her weapon and nudged the door the rest of the way open. A familiar disaster area met her eyes—furniture toppled, toys and books strewn, pillows sliced open, their guts spilling out.

Like the previous home invasions.

"One last piece of the puzzle . . . We're very close . . ."

"Police!" she called, the sound of her voice foreign to her own ears. Deeper. Hardened. She called out again and stepped into the main room, swinging left to right. She heard Zach behind her, mimicking her movements.

"The perps are gone," Zach said, stopping.

She looked at him. He stood with his face lifted slightly, eyes closed, collecting energy.

"Was it the same . . . Seth and—"

"Yes. Wait—" He held up her hand. "Hear that?"

A squeaking sound. Almost inaudible.

"The bedrooms," she said. "You take Zander's, I'll take Jax's."

She found Jacqui gagged and hogtied on her bedroom floor. They'd blackened her eye and bloodied her nose. She must have fought like a wildcat.

Micki ran to her, untied the gag first, then went to work on the ropes.

"Zander," Jacqui managed, struggling. "You've got to—"

"Zach went for him . . . Hold still, Jax. I've almost got them."

Last knot untied. With a cry, Jacqui tried to scramble to her feet, but ended up on her knees, sobbing.

"Take it slow, Jax. You're okay. You just need to let the blood return to your legs and feet." She squatted beside her. "C'mon, I'll help you."

"No—" she grasped Micki's arm, "—it's too late . . . Zander . . . they—"

"Mick?" She looked at Zach, standing in the doorway. At his grim expression, her knees went weak.

"They took him, Micki!" Jacqui's voice rose to a wail. "They took my baby!"

⚜ ⚜ ⚜

Back-up arrived as did the CSI team and paramedics. After making certain Jacqui didn't need hospitalization, Micki got her situated at a neighbor's, then returned to the scene.

She found herself questioning everyone and everything. Barking orders like a general on crack. Nothing they did was thorough enough or done quickly enough.

They had to locate Zander. Time was of the essence.

Zach caught her arm. "What's with you?"

"They have Zander," she said impatiently. "The last piece of the puzzle Seth was talking about."

"Yelling at people doesn't make them go faster."

"You don't understand—" she shook off his hand, "—because you don't love them."

"That's not fair." He leaned closer. "And we both know it's not just that." He lowered his voice. "You blame yourself."

She wanted to deny it. To throw it back in his face. But she couldn't and the guilt was ripping her apart.

"It's not your fault."

Furious tears stung her eyes. "Yeah, it is. I'm the connection between

Jacqui, Zander and Seth and his little band of monsters. I exposed her to them."

"That's crap."

"Because of me, Zander's in danger."

"In case you haven't noticed, you're not the center of the freaking universe."

She bristled. "Excuse me?"

"What about Zander's father?"

"I don't understand. What—"

"What has Jacqui told you about him?"

"Almost nothing."

"You don't find that odd? As close as you two are?"

Now that she thought about it, yeah. She met his eyes. "It was painful for her. Very painful. I always felt like she just wanted the memory to go away. Like maybe Zander didn't even have a . . ."

Father. The unspoken word hung in the air between them. She thought of the other home invasions, the history of those children. She recalled the things that Professor Truebell had told her that day.

This *wasn't* about her. They hadn't abducted Zander to send her a message, but because they wanted *him.*

The Dark Bearer wanted him.

That was worse. Much worse.

She struggled past the wall of fear that threatened to level her. She looked at Zach. "You don't think . . . Zander can't be . . ."

As her words trailed off, Zach picked them up. "The Chosen One? Isn't that who we decided the Dark Bearer was looking for? Isn't that what Eli and Professor Truebell thought as well?"

"But how can that be? Jacqui's just an ordinary girl—"

Who had communicated with her telepathically, she thought. Only Eli had been able to do that. Not Zach, not even Professor Truebell.

She met Zach's gaze once more. "She might not even know what she is."

"Come on, Mick, do you really believe that's possible? I think you better prepare yourself for the fact she's been hiding this from you. And considering, would you blame her?"

Ten minutes later, Micki squatted in front of Jacqui, huddled under a blanket on her neighbor's couch. When the neighbor excused herself to give them privacy, Micki found Jacqui's hands. They were ice cold and she rubbed them between hers.

"Jax, sweetie, we have to talk. I have to ask you some questions about what happened."

"They took Zander."

"Yes, I know. And we're going to get him back. But I need your help. How many of them were there?"

"Five."

"Did you recognize any of them?" She shook her head so Micki went on. "I need you to describe them to me."

"You already know who they are."

"Why would you say that?"

"They told me so."

Micki could hardly breathe. She took out a picture of Seth from her inside jacket pocket. She held it out. "Was he one of them?"

She nodded. "He had the gun."

"Why'd they take Zander?"

She looked away; Micki squeezed her hands. "I know everything, Jax. About the Lightkeepers, the Dark Bearers, and Half Lights."

"Because of Zach." She glanced at him, then back at Micki. "I wondered if he had Lightkeeper in him. Because of the eyes and then . . . Eli."

"You recognized Eli that night he showed up with Zander?" Jacqui nodded and she drew her eyebrows together. "But he didn't recognize you?"

"I was suppressing my light, so Zander and I wouldn't be found." Her eyes filled with tears. "I didn't know who I could trust."

"Tell me about Alexander's father."

"His name was Paul. He's gone now."

Her tears spilled over and Zach brought her some tissues.

"Did he rape you, Jacqui?"

She looked genuinely surprised. "No, I loved him. I tried to save him. But in the end I couldn't. The darkness was too strong."

She shredded the tissue while she spoke, tearing it into tiny pieces. "A Dark Bearer had gotten hold of him. Little by little, he transformed until—" her throat closed over the words and she tried to clear it, "—I tried to bring him back . . . with love, but . . . I failed him."

"Was it during that time you became pregnant?" Micki asked gently.

She hung her head; tears dripped off the tip of her nose. "Yes."

"Why did you hide?"

"Because I knew what Paul was becoming and I stayed with him anyway. It was a punishable transgression. If the Council found out, I knew they'd take Zander away from me and if Paul found us—"

"Wait, I thought you said Paul was dead?"

"Dead to her, because of what he'd become. Isn't that right, Jacqui?"

Micki turned. In the doorway stood Professor Truebell, Eli hovering just behind him.

She whimpered. "Yes."

Truebell crossed and knelt down in front of her. "My name's Lester Truebell and I think you've already met my associate, Eli. We're here to help you."

A sound came from Jacqui, one that said more than any spoken word could. Eli hurried across the room, and drew her up into his arms. As their bodies met, light bloomed around them.

It was the most beautiful light Micki had ever seen.

After a few moments, Eli released her. Lester held out a hand. "Come. We'll take you home."

"Wait," Micki said. "Her home is here. We need her, I need her. To help us find Zander."

"Micki's right," Jacqui said. "I have to be here. For Alexander, in case he comes home."

Truebell cupped her face in his hands and looked into her eyes. "You know who has him. You know why. If you stay here, you're vulnerable. He may come back for you."

"He won't." Tears welled in her eyes once more. "They don't need me. They have Angel to control him."

Micki's knees went weak. She took a deep, anchoring breath. "They said that?"

Jacqui turned to her. "I begged them to take me with them. I promised to do whatever they asked--I just wanted to be with Zander. But he said Alexander didn't need me anymore. That Angel would take care of him. That they would be his new family."

CHAPTER FIFTY-FOUR

Wednesday, October 28
7:10 A.M.

ANGEL CRACKED OPEN HER EYES. She hurt. Her head, her right side and arm. Pain thundered in her forearm and wrist. She tried to move it but couldn't.

A sling, she realized. She sat propped up by pillows in the big, leather easy chair by the fireplace. From the kitchen came the sizzle of bacon in the skillet, its usually mouth-watering aroma turning her stomach.

This wasn't right, she thought. Last she remembered it'd been the dead of night, not day. She'd awakened alone. Seth . . . A dream about him was what had awakened her. But hadn't she been in her studio? Her hand had been flying across the page capturing—

She frowned, searching her memory. What? Seth, the zipper . . . lowering . . .

She must have made some sound, because Seth appeared in the opening to the kitchen. He smiled. "Good, you're awake."

She stared at him, the strangest sensation in the pit of her gut. The gnawing sense that there was something about that zipper she should remember. Something important.

Seth crossed to her, bent and kissed her. "You gave us a scare."

"What—" her voice came out a croak, "—happened?"

"You fell. Caught your toe on the edge of the rug at the bottom of the stairs. Bumped your head and maybe broke your wrist."

"It hurts."

"I know, baby." He kissed her again. "Will's getting rid of the rug. He says it's way too dangerous."

"Why was I on the stairs?"

"Probably looking for me. I'm so sorry, sweetheart."

Regret beamed from his eyes, real and heartfelt. But why did he feel regret?

With her good hand, she plucked at the blanket. "I had this weird dream."

He laid his hand over hers, stilling it. "Don't you always?"

She smiled weakly. "I guess, I do."

"Hungry? I made us breakfast."

Just the mention of food turned her stomach. She shook her head. "I don't feel so good."

He searched her expression, concerned. "How about some juice?"

"All right."

She watched him hurry back to the kitchen, her thoughts whirling. If only she could think clearly. She brought her good hand to her head and found an egg-sized lump there. She gently felt it, then dropped her hand.

Charcoal on her fingers. Underneath her nails. Smudges on the side of her hand. Her memory came crashing back: waking up dreaming of Seth, that he was in trouble, racing to the studio, forcing the dream onto paper.

Through her art, releasing what fought to get out of Seth. No, she acknowledged, what he had been hiding from her.

His true self—a beast in a beautiful suit.

She heard him humming in the kitchen. A knot formed in her throat, the taste of betrayal bitter in her mouth.

The betrayal grew and swelled up in her, anger with it, as big and powerful as the ocean. Her headache abruptly ceased, all her body aches too. Adrenaline, she thought. She could feel it, surging through her veins.

She leapt out of the chair, as agile as a cat. In the blink of an eye, or so it seemed to her, she stood in the kitchen doorway, within arm's reach of him.

"I know what you are."

He stopped, turned to face her, suddenly pale. "Angel?"

"You're one of them, aren't you?"

"One of who?" He held out a hand, beseeching. "Angel, sweetheart, you've had a bump on your—"

"You tried to keep me from learning the truth, but now I know. You belong to the Dark One. So does Will."

"Angel, please . . . come sit down. I love you. You're talking crazy."

She stared at him, her head beginning to ache again, her wrist to throb. He looked so sincere, so hurt by her accusations.

"Angel, baby, trust me. I love you and you love me. We're good together."

She so badly wanted that to be true. She brought her hand to the bump on her head. Maybe she was confused? Maybe none of it had happened?

But the charcoal smudges . . .

From the other room came the sound of the patio door sliding open, then closing. A moment later, Will appeared in the kitchen doorway. He held her sketchbook. "Ah, you're awake."

"Give me that." She held out her hand. "It's mine."

"Uncle Will, would you mind giving me and Angel a few minutes? We're in the middle of—"

"There's no need for that now." He tossed the sketch pad on the counter, open at her drawing of the other Seth, the wolf in sheep's clothing.

Seeing it again, the visible evidence of his betrayal, assaulted her like salt being ground into her opened, bleeding heart.

"Angel, baby . . ." he took a step toward her. "I don't know what you think that means, but I can explain—"

Will cut him off, tone matter-of-fact. "No, you can't. Give the girl some credit, she's neither an idiot nor bound to human comprehension with only the five senses."

"We're done, Seth. I never want to see you again."

Will laughed and shook his head. "Such righteous indignation. Bravo!" He crossed to stand directly in front of her. "But such a lie, my darling Angel. You wish he could convincingly deny it all. You long for nothing more than for the two of you to live happily-ever-after in some dreadful but cozy cottage. You, my dear, need to think much bigger."

"Shut up," Seth snapped.

"I wonder," Will murmured, leaning so close she caught the smell of something foul on his breath, "what you'll long for when I explain how I engineered every detail of your relationship, from first meeting to—"

"Save your breath. I already figured that out. And I hate you both for it. But especially—" she looked accusingly at Seth, "—*him*."

Will grabbed her chin, his fingers biting into her skin, forcing her face back to his. "We followed you. Learned your routes and routines. Seth here popped into the coffee shop late, making you swoon at his deliciousness, all engineered by me."

Hearing Will detail how they'd made a fool of her while Seth just stood there saying nothing hurt more than she could have imagined. "I'm leaving."

Will laughed loudly. "Really? You'd just go? After all I've done for you?" He made a *tsk, tsk* sound. "What atrocious manners. But what should I expect from someone like you? Not even wanted by her own mother."

She jerked her head free of his grasp. Every place he'd touched her burned. "You don't know anything about me."

"But I do, child. I know *everything* about you. Including who your father is. He and I are very close."

A tingling sensation started at her forehead and travelled down, until she felt numb from head-to-toe. "That's a lie."

"He's been in contact with you recently. I understand you're having some difficulty accepting him."

The voice in her head. The one she'd thought she'd silenced. She took a step back.

"You're not leaving us, Angel. Quite the contrary, you're his—no, you're *ours* now."

"No." She shook her head. "Never."

"You can have everything, Angel. The whole world. Fame and wealth, powers you didn't know you had. And of course *love* . . ." He hissed the word and gooseflesh raced up her arms.

When she didn't respond, he went on. "You and Andrew together forever . . . oh wait, you didn't know his real name, did you? Angel, let me introduce Andrew Seth Kyles. Don't feel too bad. At least he used his real middle name."

That he hadn't even told her his real name was the final blow. She whirled to face him. "I hate you! I hate you both!"

"A lovely start to your future together. As I was saying, you two, together forever, fornicating to your heart's content, making little baby Half Things. Who knows? Maybe you'll be the proud parents of the *One*?"

With a roar, Seth lunged at Will.

In the next instant Will had him by the throat and was lifting him off his feet. Angel saw her chance and took it, sprinting for the door. She reached it, found it locked, cocked the deadbolt and yanked again, but the door wouldn't budge.

She gave up and raced to the patio sliders, but no matter what she did or how she tugged, they wouldn't open.

"Enough of that, Angel," Will said.

She heard a thud and saw Seth on the floor, struggling to get back up as he gasped for breath.

"You don't want to hurt your other arm, do you? Besides, I have a surprise for you. Several actually. Come here."

"Go to hell."

She bolted for the entryway door, but before she could reach it, an invisible force—like tentacles of pure energy—coiled around her and dragged her backward. The harder she fought, the tighter the coils.

"Are you ready for surprise number one?" Before she could answer, the television on the counter popped on. The morning news.

"Early this morning, the group responsible for the string of home invasions across the metro area struck again, this time in Gentilly. The quiet neighborhood was awakened by the terrified screams of a mother frantic for her child."

Angel's gaze went to the television.

Micki, Angel saw. And Zach. Longing, like a bitter pill, stuck in her throat and she choked back tears.

"You miss them, don't you? Poor baby, I've heard your silent pleas for them to come save you. Do you really believe I wouldn't have thought of that? That I would leave you—or us, for that matter—vulnerable to their interference? This house is a fortress, my dear. Nothing in or out, even energy."

"Officers at the scene refused to comment, but a neighbor offered—"

The newscast grabbed her attention once more. The camera panned across an apartment building, and up and down a quiet block.

She recognized that neighborhood. She recognized the apartment building. It looked like—

Jacqui's.

She shifted her gaze from the television to Will. He was watching her, his expression as cunning and as pleased as a cat's with its attention fixed on a plump mouse.

"What have you done?"

"In a stunning and tragic turn, four-year-old Alexander Clark was abducted by the perpetrators—"

"Surprise."

"No!" The word ripped past her lips and she lunged at him. Seth caught her from behind and dragged her against him.

"Stop, Angel," he said close to her ear, his voice ragged. "It won't help. You saw what he did to me. You can't beat him."

She fought, but with only one arm and still reeling from her fall, she was like a butterfly battling the wind.

"You led us straight to him," Will said. "Thank you for that, Angel. He's a very special boy. Maybe even *the* boy."

"He's just a baby! Please . . . let him go home."

He cocked his head, studying her as if she were some sort of science experiment. "Such sweet tears, lovely on you. So many turn ugly with tears, but not you. Your eyes are like pools of liquid chocolate."

"Please," she said again, "he's such a sweet little boy."

"That's the thing," Will said, "I've never worked with one so young—or impressionable—before. Your knight in shining armor here was an excellent student--so much anger to work with, such a willingness to learn. But still, already ruined. Get them young, though, raise them in the way you want them to be..."

He looked affectionately at Seth, the way a real father would, with love and pride. Yet this was the same "father" who had only moments ago choked his "son" into submission.

Will shifted his gaze back to hers. "You know, he's quite a powerful Half Thing in his own right." He saw her expression and inclined his head. "Yes. All this time you tried to hide what you are from him, afraid he wouldn't love you if he knew the truth. But, of course, he knew all along."

She felt like a fool. A love-sick idiot. Betrayal and anger bubbled up within her, a wellspring of rage--white hot, then turning cold. Icy cold.

She spied a crystal vase. Yesterday it had held a spray of vibrant fall flowers; today it stood empty. She stared at it, the taste of hatred, rancid but addictively powerful, overcoming her. She wanted to hurt Will, the way he was hurting her.

She wanted to kill him.

"Do it, child. He deserves it, doesn't he?"

Yes, Angel thought. He did. She imagined it—picking up the vase, hitting him with it, hearing his skull crack open, seeing his blood spill out.

As the images played through her head, the vase trembled.

Be rid of him.

It lifted off the counter.

Kill him. He deserves it.

Yes, she thought. He does. She'd be a hero.

Hatred exploded from her. The vase sailed toward his head.

Will stopped it by simply lifting his hand. "Oh goody," he said, "the gloves are off."

He flicked his wrist; the crystal dropped to the floor and shattered.

Angel looked a Seth. "Together we can beat him. If we work together—"

"Poor baby . . . do you really think that?" Will's voice deepened. "That little display? Nothing more than sideshow tricks and juvenile antics . . ."

His voice deepened again. A low rattle began, seeming to come from the home's very foundation. The clatter grew louder, the kitchen began to shake, table and chairs to bounce on the tiles.

Suddenly, the cabinet doors blew open, the drawers flew out. One by one, the plates launched themselves, porcelain frisbees smashing against walls, whipping around her and Seth. A symphony of destruction.

Seth drew her to him, folding himself over her. "I've got you, babe," he whispered in her ear. "I won't let him hurt you."

She wanted to cry that he already had, but she clung to him instead, terrified beyond the ability to move.

"You see, Angel," Will went on, as the din subsided, "your little show of temper doesn't worry me. It doesn't worry us. We are ancient of days, my dear. It's time, Seth."

Angel felt Seth stiffen, then shudder.

She looked up at him. "Time for what, Seth?"

Something awful, she knew. Something beyond her comprehension.

"No, Seth . . . please." She tried to break free of his arms, but he tightened his grip on her. "What are you . . . don't let him hurt me! You promised, Seth. You promised!"

"Take her back to the chair."

He swung her into his arms. "Wait, no . . . Seth—"

He carried her to the family room, murmuring over and over that it was going to be okay. Will went ahead of them. She heard him give an order, then the whoosh of the patio door opening and closing.

Seth meant to save her, she thought, tears running down her cheek. He loved her, despite everything, she knew he did.

Or Micki and Zach would burst in. Any moment now, with back-up. Or Eli and Professor Truebell. She looked to the door, willing her saviors to arrive.

But no shout of "Police!" came, no sound of wood splintering as the door was kicked in.

He didn't mean to help her. No one was coming . . . she was lost. She buried her face in the crook of his neck, pleading over and over for him not to do this.

He stopped. "It'll be over fast, baby," he whispered. "Trust me."

They'd covered the chair with a white sheet, reclined it back as far as it would go. A kind of altar.

Angle clung to him with her good arm, pleading, but he pried her free, laid her in the chair. She observed him through a wall of tears. He looked sick, almost green, like he might vomit.

"I love you," she said.

He visibly shuddered and looked away.

"I love you," she said again.

"Sedate her," Will barked, sounding irritated. He looked down at her without compassion. "This could have been pleasurable for you, but you leave us no other choice. It's time you accept who you were born to be, dear. You belong to us."

Seth stood, syringe in hand, on her other side. "Hold still, sweetheart. It will help with the pain."

She felt the sting of the needle, the hot rush of the narcotic entering her bloodstream. Its effect was immediate, debilitating.

"That's a good girl," Will said.

So fuzzy-headed. There was something. . . on her legs.

A pressure... strapping them down, at an odd angle.

Did they mean to . . . rape her?

The horror of it penetrated the drugged haze. "Why?" The word came out garbled. "Wh're . . . you doing—"

"Because you're ours now," he said. "We must mark this moment. We have the three, a trinity . . . Just as our master instructed."

"Master . . . who . . ." Her words slurred, then seemed to melt on her tongue.

Whatever they'd given her took full hold of her blood and every organ it fed. She'd lost the ability to speak. The words sounded only in her head, only for her own ears.

Angel became aware of activity. The patio doors swooshed; another arrived. Something rolling on the tile floor. A suitcase? A cart? Suddenly a bright light. Not on her face, but warming her abdomen and thighs.

Conversation between two men. Friendly. Not Seth. Where was he?

She searched for him. His back was turned, so he wouldn't have to see. She silently begged him to stop this, to save her.

He didn't even turn around.

"This should be adequate," the third man said. "Is she sedated?"

"Yes."

"If she thrashes about, I won't be responsible—"

"She won't."

Will's voice, impatient.

"Hello, Angel," the man said, smiling down at her. "How are you today?"

He reminded her of the dentist one of her foster mothers had taken her to. Is that what they meant to do? she wondered. Fill a cavity? Her teeth were fine, she thought, hysterically. This was all a mistake.

He patted her hand. "I'm going to give you a little something more, to help you relax."

He placed a mask over her mouth. She wanted to turn away, but her brain refused to respond to her plea. "Breathe deeply. It'll help."

A scream rose up in her head even as waves of lassitude rolled over her.

A buzzing sound she recognized . . . a pressure on her leg . . . then . . .

Nothing at all.

CHAPTER FIFTY-FIVE

Wednesday, October 28
11:15 A.M.

ANGEL CAME TO COTTON-MOUTHED AND nauseated. Her tongue felt thick and her eyes scratchy. She lay in the big bed that just a few days ago she had thought so luxurious, the bed that had made her feel so very grown-up.

Now, she saw the bed, these luxurious surroundings, for what they were—a prison. Her feeling of strength and independence had been built on nothing but lies and pride.

Bile rose in her throat and Angel slid out of bed to limp to the bathroom. She made it to the toilet just in time, bent over the porcelain bowl and retched.

When she was empty, she sank to the floor, resting her cheek against the cool tile. Her inner thigh burned and she moaned with pain and shame. Tears slid down her cheeks, falling from the end of her nose, hitting the tile with an almost silent ping.

"Hello, my child."

Him, she thought. It. "Leave me alone."

"You're stronger than this. Part of me, your father."

She drew her knees to her chest, curling into a ball. "No. Leave me alone."

"You've always belonged to me, but now you bear my mark."

"Your—" Her throat closed over the words. She couldn't even say it. "What do you mean?"

"Look and see."

She dragged herself to her feet, gingerly crossing to the vanity. Her reflection mocked her: her face was swollen; her forehead purpling from her fall; bottom lips puffy and bruised; dried blood on her chin. Sometime during her ordeal she'd bitten her tongue as well. She touched its tip to the roof of her mouth and winced.

And her eyes . . . She leaned closer to the mirror. Was it her imagination or were they a darker brown than before?

None of that was what he had referred to, she knew. Using her one hand, she shimmied her yoga pants down her hips. She saw her panties were in place, the same ones she'd had on before, and pressed her trembling lips together. So probably not raped. But what—

A bandage, peeking out from between her upper thighs.

And then she knew: what the buzzing sound had been, why her thigh burned, and what the bandage covered. She knew what the Dark Bearer had meant by being marked.

Not raped. Literally marked.

Praying she was wrong, Angel found the outer edge of the dressing and peeled it back.

Her legs buckled as a cry of denial passed her lips.

A triple six had been tattooed on the inside of her thigh.

CHAPTER FIFTY-SIX

Wednesday, October 28
11:45 A.M.

HOURS LATER, MICKI WAS STILL numb with shock. She couldn't get warm, no matter how many cups of coffee she drank or how tightly she hugged herself. She had gone through the motions, done her job, worn an expression of confident self-control. Now, she sat stone-still and silent while Zach filled Major Nichols in on the case.

Zander's abduction, Jacqui's secret, her grief, guilt and hopelessness over the loss of Angel and Bear had zapped her last shred of fortitude.

She had nothing left to hold onto.

"This was definitely the work of the same group of perpetrators," Zach said. "The pattern of destruction was nearly identical to that of the other scenes. Like those incidents, a blaring boom box and strobe light were used to disorient and intimidate the victim."

"With one major difference," Nichols said. "The boy. Why?" His gaze settled on her. "Theories, Detective Dare?"

"None, sir."

He couldn't have looked more surprised if she'd jumped onto his desk and broken into the Mardi Gras Mambo.

"None?" he repeated.

"Not quite, sir," Zach said, coming to her rescue again. "The victim is a single mom with no known connection to the perpetrators. She's an online college student, works part-time at the library and a lives a quiet life with her son."

But she did have a connection to the perpetrators, Micki thought. One they couldn't share with Major Nichols—or anyone else outside

LAM.

Nichols looked at her again. "But she and her son have a connection to you, correct?"

Memories of times with Jacqui, in no logical order, sprang to mind. The day Zander was born, the very pregnant Jacqui moving in with her, the first time Alexander had called her Aunty Mouse. "Yes."

"Is there a chance the perpetrators were aware of your friendship and targeted her as a way of getting to you?"

The question sliced her wide open. She curled her hands into fists. "Yes."

Nichols face softened with sympathy. "What about the child's father?"

"Not part of their lives. Ever."

Zach cleared his throat. "Amber alert has been issued. As has a BOLO for Andrew Seth Kyles. Jacqui Clark has given her statement, the crime techs are scouring her place and uniforms are interviewing neighbors as we speak."

Nichols nodded. "Judge signed the warrant for Kyles' cell phone records. Since a child's life is at risk, the company representative promised to expedite the process."

It was already too late, Micki thought. Zander was that last piece of the puzzle that Kyles had mentioned. They could be gone already.

"Dare? You able to carry on?"

She blinked. Straightened and squared her shoulders. "Yes, sir. Absolutely."

He studied her a moment, then turned back to Zach. "You lead on this. Dare starts to lose it—"

"I won't."

He went on as if she hadn't spoken. "She starts to lose it, you bring it to me. Immediately. Understood?"

Zach stood. "Yes, sir."

Micki took longer to get to her feet. When she had, she crossed to Nichols' desk, laid her palms on its top, leaned in and looked him directly in the eyes. "This never should have happened. I should have nailed this guy already. But I promise you now, I've got this."

Nichols smiled grimly. "Good. Go find this boy and bring him home to his mother."

CHAPTER FIFTY-SEVEN

Wednesday, October 28
2:45 P.M.

ANGEL SAT PRESSED INTO THE far corner of the bedroom, knees to her chest, gripping the weapon she'd fashioned out of a curling iron, cuticle scissors and rubber bands. If it failed, she'd tucked a metal nail file into her pocket. If they tried to touch her again, she'd do her best to kill them.

At the soft tap on the door, she tightened her grip.

"Angel?"

Seth. Tears flooded her eyes and she blinked against them. She was done crying over his betrayal.

He tapped again. "Are you awake?"

She crept toward the door. When she reached it, she pressed her ear against it and heard him breathing. "Seth?" she whispered.

"Thank God. Are you okay?"

A choked sound passed her lips. "You know what they did to me. No. Hell no, I'm not all right."

"I'm so . . . sorry."

"You didn't even try to stop them."

"There was nothing I could have done. You saw his power."

"Let me out of here. I'll run away."

"What about Zander? He needs you."

"I'll get help."

"He needs you now. He's scared and won't stop crying and asking for his mom."

Angel imagined Jacqui's devastation. Zander was her life. She had to find a way to make this right.

"Help me save him, Seth." She laid her hand flat against the door, imagining him doing the same on the other side. "He's a sweet, little boy. He doesn't deserve this."

"We can be a family," Seth said. "The three of us. We'll raise him. We'll—"

"Where does Will fit into this pretty picture? Daddy to us all? I'd rather die."

"Would you, Angel? Because that's the alternative. The only one."

His plainly spoken words took her breath. She complied or she died.

"Bear needs you, too."

"Bear?"

"Little Bear. His real name's R.J...."

The cub, she thought. From her drawing.

"He needs a mother, too. And a father."

"Not me. I can't. I won't."

"Will's a monster," Seth said. "The boys need our influence. Without us—"

"You are, too," she said, cutting him off. "You're a monster, Seth. I saw it and . . . and you broke my heart."

Silence followed. So long and so heavy, she began to wonder if he was even there—or if she was simply hallucinating.

She wasn't, she realized a moment later, when he spoke.

"Will is coming. He expects you to calm Alexander. I suggest you don't resist. His punishments can be . . . brutal."

And then he was gone.

CHAPTER FIFTY-EIGHT

Wednesday, October 28
3:15 P.M.

ANGEL FELT WILL'S PRESENCE BEFORE he tapped on the door. A damp cold that penetrated the walls and seeped into her skin. Almost reptilian. She wondered if it had been there all along but he had hidden it from her? Or if she had tricked herself into seeing only what she wanted to see? Whichever, her very skin seemed to ripple in response.

"Hello, dear," he said. "May I come in?"

She wanted to refuse, to barricade the door or hide. But against the power he'd exhibited in the kitchen, any resistance would be a joke. "I know I don't have a choice."

The lock turned and the door opened. He'd brought what looked to be a biker-bodyguard with him: pierced, tattooed, and muscle-bound. She noticed his eyes looked dead.

"Drew told you why I've come for you?"

"Yes." She refused to meet his eyes. "But I'm only doing it for Alexander, not because I'm afraid of you."

He smiled slightly. "Still plucky, I like that."

She pointed to the dude. "Who's this?"

"A friend."

"If you're worried about me attacking you or trying to escape, I have one arm and can hardly walk."

"I have nothing to worry about, but it pays to be careful, now doesn't it? People are hardly trustworthy."

"I've learned that." She thought of Seth—she would never think of him as Drew— and his lies. "What now?"

"Follow me."

They made their way down the central staircase. She stayed close to the left side and took it slow; every time her thighs brushed, the tat burned.

"I see it's bothering you. I'll make certain you get some ointment." She didn't respond and he went on. "How do you like our handiwork?"

"I don't."

"Examine it closely; you'll recognize the artist. I'll see that you get a hand mirror as well."

"Don't bother. I'm having it removed the minute I get out of here."

"I'm sorry, Angel, but this one goes a bit deeper. It's permanent."

She flinched. "What do you mean 'permanent'?"

"That it'll keep coming back. It's a birthday present." He paused. "From your father."

A knot of tears formed in her throat. She fought them. She would not give him the pleasure of seeing her cry.

"This way," he said, touching her elbow, steering her toward the patio doors.

"Where are we going?"

"You know."

"My studio?"

He smiled slightly at her use of the possessive and she promised herself she would never refer to it as hers again.

As they neared the doors, she recalled the way she'd felt that first day, when he'd shown her it. Remembered her sense of wonder and excitement. Of marveling that finally, someone believed in her wholly and without reservation.

He had known exactly the places she was weakest.

They stopped at the metal doors. Through them she could hear Zander crying. Her fault, she thought, sick with guilt. If only she could go back in time, she would do it all so differently.

"You will calm him," Will said as the bodyguard unlocked the padlock. "You will get him to eat, drink and rest. If you fail, both of you will face the consequences."

He opened the door. Zander sat on a pallet on the floor, his little body shuddering with the force of his sobs. Beside him sat a boy who looked to be about eight or nine, his chubby face scrunched up as if in pain.

"Alexander!" she cried and ran to him, tattoo and pain forgotten. She knelt down and pulled him close with her one arm.

He clung to her, sobbing. "I want mommy."

"I know, buddy." She rocked him, his wails tearing her apart. "We'll get you back to mommy. Somehow, I promise."

The minutes passed, with him curled into her side, his wails slowing to deep, heart-breaking sobs, then to hiccoughing cries and finally, soft mewls of despair.

Her arm had gone numb and her side ached, but she didn't stop or change positions. No pain was too great: her drawings—and stupidity—had led them to him.

And then he was asleep, his little body limp against hers. She carefully shifted so he lay across her lap.

"I'm Bear," the other boy said.

"Hi, Bear. I'm Angel."

"I know."

"Are you okay?"

"I am now." He glanced down at Zander then back up at her. "It's not your fault."

She drew her eyebrows together. "What's not my fault?"

"That Zander's here. They're real bad."

"I've figured that out, kid. Don't worry, I'm getting us out of here. Somehow."

The realization of just how impossible that would be took her breath away. She studied Alexander's sleeping face. She had to find a way. She *had* to.

"I'm sorry you're so sad."

"I'm fine," she said. "You don't have to worry about me."

"Nope." He gave his head a firm shake. "You're sad."

"What makes you so sure?"

He shrugged. "It's just something I know."

Angel studied him a moment. "Is that why you're here? Because you can read people's true feelings?"

"Uh-huh."

From the door came the sound of the padlock being opened. Seth and the bodyguard stepped inside; they held a pizza box and a caddy of soft drinks.

She turned her head when Seth looked her way. She hated him now, so much that even looking at him caused a visceral reaction in her.

"Bear," he said, "come help me with this."

The boy stood and trotted over. Seth handed him the pizza box.

"Got that?" he asked.

Bear nodded. "Got it."

"Good boy. Let's set this stuff on the work bench."

Angel felt his eyes on her. "I thought you all might be hungry."

She didn't respond in any way and he sighed. "We'll check on you later and bring some more bedding."

A moment later, she heard the door shut and the lock click into place.

"Want some pizza?" Bear asked solemnly.

She nodded. "And a drink. Could you get it for me? I don't want to wake Alexander."

He brought the pizza to the pallet, then went back for the drinks. "It's like a picnic," he said, helping himself to a slice. "I like pizza. And picnics."

She reached for a slice, her stomach growling. "How old are you, Bear?"

"Eight. How 'bout you?"

"Eighteen."

He nodded and chewed on his pizza, then took a long slurp of his soda. "Why wouldn't you look at him? He kept lookin' at you."

He meant Seth, of course. She hardened herself against the way his words made her heart ache. "Because he's bad. He lied to me and hurt me. And I hate him now."

He contemplated her, eyebrows furrowed, slice of pizza halfway to his mouth. Then he shook his head. "No."

"What do you mean, no?"

"You don't hate him."

"Yes, I do."

"Nope. You love him." He took a big bite of pizza.

"I did, but now . . . I hate him."

He looked at her in that way kids sometimes did at adults, like they were totally clueless. "Whatever he did, he's real sorry. He loves you."

She fought back the tears that stung her eyes. "You're too young to understand this, but he can't. Because he's got no love in him."

He found her hand and curled his fingers around hers. His was soft, a child's hand, warm and comforting. She held onto it like a lifeline.

After a moment, he looked up at her. "He has good in him, just like me and you."

She wanted to cry, no doubt because she so badly wanted it to be true. "I want to show you something."

Angel eased Zander off her lap. He moaned, then curled into a ball, his thumb in his mouth. She covered him with a blanket, then stood, careful not to wake him.

Will had returned her sketchbook. She limped over to the easel and retrieved it, then brought it back to the pallet and opened it to the drawing of Seth. "*That's* what he really is, Bear."

He made a face. "I don't think that's right."

"My drawings are never wrong. He pretends to be nice but he's not."

"You've got to forgive him."

"Some things are unforgivable."

"You *have* to, Angel."

"Why?" she asked voice rising.

"Because you're the same as him. Dark and light."

CHAPTER FIFTY-NINE

Thursday, October 29
4:00 A.M.

MICKI HEARD THE CREAK OF the front screen door opening. Instantly awake, she retrieved her gun from under the edge of the mattress and slid out of bed. She made her way to her bedroom door. She'd left it ever-so-slightly ajar and eased it open with her toe.

Maybe Angel, she thought hopefully.

But probably not.

Firming her grip on the weapon, she peered around the jamb. A figure at the end of the hall. Male. Tall and broad-shouldered. Something familiar about his stance, the cock of his head.

Son of a bitch, it couldn't be—

She swung into the doorway, Glock aimed dead center at Seth's chest. "Hands up, ass-wipe."

He lifted them. "Hello, Micki."

His calm pissed her off even more. "Give me one reason I shouldn't shoot you where you stand."

"How about you'll never see Angel or Zander again."

She wanted to shoot so bad her trigger finger twitched. "You piece of shit."

"Hear me out. If you don't like what I have to say, kill me. I've got nothing to live for anyway."

"Hands against the wall. Spread 'em."

He did as she ordered. She frisked him, found him clean, and pressed the barrel of the gun to the back of his head. "Kitchen. Real slow."

He did as she ordered, tone conversational. "I'm alone, Micki. I'm unarmed. Isn't this a little over-the-top?"

"Shut the fuck up." With her foot, she dragged a chair from the table to the center of the room. "Sit. Move a muscle, I kill you."

"I came to you, remember?"

"Yeah, right. Why's the question."

She retrieved a set of cuffs from a basket on top of the refrigerator, never taking her eyes or aim off him. She cuffed him to the chair, then sat across from him. "Talk."

"I need your help."

She laughed. "That's classic. And so not happening."

"I need your help," he said again, then added, "to save Angel and the boys. I can't do it without you."

She narrowed her eyes, surprised. And curious. "Why would I trust you?"

"You've got nothing else and you're out of time."

Her chest tightened. "What does that mean?"

"He's moving them."

"Where?"

"I don't know."

"Bullshit." She lifted the muzzle of the gun, training it on the spot directly between his eyes. "I'll ask you again. Where?"

"I told you, I don't know. He doesn't trust me."

"Who's 'he'?"

"Will Foreman. You won't find him in any of your databases."

"We'll see about that."

He shrugged. "You'll just be wasting valuable time. Today's the day. Once they're gone, you'll never find them."

She hesitated. "I say, I take you in, you give up your buddy and his location and we swarm the place. And you end up where you should be, in a cell."

"That's your choice. Take me in now and it's over. You'll have me but he'll be gone, Angel, Bear and Alexander with him."

The thought of that made her sick. There had to be another way, but she didn't trust him. She'd be a fool to.

But what if he was telling the truth? What if this was her one chance to rescue Zander, Bear and Angel?

"Why are you doing this?"

He looked her dead in the eyes. "Because I love her. And I hate him."

"What is he? The Dark Bearer?"

"Not 'the', but a force that's been with him for a very long time. He's quite powerful."

"What about you? What are you?"

"I'm the product of an experiment. My mother was abducted by someone she thought she knew, someone she thought she was in love with. He impregnated her, held her against her will until she was well past the opportunity for abortion, and left her."

"So, it's true."

"Yes." He looked away, then back. "My mother didn't know what she was, she didn't know what he was or who had sent him. And she certainly didn't know what she had given birth to. A Half Thing," he finished, self-loathing in his tone. "*Uncle* Will's name for me."

"He told you this story."

"Yes. I know it's true."

"And your mother? What happened to her?"

"She killed herself. I was six."

Ten minutes ago there was no way she would have believed she could feel sympathy for this man. But she did.

"And that's what you planned for Angel? You're a great guy, Seth. A real winner."

"Angel's already like me. That's why they want her."

"To turn her to her dark side and use her gift of prophecy against us."

"Yes. And for breeding."

Her stomach turned at the thought. "Angel's light's too strong. She won't cooperate. Not ever."

"I know," he said. simply. "That's why I have to save her."

Even as a part of her called herself a fool, Micki realized she had to trust him. She had to go with her heart on this one, not her head. And her heart believed.

"All right." She laid her gun on her lap. "What's the plan?"

"Will's scheduled to move them from the compound via a florist delivery truck this morning. The delivery should cause no undo attention—fresh flowers are delivered every Thursday morning. The truck backs around to the side entrance, the spent arrangements are removed, replaced with fresh."

"Only today what they remove from the house will be quite different."

"Yes. The truck will transport the group to the airport. Will has arranged for a private plane."

"Will he be with them?"

"No, and neither will I. Will wants to keep me close. He knows I'm conflicted."

"Where is he now?"

"Even the devil needs to sleep."

Goosebumps raced up her arms. "Go on."

"He's sending Angel and the boys with two armed bodyguards. They're big but stupid, nothing much to worry about."

"Except for being armed."

"Right. But no special skill set."

Just regular Joe-Schmoes, she thought. Like her.

"The flower truck is set to arrive at nine in the morning. It's Lakeside Blooms."

"A real company?"

"Yes. The driver's been bought."

"The owner's involved?"

"I don't know, but I think not. Traffic can cause a ten-minute delay. The driver will be in touch with me. By my thinking, that's our window." When he shifted in his seat, the cuff rattled against the metal arm of the chair. "You arrive ten minutes early. You'll have ten minutes to get Angel and the boys off property and out of Will's range before all hell breaks loose. And I mean that quite literally."

"I'll be coming with back-up, you know that, right? Swat team, all we've got."

"Good. You'll need it."

She narrowed her eyes. "If this is a trick or trap, I'll hunt you down myself and tear you apart with my bare hands."

He went on as if her threats were as frightening as a squeaking mouse. "When he discovers what I've done, he'll kill me."

"Not *if* he discovers what you've done?"

"No. The best I can hope for is to catch him off guard and buy a few minutes. Our timing has to be exact."

"I'm going to need an address. And I want the names of everyone who's been involved with Will and the home invasions."

"Done. Wrote it all down already." He held up his free hand. "May I?"

"No fast moves."

"So little trust, Micki?"

She narrowed her eyes. "And here I thought I was doing so well."

She watched as he slowly reached into his jacket pocket and retrieved an envelope. He handed it to her. "Everything's right there, including what we talked about." He rattled his cuff. "Maybe you want to undo this? I've been gone too long."

She freed him and he stood, absently rubbing his wrist, expression pensive. "You should know, he'll kill the three of them before he'll chance losing them to the Light. He's powerful enough to kill them without even putting hands on them."

"Noted."

"I hope so."

She walked him to the front of the house but stopped him from exiting. "During all this, what're are you going to do?"

"Try to kill him before he kills me."

Nothing left to say, she let him go. He reached the BMW and looked back at her. "One promise."

"I don't know that you're in the position to ask for promises, but we'll see."

"Tell Angel I really did love her and that . . . I'm sorry."

As his tail lights disappeared, she punched in Zach's number.

He answered, voice thick with sleep. "Harris."

"It's me."

"Mick? What the hell?"

"I'm coming over."

"Now?"

At any other time, she would have laughed at his incredulous tone. "If I could make it sooner than that, I would."

"I like the urgency, but I have a feeling I'm going to be disappointed by the reason for it."

"We have a plan."

"Wait. What do you mean we—"

"And only five hours to navigate the details, get Major Nichols on board and pull it off."

"Back up. A plan for what?"

"To rescue Angel, Zander and Bear."

"Five hours? From now?"

"Yeah. And if we fail, we'll most likely never see the three of them again."

"Whoa, partner—"

She cut him off. "No time for that. I'll fill you in when I get there. Oh yeah, better make a pot of coffee."

CHAPTER SIXTY

Thursday, October 29
5:10 A.M.

ANGEL AWAKENED WITH A START. She opened her eyes. Simultaneously Bear, facing her on the pallet directly across from hers, opened his. In them, she saw herself reflected back. Not her exactly, more like what she was thinking and feeling, the urgency to act that was surging through her.

Get it out. Get it on paper. It was important.

He mouthed the word "Go." She heard it in her head and nodded.

Beside her, Zander slept deeply. Angel slid carefully off the pallet, then tucked the blanket around him. He whimpered but didn't awaken.

She'd left her sketchbook by the pizza box and crept toward it, guided by the only light in the cavernous studio—the first glimmers of morning through the skylights.

Her drawing hand was out of commission but she laid her left hand on the book and her fingers began to tingle. Thank goodness. Still, it was going to be difficult.

She opened to a blank page. She couldn't see, but she couldn't awaken Zander . . . and she had to do this *now*.

The urgency of it beat like a drum in her head. Get it out . . . get it out . . . get it out . . .

She always tucked a charcoal pencil into the sketch book's spiral binding. Now, she worked it out of its resting place, grasped it and made one mark, then another, sketching blindly, wishing the sun would rise.

And then it did, a soft glow gathering around her, illuminating her hand, the pencil, the emerging drawing.

Not the sun, she realized, astonished. Her. The light was coming from *her.*

Light and dark. Both. Angel glanced at Little Bear. He was watching her, eyes wide.

She went back to her drawing. The image began to take shape. Her hand flew across the page, this way and that, rendering something both beautiful and repellent. She suddenly stopped. The charcoal slipped from her fingers, rolled sideways and off the page.

The beautiful Seth, she saw. Radiant like the morning sun . . . and the monstrous Seth, the angry beast from before.

But a third Seth as well, emerging from the beast. The beautiful one again.

Light and Dark. Good and Evil. He was not just one, but both.

"Oh, my God, she whispered, the pencil slipping from her cramping fingers. She looked at Bear. "You were right, come see."

He did, tiptoeing past Alexander. He knelt down beside her and stared at the drawing a moment, then looked at her. "He does love you."

"Angel?"

She looked over her shoulder. Alexander was sitting up, rubbing his eyes.

"It's okay," she whispered, "I'm here."

"I didn't know." His little boy voice was thick with sleep.

"Know what, buddy?"

"That you really was an angel."

She started to tell him she wasn't, then looked down at herself. Her hands, arms and chest still glowed, though faintly. She lifted her eyes to the skylights, to the burgeoning light. A new day. A gift.

The possibility of escape.

"I've got to go potty."

She went to take him, stopping when she heard someone at the studio doors, unlocking the padlock.

"It's Seth," Little Bear said. "He's nervous but excited, too."

"You can pick that up?" He nodded and her heart began to pound. "Bear, can you take Alexander to potty? Don't hurry back. You understand what I'm saying?"

"'Course," he said and held out his hand. "C'mon, Zander. I'll take you."

They trotted off just as the door opened. And just as Bear had said, there was Seth. He had a box of donuts and a travel tray with three cartons of milk and what looked like a cup of coffee.

The bodyguard was with him. When he started to enter, Seth stopped him. "Wait here. Nobody in or out except me or Will."

The man nodded and stepped back outside. The heavy door snapped shut. Seth turned but didn't meet her eyes. He crossed to the workbench, set the box and tray on it. "I brought you breakfast. Make sure the boys eat. It's going to be a long time until—"

She ran to him and hugged him, pressing her cheek to his chest. He stiffened with surprise, then melted against her.

"I'm sorry," he whispered, mouth to her ear. "So very sorry."

"I love you."

"Shh . . ." He pressed his mouth closer. "Micki and Zach are coming for you. Soon."

"I'm not leaving you."

"You have to take the boys and go."

"Then you have to come too."

"No, sweetheart. It's too late for me."

"No! If it was, you wouldn't be doing this for us."

"You'll know when the time is right. It's all arranged."

He moved to let her go, but she tightened her arms around him. *"I'll only go if you promise you'll come for me."*

Behind them, the bathroom door opened.

"I've got to go. I love you." He kissed her hard, then was gone.

Angel wiped the tears from her cheeks and turned to the boys. Bear looked hopeful, Alexander worried as he clung to Bear with one hand and sucked the thumb of his other.

"Who was that?" he asked, words coming out garbled around his thumb.

"A friend," she said and forced a smile. "He brought us donuts."

They wasted no time digging in. As the boys were eating their second, Angel realized that Seth hadn't promised to meet her. He'd said he loved her instead. Like a good-bye.

The blood rushed from her head and she had to sit down. Breathe, she told herself. He would be at LAM. He would meet her there.

He had to.

CHAPTER SIXTY-ONE

Thursday, October 29
8:35 A.M.

ZACH SECURED THE KEVLAR VEST, making certain it was snug. Beside him Eli did the same. Six feet across the parking lot of an abandoned strip mall, Micki was giving the FBI swat team final instructions. The Bureau had been called in because the case involved child abductions. The Fed's personnel and toys; Micki's plan.

Zach hoped to God they had made the right decision, trusting Kyles, putting all their eggs in this basket. Micki was convinced this was it, their only chance.

So he'd backed her up despite his doubts. A part of him worried that Kyles coming to her for help "saving Angel" was nothing but slick sleight-of-hand. They and their army would descend on one place while Kyles and his crew were miles away, going in the opposite direction.

"This on right?" Eli asked, voice tight.

Zach checked the vest, nodded. "You're good." He handed him the short-sleeved collared shirt with the florist's logo embroidered on the left pocket—*Lakeside Blooms.*

"Piece of cake," Zach said.

"Easy for you to say," Eli muttered. "I'm a lover, not a fighter."

It came out so deadpan that Zach laughed. Eli brought a whole new meaning to that saying.

Their roles were set. Zach would drive the florist's van, Eli ride shotgun. Parker had pulled strings to get Eli approved. A medic, he'd said. In case one of the kids needed immediate, medical attention. Not a lie, Zach thought, just a different kind of medicine.

Micki finished giving the swat team instructions and headed over to them. She was in full tactical gear.

"You look ready for war," he said.

"I am." She squinted up at him, then at Eli. "You both know your parts, right?"

"We retrieve the kids and transport them to the rendezvous point where the Bureau, NOPD and Jefferson Parish Sheriff's Department will be waiting with Jacqui and Bear's Grandma. Smooth as silk."

"Ears in."

They'd both been outfitted with earpiece receivers and neck loop transmitters. Zach inserted his; Eli followed suit.

"Audio check."

"Got you," Zach said.

Eli nodded. "Check."

"Good." She nodded. "The moment you're off the property, you radio me and we move in."

"Got it."

"Your number one priority is the safety of the two minors and Angel."

"Yes, ma'am."

"And then yours, you understand? No stupid heroics."

"That hurts, Mick." Zach forced a cocky grin. "It really does."

She scowled at him. "Don't get killed." She looked at Eli. It seemed to Zach that her gaze lingered on the other man a moment longer than necessary. "Either of you."

They climbed into the van, buckled in. Micki tapped on his window and Zach lowered it. "We'll have eyes on you the whole time. Do not deviate from the route or the plan."

"Aww c'mon, Mick, you're no fun at all."

She made a sound of exasperation and shifted her gaze to Eli. "Don't let him do anything stupid. Please."

"If it's the last thing I do," he responded solemnly.

"So. Not. Funny." She checked her watch. "It's go time."

Zach started the van, eased forward, then leaned his head out. "Hey Mick?"

"Yeah?"

"You be careful."

She tugged on the bill of her cap in acknowledgment, turned and walked back to the feds. Zach watched her in his rearview, then turned to Eli. "Ready?"

"As I'll ever be."

The drive from the strip mall near the airport to the upscale residential area took less than ten minutes. The guard at the gate waved them through. "We're in the neighborhood," he said, for Mick's benefit.

"Good. Follow GPS route. You're two point five minutes from destination."

He had to admit, having Mick in his ear was sort of reassuring.

Sure enough, two and a half minutes later they arrived at the palatial home. "Right on time." He pulled up to the gate, glanced at Eli. He looked paler than usual. "You okay, man?"

"This is a dark place. I suggest we get in and out real fast."

"That's the plan." Zach rang the buzzer. "Lakeside Blooms," he said "Pick-up and delivery."

The gate swung open. Zach drove to the circle, then backed around the side of the house, to the kitchen entrance. "You wait," he said to Eli, who nodded and sank down in his seat.

Zach climbed out, went around to the back of the van, opened the panel doors.

Kyles appeared. Zach met his eyes; something in them set off alarm bells.

"This way."

Zach hesitated. "Where are they?"

"Coming."

Something was wrong, Zach thought. The energy. Something . . . a trap. He took a step back, hand going for his weapon.

And then he saw them. Angel carrying Alexander. Little Bear walking beside her. A tattooed goon with them.

But Angel only had eyes for Kyles.

They reached the van. Zach scooped up Bear, set him in the van. Angel didn't move.

"We have to go," he said, tone low, "Now."

He took Zander from her. The boy wrapped his arms and legs tightly around him and buried his head in his neck. He went to set him in the van, but the child refused to let go.

He looked back at Angel. "Snap out of it," he murmured. "Alexander needs you. He's terrified."

She blinked, then nodded. "Come on, Zander. We've got to go. Can you climb in and sit next to Bear?"

Bear held out his arms. Zach let out a relieved breath as Alexander scrambled over to Bear. Angel took one last glance at Kyles and climbed in.

Zach slammed the doors shut. He didn't like the way the goon was staring at him, with those lifeless dark eyes. He nodded curtly at Kyles, hurried back around to the driver's side and climbed in.

"Packages delivered," he said into the transmitter. "Getting the hell out of Dodge now."

"Gotcha," Micki replied, "Let me know when you're through the gate."

Zach shifted into gear. Gripping the steering wheel so tightly his knuckles turned white, he rolled forward. For a single, agonizing second he thought the gate wasn't going to open, then it slowly swung in.

"Stop the van!" Angel cried, pounding on the partition window. "Stop the van now!"

Zach hit the brakes and the van lurched to a stop. He twisted around. "What's wrong? What's—"

"I can't leave him!" The back panel doors flew open. "Tell Micki I'm sorry."

"No, Angel! Don't—"

She slammed the doors behind her. Alexander began to wail.

"What the hell's happening!" Micki asked in his ear.

"Angel took off. I'm going after her—"

"Oh hell no, you're not. Proceed through the gate, I'll be there in five minutes. I repeat, proceed through—"

He looked at Eli. "Get them out of here. See you on the other side."

"Stay on plan, Hollywood," Micki ordered. "Remember, no stupid hero—"

Zach popped out his earpiece and tossed it onto the console, then leapt out of the vehicle.

No stupid heroics, he thought. Just necessary ones.

CHAPTER SIXTY-TWO

Thursday, October 29
9:23 A.M.

ANGEL PEERED THROUGH A SIDE window into the kitchen. Empty. As HGTV-perfect as ever. Heart pounding like crazy, she grasped the door handle, twisted and eased open the door. Absolute quiet, not even the whir of the AC running. As still as the grave.

She stepped inside. Shut the door behind her.

"Seth," she silently called, *"where are you?"*

Silence. No voice in her head. She scanned the kitchen. Her sketchbook, open on the counter. A black marker on the counter beside it. As she moved closer, she recognized her last drawing of Seth.

Someone had used the chisel tip marker to strike a bold 'X' through it.

Cold slipped down her spine. Not somebody. Will.

He knew. Everything.

Her mouth went dry. She tiptoed through the kitchen and into the living room. There, just beyond the doorway, lay the bodyguard. Obviously dead, but something about the body . . .

Then it struck her. His head looked as if it were on backwards. Her stomach lurched to her throat and she quickly brought a hand to her mouth. What kind of force had it taken to do that?

Fear, real and icy cold, settled over her. She and Seth didn't have a chance against a power like that.

She had to find him before Will did.

Unless he already had him.

She looked down at the bodyguard, then quickly away, tears stinging her eyes. Of course he had him. The bodyguard had paid the ultimate price for his stupidity.

"What have you done with him?" she called out. "I know you have him!"

A low rumble shook the house. *"Of course I do, ungrateful child. I'm so disappointed in you."*

"Where is he?"

The rumble came again, morphing into laughter. *"He's waiting for you in your studio."*

Angel didn't hesitate. She ran around the bodyguard to the patio doors. Once through them, she practically flew down the garden path to the studio. As she reached the door, she heard a sound coming from within. Like wind or—

She pulled open the door.

A storm swirled inside. Dark clouds, the howl of the rushing air. Flashes of lightning in the clouds, the rumble of thunder.

Before it all stood Will, both creator and conductor; orchestrating his symphony of chaos. He looked over his shoulder at her. "Beautiful, isn't it?" He motioned toward the ceiling. "Do note the tableau's centerpiece."

She lifted her eyes. Seth hung six feet above the floor, arms stretched out as if affixed to an invisible cross, his face contorted with pain.

"Seth!"

He saw her and cried out in agony. "Why'd you come back? You should have gone!"

"I couldn't leave you!"

She rushed forward. The wind caught her and threw her backward, crashing into an easel that tumbled with her to the floor. She dragged herself to her feet.

"Run," he managed, voice fading in and out. "Micki . . . the police . . . here soo . . ."

The swirling wind became a snake-like coil, squeezing around him. He screamed in pain, face twisting into a horrific grimace.

"Stop!" she shouted. "You're killing him!"

"Why, yes, I am." Will smiled. "Isn't that the point?"

"No, please . . . I'll do anything you want, just let him go."

"I'm sure you would, stupid girl. But it's too late for that." Will turned his black, liquid eyes on her. "As I was asking dear Andrew a moment before you arrived, what use do I have for him now? None is the answer. You, my dear, were his ticket to living."

"I'm here, aren't I? Please, it's not too late! I'll do anything!"

"Disobedient children should be punished. He understands that but chose to defy me anyway."

"Then take me, too! I'd rather die with him, than live without him!"

He narrowed his eyes, then shrugged. "Very well." With a sweep of his hand, the tail of the snake lashed out and caught her, dragging her into the vortex.

She slammed into Seth, the force of it knocking the wind out of her, causing her to see stars.

His arms went around her, steadying her. He pressed his lips to her ear. "Breathe, babe. I've got you."

She sucked in a breath as best she could, both terrified of her imminent death, and strangely at peace. She sought his eyes, willing to die lost in them. "I couldn't leave you."

"I wanted you to live. You . . . deserve . . . but I—"

The pain ebbed. She felt oddly weightless. So this is what dying felt like, she thought. What had she been so afraid of?

"You saved us." The stars in her head met and melted, creating a deep glow. *"Even knowing he would kill you."*

"No, you . . . saved me." His body softened, as if he, too, had lost the ability to respond to, let alone fight, their attacker. *"I was dead. You brought me back to life."* He shifted his mouth close to hers. *"I'll love you, forever."*

Around them, the violence of the storm grew—yet it didn't touch them. Angel held him, and he her. Together they dipped and swayed in a sort of dance, while their mouths met and mated. She felt warm and oddly, completely protected. Alive in a way she had never experienced before.

If she was going to die, she acknowledged, there was nowhere she would rather be.

The building shook; the metal panels creaked, the supports bowed. Above them the skylights burst with a thundering crash.

The glass rained down but didn't touch them. She imagined them glittering like tiny white lights.

"Angel," Seth whispered, "open your eyes."

She did. They were in a spotlight, but one of their own making. A brilliant glow cocooned them, protecting them from the storm. Nothing could touch them, she understood. Not when they were together.

She felt Will's frustrated fury, and searched him out, shocked to find him no longer handsome. His mask of beauty, stripped away, revealed a beast.

Like her drawing. What had been inside Seth.

Then she saw Zach. Slipping through the metal doors. He'd come after her. With nothing but a gun to protect himself.

Will would crush him.

Angel screamed his name. As she did, pain rocketed through her. She grabbed for Seth but the wind ripped her from him and sent her sailing toward one wall, Seth the other. She hit hard, the pain from a moment before nothing compared to this new torture.

She was aware of landing on the concrete floor, feeling as her body had broken in a dozen places. As the thought registered, she heard a distinct *pop,* followed a moment later by another. The wind died, its roar fading to a weak mewl.

Over, she thought. It was over.

"Seth, where are—"

Her words were swallowed by a low rumble that shook the building. The rumble was followed by a groan. The floor moved beneath her.

"Angel," Zach called. "Where are—"

"Here! Is Seth—"

"Take . . . cover—"

A grating sound of metal against metal. The deep snap and crackle of the cement seizing, buckling.

"The building," he said, "it's coming dow—"

"I can't move!"

"Hold on, I'm—"

A mighty groan cut off his words. Angel looked upward as the roof gave. Her last thought was of Seth.

CHAPTER SIXTY-THREE

Sunday, November 1
9:46 A.M.

MICKI STOOD BESIDE ZACH'S HOSPITAL bed, willing him to open his eyes. Three days. And counting.

"Wake up, Hollywood. Let me see those baby blues."

But same as every time before, he didn't.

She let out the breath she had been holding. Even in a coma, the man was so damn irritating.

"What were my last words, dude? No stupid heroics." She swallowed hard, looked away, composing herself. "And what do you do? C'mon, that was supposed to be me. Rushing in, all big and bad. And now look—"

Micki stopped, pulled the chair over and sat. Her hands shook. They hadn't stopped shaking since she'd fought her way through the rubble of what she now knew had been an art studio and found Zach, unmoving, covered with debris, the area around him stained red.

Micki flexed her fingers, reliving the moments. Even as she reminded herself it was over, that both Zach and Angel were alive, her body responded as it had then: pulse elevating, heart racing, breath coming quick and short.

She'd pressed her fingers to his throat, felt a pulse and shouted for paramedics. To the agents at the scene, she'd been a machine—calm, cool and collected. Inside, she'd been totally freaking out.

It'd taken longer to find Angel. Tucked into a back corner, she'd been the miracle. Roof and wall had fallen in such a way she'd been totally protected, sheltered by a haphazard lean-to of debris.

She'd started to cry when she saw Micki, silent tears rolling down her cheeks. The expression in her eyes, Micki would never forget: raw with regret, relief, and grief.

Micki flexed her fingers again, blinking against tears of her own. She looked away. Stupid, she told herself. Weak.

"Are . . . you. . . crying?"

She jerked her gaze back to the bed. Zach, his eyes open. And though his words had been thick and raspy, she had understood them.

"Mad Dog doesn't cry," she said. "Mad Dog crushes skulls."

He didn't smile. He tipped his hand palm up, silently asking her to take it. She did, curling her fingers around his. He closed his eyes.

They stayed that way, and as the moments ticked past, the tension coiled inside her eased. For the first time in seventy-two hours, she felt as if she could fully catch her breath.

"Angel?" he asked, holding her hand more tightly.

"Alive. Busted up. Broken leg and arm, five cracked ribs. Cuts and bruises. But it's her heart that's taken the biggest beating."

"Kyles didn't make it?"

"He wasn't there."

"He escaped?"

She frowned. "He was never there. Abandoned Angel to save his own skin."

"That's not . . . I thought—"

He let the thought trail off and she frowned. "What?"

"I thought I saw . . . him. But now, I'm not so sure."

She leaned closer. "What did you see?"

"Foreman had her—them, I thought. They were . . . suspended . . . encased in . . . light."

"In light?" she repeated.

"Like a bubble, or capsule. Then it evaporated."

"And?"

"And I shot Foreman."

Zach drew his eyebrows together. He seemed to be struggling to process his thoughts. "Angel asked me about Kyles. I'm sure of it."

"So you didn't actually see or hear him?"

"I guess not."

They fell silent a moment. Micki slipped her hand from his. "By the way, partner, that was some good aim. You nailed Foreman once dead in the chest, the other right between the eyes."

"Detective Harris?"

They turned toward the doorway. A nurse stood there, smiling from ear-to-ear. "You're awake."

"A few minutes now," Micki said.

"Excellent!" She hurried across to the bed, bright blue eyes sparkling. "Let me get your vitals, then I'll call the doctor."

She did, chattering the entire time. A moment later, she was gone and Micki stood. "I'll let Major Nichols know you're awake and give the gang at LAM a call."

She started for the door, but stopped to look back when he called her name.

"I guess this makes us even."

"Seriously?" She cocked an eyebrow. "A little bump on the head and we call it even?"

"Yeah." The corner of his mouth lifted in a lopsided smile. "What?"

"A YouTube video, Hollywood? The Nova, totaled twice—"

"Second time wasn't my fault."

"*And* I took a bullet."

"Hey, Mick."

She stopped and looked back again. "Yo?"

"Thank you."

"For what?"

His eyes crinkled at the corners. "Caring so much."

Micki worked to keep from showing how vulnerable his words made her feel. "You reading my mind, Hollywood?"

"Couldn't help myself."

She mock-scowled. "You get a pass this time. But you use that mind-reading, mojo bullshit on me again, I'll kick your ass."

CHAPTER SIXTY-FOUR

One week later

MICKI AND JACQUI STOOD BESIDE a white mini-van in the parking lot behind LAM. Inside the van, Bear and his grandma waited patiently and Alexander watched a cartoon on Jacqui's tablet.

The suitcases in the back contained the personal items they were being allowed to take with them.

They were being relocated. LAM's version of the witness protection program. New identities, new home and school. New everything.

Even friends.

Jacqui squeezed her hands. "I'm going to miss you like crazy." Her eyes welled with tears. "What will I do without you?"

"You'll be fine," Micki said evenly. "Alexander will be safe."

This was the best for them. Micki had reconciled herself to it by focusing on their safety. How she felt didn't matter—even when a part of her was dying inside.

"His safety, yours and Bear's, that's all that matters, Jax."

"I know." A tear ran down Jacqui's cheek. "But we're not even going to be able to talk. How am I going to explain that to Zander? You're his Aunty Mouse."

"Stop it," Micki said, voice cracking. "You just are. No communication by *any* means. You will make this work."

"Yes." Jacqui dropped her hands, wiped the tears from her cheeks. "You couldn't change Angel's mind and get her to come with us?"

Micki shook her head. "She said Seth wouldn't be able to find her when he came back for her." She shook her head again. "I don't get it."

Their driver lowered the window. "We've got to go," he said, expression apologetic. "Sorry."

Jacqui nodded and hugged her hard. "I love you, Micki. I'll never forget you."

Micki hugged her back then stepped away. "Love you, too."

"Alexander, Bear, come say bye to Micki!" They both barreled out of the van. Zander hugged her first. "Bye, Aunty Mouse!"

"Be good," she whispered. "Remember Aunty Mouse loves you no matter what." She held him a moment too long, and he squirmed. Releasing him was one of the hardest things she'd ever had to do.

Bear hugged her next. "Don't be sad," he said.

"I'll try not to, buddy." She kissed his forehead. "Keep watch over Zander, okay?"

He nodded in that serious way of his. "I promise. And tell Angel I said goodbye."

"I will."

And then there was nothing left to do but watch them drive off. Zach had joined her and laid an arm across her shoulders. "You okay, partner?"

"They're going to be safe, and that's all that matters."

He gave her shoulders a squeeze and dropped his arm. "That's my skull crusher."

"Considering recent events, perhaps another description . . .?"

He laughed. "Maybe so."

They headed inside, and took their seats at the conference room table. Micki noticed two empty chairs. "Are we waiting for anyone else?" she asked.

"Not anymore."

All eyes turned toward the doorway. Parker, looking five years older than the last time she'd seen him.

"P," Zach said, getting to his feet. "It's good to see you, man."

They hugged briefly and clapped each other on the back.

"Way to miss all the excitement."

"Hear you took a pretty good blow to the head."

"It didn't help," Micki said dryly. "He's still as irritating as ever."

Truebell spoke up. "You have the package?"

"I do, indeed." Parker turned back to Zach. "There's someone I want you to meet. Someone who's anxious to meet you."

A woman stepped into the doorway. She had eyes the color of a clear, summer sky and a wistfulness to her smile that suggested a much younger woman.

"Hello, Zach," she said, clasping her hands in front of her.

He stood, looking from her to Parker. "P?"

"I was wrong," Parker said, a slow smile transforming his face. "Zach, I'd like to introduce you to your mother."

They stood staring at one another a moment, then moved into each other's arms. As they clung to one another, the rest of them filed out, closing the door behind them.

Truebell touched Micki's arm. "Come with me. There's something I have to tell you."

She followed him to his office and sat in the patches of colored light that fell through the stained glass window.

His expression was almost gleeful, and she frowned slightly. "What's up?"

"Some days ago, you asked Eli what he meant when he called you one of us. He told you you'd have to wait a little longer. Do you remember?" She nodded and he went on. "After Kenny shot you the second time, he gave you something for safekeeping."

She searched his expression. "What?"

"The last of his light force."

For a moment, Micki simply stared at him. Then she blinked. "Excuse me? Did you just say—"

"I did."

"This is a joke, right?"

"No joke, I'm delighted to say."

"But how . . . y'all can do that?"

"Only because somewhere in your family's distant past, Lightkeeper was introduced to your line, so Kenny was able to attach the flicker of his light to yours. Eli realized it that night when he connected to you. That's why you could communicate telepathically with him."

"You've got to be shitting me."

He laughed. "Afraid not. But don't expect to be able to communicate with others that way. Not only is Eli a Full Light, he's particularly skilled in that area."

Micki struggled to process what he was saying. "I had Lightkeeper in me?"

"Have Lightkeeper in you," he corrected. "Such a very small amount that neither Eli nor I picked up on it before. But enough for Kenny to attach his to. You may have noticed some small changes in your perceptions, dreams or even what most people call their gut reactions."

"And that's it? No super-slick voodoo powers? No mind-reading, scene-stealing, bullet-dodging magic?"

"Nope. Sorry."

She paused, cleared her throat. "I'm not sure what to say."

He stood. "Don't say anything. Just live with it a bit, see how it fits."

She followed him to his feet, crossed to the door. "I suppose I will."

"Detective Dare? Welcome to the club."

ACKNOWLEDGEMENTS:

THANKS AND APPRECIATION TO THE entire Trident Digital Media & Publishing team, particularly Scott Miller and Nicole Robson. To my family, friends and writing retreat 'Girl Power' gal pals Hailey North and Robin Wells: love, hugs and deep appreciation for your support.

ABOUT THE AUTHOR:

ERICA SPINDLER IS THE NEW York Times and International Chart bestselling author of thirty-two novels and three eNovellas. Published in twenty-five countries, she has been called "The Master of Addictive Suspense" and "Queen of the Romantic Thriller."

The Lightkeepers is Erica's first series, something she's wanted to do for years. All she was waiting for was the right characters. She found them in Micki Dee Dare, reformed southern belle turned kick ass cop, and Zach "Hollywood" Harris, a charming bad boy with some very cool, save-the-world skills.

Erica splits her writing time between her New Orleans area home, her favorite coffeeshop, and a lakeside writing retreat. She's married to her college sweetheart, has two sons and the constant companionship of Roxie, the wonder retriever.

Erica is currently at home in New Orleans, writing Micki and Zach's next adventure, FALLEN FIVE.

CPSIA information can be obtained
at www.ICGtesting.com
Printed in the USA
LVOW08*1459151216
517421LV00005B/95/P